moving to the UK with her British husband and daughters. *The Downside Ghosts* is her first urban fantasy series.

Visit her authorized website at www.staciakane.net

Also by Stacia Kane

THE DOWNSIDE GHOSTS
Unholy Ghosts
Unholy Magic
City of Ghosts
Sacrificial Magic
Chasing Magic

STACIA KANE

UNHOLY MAGIC

Book Two of the Downside Ghosts

HARPER
Voyager

HarperVoyager
An Imprint of HarperCollins*Publishers*
77–85 Fulham Palace Road,
Hammersmith, London W6 8JB

www.harpercollins.co.uk

This paperback edition 2010
3

First published in Great Britain by
HarperCollins*Publishers* 2010

A catalogue record for this book is
available from the British Library

ISBN: 978-0-00-734325-6

MIX
Paper from
responsible sources
FSC
www.fsc.org
FSC™ C007454

FSC is a non-profit international organisation established to promote
the responsible management of the world's forests. Products carrying the
FSC label are independently certified to assure consumers that they come
from forests that are managed to meet the social, economic and
ecological needs of present and future generations,
and other controlled sources.

Find out more about HarperCollins and the environment at
www.harpercollins.co.uk/green

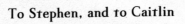
To Stephen, and to Caitlin

Chapter One

> The penalty for summoning the dead back to earth is death; if the summoned spirit does not kill its summoner, be assured the Church will.
> —*The Book of Truth*, Laws, Article 3

Ghosts were stronger underground; no witch willingly went below the surface of the earth, not without a Church edict or a death wish. Chess had both to varying degrees, but that didn't make the doorway looming behind the skinny man holding the cup any more appealing. The doorway, and the stairs. Down into a basement, down into the ground.

Chess's skin crawled from more than just the squat-faced, wizened appearance of the man, more than the bizarre energy in the dirty shack. Something told her this was not going to end well.

But then, things so rarely did.

She could have busted the bastards simply for having a basement. The Church decreed they were illegal, and the Church was not to be disobeyed. But she needed more than that—a month of investigation *demanded* a more satisfactory resolution than that—so instead she pasted what she hoped was a smile with the right touch of nervousness on her face and handed the skinny man the picture she'd brought, careful not to touch his grimy fingers.

The picture was of Gary Anderson, a fellow Debunker, but the skinny man didn't know that. At least Chess hoped he didn't.

"My brother," she told him. It would have been better if she'd been able to squeeze out a tear, but the Cepts she'd taken didn't allow it. It was hard enough to feel emotions when she was high, let alone emotions intense enough to make her weep. Hell, that was one reason why she kept taking the fucking things, wasn't it?

The skinny man focused his rheumy eyes with effort on the photo, then nodded.

"Aye, seein a lookalike," he mumbled, scratching his bony chest through a hole in his ragged green sweater. He shoved the cup forward, narrowly avoiding hitting her with it. "You drink, aye?"

"Thanks, but—"

"Nay, nay, lil miss. You drink, or you ain't get down, aye? All must drink." His chapped lips stretched and flaked in a gruesome semblance of a smile, like a fat worm crawling across his face, revealing broken, graying teeth. "All must drink, or the energy, she ain't work."

Shit. Who the fuck knew what was in that nasty cup? Even if the "tea" was harmless—which she doubted— the thing looked like it hadn't been washed since before Haunted Week. She could practically see germs crawling along the rim.

The bonus on this job would be a couple of grand, she reminded herself, and snatched the cup from his dry, bony hand.

His gaze locked on hers. She held it while she tilted the cup and poured the contents down her throat.

For a second the room spun around her, whirling on its side like an amusement park ride. The concoction tasted of bitter herbs and glue, of seawater and sewage. It was the most revolting thing she'd ever put in her mouth, and that was saying a lot.

She held it down through sheer force of will, and was rewarded with another flaky smile. Something lurked behind that smile, but she didn't have time to analyze it.

His hand was on her sleeve, urging her into the dark mouth of the stairway, and her feet clumped on the wooden slats as she made her way into the damp cave below.

The others were already there, sitting in a circle beneath flaming torches, around a scarred wooden table. Across one end of it was draped a blue silk scarf, stained with blood or wine—or perhaps someone else's stomach had lost its battle with the tea.

No time to think about it, even if she'd cared to. Instead she made her way to the table, to the straight-backed wooden chair someone had pushed out for her.

"Someone," she saw, was a five-foot-tall human parody of indeterminate sex wearing a belted garbage bag and white face paint. Heavy black rims surrounded its beady, pupilless eyes, and its voice was barely more than a dry whisper, like a knife cutting through cardboard.

"Sit ye down, lil miss," it rasped. "Sit ye down, and the Ladywitch, she'll be out."

"The Ladywitch" was Madame Lupita, formerly known as Irene Lowe, and as soon as Chess had the evidence she needed—in the form of her own eyewitness testimony and whatever the minirecorder concealed in her bra picked up—Madame would have a date with a guillotine. The Church did not take a forgiving stance on illegal ghost-raising or séances, even fake ones such as Lupita was rumored to run.

Rumor, hell. What was about to happen here was obvious, was even more so when a black-painted door opened opposite Chess and an enormous woman thrust her bulk into the room.

Her face was white, her eyes black-ringed, a garish parody of Church Elder makeup. Any resemblance stopped there. Madame Lupita wore a shiny silver caftan, on which were painted various runes and magical symbols. Small pieces of iron hung from it, too small to offer any real protection. Chess supposed they were there for effect, as was the heavy iron-and-amber necklace around the woman's short, fat throat or the matching silver turban covering her head.

Whatever they were for, Lupita's appearance was obviously what the other people around the table expected. Chess felt rather than heard their sigh of satisfaction, their belief that they'd done the right thing in coming here. For those who couldn't afford to pay a Church Liaiser to contact the spirits of their dead loved ones, amateur séances like these seemed the answer to the prayers they were prohibited from uttering.

Too bad they were illegal, which was why Chess was there to begin with. Helping the Black Squad make a case against Lupita meant some extra cash for her.

And too bad it was all fake. If Lupita and her ilk were truly powerful enough to raise ghosts, the Church would have found them through the tests every child in the world underwent at the age of fourteen, would have trained them and hired them. Many of them had a glimmer of power, enough to send a shiver through the air and fool their clients, most of whom had no idea what real power, real magic, felt like.

Chess did. Knew the feeling—loved the feeling— almost as much as the cool, smooth peace of her pills, or the foggy bliss of Dream smoke, or the sparkly, fizzing sensation created by the occasional line of speed. She knew them all, loved them all, because anything that distanced her from reality was a blessing in a world where blessing was against the law.

Of course, her drugs were illegal, too. But that hadn't stopped her from doing them, hadn't stopped her dealer, Bump—or her whatever-he-was, Lex—from selling them. It just meant they all had to be a lot more careful.

Speaking of careful . . . Madame Lupita settled herself at the table, clapped her hands. Something clinked behind Chess. She didn't turn around, but she heard it, soft wings beating the air. A psychopomp. Madame Lupita knew how to put on a show.

"All hold hands," she commanded, in a deep, liquid voice. "No messin, aye . . . hold hands, or they don't come."

To Chess's left sat a rake-thin young man. His fingers were sweaty, his face wet with tears as he stared at the picture on the table before him. Chess couldn't make out the image.

To her right was the female half of a middle-aged couple, clad in a cheap fake silk dress. Her hand shook against Chess's palm.

Lupita reached across the table and grabbed the picture in front of the woman. "What be this girl's name?"

"A-Annabeth. Annabeth Whitman."

Lupita bowed her head. The others did the same, including Chess, who used the opportunity to look around the room from under her lashes.

The psychopomp settled on a perch behind Lupita's left shoulder. A crow, its black feathers gleaming in the firelight. To Chess's right, against the wall, row upon row of skulls grinned blankly at her. Most were small animals, cats and rats and the occasional dog. To her left a wall mural; spirits straining for the sky, their long arms and spidery fingers gruesome and sad.

Sweat beaded on her forehead and trickled down the side of her face. Had it been that hot in there a few minutes before? No one else seemed to be sweating, why was she?

Of course, no one else was wearing a high-necked, long-sleeved sweater, either, despite the cold outside. Chess had no choice; every inch of her arms and chest was decorated with the tattoos marking her as a Church employee, magical symbols that focused her power, warned her, protected her. They tingled now, but whether it was from the heat or her nerves or the tremors in the atmosphere, Chess didn't know. It was nothing serious. She'd been right. Lupita didn't have anywhere near the kind of power required to raise a ghost.

Good thing, too, as she hadn't even bothered to mark her "guests" with basic protective sigils or circle the floor with salt or anything else Church employees learned in their first year of training.

Chess wondered what they might see. Holograms, probably; their technology had advanced to the point where it was difficult or impossible to tell the difference between a real ghost and a fake one—at least if you didn't have any natural abilities in that direction—and if Lupita brought in this kind of money on a regular basis, she could probably afford the top of the line.

Or it could be some of the old-fashioned tricks, the kind used by charlatans long before Haunted Week. Dim lighting, the bizarre and disgusting tea that was probably mildly hallucinogenic, the power of suggestion. Mirrors and shimmery fabric and the customer's own desperate need to believe would take care of the rest.

At least it was safe. A real ghost—a real ghost was something to inspire nightmares. A real ghost, outside of Church control, wasn't going to have a nice little chat with its mommy or beloved friend. A real ghost was going to have one thing on what remained of its mind, and one thing only: to kill. To steal the energy of everyone it came near, to use its life-force to make itself stronger, a parasite that would grow fat on the blood of its victims.

Not one of the people in that room had any fucking idea what it meant to face a real ghost. Lucky for them, they weren't going to find out, either. As soon as Lupita got her little show on the road they could shut her down, and the closest they'd get to a ghost was that hideous mural.

Orange light flashed off silver. Chess looked up along with everyone else, and her already nervous heartbeat kicked into high gear. Madame Lupita held a knife, high over her own exposed forearm. Blood magic. Oh, that was not good. Blood magic, with no circle, no words of protection. Lupita might be powerless, but this was—

The knife descended. Lupita's blood spilled out over her tattoos—so like Chess's, but illegal, another crime to add to the growing list, as if Lupita needed anything more to damn her—onto the silk tablecloth.

"*Kadira tam*, Annabeth Whitman," intoned Madame Lupita. "*Kadira tam.*"

A drop of sweat landed on the table in front of Chess. Her breath rasped in her throat. Shit, she really felt sick. Weak. Exposed, like all her psychic shielding was failing and her power fought to escape.

Escape . . . as Lupita pushed with her own weak power, as she leeched from all of them, Chess felt it, like she was a battery being drained, and in that second, just as the temperature in the room dropped about twenty degrees, she knew something was very, very wrong.

No, Lupita didn't have the power to raise a ghost. But Chess did, and Lupita was pulling it from her. Somehow the woman was reaching into her, *through* her, sucking Chess's strength and focusing it—focusing it on her spell, fuck—

Chess fought, threw as much energy as she could to her shields, but she felt like a child struggling to play tug-of-war against a giant. She couldn't think, her energy was draining away and she couldn't . . . couldn't hold on to it . . . her stomach roiled, her eyelids fluttered.

The crow flapped its wings, danced on the perch for a minute, then took flight. It circled the room, faster and faster. Chess's skin crawled and stung, her tattoos screaming the warning her mouth couldn't seem to form . . .

Lupita's deep chant turned into a screech. Through a bleary haze Chess saw the woman heave herself from her chair, her black-ringed eyes widening in terror. Staring . . . staring at the pale haze taking shape in the corner.

The haze of Annabeth Whitman.

Chess gritted her teeth so hard she thought they might crack and yanked her hand away from Annabeth's mother's. The microrecorder had an emergency button, in case her fellow Church employees weren't already on the way. She had to get out of there, had to have help. Whatever was wrong with her was too much, too bad, for her to hope to defeat the ghost, and if someone didn't do it soon, Annabeth would kill every person in the room.

She found the button, pressed it. And kept pressing it as the pale column grew, as a head appeared. Long tendrils of white formed arms; the shape solidified, growing more detailed with every beat of Chess's panic-stricken heart. She'd lost count of the number of ghosts she'd seen, but the fear never left, never lessened. A ghost—one like this, free of its underground prison, free from Church safeguards and protocols—was a loaded gun, a sword in the hand of a lunatic.

And Chess and everyone else in this flaming pit of hell were the first who'd feel the weapon's rage.

The others didn't seem to understand that something was wrong. Mrs. Whitman was standing, holding her hands out in supplication. "Annabeth . . . my baby . . . we miss you, we wanted to—"

Annabeth's features had formed now, translucent but perfect. She'd been a beautiful girl. Long pale hair hung down over her shoulders; the vague outline of her body beneath her gown was petite and sweetly curved.

Her eyes widened. Chess held her breath for one heart-stopping, hopeful moment. They weren't always vicious, not always. Only ninety-nine percent of the time . . . There was a chance Annabeth would—

No chance. Those innocent eyes narrowed, the perfect lips pulled back in a snarl. Chess barely had time to open her mouth before Annabeth dove for the bloody knife on the table.

In her bag Chess had graveyard dirt and herbs. She couldn't do a full ritual, didn't think she'd have the power to do one even if she had the equipment, but she could freeze Annabeth, stop her from harming anyone.

Her fingers still worked. She tore at the tab of her zipper, yanked it open. Keeping her eyes on Annabeth, she shoved her hand into the bag, past her pillbox and compass and tissues and cash and wipes and all the other crap to find her supplies at the bottom.

Madame Lupita screamed and tried to run, but her weight and flair for the dramatic caught her. She tripped over something—Chess assumed it was the heavy folds of her ridiculous robe—and fell with a thud.

Sweat ran into Chess's eyes. Acid bubbled in her stomach, leapt into her throat. Shit, she was going to be sick, her gut felt like somebody had shoved in a knife and twisted. This wasn't normal. Magic, especially not her own magic, shouldn't make her feel this way, she was— *what was in that tea? What the fuck was in that tea?*

The assistant, the little one, cackled in the corner. "Feelin awry, Churchwitch? Feelin sick?"

Oh, no. They knew who she was—knew what she was. Had known when she walked in the door.

Annabeth lunged for her mother. Chess threw a handful of asafetida and graveyard dirt, tried to put some power behind it as she forced words out of her gummy throat. "Annabeth Whitman, I command you to be still. By the power of the earth that binds you I command it."

Annabeth faltered but kept moving. Not enough power. Shit!

A loud bang, the clattering of footsteps on the stairs. Reinforcements, oh, thank the technology that brought them here, they'd arrived.

Chess spun away from Annabeth. The others would take care of her. Instead Chess dove for the bizarre figure in the garbage bag, straining to focus. The handle of her knife felt cool, solid in her hand, better than almost anything else could.

Up close Chess realized it was a woman behind the makeup. She grabbed the tangle of hair on her head, held the knife at her throat. "What was in the tea?"

The woman giggled. The acrid, silvery odor of speed sweat assaulted Chess's nose. Just what she needed. A fucking Niphead lunatic holding her life in her filthy hand.

"What was in the fucking tea? You don't want to die right now, you'll—"

"You ain't kill me, Churchwitch. Ain't got it in you."

Chess pushed the knife farther up, so it dug into the woman's throat, and focused. She'd killed before. She hadn't wanted to do it and she hadn't liked doing it, but she had. And better yet, she knew people who did it without batting an eye, knew people who'd done worse—hell, if she went back far enough she knew people who'd done worse to *her*. People who made hate rise, boiling and putrid in her chest. She thought of them, let those memories wash over her and crystallize in her head, become something solid and hard.

Behind her all was chaos. The Church employees shouted. The scent of banishing herbs rose thick and dry. Chess ignored it all and stared at the woman at the point of her knife. She stared, and she believed, deep down, that she would drive the knife up, and she let the woman see that belief.

It worked. "Tasro." The woman looked down. "Were tasro."

Poison. Tasro was poison. Chess's head swam.

"Chessie? You okay?"

Dana Wright, another Debunker. Her eyes were wide with concern, her hands still full of herbs.

"Tasro. They put tasro in my drink, they knew me before I even got down the stairs. Is the kit in the van?"

"I'll go with you." Dana reached for her, but Chess ducked away. She didn't want to be touched. Didn't think she could stand it.

"No, just—take this one, okay? I've—I've got to—"

She didn't bother to finish. It felt like she'd swallowed a razor blade and she didn't have much time. Not to mention the tiny prick of uncertainty, of worry. The antidote shouldn't react with her pills, but . . . better to be alone. Just in case.

"You're not supposed to self-administer—"

"I'm fine."

Dana looked like she wanted to say more, but Chess didn't stick around to listen. She ran up the stairs, out the door, and let the icy wind dry the sweat on her forehead.

The Morton case three months before had forever changed her position in the Church. Not just her job itself—in addition to Debunking she now worked occasionally with other departments, which was how she'd gotten to run point in tonight's deadly party—but in the eyes of those she worked with. Half of them looked at her like she was the great Betrayer and the other half seemed to think she was some sort of fucking genius for banishing Ereshdiran the Dreamthief—but only *after* he'd killed Randy Duncan, another Debunker. That Randy had summoned the entity in the first place made a difference only to some.

Chess didn't give a shit either way. The only thing she

minded was that the anonymity she'd once prized had disappeared, and now she felt eyes on her everywhere she went. Which sucked. Who knew what they might see if they paid attention? Church employees were not supposed to be addicts.

Her skeleton key unlocked the van's back door and she yanked it open with a bit more force than necessary. Somewhere in the back was a first-aid kit with a variety of antidotes along with basic remedies like bandages and antibiotic ointment.

She climbed in, leaving the door open so more cold wind could blast her. It wasn't just the air of the shack that had made her warm, wasn't just the poison either. She'd taken an extra Cept before entering the building, not knowing how long the ritual and resulting paper-work would take and not wanting to be caught out if it took too long. If she sat still and focused, she'd be able to feel the high, but there wasn't time. Not unless she wanted it to be the last high she ever felt, which she didn't.

The kit was hidden beneath the back bench seat. Chess dug it out and opened it. Fuck. Somewhere in the back of her mind she'd hoped the antidotes weren't kept in syringes anymore. So much for hope . . .

The needle was cold, too. Great.

Voices rode the wind into the van. She had no idea how far away the others were, but she preferred to have this done with before they returned. Nobody would think twice about it, not after Dana told them what had happened. But that didn't make the thought of being found in the back of the van with a spike in her vein any more pleasant. Too close to the truth, perhaps, the undeniable fact that she was only a short jump away from that fucking needle turning into a vital part of her life, that only fear and willpower had kept her from it so far.

The rubber catheter was stiff, not wanting to be tied. Chess could relate. She didn't want to tie it. Fear curled in her stomach and sat there like a lump of half-rotten Downside meat. She tied off, clenching her fist to pop a vein, slapping the crook of her arm. Something she'd sworn to herself she'd never do. That she was doing it to save her life—doing it with Church sanction, the way they'd been taught to do—didn't seem to count, not when she'd seen this moment coming, dreaded this moment almost every time she opened her pillbox.

She shook her head. This was ridiculous. Everything was under control, *she* was under control, now more than ever. She didn't owe anyone money, she had plenty of pills, she *maintained*. A happy medium.

One quick stab, that was all it would take. She could do that, it would be easy. She'd barely feel it, right?

Not right. The freezing needle buried itself into her vein and when she shoved the plunger down, cold shot up her arm like a crack in ice. Tears stung the corners of her eyes and she turned her face away while she yanked the catheter off, not wanting to watch the syringe bob in time with her pulse while she fumbled in the kit for a cotton ball.

It only took a few seconds for the antidote to warm up. Another few to find the cotton and press it into place after she withdrew the needle. It was over. She'd done it, and it hadn't been so bad.

That was the scariest thing of all.

Chapter Two

Madame Lupita's curses and screams as she was
dragged into the Church van still echoed in Chess's head
when she walked into Trickster's Bar a few hours later.
It was early by Downside time, not quite one o'clock.
The Rolling Ghosts were playing and she wanted to
catch the tail end if she could. At least that would chase
the memories and sounds away.

And at least it was warm, in the sweaty, stifling way of
bars. Her earlier sensation of being overheated had
vanished by the time she finished giving her report at the
Church and headed back home to Downside. Even if it
hadn't, the drafts from the stained-glass window that
made up one entire wall of her apartment and the lazy
water heater that turned showers in winter into a gamble
would have finished it.

Thanks to the Dreamthief case, she got most of her
drugs for free—not through her regular dealer, Bump,
but through Lex, who worked for Bump's chief rival,
Slobag. She didn't know what exactly Lex did for Slobag.
Not only had she never bothered to ask, she doubted he
would tell her if she did. Their relationship, such as it
was, worked a lot better when they kept their mouths
busy elsewhere, but the fact remained that since she

didn't pay for most of her drugs, she could have afforded to move.

Could have, and probably should have. Somehow, despite having more money in theory, it didn't quite work out that way. Instead of more money she ended up with more drugs. Something told her that was probably not healthy. Something else in her didn't give a shit. And the rest of her was realistic enough to know it didn't matter.

Lex was fun. She liked him, and he gave her what she wanted in more ways than one. But dependable he was not—maybe she wouldn't have liked him as much if he had been—and she couldn't count on free drugs forever. Sooner or later she'd need to supply herself again, and living cheap was the only way to keep up.

Besides, Downside was her home, and there weren't many better places available. At least her building—a converted Catholic church, one of the few that hadn't been destroyed when Haunted Week ended twenty-four years before—was quiet. Even the hookers on the corner kept it down most of the time, which was more than could be said for most of the neighborhood.

The bouncer stepped aside for her, admitting her into the dark red interior of the bar. The Rolling Ghosts hadn't gone on yet. Instead the Clash blared out of the speakers, loud enough to turn the talking heads in the room into ghosts themselves, silent but trying to overcome it.

She didn't want to think about ghosts. She held up a finger at the bartender and gripped the beer he handed her with fingers that were finally starting to lose their stiffness.

Terrible stood in his usual spot near the back. She headed for him, watching the red lights play off his shiny black hair and illuminate the breathtaking ugliness of his profile. She didn't notice it anymore, not really; even now her eyes simply slid over it. He was Terrible, that was all. He was her friend . . . sort of.

But she knew it was what everyone else saw. The heavy, jutting brow; the crooked nose that looked as though the bones were trying to break out through the skin; the scars; the jaw like the prow of a ship. They saw the thick muttonchop sideburns, the impenetrable darkness of his eyes, and backed away. A face like that was a walking advertisement that the man behind it didn't give a fuck, and a man who didn't give a fuck was a very scary man indeed, especially considering he made his living as Bump's chief enforcer, especially considering his size. Someone catching sight of him expected the shoulders to end before they did, expected the chest to be less broad. They didn't, and they weren't.

Chess watched him lurking back there for a few more seconds before he caught sight of her. His chin lifted in a greeting, but he made no other move. Something bothering him, then, and no way to ask. They'd tried to have a deep conversation in a crowded bar once before. It hadn't ended well. Chess tried not to think about it.

"Hey, Chess," he said. She got the words not so much from his voice, barely a rumbling murmur over "Garageland," as from watching his lips move. "Figured you ain't coming after all, getting so late. You right?"

"Yeah. Right up. The job went on longer than I expected."

"Lookin pale."

She shrugged and drank her beer. No point discussing it, not when they could barely hear each other. "When are they going on?"

"Few minutes, maybe. Not long. They—Hold on." From his pocket he produced a small black phone and flipped it open. The stark white glow of the screen invaded the darkness of the corner and highlighted his furrowed brow. "Fuck."

"What's—"

He cut her off with a look, a quick jerk of the head to

indicate she should follow. This she did, trying to stay in his wake as he cut back through the crowd to the front of the room, narrowly avoiding razoring her cheek on some guy's Liberty spikes, and out the front doors.

Desultory clumps of people huddled outside, braving the cold to get a free listen once the band started playing. They shuffled out of the way when Terrible headed for the side of the building. Chess followed. For a second the cold soothed her heated skin before it became too much and she shivered. She should have brought a jacket, but they were such pains in the ass to hold on to in a club.

"Got problems." He didn't look at her as he dialed the phone and lifted it to his ear. "You know Red Berta, aye?"

"I know who she is." Red Berta handled all of Bump's girls—which meant she handled all of the Downside prostitutes west of Forty-third.

"Well—Hey." Whoever he'd called must have answered. "Aye, she—When they find it? Shit. Aye, hang on. I'll be there."

She knew before he snapped the phone shut that he wanted her to go with him. What she didn't know was why.

"What's going on?"

He stood for a moment with his eyes narrowed, sliding the phone back into his pocket without paying attention while he worked out whatever it was he needed to work out. "Feel like riding with me?"

"What's going on?"

"Dead body." His other hand went into his pocket. The movement made his shoulders look even broader, but the threat of his size had never been less evident. "One of Bump's girls. Third one they find."

"Somebody's killing hookers?"

He shrugged. "Looking like a ghost doing the killing. Wouldn't ask otherwise."

"What, just in the streets?"

"Ain't you cold? Whyn't you come on, Chess. Warmer in the car, aye? Just take a look." His head turned back toward the huddled crowd. Right. Probably not a good idea to discuss this in public. So she nodded and followed him across the street while the music kept playing inside the bar.

Terrible's '69 BT Chevelle straddled the curb two doors down, making the streetlight look like it was set up just to display it. New black paint gleamed in the orange glare. Chess was almost afraid to touch it, the way she would be afraid to approach any predator. The car seemed ready to leap forward on its fat black tires at any moment and start swallowing the road.

Sitting on the leather seat was like sitting on a block of ice, but Chess didn't mention it. Terrible didn't seem in the mood for jokes. Instead she waited for him to talk, knowing he'd get to it in his own time.

They'd gone about ten blocks through the abandoned streets west of Downside's red-light district before he did. "First hooker," he said. "But the third body, dig? Bump ain't paid much attention before, outside getting pissed. Dealer first. Slick Michigan, know him?"

She shook her head. The heater was starting to work; she could have relaxed if it weren't for her nerves. The last thing she wanted to do was get involved with a murderous ghost. Another murderous ghost, that is— she still hadn't fully recovered from the Dreamthief.

Terrible kept talking while she fished out her pillbox and popped a couple of Cepts, washing them down with the beer she still held. "Found him maybe five weeks ago, down by the docks. Nobody think much of it. You know how them docks get. And Slick weren't exactly the calm type. Figure he gets into a fight, aye? Plays with some boy got a quick knife hand."

"He was knifed?"

"Aye."

"But then—"

He glanced at her. "Second one came a couple weeks ago, guessing. Little Tag. He a runner, aye? Ain't sell, ain't handle much. Just carryin from one place to another. Found him in an alley off Brewster."

"I didn't even know there were alleys off Brewster." She looked out the window. They'd gone south first, down to Mather. Now Terrible swung the big car left against the light. What was a hooker doing this far off the drag, this close to the end of Bump's territory?

"Aye. Ain't much good in them places, neither. Nobody even sure how long he was there. He body . . . ain't pretty, if you dig. Hardly any left." He took a long pull on his own beer and set it back down between his thighs, then took two cigarettes from his pocket and lit them.

Chess took the one he offered her and leaned back in her seat, letting the smoke curl out of her mouth and up toward the roof. "And now a girl," she said.

"Aye."

"You still haven't told me why you think it's a ghost."

"Ain't sure it's a ghost. Not me, not Bump. Got others thinking so, though."

"So you want me to come in and say it isn't?"

"Be a help, aye."

"But what if it is?"

He glanced at her as he pulled the car up by a burned-out building. "You think be a ghost, Bump gonna call the Church, ask them take care of it? Or you think he come to you?"

Shit.

His jacket practically swallowed her when she slipped it on. She shrugged it off and handed it back. Best not to look like a little girl. Probably best not to show up wearing his clothes, either. Their casual friendship already sparked enough rumors—although those probably wouldn't have been as fierce if she hadn't lost her head and let half of Downside see her practically fucking him in a bar three months before. She shrugged the memory off, too, tried to focus on what was in front of her instead of what was behind.

Fires in steel trash cans added a little heat to the air and cast eerie shadows against the blank, broken walls along the street. Forty-fifth was practically no-man's-land this far down, a street constantly under siege from Slobag's men as they struggled to gain more territory. Here and there lights flickered in broken windows, indicating human inhabitants, but for the most part only shattered bottles and dirty needles called the street home.

Chess glanced to her left, across the street. A block away Slobag's buildings started. Ten or eleven blocks farther north and a few east lived Lex. She shivered and had to force herself not to cross her arms over her chest. If she was going to suffer the cold in order to look tough, she needed to do it right.

The cold was abating a bit anyway as those last two Cepts worked their way into her system. Speaking of Lex, she'd need to go see him in the morning.

A tall woman with a mane of red hair so bright it glowed in the light strode away from the ragtag crowd and headed toward them. Her long legs were wrapped in woolly tights almost the same color, finished with thick knee-high orange-striped socks that peeped from the toes of her red high-heeled sandals. She wore no skirt, only a thick green sweater, and over her shoulders hung a sleek black fur coat. On anyone else Chess would have thought it was rat, but this was Red Berta. It could have been sealskin from before Haunted Week, or just about anything else. She looked terrifying, like a doll dressed by a homicidal child.

"Terrible," she said, and beneath the brashness of her tone Chess heard her fear, felt it tingle. "Took you long enough."

He didn't reply, just pushed his way through the ring of people and glanced back at Chess. She followed, her steps slowing against her will. A dead body was not what she'd had in mind when she went out for a drink. A dead body, in fact, was never what she had in mind for anything, and feeling so many eyes on her did not make it easier.

Some watched with curiosity, some with hostility. Those she could ignore. It was the hope that drove a knife into her stomach and twisted it. A few girls in short skirts, their pale legs the ashy pinkish-white that indicated the beginning of hypothermia, huddled together and stared at her as if she could wave a magic wand and bring their friend back to life. Very few people realized she really wasn't that powerful. Usually it made her life easier. Tonight it didn't.

Neither did the unmistakable evidence that at least a few of these girls were using some low-level sex magic. Not unusual for those in their profession, but not comfortable for Chess. Their energy licked over her skin, damp and insistent. Molesting her. Heating her blood against her will. The warmth was welcome; the reason for it was not. Neither were the memories it brought back. She never used sex magic.

Terrible caught her eye. His were shadowed, both from the absence of light and from something like sadness. Not good, then. She steeled herself and went to his side.

Empty eye sockets stared at the sky, filled with blood. It was all Chess saw for a long minute, that dark space where life should be. Whoever had killed the girl hadn't just taken her eyes, he'd cut the flesh around them so bone peeped from the ragged edges. Chess closed her own eyes and set her feet more firmly on the cracked sidewalk. Not just because of the sight before her; that same invasive magic hung in the air around the girl, stronger than from any of the others.

That didn't make sense. The girl was dead. Her spell should have died with her instead of insinuating itself farther into Chess's own energy, curling and spinning, tinged with a throbbing darkness Chess didn't understand. Instead of running hot it felt cold, dank, and oppressive. Like being shoved into a cave. She knelt by the girl's pale, motionless arm, hoping to steady her trembling legs.

The girl's age was indeterminate, in the way of most prostitutes. She could have been fifteen or fifty; the slack, ruined skin of her face told Chess nothing.

Neither did her body. Beneath the blood already freezing into a crackled coating, her limbs were slender, but it was rare in Downside to find people who managed to eat more than a few times a week. Almost everyone was thin, even painfully so.

The only thing that stood out about the girl, save the obvious, horrible fact of her death, was the thick sex energy wrapping itself around Chess, sliding up her arm when she touched the girl's ice-hard flesh. It couldn't be hers, it couldn't belong to her. It had to be an aftereffect of her death. Part of the ritual, perhaps? Had they somehow used sex magic to kill her? The darkness hiding in that energy, smooth and secret as an intimate chuckle, indicated that whatever it had been, it was not a regular sex spell.

"It be the Cryin Man," someone said helpfully. "He tooken she eyes, so she ain't see him even in the City, aye?"

"Left his mark on her, too," another voice piped in, younger and higher with fear. "On her, and on yon wall."

Chess glanced up, finding the speaker's pointing finger and following it to the symbol scratched into the wall. Not a rune, as she'd originally feared. A glyph of some kind, like a gang sign. A triangle, decorated with upside-down arrows and crosses. It looked more like a bizarre doodle than something to inspire fear, but the hairs on the back of her neck stood up just the same.

Finding the symbol on the girl took a minute. Chess expected it would be carved into that too-pale skin, but it wasn't. The mark covered her left breast, just below the plunging neckline of the girl's hot-pink top. Not cut in. Burned. And burned before she died, because blisters had started to rise on the wound.

"Did anybody hear anything?" She had to clear her throat to get the words out, to busy herself with snapping a couple of quick pictures of the mark to keep from seeing the entire body, as if she could filter away the girl's lost humanity by viewing it through the lens.

"Cryin Man ain't let she scream," someone told her. "Nobody hear nothing."

"Was anyone with her?" Did it matter? Shit, how was she supposed to do this? Yes, Debunkers sometimes investigated witchcraft-related crimes, but only as they related to cases like Madame Lupita's or ghost abuse. She wasn't a detective. How the fuck did Terrible or Bump expect her to look at this poor dead girl and know whether or not a ghost had done this?

Of course . . . shit, she already knew one hadn't, at least not alone. Ghosts couldn't do magic. Unless the girl had been trying out an incredibly strong new spell—not likely, as the kind of power Chess felt wasn't the kind just anyone could project—her murderer had definitely been human.

Red Berta shoved someone forward, one of the hookers standing in the circle. The girl stumbled on her teetery shoes and righted herself, but not before Chess saw how high she was.

"I hadda go get somethin," the girl mumbled, swaying in place.

"You left Daisy alone to die." Red Berta fixed her with a glare that would have made a sober person quake. At almost six feet tall, Berta wasn't someone to mess with. She'd been a showgirl before Haunted Week—Haunted Week and an attack from a razor-wielding ghost. Berta had survived. Her looks had not.

Chess stood and glanced at Terrible's impassive face, then back at the girl. "Did you see anything? When you got back?"

"Bettin she saw lotsa things," someone whispered in the back. "Flowers an puppies floatin upward the sky, aye?"

"Saw the spook." The girl hugged herself. "Saw it disappear when I come back."

"You saw the ghost?"

"Aye."

"What did it look like?"

"Wearin a hat."

Fear rippled through the crowd as everyone took a step back. "She seen the Cryin Man. Cryin Man wear a hat."

Before Chess could reply, Berta spoke up. "Terrible." She nodded across the street.

Chess followed the look with the slow sinking feeling of someone whose night had just gone from worse to deadly.

Slobag's men watched them from the alley.

Chapter Three

It wasn't a large crowd. Five, perhaps six men stood in the shadows, caught by the firelight. They didn't move when all faces turned toward them. Somehow that stillness was more threatening than sharpening machetes or playing with guns would have been, as if they knew beyond a doubt there would be no reliable defense against their attack.

Then Terrible stepped forward, lifting the bottom of his bowling shirt so the diamond-patterned handle of his knife showed. Chess tried not to respond. On his opposite hip the brushed steel butt of a gun reflected the watery moonlight. When had he started carrying a gun? Usually he didn't, at least not so obviously.

Next to Chess, Berta reached up and extracted what looked like a machete from the crimson bird's nest of her hair. In an instant the mood changed from terrified sadness to hot rage. Excitement. Butterfly knives opened in a blur of metal, zippers gave way so sharpened nail files and pipes could be pulled from cheap nylon purses. One of the girls flicked open an ivory-handled straight razor that had to be a hundred years old. Nobody spoiled for a fight like a group of Downside hookers around the corpse of one of their own.

Slobag's men didn't move. Fuck! What was she supposed to do here? Slobag's men were Lex's men, and she doubted he'd take too kindly to her fighting with them, no matter how much he liked having her in his bed. On the other hand, Terrible was her friend, and the people around her were—well, they were his friends, or his to protect, anyway.

Not to mention the dead body turning to ice on the pavement at her feet.

"Chess," Terrible said, his lips barely moving. He held his head like he was sniffing the air for prey. "Whyn't you head back into yon alley, aye? Get yourself offen the street."

"I have my knife."

"Naw, naw. Get on out. Ain't your fight."

Wasn't going to be a fight at all, if she had anything to say about it. She held up her hand, intending to pat him on the back or arm, something to show her thanks, but she dropped it before it reached him. It would only be a distraction.

Instead she pulled her phone out of her bag as she picked her way through the black alley. Things rustled and moved in the garbage piled along the battered walls. Rats, probably. Maybe cats or small dogs. She stepped carefully, hearing the sliding *shink* of Terrible's knife being drawn as she opened the phone.

The bright screen hurt her eyes and made her feel like a fucking target, standing there in a pool of light. It hit her then what she'd done. Left the fight, picked up a phone. Target indeed. She didn't have much time.

Her fingers didn't shake as she scrolled down to Lex's code name. He was only one of three numbers she had programmed into the phone.

Her ass hit something hard and sharp-edged when she crouched down. A metal box of some kind. Her mind automatically took note of it—it looked like just the sort of place to hide electronic equipment of the kind used to fake hauntings—but Lex picked up before she had time to really register it.

"Hey, Tulip, what you up to this night?"

"Call them off, Lex," she whispered, but as the words left her mouth she knew she was too late. Someone shouted. The fight was on. They clashed in the middle of the street opposite the alley, giving her a perfect view of what was happening. Not just five or six of Slobag's men; at least as many again poured onto the street from somewhere. How many had been waiting, and why? Did they just keep an eye on the street, or what?

"Call who off? Ain't know what you saying. You right?"

"No, I'm not fucking right. Your men, Lex. Slobag's men. They're here, they're—" A scream cut her off. Red Berta in full battle cry, the voice that used to belt out show tunes, striking fear into the hearts of anyone within a few miles. The machete sliced through the air and grabbed a piece of one of Slobag's men. He howled and stumbled sideways.

Terrible didn't miss a beat, grabbing the man's hair and slamming a heavy fist into his face. The man fell. Terrible turned to the next one.

All around were the hookers, stabbing at the men with their small blades, wielding pipes like pros. Sharp heels dug into soft leather shoes. They were holding their own, but they were outnumbered. Even as Chess watched, one of the girls went flying, her screech ending abruptly when her face hit the street.

"The fuck is that sound? Where you at?"

"I'm on Forty-fifth, dammit, Forty-fifth and Berrie, and there's a bunch of your guys here and they've started a—"

"What you doing there? Ain't nowhere near your place."

"Can we talk about this later? Call them off, *now*."

Metal scraped the pavement. A long, slim knife skittered on the sidewalk across the mouth of the alley, the blade sticky and dark. One of the men fell. His blood steamed in the cold air.

"Shit. A fight? You safe, Tulip?"

"For about the next two minutes. Lex, I'm not kidding here. There's a fight, and it's on Forty-fifth and I'm stuck in the fucking middle of it, please find out who it is and call them off!"

Another scream. Blood spurted from one of the hookers' arms. Chess couldn't tell which one she was, and in a moment the girl had disappeared, another wounded fighter in a crowd full of them. Over it all Terrible's face, oddly peaceful, totally absorbed. As she watched he ducked down, catching a man midleap and shoving him over his shoulder and onto the street. His knife flashed in his fist.

"Stay on, aye? Gimme a minute." Over the screams and shouts of the brawl she heard Lex speaking Cantonese to someone, heard several different voices answer.

Chess crouched lower in her not-very-good hiding place, her stare focused on the fight. Berta kept swinging her machete, southpaw. Chess expected to see heads start flying at any second. With her free hand she found her knife; her palm was so sweaty it took her three tries to get a grip on it and pull it out. Just in case . . .

"Tulip? You there?"

It took her a few seconds to find her voice. "Yeah. I'm here."

"Aye, hang on there. All be over soon. You all hidden up? Stay out of sight. Them dudes, they ain't know you, dig?"

"Yeah. Yeah, I get it."

"What you doing on Forty-fifth?"

"Terrible asked me—"

"Terrible's there? All by hisself, aye?"

"No, not by himself. There's a fucking army here, okay? And even if he was by himself—which he isn't—I wouldn't tell you."

"Thought you was fun."

"I'm not."

"Why he ask you to go there for, anyhow? Ain't safe there, you know that."

"There's a—there's a dead girl. One of Bump's girls." Hell, he was going to find out anyway, if any of his men made it back safely. Which she guessed they would. A voice rose over the shrieks of the girls on the street, Cantonese ratcheting through the empty air. A call to retreat, she hoped.

"Oh? Looks like somebody getting some payback," Lex said with satisfaction. The empty eye sockets of the dead girl flashed into Chess's mind. If he'd been standing in front of her, she'd have tried to slap him.

"What? What are you talking about?"

"Ain't talking about nothing. Just saying, is all."

"What's that—I gotta go." She snapped the phone shut as Terrible appeared at the end of the alley, his broad form blocking out what little light there was. Behind him she saw Slobag's men becoming shadows again, disappearing into the spaces between the buildings.

"Come on out now, Chess."

Her legs didn't want to support her as she stood. More bodies appeared—Red Berta, a few of the other girls, Chess couldn't tell which ones. All were panting like they were being paid extra to get into it, but they were alive.

Most of them, anyway. The hooker Chess had watched fly through the air did not get up. Neither did four of Slobag's men. Red Berta and her girls emptied the dead men's pockets with crisp efficiency, like murderous bank tellers.

Chess dug into her bag and pulled out some tissues, which she used to dab at the deep, swelling cut under Terrible's eye. She had to brace her free hand against his chest and stand on tiptoe to do it, putting her face only inches from his when he looked down at her.

Their eyes met, and heat flooded her skin. Her heels slammed back onto the sidewalk. "Sorry, maybe, um, maybe you should—here."

She shoved the wad of tissues at him, felt him take them from her. Too bad he couldn't take away the confusion—and something like panic—making her stomach feel like someone was tickling it from the inside. Stupid sex magic.

She cleared her throat. "Another half-inch to the left and you'd need a hospital."

Orange light caught the wet spots on his shirt and illuminated a long rip in one sleeve. Beneath it the flesh was almost as raw as his knuckles.

"Naw, I'm right." He took the tissues away, sniffled, and pressed them back against his face.

"It'll scar."

A deep rumble of laughter. "Guess another scar make a difference?"

He had her there.

"What's your thinkin on Daisy?"

"Wh—oh." The dead girl still lay on the pavement. Whitish frost on her skin turned her into an eerie sculpture, like the statues of the original Church leaders outside the Government Headquarters up Northside. Those were carved from white limestone, coated with diamond dust to make them gleam. The rime on Daisy's dead body created the same illusion, making her mutilated form beautiful.

"I don't—I don't know. If it was a ghost, I mean. It's really too soon for me to tell, it's so dark and . . ." Chess shivered. She'd have to tell him about the sex spell, but not now. Not when her blood still simmered a little too fast for comfort.

"Aye. Don't worry on it, Chess. Maybe you free tomorrow, come back for another look? In the daylight, dig at the walls an all. Bring yon Church stuff, them little machines and all you use."

"I thought you didn't think it was a ghost."

His eyelids flickered and he nodded toward the huddle of girls, counting their money and lighting the dead men's smokes. "They do. Bump an me, we ain't so sure. You ain't think it's fair chances, them showing up here this night, aye?"

"You think—"

"I pick you up tomorrow round midday, cool?"

She didn't want to. It wasn't that she didn't want to help him; it was that Lex's words about payback wouldn't stop echoing in her head. If this was a gang thing, some sort of territory struggle, she did *not* need to be involved. Her life worked, as much as it could. Getting in between the people to whom she owed her loyalty—the one person to whom she owed loyalty, anyway, all Bump did was sell her pills and run the closest pipe room to her apartment—and the one with whom she swapped bodily fluids probably wasn't the best way to make sure it kept working.

But there really was no good way to refuse. It wouldn't just look suspicious, it would be . . . it would be wrong.

She glanced again at Daisy's body, abandoned like a busted Dream pipe on the cracked and pitted sidewalk. If it weren't for the Church, that could have been her. Probably would have been her. Certainly it was what she'd grown up expecting.

So she nodded. "They told me not to worry about coming in tomorrow, not after what happened tonight. No new cases anyway."

"They give you the day off? How bad your night go?"

"Oh . . . it was nothing. I got poisoned a little bit. They had an antidote, no big deal."

He cocked an eyebrow.

"Don't look at me like that. I'm here, right? No problem. Where's the girl who saw the ghost?"

He started to say something, then stopped himself. "Laria. She name is Laria."

"Yeah, her." Chess scanned the little crowd of women, picking out the frizzy brown head. Laria stood near the back, a confused look on her face. Chess tried to catch the girl's eye, but she wasn't sure if it was possible for anyone to catch the girl's eye at this stage; she looked like she was ready to keel over backward.

"I get her."

Laria looked younger close up than Chess had thought. Sixteen, perhaps, or seventeen at the oldest. Her pale blue jacket had stains on the sleeves and a tear in one elbow. When she squeezed her arms tighter around her chest her pinkish-white skin poked through the hole like a turtle peeping from its shell.

"Laria, I'm Chess. Could you tell me what you saw earlier? The man who killed Daisy?"

Laria shook her head. Her clouded brown eyes filled with tears. "Ain't seen nothin."

"You said earlier you saw—"

Laria shook her head again. Her hair moved with it like a clump of dirty steel wool.

Chess glanced at Terrible, not bothering to hide her irritation. She had sympathy, sure, but it was late and freezing cold and she just wanted to go home, and Laria's reticence wasn't helping anyone.

He gripped Laria's arm. "You tell she, girl. Only way for us to catch him, dig?"

"I ain't—"

"Ain't nothing. You the one left she alone so's you could go stab up, aye? Least you owe she some knowledge."

Laria gasped; Terrible's fist was so tight around her arm that his thumb pressed the second knuckle of his middle finger. "Terrible, you hurting—"

"Be hurtin worse, you don't talk up."

Chess held out her hand. "We can do this tomorrow, can't we?"

"Come the morrow she won't get any recall," he said. "Gotta get what we can now."

Laria's cheeks were wet. "He had a hat on. All's I remember, he had a hat on."

"He big? Small? You see through him?" Terrible's grip relaxed, his voice softened. "Come on, Laria. You recall it, aye? You just gotta think on it."

"He weren't big. Ain't much bigger'n me. He were bendin over her when I come close enough to see—he stood up and he was . . ." Laria swallowed once, then again. "I seed through him."

"He was transparent?"

"Could see through him," Laria whispered. "'Ceptin he looked up at me, under the brim o' his hat, aye . . . funny hat, with a point in the center and them flaps on the side, on the ears? All of him clear, his clothes and all, 'ceptin . . ." She raised a hand to her face, patted trembling fingers beneath one eye.

"His eyes?" The chill creeping up Chess's spine had nothing to do with the temperature of the air.

"Not his eyes," Laria said, and it came out like the low moan of a wounded animal. "Hers."

"What?"

Laria started to cry. "Him were wearin she eyes."

Chapter Four

You must always be vigilant in guarding against the desires of the flesh. Even those acts not deemed illegal can stain the soul in some situations.

—*The Book of Truth*, Rules, Article 278

The knock on the door came just when she'd started to think it wouldn't. Typical Lex. She opened it, determined not to let her tiredness loosen her lips.

Of course there were other things to do with those. Despite the way she'd hung up on him earlier, he seemed to be in a good mood—at least his kiss indicated he was. She was almost dizzy by the time he pulled away and set a plastic baggie in her hand. More pills.

"Plan on giving me the clapperclaw, Tulip?" His dark eyes gleamed with amusement—or desire. She didn't bother to analyze.

"It's no more than you deserve, being so flippant. I thought I was going to get killed in that damn alley."

"But you ain't killed." He opened her fridge and grabbed a couple of beers. "Look, you still here. So whyn't you tell me what was on the happening?"

She stiffened. "Why do you want to know?"

"Ain't I allowed some curiosity? You get stuck in the middle of some road brawl, I can't ask why you was there in the start? Why you always so mean to me?"

"I'm not mean."

"Aye, you sure is mean." He kissed her forehead and handed her an opened beer. She watched him slump gracefully onto the couch and lean back, his Buzzcocks T-shirt riding up to expose a thin line of flat stomach. "Especially after I called them men off. But no matter. Come on in here and sit down."

She drank off half her beer in one nervous swig. She did not want to sit down. If she put herself within easy reach of him, they'd never get around to discussing anything, even if she wasn't still jacked from the sex magic around that poor dead girl. "Tell me what you meant first."

"Meant by what?"

"You know what. You said it was about time Bump got some payback. What did that mean?"

"You ain't really wanna talk about dead folks and that Bump, do you? I ain't seen you in a week."

"Just tell me what you meant, and then we can talk about anything you want."

She didn't want to ask him if Slobag's men were responsible for the dead girl. Didn't want to ask, because fear coiled in her stomach when she thought about what his answer might be. Payback could mean a lot of things, yes, and she honestly couldn't believe he would have anything to do with men who would cut the eyeballs out of a human head, living or not. But still . . .

Finally he shrugged. "Lot goes on here, you know that. Sometimes people turn up dead, and no way of knowing who did the killing."

"That's not an answer."

"You ain't asked a question."

"Do you know anything about the dead girl? Do you—do you know who killed her?"

He didn't act offended, or as though he didn't understand the question. That, more than the way his gaze grabbed hers and held, made her believe him. "Nay, Tulip. Ain't had nothing to do with it. Nothing at all. Don't know who does—order ain't come down from us, dig?"

The breath she hadn't realized she was saving left her in a quiet rush, only to catch again when he said, "Coursen, Bump ain't say the same thing."

"What?"

"You hearing right. Can't say as that girl ain't payback from somebody decided to take matters into they own hands."

Without thinking Chess reached into the baggie he'd given her, still dangling from her clenched fist, and extracted a couple of pills, swallowing them with more beer. Hey, she didn't have to get up early in the morning. Good thing, too, as it was after three.

"'Specially with she so close to us, hanging the border like that. Why she up there? You ask Terrible that one?"

"No."

"Maybe you oughta."

Talking to Lex about Terrible made her twitchy, as it always did. It felt like they were talking around something rather than through it. She crossed the open space between the wall and the kitchen and leaned on the countertop, hiding her lower body. "I wish you would stop hinting around and say whatever it is you're trying to say."

"I'm saying, you gots a dead hooker. Only it ain't the first dead hooker I seen about."

"What? Wait. You mean somebody's been killing hookers on your side? Slobag's girls?"

He nodded. "See? I keep thinking you smart, you keep proving me right."

"And you think Bump's behind them."

"Who else?"

She blinked. "No offense, Lex, but they're hookers. I can think of a lot of who elses." Like the Cryin Man, she thought, but did not say. Life had taught her ghosts were real, but the Church had taught her to be skeptical when faced with rumors of one, even if the magical evidence of human involvement wasn't making fine sweat break out on her skin.

"Aye? Like who. They ain't with a trick, dig, when it happen. Just picked right off'n the street. You think—hey." Chess watched the nimble movements of his hands as he lit a cigarette and exhaled thick bluish smoke, more fragrant than the cheaper smokes everyone else she knew bought. "You figure it for a spook, aye? Bump bringing you in to catch a ghost."

"I didn't say that."

"Ain't gotta say it. You ain't got such a stiff face as you suppose, least not with me. I got some practice with you, aye? So Bump bringing you in to see if you gotta kicker doing the killing. Lemme say, Tulip, you sure do get yourself in demand."

She raised an eyebrow. He grinned. "Oh, you in demand with me, and you know it. How Bump trick you into checking this one out?"

She blinked. There hadn't actually been a trick, had there? Only the vague, implied threat that if she didn't do it, Bump might make trouble for her. Maybe invent another debt—she still bought from him, despite getting most of her drugs free from Lex, simply because to stop buying from him would raise suspicion. And she wouldn't dare visit Slobag's pipe rooms. Not everyone in Downside stayed with Bump or Slobag. Some switched back and forth. The last thing she needed was to be recognized, even if most of the Chinese gangs—like Slobag's gang—didn't hate Church employees on principle.

Not that she didn't understand. When so much of your culture was based on ancestor worship, to be suddenly told you had to pay to commune with their spirits in a Church-approved fashion had to be a bite. Understanding didn't make life easier, though.

"No trick," she said finally, realizing he was watching her decide what to say.

"Just doing it outta the kindness of your heart, aye?"

She nodded. The trap was there, she knew it and she knew what it would be. What she didn't know was how to get out of it.

"So you gonna help me too, aye?" He stood up and came toward her, his footsteps silent on the floor. She watched him advance, again seeing the trap and this time not caring. Quite the opposite, in fact. She was ready to fling herself into its steel-sharp teeth by the time he stood behind her.

His hand slid over her hips and forward, palm flat on her stomach, fingertips working their way under the waistband of her jeans.

"Maybe ghosts on my side of town, what do you guess?" Smoke from his cigarette touched her skin when he pushed her hair back from her shoulder. His teeth scraped her earlobe and nibbled a line down so he could suck gently on her neck the way he knew she liked. "Think you come over there, help me out?"

"I think I help you out enough already," she managed. He popped the button on her jeans, slid the zipper down to give himself room to get his hand into her panties. She gasped.

"Think we help each other here, ain't you? Got anything I can help you with, Tulip?"

"Maybe." She reached back, finding him hard and ready beneath his jeans and opening them.

He made a low, satisfied sound in the back of his throat, one she'd come to associate with him and the time they spent in his bed. The cigarette flew into the sink and landed with a tiny sizzle. His palms slid up her ribcage under her shirt, under her bra, then back down to shove her jeans and panties off her hips.

"What you say? Gonna help me? Come round my neighborhood, check the sights?" His hand on the back of her neck forced her gently down, bending her over the counter, while one knee pressed the inside of her thigh and urged her legs apart as far as they could go with her jeans pooled around her ankles. His erection butted up against her, hovering, waiting. "Sure could *use* you, Tulip."

"Yes," she managed.

"What's that? Ain't sure I caught it."

She drew as deep a breath as her tight throat would let her. "Yes."

One hard thrust told her how much he appreciated her answer.

Eight hours later she crossed the empty square in front of the Church with her sunglasses on and a few lines of speed making her heart beat fast enough to get her moving. Lex had hung around until almost five, and she'd woken up to the sound of the phone ringing just after ten. Elder Griffin calling. A new case had arrived unexpectedly, could she come down and start it up?

She pushed the sunglasses up on top of her head once she was inside the dim, blue-lit interior of the hall. It was warmer here, enough that she could take off the coat she was wearing for appearances. All that speed was like carrying a radiator inside her chest anyway.

The hall buzzed with people around her. Other Debunkers, Elders coming from their weekly meeting, Goodys carrying files. Thursday was the busiest day for the Liaisers, those who communicated directly with the dead. The benches along one pale wall were thick with people waiting their turn to be escorted down to the Liaising Rooms, to wait while their assigned Liaiser rode the long train deep into the ground to visit with the pale, emotionless shades of their loved ones or distant ancestors.

Chess suppressed a shudder. That train, and the City itself, were the reasons why she'd chosen Debunking rather than Liaising; she'd shown talent for the latter but couldn't stomach it. Some days the only thing that kept her alive was fear of the City, and she still hadn't quite gotten over the night she'd been trapped in the dark on the train platform.

Elder Griffin wasn't in his office yet. Chess settled herself on the dark, shiny wooden chair next to his door and tried to still her jiggling feet. Maybe that third line had been too much.

"Good morrow, Cesaria. Thank you for coming in. Are you well? No ill effects, I trust?"

She bounced up from her seat and bobbed a quick curtsy. "Very well, sir. Good morrow."

He turned the ornate iron key in the lock of his office door and ushered her in, closing the door behind them. "Sit down, my dear."

She did, waiting in the cushioned armchair across from his massive stone desk. She'd always loved this room, loved how peaceful it felt. But then, she'd always liked Elder Griffin as well, and knew the feeling was mutual, so perhaps it wasn't just the décor that made the room feel like a sanctuary.

He sat down at his desk, the tall window framing him. Pale sheers turned the harsh winter sunlight into a hazy glow that illuminated his hair like a halo and touched every inch of the room. Ivory walls, soft gray stone, leather, dark wood. An antique globe in one corner had always fascinated her; she could have spent hours studying all those lines and shapes where the old country boundaries used to be.

And books everywhere, lining the walls, stacked under glass-topped tables with their spines out. The shelves bowed beneath their weight, and where there were not books there were bowls of herbs, rows of consecrated skulls and bones to be used for spells. On the wall behind her was a flat television tuned to the news service with the volume down and the captioning on; when she left, she knew, he would put the sound back up to keep him company while he worked. It was touches like those that made her comfortable with him, made so many others comfortable with him as well.

Today, though, he didn't look comfortable himself. Without the makeup that made his face a pure mask on Holy Days, she could see shadows under his eyes, and his brow furrowed as he used another key to unlock his desk and extract a file.

"This came in two days ago," he said, placing the file on the desk with exaggerated care, as if by placing it in the exact center he could emphasize its importance. "The Grand Elder and I have had several discussions about it. Yea, we have found ourselves concerned about it, and decided in this case to circumvent the normal process and give the case to you."

"I thank you, sir," she said, leaning forward in the chair, "but I'm a little confused. Why me?"

"Your . . . your handling of the Morton case, my dear. You proved to all of us then that you were capable of discretion, as well as being a fine investigator. This is a sensitive case. Are you familiar with Roger Pyle?"

Had there been a drop of moisture in Chess's mouth, she would have spat it out. As it was, she tried to swallow and managed only to produce a dry clicking sound. "The actor?"

Elder Griffin nodded. "I believe he is, of some sort."

"He's haunted?"

"He is reporting a haunting, yes. Apparently he has just moved into a new house and has been having some problems." He pushed the file forward so Chess could take it. "It's all here."

Papers and photos slid out from between the pale covers of the file when she opened it. "He took pictures?"

"He has a lot of documentation."

She didn't respond. They both knew how easily documentation could be faked, especially documentation like this. Pictures of hazy gray shapes, of walls covered with shiny streaks that looked like ectoplasm but could have been anything. The deed and blueprints to the house, and a clipping from an old BT newspaper. Chess scanned it.

She looked up. "The previous dwelling was a murder scene?"

"That seems to be the case, yes."

What was it with murder this week? Hearing about murders, seeing dead bodies, now the possibility of tangling with the ghosts of murder victims—hardly her ideal way to spend a few days.

Elder Griffin shifted in his seat. "It was the decision of the Elders that given your . . . experience with malevolent entities, your handling of Ereshdiran . . ."

"I'm the go-to girl for murderous ghosts?"

His eyebrows rose. She couldn't tell whether he was amused or displeased. "We felt you were the logical one for the case, yes. If you find yourself uncomfortable, we can assign another Debunker, of course, but I don't have to tell you what a case like this could do for you."

She waited for him to continue. She'd take the case, she already knew that. When the Elders made a decision it was best to abide by it.

And she couldn't help it. The thought of handling something like this, a career-making case, appealed. Agnew Doyle was still coasting along on the success of his Gray Towers Debunking, and probably would for years.

Doyle. There was a name she thought of as little as possible. He stayed well out of her way these days. As well he might—after Terrible beat the hell out of him for hitting her, Lex had taken his shot, too.

Time was the only concern. Helping both Bump and

Lex would put enough on her plate as it was. She didn't have a choice there, and she was beginning to feel certain she didn't have a choice here, either.

"The bonus offering on this case is a tidy one," he said finally. "Forty thousand dollars."

Her car was on its last legs. Her couch sagged. Her jeans were developing holes in the knees. Even with the money she saved getting her pills free from Lex it was hard to make ends meet, hard to afford the pipes and the pills she bought from Bump to keep up appearances and the beer and cigarettes and CDs and . . . Forty grand bought a lot of time in dreamland.

She nodded. "I'll take it."

Chapter Five

> The dead do not offer forgiveness. They do not feel. They
> do not advance or grow. They remain frozen as they were,
> save for the replacement of love with hate.
> —*The Book of Truth*, Veraxis, Article 329

Normally she would have gone up to the library to
research Pyle's address and put in a request for his financial records and employment history, but in this case
there was no need. The newspaper clipping and blueprints gave her what she needed to figure out the address,
and the financials were already there.

Besides, Roger Pyle was famous. So famous even
Chess knew who he was. He'd parlayed a clever stand-
up act into a TV series, and rumor had it he was about
to make the move to the big screen. She'd never watched
his show, a spoof of a BT religious order, but she didn't
need the pictures in the file to know what he looked like,
that was for sure.

Nor did she need the financial records to know how
wealthy he was. Pyle couldn't be faking a haunting for
the money. Even if there were numerous entities in his
new house, the most he could hope for would be, what,
maybe a couple of hundred thousand? A drop in the
bucket for someone like him.

Still, there were other reasons to fake a haunting, and
forty grand was a lot of money for her. She needed it,
and she needed to prove he was lying.

But first . . . The image of those empty eye sockets

haunted her, the image and the knowledge that this would happen again if she didn't do something about it. Whether it was a ghost or something else, she didn't know, but the Church's extensive library was as good a place as any to start finding out.

Goody Glass squatted behind the desk like a troll on a heath, right down to the malevolent facial expression. With an effort, Chess kept from returning the disdain. Goody Glass had never liked her, not from the first week of training when she'd caught Chess eating crackers—crackers stolen from the kitchens—in the stacks.

A minor crime, but it wasn't the crime itself for which the Goody held a grudge. It was the way that discovery had led to a deeper, uglier one: that Chess had stolen the food because she wasn't used to being fed on a regular schedule, that she had no ancestry, no family. A fairly common situation since Haunted Week, but not for Church employees.

The Goody's thick eyebrows rose over her beady eyes. "Art thou working on a case, Miss Putnam?"

"I am, Goody." Chess waved the file.

She got no reply, but she didn't expect one. Instead, the door to her left clicked and she entered the Restricted Room, charmed as always by the displays of religious artifacts from the past, all sitting beneath the bright lights as if waiting, hoping, that one day they might be useful again, be something more than relics.

She knew it shouldn't, but the benevolent smile of the fat golden Buddha in the corner made her feel safer. She smiled in return and set her file and her bag on one of the long, empty wooden tables.

Beneath the glittering gold cross on the far wall—another symbol of religions past—the Church kept shelves full of magical reference books. Chess knelt in front of them, scanning the titles. Eyes . . . eyes.

She'd used eyes before in magic, of course, but only as

ingredients in other spells. Salamander eyes were sometimes used in poultices to heal energy deficiencies. Raven
eyes could be dried and powdered and used in protection
spells. But she'd never heard of human eyes being used
for anything of the sort, much less being used in sex
magic, and she had a feeling the eyes were more than
simply spell ingredients anyway.

Finally she grabbed a couple of books and sat down
with them. The first was a slim volume on sight magic;
she had hopes for it, but it related more to psychic
visions and spells for out-of-body investigating. That
sort of thing was done by the Black Squad, Church
government employees, as opposed to regular Church
employees like Chess. They handled crimes mundane
and magical, the breaking of legal codes as well as moral,
whereas Chess dealt pretty much exclusively with the
crime of fake hauntings—"conspiracy to commit spectral fraud," was the official term—and with banishing
the ghosts if they did exist.

The second book offered a little more information. It
opened with a quote she'd heard before, about eyes as
windows to the soul, and studied that idea from the
perspective of magic.

Perhaps that was what the glyph meant, the sigil
branded into Daisy's skin and marked on the wall behind
her? Chess pulled out her camera to examine the image
from the night before, her mouth instinctively tightening
at the sight of that horrible fallen face. She scrolled
through the images until she found the one she wanted.

It didn't look like a face at all, not really. Faces weren't
shaped like triangles. But the symmetry of it suggested it
could be a face, or perhaps another body part. Terrible
had said that Daisy's was the first female body found,
that not much had been left of the second victim—Little
Tag, if she remembered. Was it possible someone was
building a new body, a vessel for a lost soul?

Such things were rare, of course. She'd only heard of it happening, had never been faced with such a crime or even the faintest evidence of one. But eyes deteriorated quickly when not frozen; if they were indeed being used to give sight to an earthbound spirit, that spirit's companion or Bindmate or whatever would need a fresh supply.

More deaths.

She pulled the sleeves of her red sweater over her hands and hugged herself, but the chill slithering up her body had nothing to do with the air in the room. Ghosts didn't care who they killed; last night's experience with Annabeth Whitman would have been a sharp reminder of that if she'd needed one. But the ghost's summoner, the one who kept it earthbound, who fed it energy . . .

It shouldn't have surprised her. Didn't she know better than almost anyone what sort of filth humans were capable of? But it did, every time, a sort of weary, miserable surprise that someone out there had found a new way to create pain.

She flipped through the rest of the book but didn't find much else, barely enough to fill a page in her notebook. She'd talk to Terrible about it later, he might have some ideas, might know more that would help. Probably would, in fact.

With a sigh she reshelved the books and checked the clock at the far end of the room. Almost noon. She'd have to look through the Church's rune and sigil libraries another time—she already knew she'd never seen the glyph before.

One more place to check. Goody Glass frowned at her as she left the Restricted Room and headed for the long wall of files in the regular library. Chess ignored her.

The files contained—or were supposed to contain, as almost everyone forgot to update them half the time—all the information about every haunting or suspected haunting in Triumph City, about every building, every vacant lot.

And the files at the end . . . those were full of worse things than hauntings. Here lived the executed criminals and those who'd died of natural causes, both before and after Haunted Week. As she'd just discussed with Elder Griffin, murder scenes carried their own resonance; victims often hung around, trapped in the moment of their death, just as murderers often attempted to recreate their crimes.

Whoever the Cryin Man was, he'd be here, if they had any information at all.

The picture she found when she opened the file nearly made her drop the whole thing. As it was, she gasped loud enough for Goody Glass to give her a disapproving frown.

The Cryin Man—aka Charles Remington—had murdered ten prostitutes, all in the area that now covered Downside, back in the early nineteenth century.

And he'd taken their eyes. The photograph on the top of the stack of yellowed documents could have been the one on the memory chip in Chess's camera, from the ragged, sawing cuts to the ice crystals forming in the coagulated blood. The poor woman.

Fuck. Just what she needed. A murderous ghost, come back for another round. So much for not getting too deeply involved in this one.

Her first glimpse of Pyle's house—or rather, of the white stone wall surrounding it—did nothing to dispel her concerns or take her mind off the uneasy *waiting* sensation she'd had ever since she photocopied that file. The wall, broken by a wooden gate, hid the building itself but allowed a glimpse of treetops and the crest of a gray slate roof. Chess pulled up before the gate and rolled down her window, shoving Charles

Remington, his victims, and Daisy out of her head. Time to work.

A mechanical voice emanated from a small steel box. "Name and business, please?"

"Cesaria Putnam, from the Church. I've come about your haunting."

The gate glided out of the way and she drove through. No, money was probably not a concern for Pyle. White walls, interrupted by shining windows, stretched wide across the winter-dead lawn. The house stood between naked trees, branches jutting aggressively like arms trying to hold it back. It might have been graceful, even beautiful, in summer, when the grass was green and the leaves softened the sharp edges. Now it simply stared at her with dozens of blank eyes, daring her to discover its secrets.

Chess followed the curving drive along the front—it seemed to have been designed so those approaching were forced to watch the building for as long as possible, or vice versa—until she reached a gleaming guard shack.

A second guard stepped out, clad in bulky dark-green trousers and a jacket of the same color that turned his shoulders into mountains. Not as big as Terrible, but not far off. A hat turned his features into a generic authoritarian blank, and he carried a clipboard like a weapon.

"Miss Putnam?"

"Yes, that's me."

His blue eyes ran over every detail of her face, impersonally, as though she were a sculpture he was going to have to draw from memory later. Finally he gave her a short nod. "Pull your car around there." His pen stabbed at the air to his left. "Someone will escort you inside."

"Where—," she started, but he'd already turned away and encased himself back in his little booth. Warmer in there, she imagined, although for winter it was actually rather balmy outside.

She rolled her window back up and followed the drive farther until it cut back behind a copse of pine trees. There a garage sprawled, large enough for six cars, with a wide blacktop in front of it. Several more guards stood at the edge waiting for her. Was this a private home or a fucking prison? They looked like they were expecting a riot any minute.

For a moment she sat there in her car, feeling a little like she was in a standoff, before turning the key. The engine coughed into death and she opened her door, feeling their eyes on her. She should have bumped up before she arrived; comedowns made her edgy.

"Chessie?"

Her bag fell from her hand as she spun around, into the face of one of the guards. He looked familiar, yes, even under that damned hat, but she couldn't quite place him . . .

"Merritt Hale, remember me?" He took off his hat, and the memory snapped into place.

"Merritt? Wow, how *are* you?"

They shared an awkward moment, unsure if they should hug or kiss or shake hands, and finally settled into a clumsy half-embrace.

"Been a long time, huh?" he asked, his face splitting into the wide, crooked grin she remembered. "Ten years? Nine?"

"About that, yeah."

"Since you left to study with the Church." He nodded at her bag. "Guess you made it, huh? I finally got out when I hit seventeen. Well, you remember, they'll only keep you until then."

"I remember." She didn't want to, but she did. Corey Youth Home, they'd called it, but it wasn't anything like a home. More like a zoo, but instead of standing and watching the animals they locked you in with them.

Merritt seemed to be thinking the same thing. His blue eyes clouded for a moment, and he put the hat back on to cover his sandy-blond hair. "Anyway, I guess you're here about the ghosts."

She nodded. "Have you seen any?"

"I haven't, but I'm day shift. I know a couple of guys did, or thought they did, anyway. Come on. I'll escort you in."

His hand on the small of her back guided her across the blacktop and past the other guards watching with narrowed eyes. Merritt held up a hand. "I know her."

"Why are they watching like that?"

"Normally they'd search you, make sure you don't have weapons or anything, you know."

Chess thought of her knife, tucked into the side pocket of her bag, and of her full pillbox. If she was going to get searched every time she came here . . . she'd have to be careful.

"What, just my bag, or my person?"

His glance flicked over her entire body, from feet to top of head, while he grinned again. He always had been a hound. And she should know, having given him a try once or twice. There wasn't much else to do in the Corey Home, and sex was the most valuable currency she'd had.

Still was, if she thought about it, but she didn't really want to. She wasn't with Lex for drugs. Technically.

"Everything. Mr. Pyle doesn't take chances, and neither do we."

She filed that away for future use. She wouldn't be spending long hours here, that was for sure, not if she couldn't bring her Cepts. The last thing she needed was to start itching and getting sick while with a subject.

Merritt led her to what looked like another room

attached to the far wall of the garage, with an outside door. It turned out to be a hallway. Fluorescent bulbs cast a garish, shadowless light along its length; it felt like walking through an operating room. She pulled her sunglasses back down.

Merritt smiled. "Mr. Pyle likes bright lights. And with everything going on . . ."

That was a point in Pyle's favor, certainly. It was something those who faked hauntings never seemed to think of, people's almost instinctual desire for light when scared. Odd, but true.

Of course a point in Pyle's favor was a point against her, but no way was she giving up this early.

Merritt opened the door at the end of the hall and ushered her through to a small, plain room, still blindingly light but empty. He gripped the bright gold doorknob. "Ready?"

"I don't know, what do you think?"

"I know I am," he muttered, but before she could respond he stepped through the doorway, tilting his head to the side to indicate she should follow.

The ceiling rose above her, cresting so far up it was hard to see the ridge. Pale wood beams crisscrossed below it, giving an illusion of intimacy Chess wouldn't have thought possible.

That bleached wood was echoed in the huge mantel over the fireplace, big enough Chess figured she could almost stand in it, and the chairs and couches with their ivory cushions and pale orange throw pillows. The carpet was the same pale orange. It was a beautiful room, ostentatiously cozy.

In the center of it stood Roger Pyle. He exuded charisma the way Bump oozed sleaze; it felt like he'd physically hit her in the chest with charm, and she fought the reaction. Wouldn't do to start liking the subjects.

But she couldn't help liking him a little when he

crossed the room with his hand outstretched and an eager, uncertain smile on his face.

"Miss Putnam, is it? Thank you so much for coming. We're really . . . we're really at loose ends here, don't know what else to do." He raised a hand to scratch his stubbled chin, and she noticed the bags under his eyes she hadn't seen when he was smiling.

"I'm here to help any way I can, Mr. Pyle." They always thanked her for coming at first. Very few of them thanked her later.

"Please, please, call me Roger. And, oh, sit down. Where are my manners—Merritt could you ask one of the maids to get Miss Putnam a drink? Drink, Miss Putnam? What would you like? We have everything, you only have to ask. Snack? There's plenty of food, all kinds of things, cold meats and chips and shrimp cocktail, it's all in the kitchen, we can get you anything you like . . ." He looked around, shoved his hands in his pockets like a guilty child who'd just been caught talking during class and was being made an example of.

Chess took pity on him and pulled her water bottle from her bag. "I'm fine, thanks."

"Oh, you have a drink. Excellent, excellent. Well, let's see, where do I start? What do you need to know? Did you look at the file I gave you? I mean, not you, but the Church? I put everything in there, everything I know, and the pictures and everything."

"I've looked at it, Mr.—Roger. It's very detailed. Before we discuss it, though, we really should get your family in here as well. Are they available? It saves time to talk to all of you together."

It also made it easier to gauge their reactions and see if they tried to help one another out, but she didn't mention that.

"Oh, of course, of course. Merritt can you please get Kymmi and Arden? I think Kym's upstairs trying to get some sleep, and Arden—I don't know. Maybe the rec room, or something? Her room? She could be watching TV, that's possible."

Merritt nodded and left the room, giving Chess a reassuring glance as if he thought she'd be nervous at being alone with Roger.

Nervous wasn't the word for it, though. A suspicion, one that didn't surprise her but piqued her curiosity, had already started worming its way into her head. Perhaps most celebrities talked this much. She didn't much care about them or their lives, but it was difficult to escape the occasional headline or news story or bit of gossip, and she knew most people assumed famous people had incredible egos and talked just for the sake of it.

She didn't think that was the cause of Roger Pyle's unexpected loquacity, though. Or nerves. And when he sat down on the polished wood coffee table to face her, she saw she was correct.

Roger Pyle was high as a kite.

His pupils were just black spots the size of dust specks in the famously golden brown of his irises, and they veered around, never quite settling on anything. He rubbed the tips of his thumbs against the balls of his index fingers, back and forth, back and forth, as if he was playing a tiny violin, and she could see his pulse practically jumping out of his neck. He certainly wasn't lying about having a hard time sleeping. Looking at him, she doubted if he'd be able to sleep in a vat of liquid Dream.

"I'm so glad you came," he said again, looking up at the ceiling, out the windows, down at his tapping feet. "We've only been here three months, you know? Had the place built, moved in . . . It was our dream house, Kymmi and me. My wife, Kym, I mean, and our daughter, Arden. Well, you'll meet them when Merritt gets back with them."

"What made you move here?"

"I do a television show, *The Monastery*? It's a comedy."

"Of course."

"And there's been talk of a film. For me, I mean, not for the show, so I wouldn't need to work so much, so I don't have to stay in Hollywood. We thought, for Arden . . . not living there might allow her a more normal upbringing. We wanted to be somewhere less crazy, more wholesome. I told my producer I wanted to set up a studio here, film the show from here."

She hid her amusement by picking up her bag and getting out her notepad and pen. Was he serious? Triumph City was a cesspit. She'd spent the night before examining a murdered prostitute and watching a fatal gang fight.

Then she caught herself. For men like him, Triumph City *was* more wholesome. He didn't live in Downside, he didn't even live in Cross Town or Northside. The white brick monstrosity he and his wife had built sat outside the city limits, out where the streets and houses grew wider and the range of experience grew narrower. What used to be a bustling suburbia and was just now starting to be rebuilt after Haunted Week had decimated the population and driven everyone into the perceived comfort of semi-communal living.

Just the thought of all that empty land outside the walls of the house made her feel she was being watched, not to mention that sitting in the presence of someone speeding into the next dimension was enough to set her twitching. She gripped her pen more tightly and looked up, hoping to ground herself somehow.

She *was* being watched. A blonde woman whose pert nose was as artificial as the deep lavender of her eyes studied Chess from the doorway. The woman's hair hung in loose porn-star curls around her shoulders, and the snug ivory dress displayed her swelling bosom and an abdomen Chess imagined she could bounce a quarter off of, but there was nothing sexy about her—no spark of warmth or intimacy, no sense that anything of interest hid behind those startling eyes.

"Kymmi, darling," Roger began, jumping to his feet, "this is Cesaria Putnam, from the Church, she's come to take care of—"

"I know who she is." Kym Pyle gave her husband a look that could cut glass. "And don't sit on the coffee table, please. I've asked you before."

So much for the loving family. Maybe it wasn't muscle and silicone beneath that soft jersey dress. Maybe it was steel and microchips.

"Sorry, sorry, sweetness. I forgot."

Kym ignored him, turning the weight of her disapproval onto Chess. For a second Chess saw herself as this woman must: her dyed-black hair with its Bettie Page bangs, her faded red sweater and black jeans, her dusty down-at-heel boots. Nothing. No one of importance, an urchin, someone with no ancestry to speak of. Never mind that Chess deliberately sought to give that impression when she went on a case. It still stung a little.

Then the moment passed. She wasn't here for a social visit. She was here to bust someone's ass for defrauding the Church, and she was damned good at her job.

So she met that bitch-queen stare with one of her own and plastered a smile across her face. "It's lovely to meet you, Mrs. Pyle. Why don't you sit down too? I have a lot of questions."

Kym raised a sculpted eyebrow but said nothing as she placed herself in one of the armchairs, her legs crossed tidily at the ankles.

They sat for a few minutes listening to Roger grind his teeth before Arden Pyle entered. Chess put her at about fourteen, pretty, with grayish eyes and a sullen air. A shapeless blue sweater covered her from neck to midthigh, with blue jeans below, and her bare toenails were painted black. For some reason the sight made Chess smile.

"Okay," she said, "so why don't you all tell me when this started. When did you first see the spirit, or the first spirit? Dates, places, whatever you can remember."

"There's no point to any of this," Arden said, her tone belying the sweetness of her round little face.

"Arden dear, now you let Miss Putnam—"

"There's no point"—Arden glared at her father—"because I know you're faking it."

Chapter Six

Not every family situation will be pleasant; not every home is happy. Your job will be to determine whether that displeasure has drifted into dishonesty.
—*Careers in the Church*: *A Guide for Teens*, by Praxis Turpin

"Arden!" Kym Pyle's skin reddened beneath the perfect mask of her makeup. "How dare you say such a thing!"

Roger cast an anxious look in Chess's general direction—she doubted he would actually be able to focus on anything—and said, "Arden, honey, you know that isn't true. You're being very unfair, Mommy and Daddy would never do something like that."

Arden's pretty little face scrunched itself into a glower. "Give me a break."

"Miss Putnam, I assure you we're not doing anything of the kind. Our daughter has a very active imagination."

Maybe, maybe not, Chess thought. She'd have to make sure she got a chance to talk to Arden Pyle alone at some point. Not today—they'd be watching her too closely—but at some point. "That's okay, Roger. Let's just get back to the question, shall we? When did you first see the entity?"

"This is bullshit," Arden said. Chess steeled herself for more delaying on the part of her parents, but neither reacted.

Instead, Kym spoke up. "I was in my work room. Embroidery. I'm putting our family tree on a tapestry for that wall." She nodded to indicate the wall behind Chess, who didn't turn around.

"I was just finishing my great-grandmother's name when I realized it was quite cold, despite my sweater. So I got up, planning to call one of the staff members to turn up the heat, and . . ." Her hands clenched in her lap. "It was a woman. She looked terrified, and I spun around to see if something was behind me, but nothing was. When I turned back around to ask her what she was looking at—I thought maybe she was one of the staff—she was gone."

"I saw a man," Roger said. "In one of the guest rooms. I'd gone in there to check and see if we needed anything—we were having some friends stay that weekend—"

Arden snorted.

He ignored her. "—and I thought I'd check the bathroom of the room they'd be staying in, make sure we had shampoo and toothpaste, you know, the things people need. I didn't see him so much as glimpse him, standing in front of the window—I think it was a man, anyway, taller and broader than a woman—but by the time I realized it wasn't one of the staff, he'd disappeared."

"Did you feel anything? Cold, nerves, fear, anything unusual?" Not everyone did, but then not everyone knew that.

"No. Like I said, I assumed he was staff, waiting for me, or taking a few minutes for himself. I don't mind if they do that, as long as everything is done . . ." He caught Kym's disapproving eye. "Well, I *don't*. I thought it was odd he didn't respond when I said hello, and then he just . . . poof, gone."

"This happened during the day?"

"Technically, I guess. It was about five in the afternoon. But it gets dark so early now." He shuddered. "The nights are so long."

"And the sightings have grown more threatening since?"

Both Pyles nodded. Arden stayed as she was, with her arms folded and a bored look on her face.

"We were attacked in our sleep two weeks ago," Roger said. "Kymmi was injured. It's gotten worse since. We don't shower alone. We don't go anywhere alone at night, anywhere in the house."

Chess shuffled through the stack of photographs balanced in her lap until she found the one she wanted. She assumed it was Kym; the image was of a woman's toned back, covered in long shallow scratches. She held it up. "This was your injury, Mrs. Pyle?"

"Yes. The marks are still there."

"Show her, Mom." Arden turned to Chess. "My mom likes to show people her body, don't you, Mom?"

Kym looked as if she wanted to slap the girl, but she kept her composure. "Do you need to see them, Miss Putnam?"

"If you don't mind, that would be helpful."

Kym rose from her seat and turned around, crossing her arms in front of her to grip the hem of her dress. Chess opened her mouth to speak—she hadn't meant for the woman to do this in front of her child—but it was too late. The dress slipped up, displaying Kym's silky thong and the lean expanse of her back, interrupted by a bra strap in matching pink.

Trying to behave as if this weren't creepily inappropriate, Chess stood up to look closer. The scratches had faded. No longer the angry, puffy wounds in the picture, they were thin and scabbed over. "This happened two weeks ago?"

"They didn't want to heal," Roger said. "We tried everything. They've only just started to get better."

"Actibac?" Chess asked, unable to resist.

"Yes, how did you know?"

"We get injured a lot, so we keep up on stuff like that." She resumed her seat, hoping Kym would get the hint and lower her dress, but it took a good thirty seconds before the woman finally let the thin fabric slide back down over her body.

"See, I wish I'd known that, we could have just called the Church and asked them, wouldn't that have been good, Kymmi?"

Kym gave him a tight smile, but her gaze stayed focused on Chess.

If that bitch thought she could make Chess uncomfortable, she was wrong. Chess allowed herself a tiny eye roll as she looked away and grabbed her Spectrometer. "Okay, why don't you give me a tour of the house? Show me where the sightings and attacks have taken place? We'll see what we can find."

The Church operated a few living museums for the benefit of its employees; Chess especially liked the synagogue one, with instructors wearing those little hats they used to call yarmulkes. The Pyle home reminded her of one of those museums, as intensely and carefully decorated as the living room she'd already been in, and as impersonal.

They trooped up the graceful, winding staircase into a long hall. Windows at each end were blank white holes covered with blinds. Any light they might have let in was rendered useless by the bright electric bulbs at short intervals down the hall's length. It must have cost a fortune to keep all those bulbs burning.

Ten rooms, including the master suite, Arden's room, a computer room, library, and separate spa. The rest were guest bedrooms, unique only in their nondescript colors.

Chess's Spectrometer gave off the occasional blip as she followed the Pyles through each guest room and bathroom, but not frequent or strong enough to give her any information. She took careful note of the layout. If the Pyles weren't sleeping at night, it would be next to impossible to sneak in after dark and use her Hand of Glory to deepen their sleep so she could investigate. Of course, with all that security, paying an after-dark visit would be difficult whether the Pyles slept or not. She had a feeling their security didn't. Maybe Merritt . . .?

No. Even if it were the sort of thing she could ask, she couldn't ask. Trusting him would be foolish. A year or so of shared history didn't make them friends.

"Roger," she asked, interrupting him in the middle of showing her where he'd seen the ghost of a young man coming out of one of the bathrooms, "do you know where the boundaries of the original house stood? The one where the murders took place?"

"As far as we can tell—the foundation had been filled in and the walls demolished before we bought the land— the north walls aligned where our bedroom is. But from the measurement estimates we got from the surveyor, that house ended just after this room." He indicated the doorway. "We haven't seen any ghosts in that part of the house, not yet, anyway."

"Have you been sleeping there?"

The Pyles exchanged glances—even Arden, who hadn't spoken a word throughout the tour.

"We just haven't been sleeping at night," Kym said. "In any of the rooms."

"Arden stays with a friend some nights," Roger added. "And Kym and I stay in the living room."

Chess nodded. She could probably use a warding spell to keep them off the top floor while she investigated up there, but it would make things more difficult. If she could even figure out a way in.

They headed back up the hall toward the master suite,

the last room on the right. Chess had expected gran-deur. She hadn't expected the bed to be quite so barge-like, a slab of mattress covered with silk sheets. She definitely hadn't expected to see hanging over it an enormous painting of a naked Kym. Was this what Arden meant when she said her mother liked to show off her body?

She certainly seemed to be enjoying it. Lying on her side on what looked like a fur rug—how original—with one hand demurely not quite covering the pale curls between her legs and the other thrown back behind her head. A lovely piece of work, Chess had to admit, but still . . . No wonder Arden was so grumpy, having to compare her own developing figure to the best body money could buy.

That was one problem she herself hadn't had to deal with. Of course, in her case it would have been an improvement to be worried about how she measured up to the naked women she saw, rather than worrying about what they planned to do to her or make her do to them that time, but . . .

"The night you were attacked in here," she said, "what exactly happened?"

"It was dark." Roger looked as though he might have been coming down a bit; his eyes weren't quite so glassy. "I don't remember falling asleep or even waking up. Just . . . just hearing it, movements in the room, and Kymmi screaming, and I couldn't seem to feel my hands . . . and it laughed and screamed." His eyelids fluttered, blinking back tears. Chess reminded herself the man was a profes-sional actor. "It was terrible."

Kym herself was silent. Chess made a mental note to search for her private financial records. The file contained statements from several accounts, but they were all joint accounts. If Kym was looking for a good way to end the marriage and get as much money as she could, faking a haunting could be an effective, if roundabout and chancy, way to do it.

It was also a very public way, one that could end Roger Pyle's career.

She studied the rest of the room in a slow, careful sweep while the Spectrometer beeped quietly from its new holster around her waist. Two dressers, two bedside tables with ornate handles on the bottom doors. Everything in the room had a twin, a mirror image of itself. How imaginative of Kym. If she hadn't married whom she married, Chess thought, she probably would have been one of those women who hung plaster ducks on the walls and collected painted plates.

The Spectrometer found a steady beat while Chess paced the floor, speeding up by the bed, slowing down by the window, finally beeping faster outside a closed door on the right-hand wall. She glanced up.

"Bathroom," Roger said.

Chess went inside.

No, Kym Pyle was not a woman with a lot of inhibitions. The window in the bathroom had no blinds or shades; cold white light spilled over the marble tub and floor and filled the mirror to Chess's right. In summer it might have been pretty. Now it felt sterile, and hushed like a cemetery.

Something of life was in the room, though. The Spectrometer continued beeping, the high-pitched sound bouncing off the marble until it sounded more like one long continuous whine and Chess's heart started pounding. Whatever noise her boots made on the shiny floor was lost while she walked this way and that, trying to determine the source of the beeps. Trying to find the ghost. Her shoulders tensed. She was not alone in this room, she knew it. Dead eyes watched her from a place she could not see. Her skin crawled and tingled, her tattoos warming, waiting for it. Whatever it was.

But nothing happened. After a few minutes she started to relax. The Spectrometer's beeps didn't have to mean a ghost was present, just that one had been—and there were ways, illegal ways, to fool even the Spectro. She didn't see how any of those could be used here—there wasn't much room to hide them—but still . . .

She shook her head. It was not time to start thinking of this as a real haunting yet. She was spooking herself. A bad move. Time to get going.

It wasn't until she turned around to leave that she became aware of the smell. It had been there almost from the moment she stepped into the room, but subtle, almost undetectable. The minute she caught it, recognized it, it grew stronger still. Death. Decay. Rotting things, squirming things buried in the earth. Everything foul and wrong hid inside that smell, was caught by it and transmitted to her through it.

She still felt safe enough; even her tattoos had stopped tingling. But the odor remained, wafting through the air like a whisper. She checked the tub drain, wondering if perhaps the scent came from inside, but it was no stronger there than anywhere else.

That left the double sinks below the mirror. Her feet moved as if through mud. The smell was all she could think of, all she could focus on; it blurred her vision, made her ears ring and her head hurt.

The sinks were white, gleaming and pure in the dark green countertop. Chess thought the smell might be stronger there but couldn't be sure. She was beginning to doubt she would ever breathe fresh air again. The thought of all the bacteria that must be carried in that smell, the thought of plagues and epidemics, made it almost impossible to check the other sink.

She didn't have to. Movement caught her eye. She turned automatically and saw a cockroach crawling over the lip of the sink, its horrible black body an abomination against the spotless marble. Another appeared, and another. Chess forced herself to take a step closer, being careful to keep her body away from the counter itself, and saw movement in the drain, heard the dry rustle of scabrous exoskeletons rubbing together.

Her fists clenched. A spot of red liquid flew from the drain and landed on the mirror. Her insides twisted as one drop became two, became three, and blood burbled up from the drain, viscous bright blood filled with squirming bodies, rising in the sink.

She didn't realize she'd been moving until the back of her thigh hit the high, cold side of the tub. For a second she teetered, trying not to fall, unable to take her eyes from the groaning, bubbling sink.

Her hand hit the edge of the tub to brace herself. She would not throw up, would not, could not. This too could be faked. It wasn't a difficult trick to do. Even the smell of the blood, a coppery tang beneath the stronger odor of decay, could be faked. She'd never seen anything this elaborate on a case before, but she'd never investigated millionaires, either.

"Okay. Okay." Her own voice soothed her, brought her back into herself. It was time to leave this room. Every cell in her body screamed at her to get out. She'd come back later, examine, investigate. She had the layout of the house down, she had an idea of how the family worked and what their relationships were, it was all she needed.

Her composure thus regained, she strode out of the bathroom with a smile that made her cheeks ache. Church policy for Debunkers: Never, ever indicate you've seen anything out of the ordinary or been scared by anything you've seen. If they'd staged it, they'd wonder why she hadn't mentioned it and it would unbalance them. If they hadn't, mentioning it might sound like an admission.

"Okay," she said. "I think I have basically everything I need, so I'll get back to the Church and start writing everything up, and I'll be in touch soon."

"Soon? How soon?" Kym did not look pleased.

"Oh, um, tomorrow, maybe, after sunset. We don't really work on Holy Day, of course."

Kym frowned. "We're having a party tomorrow night. Arden won't be here."

Yes! Finally, something going right. Her chances of getting into the house would be much easier if there were a lot of people around anyway. And if Arden wasn't home . . .

"I haven't seen Arden's room yet." She turned to the girl. "Would you mind showing me before I go? That way you can be there while I look at it, it's less like an invasion of privacy."

Arden didn't look convinced, but led Chess down the hall to the second door on the left—odd, wasn't it, that her room wasn't directly opposite her parents'?—and opened it.

Dark curtains on the windows turned the room into a cave. Chess picked her way across the floor, through the colorless, limp shapes of discarded clothing, and pulled the curtains. It only took a second to pop the wire out of the security alarm to disable it, and to unlock the window itself. It might be detected, sure, but it at least increased her odds of getting in easily when she came back later. She palmed the wire as she turned around.

The room was . . . just a room. Posters of pop stars covered the walls—apparently Arden was not into movie stars, which wasn't much of a surprise considering what her father did for a living—and clothes and schoolbooks covered every available surface. A sparkly pink cell phone and matching laptop sat on an ornate white desk, which was itself almost hidden by stickers and pictures and scribbled phone numbers.

The rest of the room was dark blue and yellow, a surprising choice, but one Chess imagined Arden hadn't made herself.

More clothes exploded from the closet, and Chess suspected from the anxious sidelong glances the girl kept giving the half-closed door that she had something hidden in there as well, but there was no point in trying to find out what. Not when she could look the next night with a lot more ease.

She gave Arden's yellow bathroom a cursory glance—staying well away from the sinks—and made her good-byes, taking with her Roger Pyle's business card and a burning desire never to return.

Merritt was nowhere to be seen as she climbed into her car and pulled away from the garage. They'd searched the vehicle—expertly, but she knew they'd done it. She could smell them, sense them, hard hands rifling through her belongings, feeling around beneath her seats.

The wooden gate crept open for her once again and she was gone, speeding down the road, managing to get out of sight of the walls before she had to pull over and take her pills.

Chapter Seven

Worse still are those who commit the ultimate evil, who bind themselves unto the dead. No good can come of such an act; at the end of it lies only misery.
—*The Book of Truth*, Rules, Article 37

"He could have made the brand, yeah," she said, as Terrible slid the car up on the curb. The Johnny Cash CD cut off with the ignition, leaving too-loud silence in its wake. "It's not something ghosts normally do, but it's possible. Or he could have found it, or—I don't know. It had to have happened right before she died, but I have no idea why."

"He brand them dames before?"

"No. At least it wasn't in the file, and there were—there were pictures." More dead faces to add to the gallery that already followed her: Randy Duncan, Brain—the teenager she'd failed to protect a few months back . . . Brain's pale little face refused to leave her. She'd had to put her new bed in a different location, against the opposite wall. Every time she walked into her bedroom she'd seen the shade of that still, wide-eyed figure, silent and cold on her old bed.

"So he pick up new tricks, aye, in the City?"

She shook her head. "I don't know."

He accepted this without comment and left the car, the removal of his weight lifting his side by several inches. Chess waited in the still-warm interior until he came around and opened her door for her, a habit of his she'd gotten used to.

Without the dead body on the ground, the street somehow managed to feel even more threatening than it had the night before. More empty. Daisy was gone, and already forgotten, as if by dying she'd erased herself from memory as well as the world itself.

Chess looked away from the spot where the girl had lain and nodded at the alley. "In there first, I guess. While there's still a little light."

Beneath her clothes her skin felt raw from the vigorous shower she'd practically thrown herself into when she got home. Raw, and a little tingly. The energy wasn't anywhere near as strong as it had been the night before, but it lingered.

"Brought one along," Terrible replied, pulling a long steel flashlight from the trunk of his car. When he leaned over, the butt of his gun and the thin round handle of some other weapon poked at the fabric of his shirt. The sight reassured her—not that she'd doubted. Terrible didn't take chances.

Neither did she. In her bag was everything she thought she might need if the ghost of Charles Remington showed up again, and a few things she thought she might not but grabbed anyway.

"After, you wanna see Red Berta? Maybe she got more for you. Them dead ones, they ain't forgotten, if you dig."

"What, you mean the hookers still remember them?"

"Aye. Ain't something they allow me into, but they got—they got secrets, aye? Knowledge they don't share, least not with me or Bump. Not with men."

"Yeah, okay. Is she going to be free tonight?"

"I give her a ring up, you want. After."

"Okay." A glance around told her the street was empty, but trusting your eyes was folly here, where shadows multiplied with every passing second. She squared her shoulders and stepped into the mouth of the alley. Another rush of sex magic swirled around her, then settled. "Think we're going to be alone this time?"

"Slobag always tryin to make a grab," Terrible said. Not really an answer, but an answer just the same. "Back round Festival time he tried making some deal up on Fifty-first, get his hands on a building. Figured he planned to set up there, Bump and me did."

"What'd you do? Burn it down?"

"Aye."

Chess's fingers brushed Terrible's as she took the flashlight from him. Normally she would start looking up the walls, at the ceiling had there been one, but that was going to be difficult in this instance, so the ground would be first. She scanned back and forth, slowly, studying every inch revealed by the circle of light.

She didn't bother asking him if anyone had been inside the building when the fire was started, figuring the odds on it were probably about fifty-fifty. Not her business, anyway.

"He knows it was you?"

She didn't see him shrug, but knew he did. "Guessing he do. No matter though."

"Because you're safe here?"

"Because he always after us. Reason ain't important."

A spark of light shot off the flashlight's beam, but when Chess bent down she saw it was only a bit of broken glass. She shone the light on the base of the wall to her left, listening as the creatures who'd eavesdropped on her phone conversation the night before once again skittered out of her way. Skittered, like roaches . . . ugh.

"Some things are—" She stopped. "Hey, come look at this."

He crouched beside her, his arm bumping against her shoulder. "Aye?"

"There. The feather." Inside her bag was a small box of surgical gloves. She handed the flashlight back and slipped one on, then picked up the feather between her thumb and index finger. Even with the gloves on, a slight tingle ran up her arm. Definitely connected.

Terrible shone the light directly on it, and she could see the buff tinge on the hairs, the stripes and mottling. "Shit."

"What?"

"It's an owl feather," she said.

"Aye?"

"Yeah." She turned it in the light. "I'm not sure what kind. I think it's a Great Horned Owl, but I didn't do as well in ornithology as I should have."

"Ain't know the Church teach you birds."

"Birds are psychopomps. Especially birds of prey. Especially owls."

"Taking souls to the City, meaning? They what you use?"

"No. I mean, yes, they do in normal circumstances, but no, we use specially trained dogs. Birds are too unpredictable, they can be hard to work with in ritual."

"Why a ghost use a—a bird? Ain't need it get up here, aye?"

"I'm not sure. No, he wouldn't necessarily use it to get up here, but—" With her free hand she found some plastic pouches in her bag and dug them out. "Open one of those, will you?"

He did, holding it out for her to slip the feather into. She felt better once it was sealed away, but not much. "Ghosts don't use psychopomps, no," she said slowly, trying to force her recalcitrant brain into thought. "They're not capable of magic—I mean, they can only feed off energy, not create it."

"The psychopomp give them it?"

"No. They have energy of a sort, but it's not the kind

a ghost can use."

Terrible caught the implication, as she knew he would. "So somebody working alongside yon ghost, aye?"

She nodded. The walls of the alley loomed over her, stretching into the dim sky like broad hands trying to cup over her and squash her. She hadn't mentioned the energy from the night before, but she couldn't put it off any longer. "Last night . . .," she said, then cleared her throat and tried again. "Last night I noticed, I felt the energy from the magic they'd been doing. Sex magic. They were doing sex magic."

Pause. "Them who killed her?"

"Yeah, I think so. I'm pretty sure. It was really strong, on her body and everything."

"Lots of whores use magic. Makes them work go faster, if you dig. Maybe were them other dames you felt?"

"No. I wondered that too but this was . . . blacker, if you know what I mean. It didn't feel right. And it didn't feel like any of those girls could have made it. Too powerful, for one thing. And it felt male."

Funny, she hadn't really thought of that the night before, but it was true. It had felt male; too strident and aggressive to be a woman's magic, even a woman like Red Berta.

"Ain't know you could tell."

"Yeah. Everyone's magic feels a little different, it's kind of like fingerprints. Or how everyone smells like themselves, it's all chemical, you know what I mean? The energy from one of my spells wouldn't feel like the energy from yours, or anyone else's. It's unique."

"So you can say who done it from the feel?"

She nodded. "Usually, if I have something to compare it with. Like with the Lamaru, since it was a lot of people doing the spell, the energy was mixed and I couldn't identify it. But if it's a single practitioner, yeah, I could."

"Damn. 'Sfucking cool, Chess. You like—cool, is all."

To hide her blush she focused on tucking the plastic-encased feather into one of the pockets in her bag. "Thanks."

"Ain't think birds lose feathers in winter," he said, standing up. She did the same, the movement making her legs ache.

"Some do, it all depends on—no. No, you're right. Great Horned Owls don't molt in winter. It's their mating season."

"Ain't just fall out, aye? Got pulled out."

"Well . . . I guess it could have caught on something, but yeah, chances are it got pulled out."

She took the light back and shone it around, looking for something the bird could have landed on. The alley was full of sharp edges, but nothing looked like it could have snagged a feather.

"That's some serious, aye? Taking a feather? You figure maybe it's part of it?"

"I don't know, really. It's not as serious a crime to hurt a psychopomp as it is to kill one, but it was probably an accident anyway. You can use the feathers in ritual, but I can't think of any where you leave it behind after, or where the ritual doesn't destroy it. You know, like burning it or something."

"Hey, look here." Terrible shuffled a few boxes, bent down. The light sparked off the piece of mirror he held. His hand engulfed it, but she could see the leather wrapped around its lower half, turning it into a crude knife. "Were Daisy's."

"How do you—oh. You knew her, I keep forgetting."

"Know em all." He turned the makeshift blade in his hand, studying it with perhaps more intensity than was necessary. "She not a bad one, Daisy. Pretty little thing."

"I'm . . . I'm sorry. I didn't think—"

He shrugged; getting too attached to people in

Downside was foolishness. "Ain't know her close. But she ain't stupid, Daisy. Looks like somebody here with the ghost right up, aye? Don't grab no weapon against something ain't there."

Chess took the little mirror knife from him. "Unless it just fell out of her purse."

He snorted. "Nothing just fall out a whore's purse, Chess."

"Oh. Right. But—where was her purse? I didn't see it, did you? Did one of the other girls have it?"

"Ain't think so. One of em would say, she had it." His brow furrowed. "They keep all sorts in there, dig. Like everything they got."

"Money?"

"Aye, what they ain't pay off to Red Berta for Bump, but . . . whore's real catchy about her purse. Don't like nobody touch it up, don't let nobody look in. Keep she magic in too, if she use it. Like superstition, dig? Bad luck touching another whore's purse, letting any else touch yours." He shrugged. "Them bodies ain't just theirs, dig? So they keep the purse private. Ain't for nobody but them."

She cleared her throat. "Makes sense. Come on, let's keep looking."

The sun had sunk almost completely below the horizon, too far to cast shadows; when she looked at the empty buildings across the street they were black shapes against a blazing red-orange background. She shoved her hands into her pockets for a second to warm them, then headed farther into the alley.

Terrible's phone rang, startling her. She didn't stick around to hear his half of the conversation. Somewhere near the back was the metal box she'd sat on the night before, and she wanted to find it.

Her feet scuffed through old newspaper that disinte-grated when her shoes hit it, through layers of dust and

grime. The flashlight's beam bounced off the walls, off
the piles of garbage and furniture so broken and filthy
even Downside residents found no more use for it. Two
red orbs glowed at her briefly. A rat, watching her invade
its territory.

The box was still there. That alone made her think it
was probably unrelated. The killers might have missed
the owl feather and Daisy's weapon hidden beneath the
rubbish, but they wouldn't have left this and not come
back for it. Still, she might as well search everything.

"Aye. Aye, when I can." Terrible snapped the phone
shut behind her. She glanced around.

"Everything okay?"

"Dame I know. I forgot calling her."

"Amy?"

"Ain't seen Amy in weeks."

She knelt in front of the box and slid her gloved hand
along the edge, looking for the catch. "Oh? Why, what
happened?"

"Nothing happen. Just ain't seen her."

"And now you're seeing someone else and you're not
even calling her when you say you will. Shame on you."
She flipped up the hook and pulled the lid back faster
than she should have. Her hands didn't seem quite
under her control. Made sense, with that damned magic
still hovering around her like cloying perfume, making
her ache a little bit right where she did not need to be
aching.

It was empty. Too empty, its spotless, shiny-clean interior a stark contrast to the thick layer of grunge on the
outside.

"She get over it," he said. She felt him lean over,
inspecting the inside of the box. "Look awful clean in
there for some box sitting in an alley, aye?"

"That's what I thought." She tipped the box toward
her so she could shine the light into all the corners. A

faint fragrance hit her nose. Familiar, musty. Not at all like the odor from the Pyles' place earlier. This smell made her think of Church, of bluish light and warm afternoons in wortcunning classes. The smell of ritual.

All she could do was make a note, inhale deeply, and try to memorize it. Whatever it was, they hadn't used it often or she would have recognized it more quickly, so she could rule out the major banishing herbs. She hadn't smelled it in a while, either, so it wasn't one of the conjuring herbs Madame Lupita had used the night before.

Terrible sniffed. "Smells like that dude Tyson," he said. "He skin were kinda like that."

"Really? I don't remember."

"You ain't got as close as me."

That was certainly true, and she was glad, too. Tyson was a Host, someone who'd made a deal with a spirit to share his body in exchange for power—as opposed to a Bindmate, where the energy was shared but the body kept separate. Not an ordinary spirit in Tyson's case, she didn't think, but she hadn't wanted to stick around to find out, especially not after Terrible attacked him and his guest decided to make an appearance. It felt like it had happened years before. It had only been months.

"Thinkin maybe they use the box, then leave it here? Ain't straight, aye?"

"No, it isn't." She closed the box. "But who knows why people do things. Maybe it just didn't work as well for them as they'd hoped, or maybe it was already here and they used it and didn't take it with them."

"It feel off to you?"

"Vibes like everything else. The same energy, I mean."

He nodded. "What else need a checkout back here?"

"Shit. As much of it as we can, really. There's probably not much point using the Spectrometer, not if it isn't an active haunting—the ghost involved is a traveler, you know?—but we should see if there's anything more about the human Bindmate or witch who summoned the ghost, in case that's what the psychopomp was for."

Together they moved around the walls as best they could, Terrible behind her with the light. The bricks hummed with energy when she ran her bare palm over them. Something had definitely happened in here. She just had no way of knowing when.

"Can you move that chair? I want to get behind it."

He was only a deeper shadow in the now dark alley, picking up the broken skeleton of the chair and hauling it out of the way.

Her foot landed on something squishy. A rat. It squeaked at her, shrill in the night, and she gasped and leapt back. Terrible caught her shoulders, but she didn't need it. She had her balance.

Still, she stood for a few seconds longer and let him touch her, fighting the rising tide of desire caused by that damn spell but unable to fight the simple need to be touched, in the cold darkness where a girl had been murdered. How his hands stayed so warm, even in the winter cold, she didn't know, but the heat seeping through her sweater and coat felt fantastic.

It probably would have felt even better if she weren't afraid the ghost would reappear at any moment—the ghost or, worse, Slobag's men again. With just Terrible and herself here there was no way she could call Lex and put a stop to it. The thought made her shudder. At least that's what she thought it was.

"You right, Chess?"

She cleared her throat, pulled away from the weight of his hands. "Yeah. Yeah, right up. I just want to get this done with. It makes me nervous."

"Naw, no need. Nothin show up we ain't handle, aye? You an me." The light started moving again.

She turned away, not sure how to respond but pleased anyway. "Yeah. I guess you're right."

"You want me ring up Red Berta, see if she free for a chatter? Be good to get the knowledge sooner."

"Yeah, okay."

Where was her speed? This day was taking much longer to end than she'd hoped. The image of her couch, her semi-warm apartment, the cold beer in the fridge, hovered before her. She sighed.

Normally she didn't take speed when she was trying to work; experience had taught her it interfered with her body's reactions to ghosts, masked them. But she wasn't trying to detect a ghost at the moment. That a ghost existed was Fact and Truth; she didn't need her abilities to tell her that. All she needed at the moment was whatever clues she could see or find, and she was fucking tired, too, running on less than five hours' sleep and an empty stomach in the wintry air.

Terrible handed the light back to her, picked up his phone. She wondered how many numbers he had programmed in his. More than three, she guessed, choking down a couple of Nips.

The light picked up a few smears of ectoplasm on the bricks while Terrible's voice rumbled behind her. No surprise there, but further confirmation. A ghost and its Bindmate. Just your average cozy, unholy, psychotic couple.

"Berta ain't free."

She glanced back and saw him standing there, a rueful look on his face. "Say she house too full to think. Got all the girls there, dig, keepin off the street. Try again on the later."

"Yeah, okay."

"Hungry?"

Not with that much speed in her system, she wasn't, or rather she wouldn't be once it kicked in. But she could have a Coke, nibble at a few fries or something. "You buying?"

"Aye."

"Then yeah, I guess so." What the hell. At least the restaurant would be warm—she knew where he'd take her, where he always took her, the diner a few blocks from her place. He liked their shakes, and the burgers they gave him—and by extension her, when she was with him—had a much higher beef content than what everyone else got, so they were actually decent. She also knew it would be loud and crowded and bright, and at that particular moment nothing sounded better.

She could use some life around her just then.

Chapter Eight

Punishment of both crime and sin is the exclusive domin-
ion of the Church. That punishment begins before death.
Be assured it continues after it.

—*The Book of Truth*, Veraxis, Article 220

There were lots of better ways to spend the free hours
after Holy Day services, but Chess wasn't in a position
to enjoy any of them. A pity, that. She had a few keshes
freshly rolled at home, a blanket without too many holes
in it, and a disc copy of ten episodes of Roger Pyle's
television show—not her usual thing, but she figured it
could be a decent afternoon. And a decent afternoon
was worth a lot these days.

Instead she was walking down the long corridor
connecting the main Church building to the outbuild-
ings, ready to go farther still into the spirit prisons.
According to the Log Books, Charles Remington
resided in Prison Ten; Chess intended to see if he was
still there.

She wasn't sure if she preferred him to be or not.

Her footsteps echoed around her in the tunnel-like
hallway, making it sound as if she wasn't alone. As if
there was an army following her into the sterile misery
of Prison Ten. She resisted the urge to turn around and
check. This hall was for Church employees only. She'd
had to press her index finger to the ID pad and use her
key to get in; the door locked automatically behind her
and she hadn't heard the buzz of it opening again. Pale

gray light filtered through the smoked glass skylights, pale blue joined it from the special bulbs lining the join-ture of wall and ceiling. Of all the places in Triumph City she could possibly be at that moment, this was undoubtedly the safest.

The hair on the back of her neck didn't quite believe it, but her brain did, and that was all that mattered. And bad as the spirit prisons were—and they were bad—at least they weren't quite as awful as the City itself.

Most people wouldn't take that view, but then, most of them didn't see the eternal silent peace of the City as a terrifying, isolating vacuum, either.

She pressed her finger into the pad by the door, used her right hand to turn the key. The door buzzed and opened, and Chess entered the prison anteroom.

Goody Chambers, the prison Goody, sat behind her desk, her black bonnet neatly tied beneath her pointed, whiskery chin. Sometimes Chess wondered exactly how old the woman was; she hadn't visibly aged a day in the nine years Chess had been with the Church, as if she'd become a septuagenarian in early middle age and stayed there.

"Good morrow." The Goody reached for her pen, poised it over her log. "Have you a message, or are you here to see a prisoner?"

"A prisoner."

"Name and date of death?" Chess told her. "Sign here, please."

While Chess scrawled her name the Goody took a pale blue velvet robe from a hook. "You'll need to put this on. You visited the prison during training? Very well. You may leave your clothing and effects in the dressing room there. I'll call the elevator for you."

Chess's fingers shook as she unlaced her boots. She did not want to do this. She glanced over her shoulder, checked the closed door for holes and saw none. Good.

A chance to shove a couple of pills down her throat, hope they calmed her nerves a little before she got on the elevator. Showing any sort of emotion—especially fear—to the dead was a huge mistake. To show it to imprisoned spirits, trapped in iron cages, subjected to punishments, was like slicing open a vein and waving it around in front of a starving tiger. Not a good idea.

She pushed the image from her mind and focused on the black chalk she pulled from her bag, focused on putting power into the sigils she drew on her forehead and right cheek, on choosing which of her unfinished tattoos to activate by completing. Most of her tattoos were done, but a few were too powerful to keep active all the time.

By the time she was done marking, her entire body felt warm and tingling with power. The pills hadn't kicked in yet, but it didn't matter; she knew they would, and she knew she could do this. This was her job. This was the one thing in the world she was good at, and she refused to be afraid.

The robe smelled faintly of incense and smoke, comforting smells because they reminded her of Church and of . . . well, she didn't know why smoke would be comforting, but it was just the same. It made her feel safe, as if the thin napped fabric was armor. Which in a way it was.

Goody Chambers handed her a file folder—Remington's file—and a bag of graveyard dirt. "It's only generic, but it will help if there's a problem."

"Thanks." Chess had some melidia as well, which she tucked into one of the robe's pockets. It wasn't great, but it would have to do.

"You have fifteen minutes," the Goody informed her as she held the elevator door open. "After that we sound the alarm."

Chess nodded. "Thanks."

"Good luck. Facts are Truth."

"Facts are Truth," Chess replied, and the elevator door slammed shut, leaving her alone to descend deep below the surface of the earth, to the realm of the criminal dead.

Silence prevailed in the City of Eternity, expectant, pained silence like the hush before the guillotine blade falls. Occasionally metal clanked against metal, echoing in the empty space.

Prison Ten was not the City, though, and the first indication of that difference was the blast of heat from the roaring fires, the sizzle of ectoplasm on hot coals. Chess was grateful for the thin robe; her regular clothes would have been soaked with sweat in minutes. Ghosts hated heat and disliked fire. Chess wasn't particularly fond of them either, but if the ghosts down here could take their punishment, so could she. Especially since after she'd checked whether Remington was in here, she could leave.

The iron walkway rattled under her feet as she made her way into the prison, a cavern so large she couldn't see where it ended. Across the red-hot expanse, bottomless and spiked with flames, all she saw were ghosts, hanging from the ceiling in iron cages through which mild electrical currents ran, forcing them into solid form and making escape impossible—or more impossible, given that every object in the room had been charmed and bolstered with magic.

And they watched her, the dead, with their empty eyes and wide-open mouths. Her skin itched like heavy withdrawals, crawled and tingled so hard she imagined they could all see her vibrating on the walkway. Power thrummed through her body like a line of speed times ten as her tattoos reacted to their energy and her muscles to their hate.

Sparks flew into the air on her left; gears in need of oil screeched high in the smoky, too-thin air. It took her a second to realize what was happening, to remember what to do, but she made it in time, ducking below the hot iron railing before the first metal cage passed over it. Every hour or two the ghosts were moved to a new torture station. Some got a respite. Chess knew better than anyone how that could be the worst form of torture, that brief peace. Even a ghost knew it wouldn't last, had to wait as the minutes ticked by too fast, knowing the pain was coming again.

Through the slats in the railing she watched the cages glide over her head. Ectoplasm dripped like sweat onto the walkway and oozed through the diamond-shaped holes.

She stood up again, kept walking, careful to keep her gaze straight ahead. How long had she been down there? Five minutes, seven? The last thing she wanted was for an alarm to sound.

The walkway turned and twisted, angling between the fires. To her left iron spikes drove themselves through the cages, through the ghosts. To her right two cages swung back and forth through high bluish flames. Minor punishments. The serious stuff was farther in, farther than Chess would go even to find Charles Remington. If he was there to be found.

Sweat dripped into her eyes. She wiped it away, turned another corner. Each cage had a plaque bearing the spirit's name; Remington should be in this sector.

He was.

His cage hung upside down over a vat of boiling water, dipping down, hanging for long minutes, then coming back up. Luckily she caught him on an upswing, got a good enough glimpse to know he was indeed Charles Remington.

Or not so luckily. Much as it pleased her to see him

getting the punishment he deserved—those mortuary photographs, those empty eye sockets, would stay with her for a long time—this opened up a whole new set of problems.

Remington was in prison, his spirit bound in iron and tortured. In prison, and therefore not on the streets of Triumph City killing prostitutes.

So if it wasn't Remington . . . who was it?

This time of day the library contained only a few people; the library Goody—Goody Martin today—and a couple of students at the far end, huddled together at a table in the Basics section. Chess had felt their gaze on her a few times already, ignored it. None of their business who she was, what she was doing, or why her hair still stood in sweaty spikes off her forehead.

This was pointless. A ghost was killing hookers, a ghost she had no idea how to track or find short of catching it in the act, and there was no way she would ask any of the girls to act as bait. Not just out of altruism, either; who knew what Bump or Lex would do if she got one of their girls killed?

The Lamaru could be responsible, no question there. But she didn't think it was them, not this time. They always identified themselves. They were far bolder than this. And frankly she just couldn't see any possible way the deaths of a few hookers could connect to the Lamaru's incessant drive to overthrow the Church.

Chess shook her head and dug out her camera. The symbol branded onto Daisy's skin had to tell her something. Anything.

It didn't. The image sat on the digital screen as silent as Daisy. She'd never seen those symbols before, she was certain of it.

Okay, so they weren't runes. What then?

She grabbed a pen and her notebook and opened to a

fresh sheet. Copying sigils could be dangerous. Most of them only needed to be created in order to be activated, and since she had no idea what this one meant or what it would do, she wasn't about to copy it straight out. Instead she tried separating the elements, piecing them together one at a time.

It probably wouldn't help. Even if she could see what each individual part was, she'd have no idea what it meant. But it was something, and she needed to do something.

That bit there, if she followed the line around, could be an A . . . that part could be a rune, maybe Higam? Higam was protective, though, and she couldn't imagine why someone would brand a protective rune onto the breast of a woman they were about to ritually murder.

Damn! If only she had some way to tell which layer was which, what elements overlapped, she could make so much more progress with the fucking thing. As it was, she—

"Good morrow, Cesaria. Do I find you well?"

Her guilty fingers flexed, trying to crush the paper, but she caught herself before they tore it completely from her notebook. No better way to convince someone that something unethical was happening than to destroy evidence in front of them.

Elder Griffin probably wouldn't suspect anything no matter what, but still. "Very well, sir. And you?"

He nodded. Without his hat, his pale hair rose in waves from his high forehead and caught the light from the fluorescents overhead.

He sat down opposite her, folding his nimble hands on the tabletop in front of him. "How goes your case?"

"Okay, I guess. I'll know more tonight when I go back."

"Most interesting, that one," he said. "I admit I have my own doubts."

"Doubts?"

"Roger Pyle has such a reputation for honesty and good works. His anti-drug charity alone . . . Well, you saw the information in his file."

Anti-drug charity? Shit, she hadn't even bothered to look it up. Yet. She would have, she hadn't forgotten, but she'd never heard of the Daylight Fund before. Anti-drug anything wasn't exactly on her radar.

She nodded, keeping a smile plastered across her face. "Of course. He is a very nice man, actually."

He'd also been high as shit when she met him, no question. Hypocrite.

"Do you think you'll have an answer quickly?"

Another nod, an emphatic one. "Absolutely."

"Excellent. I do enjoy his show. I hope very much he proves to be innocent of any wrongdoing."

"Surely you don't want him to be haunted?"

He gave a little laugh, one of the few she'd ever gotten from him. "Of course not. But I understand he has some rather . . . unscrupulous companions. Well, one can hardly help it, I imagine, in that sort of industry. I don't wish ill on anyone, Cesaria, but I would be quite disappointed to hear that someone who brings joy to so many people is a liar and a criminal, one who denies the Truth for his own gain."

His black-ringed eyes glittered faintly as he shook his head. "I apologize, Cesaria. I find myself in a rather philosophical mood today."

"Anything I can help you with, sir?" The minute the words left her mouth she realized how much she meant them. It wasn't simply that she'd always liked him; it was the desire to deal with problems that had a possible solution. Or at least problems that belonged to someone else, for a change.

But he shook his head. "Thank you, no. 'Twill pass. What are you working on?"

"What?" Her hand covered the paper as much as it could. Not enough, though. Some of the squiggles and half-runes she'd drawn peeped out from around the edges of her palm. "Oh, nothing. Just playing, you know."

"May I see?"

Shit. How could she say no without looking suspicious?

She couldn't. So she handed the notebook over, while her cheeks started to ache from artificial cheer.

"Creating a new sigil?" He glanced up to see her nod. "Interesting. What's it for? Protection, I assume, since you have Higam there. But what are these for?"

"Actually, I'm trying to recreate a sigil." Seized by madness or inspiration, or a mixture of both, she grabbed the camera and turned it around. The photo had been taken close up, so close Daisy's dead face did not appear. Hell, her neck didn't even appear. Nothing indicated that the sigil she showed Elder Griffin was burned into a corpse.

If she hadn't been watching him so carefully, she might not have noticed the delicate lift of his eyebrows, the blink, before his forehead smoothed. Had he seen that before?

"I saw it the other day," she said, before he could ask. Technically it wasn't a lie. "Thought it looked interesting."

"On whom? Where did you see it?"

"Um, in Cross Town." Now that was a lie. "Just some woman in a restaurant. Why?"

"Yes . . ." He didn't look at her, though.

"Elder Griffin? What is it?"

"What? Oh, nothing. It merely reminded me of . . . well. It looks a bit like something I saw once years ago, while I was training. Did you know I was one of the first here to enter the program? Before Haunted Week proved our Truth to the world."

She nodded. Ordinarily she'd enjoy hearing his stories of the world BT and the early days of the Church, but today more important issues pressed on her mind. "What was the sigil you saw years ago, sir? If I may ask."

He shook his head. "No, on second thought I don't believe they are so alike after all."

"But—"

The camera clicked back onto the table. "I'm sorry, dear. 'Tis far later than I realized. I should go."

"Please, I just—" Fuck! "I just want to know what it's for, I was hoping . . . well, you know how pleased I am to be working with other departments, and I thought maybe if I could really expand my esoteric knowledge, I could do it more often, is all. Couldn't you please just tell me what the one you saw does? Or if you know any of the elements?"

She widened her eyes, let her mouth pucker slightly. Not enough to look like she was trying to seduce him, but enough to catch his sympathy. She hoped. Every muscle in her body tensed. Please . . . please . . .

He bowed his head, lifted it again. "I really know nothing about it. But we have better sigils, as you know. Ones that protect much more consistently. Some of those we learned in my youth were not as sa—not as foolproof as what we now use. I appreciate your desire to advance yourself, but I fear moving down such a twisted path will not do you the good you seek."

"I just want to know what it does, is all, I don't plan to use it."

He sighed, watched her for a minute while her still dry eyes started feeling sticky with the need to blink.

Finally he spoke. "I'm sorry, dear. I cannot, not today. Perhaps another time. Good morrow, now. Facts are Truth."

"Facts are Truth," she echoed, but she didn't hear the words leave her mouth. Didn't hear the tapping of his buckled shoes on the floor as he exited the Restricted Room and reached the main library.

When he was in training, he'd said. Either he'd spoken without thinking, or he'd been giving her a hint. Either way, it took her only a few minutes to find the old training manuals, in the far corner beneath the smiling golden Buddha.

The Buddha and the other outdated religious relics lining the walls were one of the reasons she enjoyed doing work in the Restricted Room so much. Of course the Archive building contained even more: Christian Bibles hundreds of years old, printed on paper so fine she could almost see through it, an entire room full of Nativities, a Buddhist temple reconstructed beneath the high ceiling. Korans and prayer rugs, statues of Hindu gods and goddesses with gold leaf still clinging to their stone arms like a luxurious rash.

None of it meant anything anymore, but the images still fascinated her. Once they'd given humanity solace. Now they sat in a museum, viewable only by those who applied and were approved for a pass. How quickly importance deserted people and things, how quickly the revered became the forgotten.

She shuddered and grabbed the dusty books, flipping to the back to check the index, then scanning the pages to see if she could find the sigil. Mustiness rose from the pages, filling her nose, making her eyes burn. She swiped at them with the back of her hand and kept looking.

Nothing in the first three books. She was just about ready to give up when she found it.

Not the sigil she was looking for, not exactly. It appeared to be missing several lines; one entire letter or rune? No way of knowing, really. It could be one, could be three, thanks to the overlapping nature of sigil lines. Still this was better than nothing, like a sketch had been done of Daisy's before it was finished.

She'd been right. It was protective . . . but not for the dead. The sigil was designed for Church employees, to hold their souls in their bodies in case of severe injury.

The Chester Airport case had hinged in part on a dead man whose soul had been trapped in his body, held by magic and used to power a dark spirit. For a second Chess's blood ran cold. Fuck, there couldn't be another—

No. No, Daisy had been dead. The other hookers Terrible and Lex had mentioned were dead.

So why had their souls been fixed to their bodies, when their bodies had then been emptied and discarded? What were the other runes in the sigil and what did they do?

She sighed and snapped a picture of the book, zooming in to get the printing at the bottom. In the Church's early days every employee had been required to mark this sigil somewhere on their person before doing battle with spirits. Seemed like a pretty good idea to Chess; she wondered why that had changed and the sigil had fallen out of use, even out of teaching.

In her classes, starting at age fifteen and continuing until she graduated at twenty-one, they'd been taught hundreds of protective sigils, mainly to study and use as a basis for designing their own. Each Church employee was supposed to create and develop their own individual system, their own way of interacting with the herbs, symbols, and energies of magic. Grade points were taken off for simply copying the Church's designs.

So it was entirely possible that this sigil, which had apparently been designed sometime in the mid-twentieth century, had been used as the basis for the one she'd found on Daisy . . . entirely possible, given Elder Griffin's discomfort, that the variation used on Daisy had been used before. With results so disturbing that they'd removed the sigil from Church training entirely.

She closed the books and checked the ornate carved-wood clock. Its eldritch ivory face told her it was almost three. Time to go. She planned to head to the Pyle house that night and wanted to take a nap.

Besides, unless Elder Griffin changed his mind and came back to tell her everything he knew, her chances of finding out more about the sigil were nonexistent. There might be something about it in the files, but considering there were thousands of them, she didn't much want to look. Better to compare the two pictures and see if she could separate the differing elements.

Most of the employees had left already. Chess descended the wide marble staircase in the main hall in silence, nearly the only living thing in that vast space of dark wood and stone.

The Reckonings had ended for the day, too, although one man still hunched over the stocks with his wrists and neck trapped. An overnighter, she guessed. Thievery, perhaps, or . . . yes. Red gloves—now spattered with bits of food, as were his bowed head and pale stockings—indicated he was an adulterer. An unlucky one, too, if his spouse pressed the point this far.

She passed him, gave his Church guard a short nod. Icy wind cut through the fabric of her coat as she trudged through the dead grass and over the cement to her car, sitting alone along the wall at the far end of the lot.

Her keys were in her pocket, the metal still warm from being indoors. She slipped the car key into the lock, opened the door, and froze as energy raced from the door handle up her arm. Black energy, thick and hot, making heat blossom in her chest and between her legs. Her heart did a flip in her chest; not just sex, but fear. The darkness in that power, the pure voracious evil lurking beneath the boiling surface . . .

Two eyes sat on the driver's seat.

Eyes, sitting placidly on the gray fabric. Looking at her. *They* were looking at her. They knew who she was. Knew she was involved.

And whoever they were, they weren't pleased.

Chapter Nine

Being married, being joined by love and blood and magic
in the eyes of the Church and society, is a sacred trust. We
obligation.

—*Mrs. Increase's Advice for Ladies*,
by Mrs. Increase; from the Foreword by Elder Thomas

As she wound her sneaky way through the barren
forest behind the Pyles' house, she decided she was glad
she'd gone ahead and worn black. Not much of a choice,
really, as she didn't own any white clothing; still, the
prospect of scaling the broad side of the house, standing
out like an ink spot on a tablecloth, wasn't one she
looked forward to. Especially not when every time she
turned her back she felt phantom eyes marking it.

Hopefully she wouldn't be so exposed for long.
Hopefully they hadn't discovered the popped lock and
the missing wire at Arden's bedroom window.

Cold wind howled through the empty branches. Good.
It masked whatever noise she made, gave her some cover
until she reached the house. From what she could tell,
the security team made rounds every thirty or forty
minutes—she'd waited in the woods long enough to see
them go by twice—but who knew if one of them might
decide to up the schedule just for fun? She couldn't sit
out there all night trying to figure out their pattern.

That morning before the service she'd managed to get
her hands on a Church-issue expanding ladder. It looked
like nothing more than a metal tube, painted a pale gray,
with a few short spikes sticking out of it in two neat

rows. She pulled it out now and turned the dial on the bottom to thirteen feet, then knelt in the grass and pressed the button.

The rest of the ladder emerged, like a snake from its old skin. More foot- and handholds popped from the sides. The ladder wasn't sturdy, it wasn't the safest thing to climb. But it did the job, and it collapsed on itself again quickly.

She unfolded the prongs at the bottom and jammed them as far into the frozen dirt as she could, then started climbing.

The ladder jiggled under her weight but held. Hopefully her luck would do the same.

It did at Arden's window, at least. The pane slid up easily. Chess hauled herself inside and retracted the ladder, remembering to change her grip to avoid pinching her fingers when the bottom got within reach. The ladder went back into her bag; several wires and baggies came out. Much as she wanted to explore Arden's room, especially that closet, she had to set up her wards and warnings first.

The sound of laughter made her jump when she opened the door, but the hall was dark and empty. The party was downstairs, and loud enough to wake the dead. Or not, which Chess fervently hoped would be the case.

In 1924 BT, five people had died on this land, brutally murdered. The newspaper clipping Roger Pyle had included with his documents told part of the story, but she'd had to go to the Church records for the rest of it.

Mr. and Mrs. Michael Cleveden; their adult son, Andrew; and two servants. One of their neighbors—this part of the city had been a small town in its own right at that time—had stopped by that morning hoping to borrow a cup of sugar. Finding the place oddly silent, she'd let herself in through the unlatched door and found them in their beds, the rooms awash with blood. The

Church had absorbed the police records, which included photos and suspect interviews. There hadn't been many of either. The Clevedens had been popular in their small town. Nice people.

Too bad that niceness wouldn't have carried over into death. If there was anything more mindlessly violent, more full of rage, than the ghost of a murder victim, Chess didn't know what it could be. And she didn't want to find out.

"*Shedka ramedina*," she whispered, sprinkling white salt in a semicircle at the top of the staircase. With her left pinkie she etched a warding sigil into the air, felt it breathe into life and set. It wasn't perfect. She would have much preferred setting it at the bottom of the stairs. But if all went well, any partygoer planning on coming up here—not that many would, she imagined, given the supposed ghosts—would decide it wasn't so important after all.

There was a handy electrical outlet in the wall below a long table. Chess plugged her floor alarm into it and switched the alarm on, then pulled out her box cutter and made a tiny slit in the carpet by the baseboard.

The music downstairs grew louder. She glanced up, saw nothing, and went back to work, sliding the alarm under the carpet until the tiny lump at the end hit the opposite wall. Good. She'd checked the system before she came. If anyone broke the weak force field emitted by the alarm, the unit on her belt would buzz.

Time for Arden's room. Chess clamped her penlight between her teeth and started hunting.

So many clothes hung in the closet that the pole bowed under their weight. They were almost impossible to move. Chess scooped up as many as she could and set them on the floor, making careful note of their order. Next she shone the light along the ceiling. Nothing again.

Her electric meter came from the bag next. She set the sensor on the floor with no result, and tried various places along the wall. Only one spot beeped, and it was low-level enough to make her certain it was nothing more than regular wiring in the wall.

So what was dear little Arden hiding?

A small collection of decidedly inappropriate clothing, for one thing—spangly halter tops, skirts Chess imagined barely covered the girl's bottom. A small white shoe box . . .

Pay dirt. Well, not pay dirt, but items of interest. A few keshes, a little baggie with more weed waiting to be rolled. Chess sniffed it, made a face. Nowhere near as good as Bump's product. A razor blade. Hmm. No straw, though, so unless Arden clipped fresh ones every time, she wasn't cutting lines with it. Condoms. A tacky butterfly necklace made of different shades of gold. A gift from a boyfriend, maybe, that Arden's parents didn't know about? Either way it didn't matter. None of this was Chess's business.

Twenty-five more minutes of searching convinced her the girl's room was clean, which sucked. But then, nothing had ever manifested in this room, had it? So that was a point in Chess's favor.

She replaced the clothing, then set the light on the carpet by the bed in order to slide out the photo albums and various books and papers under there, but they gave her nothing either. No information on ghosts, no books on electronics, no wires or machines anywhere. Nothing. She put those back as well, and opened the door.

The noise level on the lower floor had abated somewhat. Was the party ending?

Knowing she shouldn't, but unable to resist, Chess sneaked along the hall to the top of the stairs. Her transmitter buzzed when she crossed the warning line, a nice little additional test of the system.

She lay on her belly on the carpet and peeked around the corner.

From here she could see a small slice of the couch. Men lined up behind it, their eyes intent, their hands wrapped around their . . .

They were naked. Watching the bodies on the couch, writhing together. Kym Pyle half-sitting, her skin glowing with sweat, kissing a dark-haired man Chess hadn't seen before while he kneaded her breasts like bread dough. Kym's hands reached down her flat stomach, tangling in another man's sleek, swept-back hair.

Against the wall, behind the spectators, stood Roger Pyle, his pelvis moving energetically against a woman whose face Chess couldn't see.

A swingers' party.

No wonder they'd sent Arden away. Although the girl probably knew. Her comment about her mother's exhibitionism now took on a whole new level of meaning.

Chess gave a mental shrug. The ritualized sex below, with its furtive lack of spontaneity, meant nothing to her. She was relieved to notice it didn't even call up any bad memories, though this sort of scene wasn't new to her. Those parts of her mind were blessedly silent, and she was grateful for that.

One last glance—another man had joined Roger and his partner—and she scooted back toward the Pyle bedroom.

She should start in the bathroom. Should, but didn't want to. Instead she checked along the ceiling, looking for cracks in the crown molding or the glint of projector lenses. The Pyles hadn't actually *seen* anything in this room, but this was where the most direct attack—the only violent attack—had allegedly taken place.

Next she checked the bed, pulling back the thick comforter and soft silk sheets. She hoisted up the heavy mattress and peeked beneath it, but found only the box spring.

The headboard was padded in thick gray suede. Chess felt carefully over every inch of it, but no odd lumps marred the smooth expanse of fabric.

The painting of Kym Pyle was heavy and awkward to remove, but Chess did. Pay dirt. A tiny hole, about the size of the head of a pin. It wasn't directly behind the frame, but the mere presence of the frame hid it; it blended into the shadow unless someone inspected carefully. A small camera lurked back there. A camera . . . or a projector.

It could almost have been Church-made, that setup, so small and clever was it. She couldn't remove it to find out for sure what it was, and she wasn't sure how they managed to use it, either.

Her electric meter provided the answer. Low-level readings led her to the floor, where a small flap of the baseboard was removable. The lens in the wall was nothing more than a wireless transmitter or receiver; the corresponding element sat on the floor inside the wall, and the A/V wires from it ran off to the right . . .

Into the bedside table. Chess opened it and found the machine itself. An awfully sophisticated setup. What exactly were they using it for? To record, or to project?

She pulled it out and, after making sure it was off, found that the switch on it was set to receive. Of course that didn't mean it always was. Perhaps they had something set up for her, a little display for the next time she stopped by in the early evening. Such a setup wouldn't work at night. The cone of light from a projector, even a holographic one, would be too easily seen. But at dusk, when the light took on that unusual absorbent quality and all the electric lamps in the world didn't seem to brighten the insides of rooms . . . then it might fool anyone. Might even fool her, at least until she realized it might look like a ghost, but it didn't feel like one.

Well, if they liked cameras . . . none of the video recorders she had on her were small enough, but she'd bring some next time and hide them. The curtain rods were big gold bars, with ornate finials at the end; she could run a wire and minicamera behind them without much trouble. Meanwhile she could find out what exactly they were recording on their own.

Chess opened the drawers and found a startling array of vibrators and other sex toys—a few of which she couldn't figure out—but no disks for the recorder/player.

She found them under the bed, among some boxes of black lace nighties. Seven of them, unlabeled. She'd have to find out what they were later, and with that in mind she copied them one by one on the little scanner/ recorder she'd brought. It would have been easier, and probably a clearer picture in the end, if she'd used their recorder, but she didn't want to take any chances.

She put the penlight back in her mouth to photograph the little setup, closed the door, put the disks back under the bed, and started on the dresser. All Roger's belongings. Kym's would be in the closet, which Chess would inspect next.

Six drawers filled with nothing but underwear, socks, and plain undershirts, not so much as a nudie magazine hidden under the clothes. She guessed nudie mags were unnecessary when you had not only Kym, but an assortment of willing party guests whenever the mood struck. A quick swipe with the electric meter confirmed nothing hiding beneath the drawers or the dresser itself.

Kym's closet—Kym and Roger's closet, technically, as about a third of it was devoted to men's clothing—was almost as large as the bedroom itself. Chess stepped inside and jumped, her heart pounding.

A mirror. Idiot. A wide, full-length mirror, of course. Beside it, a dressing table surrounded with darkened bulbs.

She circled the room with her Spectrometer, getting only a few random beeps, then again with the sensors of the electric meter. Still nothing. Nothing in the hundreds of pairs of shoes, racks four rows high, lining the walls. Nothing in the pockets of any of the silky trousers, nothing in the linings of the fur capes. She used her mirror on its long handle to check the shelf, just a little too high for her to see over.

There was no way to put it off anymore. She'd have to check the bathroom.

It waited for her, seeming to breathe a sigh of welcome when she stepped onto the dark marble floor. In the dim, cold moonlight coming through the frosted window the entire room looked wet, slick with something dark and unpleasant.

The unit on her belt gave a tiny buzz. People upstairs? She hadn't heard voices or footsteps, but electronics did not lie. She flattened herself against the wall and waited, straining to hear something.

But instead of what she expected, there was only silence, growing ever louder until her ears throbbed with it. What was going on? Was someone just standing in the hall—or, given the type of party this apparently was, fucking in it?

Being caught wouldn't be the end of the world. The documents the Pyles had signed when they turned in their complaint gave Chess and any other Church employees free rein to enter their property at any time with or without notice. But it was bad form, being caught. A sign that perhaps you weren't as good as you should be. Atticus Collins still hadn't lived down the time he'd forgotten to use his Hand; he'd been caught searching through a drawerful of lingerie by an angry, gun-toting husband who thought Atticus was some kind of home-invasion pervert. For months afterward he'd found panties everywhere he looked, including attached to his car's antenna.

She could just imagine what sorts of things would be tossed at her if she were caught at the Pyles' place. Ugh.

She wasn't going to stand here against this stupid wall all night, either, so after her watch ticked off five minutes she decided she'd had enough. Her head was starting to ache from standing tense in place like that anyway.

Her light scanned across the ceiling, revealing nothing. Not even a spiderweb in one of the corners, no surprise there. She did find a tiny seam of shadow on the nearest wall, which proved to be a small cupboard.

Bleach, disinfectant, scrubbing cleanser, bleach emulsion to cling in crevices, spare disinfecting toilet disks to make the water blue—why would people want to make their own bathrooms look like public toilets when you could get disks that didn't dye the water?—scrub brushes, sponges, gloves . . . The entire cupboard reeked of bleach and cleansers, as though one of the bottles had spilled. It was making her light-headed, making her eyes sting.

The Spectrometer showed some extra interest around the sink, which had been restored to its original sparkling white. Chess leaned over, ready to shine her light down the drain—

And almost jumped out of her skin when a face flashed in the mirror, just behind her right shoulder.

The penlight fell, bouncing off the marble with a series of clacks and clatters, rolling to the edge and finally falling on the floor. Chess searched the room, found nothing.

She had not imagined that face. A woman, her eyes pale pupilless orbs set in the furious visage of her face. Tangled hair hanging in clumps down over her shoulders.

Lips curled in a snarl . . . Chess shuddered, tried to get control of herself, and shuddered again.

This time it did not stop. Her hands seemed controlled by someone other than herself. She tried to lift them to push her hair back from her face, to rub her forehead, but they trembled like she was in the throes of a seizure.

She wrapped her arms around herself. When had it gotten so cold in here? The marble at her back froze her spine. She couldn't move, couldn't get enough air into her lungs.

A sound, barely audible, from the bedroom. She couldn't identify it, but when she turned to look she saw a pale shape taking form . . .

Her grip on her arms started to hurt, but she couldn't let go. The hazy mass writhed, trying to find its form, then snapped into being with sudden clarity.

A man. Faint folds and lines indicated trousers and a loose, tucked-in shirt. He hadn't seen her. His attention was focused on the empty bed, but she knew beyond a shadow of a doubt he didn't see it. He saw shapes there, sleeping forms. He must, because his translucent arms lifted and the sharp head of the axe formed a steep angle with the ceiling.

The axe came down.

She bit her lip hard enough to taste blood, but barely felt it. All she felt was a miserable sickness, fear and shame at that fear, the horror of witnessing a gruesome murder almost a hundred years after it happened . . .

The axe came up again, and down. Up, and down again. She could practically see blood spurting from the long-buried figures on the bed, practically smell the—

The smell. The smell was back, waves of choking foulness that left her gasping on the floor. She couldn't get away from it, couldn't stand it. The window was only ten feet away, across the wide expanse of dark marble floor.

As quietly as she could she reached into her bag, using every bit of her strength just to get her hands to obey. She was prepared this time, with graveyard dirt and asafetida. She'd even brought some melidia with her, just in case.

She'd take her chances with the ghost. She needed air. Had to have it, or she would die. Her stomach churned, her head pounded like she'd drunk a case of beer the night before, and spots flashed before her eyes, but the window was there.

She curled her legs beneath her, gave the figure in the bedroom one last look, and leapt for it.

Chapter Ten

A further note: The spells within contain common, legal
ingredients. You may be told you can gain greater results
by using herbs or symbols forbidden to the public. Don't
believe it! Forbidden herbs are forbidden for a reason.
— *You Can Do This! A Guide for Beginners,*
by Molly Brooks-Cahill

She couldn't see him anymore, didn't know for sure if
the figure she'd glimpsed in the mirror was gone or was
even now creeping up behind her again. Her throat
closed, rebelling against the stench. She ground her teeth
to hold in the coughing fit. It was no longer a matter of
wanting to open the window. She *needed* to if she hoped
to remain conscious.

The hairs on the back of her neck stood up while her
weak, numb fingers groped at the latch, finally lifting it.

Icy air plunged into the room, fresh and clean and the
best fucking thing she'd ever tasted in her life. She sucked
it into her lungs like it was Dream and she had only a
minute at the pipe. Risking a ghost attack, she leaned
out as far as she dared, letting the moonlight bathe her
skin, letting the wind chill it.

The second the nausea started to abate she turned
around to check the room. Nothing. For the next several
minutes she sat there on the cold windowsill, breathing
and looking around, breathing and looking around. She
still had her bag with her; now that her fingers had
returned to her control she grabbed a handful of dirt. It
grounded her, made her feel stronger.

Strong enough, finally, to get up and tiptoe back to the bedroom door.

Gone. The ghost was gone. Moonlight entered the room again. The bed was still neatly made, the walls free of blood. It looked as though nothing at all had happened.

Maybe nothing had. Highly unusual for a ghost to appear and take no notice of a living human, especially not the ghost of a murderer reliving its crime.

Of course, it was also highly unusual for her to feel so awful for no reason. The throbbing in her head wouldn't let up, hammering behind her eyes. Her throat was like sandpaper. She took a drink from her water bottle, but it tasted off, bitter and metallic, like old dirty pennies.

Her legs shook beneath her, but she managed to retrieve her penlight from where it had rolled beneath the countertop. The room was still cold, but it was a natural cold. She did not want to take the chance of closing that window again. Even now that the visitation had apparently ended she could still smell that horrible rotten odor, faint but present, like the lingering stain of a bad memory.

She was just about to straighten up when something under the sink caught her eye. A shinier spot on the silver pipe, where the metal had been scraped . . . as if the plumbing had recently been worked on. Or tampered with.

This time she shone the light down the drain, steeling herself for roaches or blood or who knew what else that might decide to crawl out of it. Perhaps there was a smaller, inner pipe in there, or—

"Check that window."

Fuck! She spun around. The open window taunted her, a blank hole in the pale wall. She'd forgotten about the security staff. They'd be making their regular rounds, of course—she'd watched them do it from the woods.

Cursing silently, she snatched up her bag and raced out of the bathroom. The unit on her belt buzzed again—were they already in the hall? She pressed herself against the bedroom wall by the door but heard nothing.

Three long, quick steps carried her across the corridor—no time to retrieve the alarm from beneath the carpet—and back into Arden's room.

She hadn't removed the ward from the top of the stairs, either. Confused male voices floated toward her, anxious chatter from women farther away. The party guests weren't pleased by the interruption, she assumed. Not that she could blame them.

Two choices. Stretch the ladder and risk getting busted at the bottom, or hide in Arden's closet. Neither appealed. Especially if they did a search of Arden's room and found either the missing wire or—well, *her*.

It would have to be the window. She yanked the ladder from her bag with her right hand while sliding the window frame up with her left.

On second thought. The voices grew louder. They'd be at the door any second. Thirteen feet . . . seven and a half feet taller than she was.

Busted, or injured? Injured won. In one motion she gripped the freezing sill and slid over it.

A second to hang there, like a target painted on the side of the house. Another to fall.

Pain shot up her legs, but she didn't think anything was broken. She stumbled to her feet and ran, glancing back once she'd reached the safety of the trees to see the guards coming around the corner of the house.

They left Lex's car on Fifteenth and walked the rest of the way; there were places below Thirtieth where even Slobag's men felt the need for caution, and the two of them were heading for one of those. Just what she needed. Not that she didn't trust him to keep her safe; she did, as much as he was able. It was just that she could think of better ways to spend a freezing night than wandering the streets. Especially when all he'd told her when he called was that he might have some information, and she should hop on over to his place.

Lex took her hand and led her into an alley. If it hadn't been so cold, she might have been suspicious, but as it was she doubted he had anything of interest in mind.

Of course, she'd been wrong before. His lips were cold, but they warmed up fast. Too bad she couldn't say the same for his hands. The second they slipped up under her shirt she yelped.

His laugh puffed against her throat. "Cold hands, aye?"

"Like ice."

"Sorry." He teased her earlobe lightly with his teeth. "Maybe you got somewheres warm I can put em?"

"In this weather? No way."

"Aw, never mind that. Just pretend we back in my bed."

"But we're *not* in your bed. We're in an alley. Someone could walk by and see, even if it wasn't freezing outside."

"Part of the fun, ain't you think so?" His teeth moved down to her neck. "C'mon, Tulip, let's us heat up."

She gave a small, choked half-giggle. "Is this why you brought me here?"

"Nay, but you looking awful cute in that Churchy coat, aye? *Like* them big buttons down front."

He kissed her, up against the dirty brick wall. She moved her own numb hands to his thighs, slid them up beneath his leather jacket and the hem of his ragged sweater until she found bare skin. He gasped and jumped back.

"Cold, huh?"

"You ain't hadda do that, now. Coulda made your point some other ways. See? Mean." But he was smiling, and so was she. "Maybe I oughta hold them hands out the way, what you say? Like this . . ."

Her wrists hit the bricks, rough and cold against her skin. Her heart rate sped up.

"Look like I got you all held up now, me."

"Looks like it," she agreed. His lips were inches from hers. "But if we're supposed to meet someone, isn't it a good idea to actually go and meet them?"

"Aw, damn. You always worryin about stuff like bein where we say we gonna be." He let go, stepped back. "But whyn't you come here anyway, share you some body heat for a minute, then we get moving on."

She pressed her back against his chest, let him wrap his arms around her. It was warmer this way, she had to admit, even if it did feel strange to be this close to him and not actually doing anything but standing. Strange, but not totally uncomfortable; it was nice to have someone there after the horror of the Pyle bathroom earlier. She hadn't wanted to come out, hadn't wanted to do anything but sit at home under her tattered blanket, but . . . people could die. Women could die. She figured a little physical inconvenience was a worthwhile price.

"So who is this guy again?"

"Huh. Name of Hat Trick, but best you ain't recall it, aye? Not a safe place we headed, Tulip. Keep that knife you got handy."

"And I get to go along because . . .?"

"Who else? Hear he maybe got some knowledge, figure best you come along. Maybe he know something bout what the ghost for, aye? Only I ain't knowing if he speak true or not. You know it. So you here."

"That's true."

They walked in silence for a few minutes. They were,

as best she could tell, by one of the abandoned ware-
house blocks growing like toadstools around Fifteenth.
Deep in Slobag's territory now, where tin wind chimes
hung in broken windows to amuse the squatters within.
Their off-key jangles rode the wind toward her, discord-
ant and disconcerting.

"You brought all them stuff you use, aye?"

"No, Lex, I left it all at home because it's such a nice
night for a walk. Of course I brought it."

"Just checking, is all. No need to get fratchy."

"I'm not, I'm just—it was just a joke."

"Aye. Sorry."

She rolled her eyes without letting him see and kept
walking. He always seemed to have in his head that she
was much touchier than she actually was.

Then again, maybe she *was* actually touchier with him
than with anyone else—and not in the physical sense.
Much as she liked him, the knowledge that there was an
undercurrent of business relationship in their sexual
relationship . . . She folded her arms over her chest. That
was not a topic she wanted to start on, oh no.

Halfway down the block now, and she felt more eyes
glued to her with every step. The windows were empty
on both sides of the street, but that didn't mean people
weren't watching.

"Hey." He touched her arm to stop her, leaned over
to kiss her forehead. "Ain't mean to get the junters with
you, I ain't. Just on the edgy side this night. You ain't
deserve it."

She shrugged. What was she supposed to do? Tell him
to fuck off and make her way home by herself? Wasn't
like there was any point in fighting with him about it
anyway. "No problem."

It felt like miles, but it was only another few blocks
before they made a left and Chess heard the music.
Barely audible at first, then louder as they drew closer to

it, a bizarre combination of pounding techno and the Pixies.

That it came from their destination she did not doubt. The building rose before them, a hulking shape guarding the street's termination point. Dozens of windows filled with flickering orange light stared at them, daring them to come closer. More fire rose from the rooftop, glowing columns of it slicing through the black sky. The Nightsedge Market.

"You ready?" Lex muttered.

She nodded, tightening her grip on the knife in her pocket.

What looked from the outside like one huge fire was in fact dozens, overflowing from fire cans or set in the center of stone circles.

Sweat formed on her brow. Her heart pounded in rhythm, "Wave of Mutilation" thundering through her head, making her high. Along the graffiti-covered walls, bodies covered sprung couches, lolling figures with half-closed eyes or couples with half-closed clothing. It stank of smoke and charring meat and sweat, of sour milk and sex, and, beneath those other scents like hot bodies beneath sheets, of Dream and burning keshes and huffer glue.

A clandestine thrill ran up her spine. In the corner a small group of bruised, skinny teenagers huddled around a one-piece hookah, spinning a knife on the floor to see who got the next hit. At the far end of the room a dice game was being played; the prize seemed to be a string of betel nuts and shrunken heads. Beside it was a display of jewelry made from syringes and bones, and farther along was a rack of Dream pipes, ornately carved and gleaming in the firelight.

There was Downside, and then there was this place. It stripped her raw, made her want to sink to the floor and burrow in. It was her own Market plus ten.

Lex tapped her arm, bringing her back to him. "Quit starin, Tulip. Get you noticed, aye?"

"I wasn't staring."

"Nay, but you was almost. Follow me."

Through the crowd they wound their way, passing a naked woman with blue swirls all over her body and a purple-haired guy doing tattoos. Chess stopped when she saw the short man at the end of the row, just past a steaming cauldron of dime-a-mouthful greenish soup. A box at his side towered over him, made of clear glass with iron bars at the corners. Inside the box was a ghost.

At least it looked like a ghost. She couldn't tell for sure. Her senses were so cranked from the energy around her, from the desire to immolate herself on the pyre of drugs, sex, and violence the entire building represented, she would have had a hard time feeling a real ghost if it had sneaked up behind her and slipped a noose around her neck.

But the thing in the box had the blank, angry stare of a ghost, the unseeing, impersonal hatred the dead took on when out of the City.

Seeing her interest, the man bared his teeth in a greasy smile and pressed a button on the side of the box. The ghost inside leapt, thrashed around for a moment, then subsided. Electric current, forcing the ghost into solidity. Ghost torture on the highest level.

"A gift for the lady," the man said as the song changed, leering at her and Lex both. "Surely the lady deserves a gift?"

Lex ignored him, kept walking. Chess followed with her head straight but her gaze darting from side to side, taking in everything, wanting to store up as much of the sweet, dangerous sleaze as she could.

Together they started up a narrow, rusty iron staircase bolted to the wall. It rattled with every step and rained flakes of corrosion onto the heads of those beneath them. She didn't ask him where they were going. It didn't matter.

The stairs led to a window, and outside the window, back in the freezing air, was the flat roof of the building next door. A man holding two pock-edged hatchets nodded to Lex, waved them both on, and before them sat Hat Trick.

Surprisingly small and dumpy, he seemed to squat on a stool too low for even the tiniest man. Chess couldn't tell his age; one minute he had the wrinkled visage of the very elderly, the next he appeared smooth and unlined as a young man. Magic of some sort, she figured, but like nothing she'd ever seen before. Everyone bought or tried to make various beauty charms, but most of them were useless—a fact the Church generally didn't bother to reveal to anyone, knowing as they did that most of the power of that type of magic lay in the belief of the practitioner anyway.

But this one worked, at least to some extent. Chess figured that had she not been who and what she was, Hat Trick would have looked like the young, handsome man whose shadow she caught glimpses of. Certainly she imagined that's what Lex saw; he had about as much sensitivity to magic as a lump of cement.

"Lex," he said, in a surprisingly normal and light voice. "And yon witch. Come closer, girl, let we focus on ye."

Forcing her face into a calm, untroubled expression, she approached, getting close enough to smell the powerful reek of herbs and unwashed body. Shit, he was *ripe* under those layers of fur. Did he ever leave this rooftop?

His gaze scanned her from head to foot. It felt like being X-rayed. Finally he nodded and looked away, digging around in the sacks by his side until he pulled something out and held it in one outstretched hand.

Even in the dim light spilling from the window she saw the deep grime under his nails and around his cuticles, saw the crusty skin of his fingertips.

She took the bag without touching those fingers and opened it. Some sort of herb, it looked like, some . . . oh.

Hat Trick caught her look. "You see what you holding, then, got it true." She nodded.

"Girl brung it me yestereen. Found it, said she. We hears, even down this way, of what happens. Such an odd, figure best to tell Slobag." He dipped his head in Lex's direction. "We are not involved, got it true. Where this found all empty now, and no seeing them there before. But we knows what it could mean, so we call."

Lex nodded. "Ain't no trouble, Hat Trick. Got no problems here, aye?"

Hat Trick shook his head. "Ye has problems, got it true. Ye just not aware until yon witch tells you."

Lex glanced at her, his brows raised in his smooth, sharp face. "What's the tale, Tulip?"

"It's althea." Tyson's place, Tyson and whatever spirit he'd bonded with. Terrible's comment that the metal box in the alley smelled like Tyson had smelled. Not just ricantha, that wasn't all of it. Althea too. Ghosts and owls, psychopomps and sex and eyes. It still didn't all make sense. But this was a piece, a big one, and her head spun.

"Aye, and . . .?"

"It's a bonding herb. It traps ghosts, holds them."

"Ain't you use them all the time?"

"No. This is a trap. It closes the door between here and the City—I mean, it prevents the soul from attaching to its psychopomp. So it can't leave."

"Creates a ghost?"

She nodded. "Creates it and keeps it there. Here. Somewhere, wherever it is they're doing this."

For a minute she considered the possibility that this might not be connected to her case. Considered, and discarded it. She had smelled this in the alley.

So what the hell were they doing, the ghost and its Bindmate? And where did they get the stuff, anyway? Althea was highly illegal. The punishment for possession was death. Not that that mattered to the ghost.

They thanked Hat Trick and headed back down the stairs, passing weapons and jewelry dealers, passing a booth where snakes were sold by the foot. She didn't want to leave. This was a place to explore, a place to spend hours getting lost in. And she didn't feel like going home yet anyway. In fact, if she was thinking of going anywhere, it was back to Lex's place with him, where they could dive under the blankets and not come up for air until at least a week had passed.

Wait a minute. Whose thought was that? A week in bed with Lex? Why in the world would she want to do that? She'd be ready to strangle him after two days.

But damned if bed didn't sound like a fantastic idea just then, while her skin felt extra sensitive and her blood thicker than normal, while her heart thudded and something dark and needy crawled up her spine like a scorpion—

Chess froze, suddenly aware as she hadn't been before of the crowds around them, strangers all, sinister. Suddenly aware that the arousal she felt wasn't her own, that it was horribly familiar, and that her heart wasn't racing along because she was turned on but because she was terrified.

They were here.

A fortune teller was busily setting up a folding table and a murky glass ball nearby. Chess stared at it without really seeing, aware that Lex was talking to her but unable to hear him. Where were they? They were here, she knew it. She felt them, the energy getting stronger by the minute.

For a moment a face appeared in the glass ball's smudgy surface, long and mournful. Its mouth stretched open in a silent, agonized wail before the image faded.

"What's troubling, Tulip?"

She shook her head. Her mouth was too dry to speak, not enough air existed in her lungs to force sound from her throat. Crowds, all these people around, all those sweaty, stinking bodies crushed together, touching one another, touching her, all those germs floating in the air, being sucked into unwashed mouths and breathed back out.

She couldn't seem to hear them. She could barely hear the Avengers song now playing as if from a great distance. "They're here," she managed, but the words felt like sandpaper against her dry throat. She swallowed and tried again. "They're here, Lex, they're here, they're right nearby."

Even here . . . even here, on the farthest, darkest edge of Downside, where not even Slobag held full sway, they were following her, watching her.

Around her the riotous colors and scents of the Nightsedge Market became a sickening, protean whirl-pool, like a bad Sizzle trip. Lex's hand held hers so tight it hurt, or maybe it was the other way around; probably it was. And all the while that energy pumped into her, through her, so luscious and awful she could barely stand up.

Stand she did, though; she stayed on her feet, forced them to move. They were here somewhere, and she would find them. She had no idea if they knew she was aware of them or not, had no intention of warning them, but if she could find them now, catch them now . . .

Without thinking she moved through the aisles,

backtracking when the energy lessened, turning when it felt stronger. Shit, it was so strong, almost as strong as the pure earth energy she'd channeled back at Chester Airport, stronger than anything she'd ever felt a human conjure. And she followed it because she had to, despite the pure terror growing in her heart with every step, despite the way every step made it harder to breathe through the soupy miasma of sick desire.

Closer now, and closer. Lex stayed at her side, the feel of his body next to hers almost enough to distract her. Almost, but not quite, because she was so close now, so close, they were right nearby, and maybe it was a trap but she had no choice because if it wasn't, if she found them before they knew she was there—There!

Lex uttered a strangled gasp when she practically yanked his arm out of the socket in her haste.

He was in the doorway. She didn't know how she knew, she just knew. Knew that the tag end of fabric disappearing around the edge of the rough rectangle cut in the wall belonged to the killer.

She could catch him. She and Lex could catch him. Lex barreled out the doorway, not even pausing to speak. Chess didn't either.

Their feet slapped on the cobblestones, the only sound on the empty winter-barren street aside from the thumping music of the Market fading behind them. Chess's breath was loud in her ears, her fingers so tight on the handle of her knife they ached. She ignored it.

Up ahead the killer kept running, glancing back once. He ducked to the right. His coat flapped behind him like a goodbye wave.

Closer. They were gaining on him, chasing him through streets she'd never seen before. They could end this now if they caught him, end all of it.

Her bag slapped and jolted against her thigh. She twisted her left hand around the strap and let it fall from her shoulder, circling her wrist to wrap the strap around it. That could be handy as a weapon too.

Candles in windows cast the occasional patch of pale light on the damp cobbles. Inside those rooms people lived their lives, told stories or did drugs or fucked or whatever they were doing indoors on a freezing night, totally unaware that fifty feet away death raced past their doors.

They followed him left again. The street was empty. Gone.

But the magic remained, and Chess followed it, trusting it.

The killer hit a trash can as he slipped around a corner; it rolled toward them, the sound of metal against stone like the slow death-grind of worn gears.

Another street. Another. Chess had some idea they were headed northwest—her sense of direction held steady—but she didn't understand why. Nothing was out here. The buildings grew farther apart, even more dilapidated than the ones on the border of Bump's and Slobag's territories. Most weren't buildings at all, just broken half-walls with empty eyes and gaping mouths where doors used to be, open in silent screams. Defeated giants of buildings, half-buried in the unforgiving cement.

She stumbled on a broken cobble. It was getting too hard to run, her legs didn't want to move, her chest screamed for air, she could barely see. But she had no choice. She couldn't have Lex go ahead without her. Even with her knife the thought of being alone on this street . . . knowing what might hide behind those charred and decaying walls . . .

Another left, a short block. He was back in sight now, their killer, a moving shadow in the darkness. No street-lights here and the moon was only a sliver above. How far had they come? She didn't know, but seeing him, knowing they were so close, gave her the strength she needed. She pushed herself, harder than she'd ever pushed herself before, breaking through the pain and finding hatred, burning black in her soul. Hatred was clean. Hatred was strong.

The killer turned right again, maybe thirty feet in front of them. They reached the corner, spun it, raising their knives in unison. So close, they were so close, and the way she felt at that moment she could have torn the fucker apart with her bare hands . . .

Nothing. Empty street. Blank wall. And ahead of them, the still-swinging door of Triumph City's principal crematorium.

Chapter Eleven

The body is a vessel for the soul, and nothing more. Once the soul has departed, the body is merely a cast-off shell, and we destroy it as all useless items are destroyed. With fire.

—*The Book of Truth*, Laws, Article 801

She didn't want to go in there. Did not want to, did *not* want to.

Too bad she didn't have a choice. He was in there, he was a murderer and he was in there, it didn't matter that she wasn't prepared for this or that her heart was speeding along out of fear now instead of exertion. The bastard was following her, would keep doing it, and she had a chance to end this now. She'd be a cowardly fuck if she didn't take it.

Without discussing it, she and Lex pressed their bodies together, leaving their knife hands free after she slipped her bag back over her shoulder and affording some kind of protection. If he leapt on them when they opened the door—which she was convinced he would—at least they would be as ready as it was possible to be.

The door should have been locked. During the day this place was, if not a hive of activity—nobody wanted to work here, it was too dangerous—busy enough. A lot of people died in Triumph City, and their bodies were by law disposed of in the ovens as soon as possible after death. There'd been some . . . issues, during Haunted Week and immediately after, as the dead tried in vain to return to their moldering corpses. As long as the body remained in existence, it was that much easier for the soul to return.

Lex glanced at her. She nodded. Together they shouldered the door open, swinging it hard enough to fly back and hit the cement wall with a hollow boom.

Nothing happened. Good thing, too, because the small high windows were barely discernible, so covered in soot were they. No light showed in the cold ovens. Chess couldn't see her hand in front of her face, or Lex beside her. But she felt him, oh yes. Sex beat against her skin, probed her, pulsed against her; she gritted her teeth and forced herself to ignore it. To fight it.

The air was warm and close, oily in her nostrils and against her lips. She was afraid to lick them, because the heaviness she smelled was death. Rendered human fat, pulverized human bones.

She tried not to breathe, ignoring her body's need for oxygen. She was choking, dying, fighting the scream of pure terror that wanted to escape from her throat. Something tickled her cheek and she realized it was a tear.

Her speed-blown pupils dilated. What little light entered found the edges of the long steel ovens, resting now after a long day of immolating the city's dead. Seven of them in this building, she knew. She'd been here once for school. She'd been threatened with another visit all her life, from one person or another.

Worse than the ovens, worse than the cloying sex-thick air, were the pale white-shrouded corpses lined along the far wall. They shimmered in the darkness, seeming to shrink and expand, shrink and expand. Were they moving? It was so hard to tell, it could be an optical illusion or it could be that the spirits of these dead had not settled yet, they were waiting . . .

Get a fucking hold of yourself!

She caught her breath, held it until her heart rate started to slow, then blew it out. This was bullshit.

Lex nudged her. She could barely make out his features, but his free hand on her wrist was familiar. He lifted it, motioning with both their arms toward the far wall. Right. The light switches were there, and the office. The other exit. Why the hell were they standing here? He'd probably escaped already, damn it.

They picked their way across the gritty floor, trying to move fast but hindered by the need for silence. Every step they took sounded like gunshots in her ears.

Or *was* that their steps? She swung her head to the right, back toward the stacks of bodies. There was movement there. Not the bodies themselves. Rats. Little more than dark spots against the white, and only a few of them, but her empty stomach clenched. Were they on the floor, crawling toward her, ready to climb up her legs . . .?

She gritted her teeth and looked away. Took another step. Her hand holding the knife swung in careful swoops through the air; she could feel Lex's shoulder and upper body move as he did the same.

Then a shattering groan rent the air, a demon's death rattle. The building shook.

The ovens roared into life. Their doors were open.

From utter darkness and silence to blazing red light in a matter of seconds. She'd felt exposed before. Now she literally stood blind in the center of a corpse warehouse, blinking furiously to try and get her pupils to shrink. White flames flashed before her eyes when she closed them, red-orange ones seared her retinas when she opened them.

The temperature in the room soared. Those doors were not supposed to open while the flames were on, it was too dangerous. Had he broken the mechanism? How the fuck—?

Sweat poured down her face. Her coat was too heavy, her bangs stuck to her forehead. She adjusted her grip on her knife with fingers already slick.

She grabbed Lex's hand. His too was wet, as was his face. Nowhere to run, nowhere to hide, not now. They stood in the center of the inferno and waited for the inevitable attack.

Over the hiss of the flames she heard pipes rattle and clang. The rats, attracted to the heat, climbed onto the conveyor belts. By the time they realized they were being drawn to the fire it was too late. She watched one burst into flame like a tiny firework.

Lex urged her forward. There was still a chance they could catch him, or at least get out. They'd made it more than halfway through the room. The killer might have ducked into the office, might be up on the metal catwalk circling the room . . .

He was right in front of them. *They* were right in front—the bastard had a ghost with him.

She leapt to the side. Lex was already moving, driving his blade forward. Chess spun around swinging her knife, her left hand finding the zipper of her bag. Fast. Not fast enough. Cold hands closed around her throat.

Oh, fuck . . . Sex roared over her skin, immolating her like a corpse in a crematory oven, reducing her to nothing in a second. She barely existed; her body jerked in a painful, hideous, hateful orgasm she didn't want, couldn't control. And she was back in bed, fourteen years old, hating what they were doing to her, hating herself because she couldn't help liking it, too, and shame washed through her like a red ocean full of dirty needles and broken glass tearing her skin from her bones. Her throat went raw but she kept screaming. Her tattoos seared like fresh brands. She was sinking, falling . . . They were winning. They were beating her. Realization hit like a sledgehammer, and in it was iron determination. She wasn't fourteen anymore. She wasn't that child anymore, and she was not going to lie there and die. Not after everything she'd been through.

Nothing to kick at, nothing to fight. The hands squeezed, cutting off her breath, and worse than that cutting off her circulation. She found the slide with fingers made of rubber and yanked it back. The whole bag moved, but the zipper opened . . . just enough. She needed air. Even the searing hot air of the room, she had to have it, her vision was growing black . . . She brought her right hand up, slashing at the ghost's hand. It was solid on her, and she could damage a ghost's solid parts. Its face . . . oh fuck oh shit, its eyes, those eyeballs suspended in the blank ether of its face—of *her* face—oh fuck no that wasn't possible—

Thankfully her arm continued to move, dragging the knife down. The hand on her fluttered enough to let her take one desperate gasp of air and dig all the way into her bag. The dirt, the graveyard dirt, there was some in there, there had to be, holy shit . . .

Lex shouted. The killer shouted. Through the ghost she saw them struggling in the center of the floor, moving ever closer to the hungry mouth of the nearest oven. The flames inside leapt, anticipating their next meal.

She swung with her knife again, missed. Caught her own cheek with the tip and opened a long stinging cut. Good. The pain grounded her, made her mad.

She scrabbled in the bottom of the bag but could not find the dirt, could not find anything. Her head swam. She pulled out her hand and swiped it through the ghost, hoping even a few specks of dirt were on it, enough to sap at least some of the spirit's strength.

It worked. Only for a second or two, but it worked, and a second or two was all she needed. She brought both hands up between the ghost's arms, shoving out as she ducked down, catching it just at the wrists where it started to solidify.

She hit the ground spinning, rolled herself back to a stand. There had to be something here, something she could use. No point hunting for more dirt, there wasn't time. The baggie must have spilled while she ran. Electricity? Her electric meter was still in her bag, she could reverse the leads, use the ghost's own power against her, but then what? It wouldn't be enough to short her out, and simply solidifying her meant nothing. She could make the ghost feel pain that way but couldn't really *hurt* her, couldn't trap her. Flames? Pure heat energy. Maybe it would work. At least it would destroy those horrible naked eyeballs, and even that would be a huge relief.

Chess cut around Lex and the killer, locked in grim battle, closer still to the oven. Not that one. The thought flashed in her mind to catch the killer with her knife, help Lex out, but the ghost made a swipe for her. She managed to duck, banging her knee on the cement floor, and the opportunity was gone.

This was going to hurt.

She sprinted back toward the front door, drawing the ghost away from Lex and the killer. If she failed, he didn't need to be distracted, needed at least a second or two to try and get away.

The conveyor belt wasn't what she'd expected. It was made of a dull flexible metal, clanking softly as it rounded the bumpers and wheels. The edges of the belt were thin iron rods. Excellent. She took a deep breath and leapt onto it.

Heat blasted her, worse even than before, worse than in the spirit prison earlier. She felt her lips crack almost immediately. Her vision blurred again. Shit, the last thing she needed was not to be able to see, this had to be timed perfectly.

The ghost lunged for Chess, manipulating her body unconsciously to land on her stomach on the belt— ghosts weren't good at jumping, for whatever reason. Good.

Her thighs burned. She wanted to scream. It felt like she was about to burst into flames . . . and she was . . .

The ghost came toward her now, her murky lips parting into what looked like a grin as she anticipated Chess's death, probably imagining sucking Chess's energy away like a milkshake through a straw. And Chess wasn't at all sure she wouldn't get the chance.

The steel frame of the oven seared her skin when she reached back and braced her palms on it. She stepped forward on the belt, forward again, to keep from stumbling. If she fell, all was lost. She could not get away—

The ghost leapt. Chess inhaled, held it. Her thighs tensed. She bent her arms and launched herself up and back while the ghost slid into the oven.

The smell of burning fabric hit her nose. Her jeans were smoking, about to catch fire. She leapt up, not waiting to see if the fire had actually overloaded the ghost. If it had, she was safe. If it hadn't, she was dead. No point in spending her last seconds worrying about it.

Instead she ran the length of the oven, her boots thundering on the steel, and leapt off the other end.

Lex's knife clanged against the cement. The killer screamed. She reached them just in time to stop Lex from bringing the knife down again in a killing blow.

Lex fought for a second, but stopped when he realized it was her. She didn't waste any time.

"What are you doing?" her voice croaked from her throat, unrecognizable. She thought of getting her water bottle but decided against it. It would look weak. "What are you doing to them?"

The killer laughed. In the red glow of the fires he looked like a demon of the old legends. Sigils and markings covered his skin so completely he appeared to be made of them, featureless, his eyes black, his teeth stained with blood. "You," he said in a steam-hiss voice. "I know you. You're very nosy, aren't you?"

Her heart rate tripled. He knew her? The eyes . . . the eyes in the car. He must have seen her with Terrible the day before, seen her in the alley . . . followed them to the diner? Followed her home? She felt Lex glance at her, willed her features to stay calm. Her palms stung; she was clenching her fist so hard her nails broke the tender, tight skin.

"Give her the answer," Lex said. "Give her the answer fore I—"

The killer almost smiled, those reddish teeth gruesome in his decorated face. "You think you can threaten me?"

Fuck this, she was thirsty, and she couldn't think straight. The first drink made tears spring to her eyes. She felt it seep through her body; it was better than sex.

Too bad she couldn't enjoy it.

He knew her, knew her car, knew where she worked . . .

The killer laughed again. Lex glanced up at her; Chess saw the danger then, saw what the killer planned, what he wanted, but it was too late.

The killer screamed something. Chess didn't recognize the words but felt their power blast over her skin. The killer's eyes rolled back in his head, pure white; his ghost, returned in his body, sprang from it fully formed. He'd summoned her, let her take form again through him. He shoved Lex off him as easily as if Lex were a child, leapt to his feet, and ran. Straight for the stairs, dragging the blind ghost behind him.

Chess lunged, tried to stop them, but missed. Killer and ghost tore up the stairs and along the walkway and had flung themselves out the window at the top before she could get up; when she and Lex ran outside to look, they were gone.

Their energy remained, thick and heavy but fading fast. Chess didn't care. Every bone and muscle in her body screamed for rest; she felt like she'd snorted a full ashtray. And the sex magic wouldn't be fading so fast if they were nearby. Maybe they had a car?

"Shit." Lex wiped his forehead with the bottom of his shirt. "All that and we get nothing for ourselves, aye?"

"Not exactly," Chess said. Those eyes . . . that face. Fuck, who was going to believe this? Would—well, Terrible would, she knew that. But . . . shit. Yeah, he'd believe her. All she had to do now was come up with an explanation for why she was hanging around in Slobag's territory at midnight with Lex. Or make up a damned good lie.

"What's your meaning there?"

"I know who the ghost is."

"Aye? How'd you get that?"

The wind blew Chess's hair from her forehead, dried her sweat, and left her feeling encased in ice from the chin up. Almost exactly how she'd felt when she'd seen the Remington file. "I've seen her picture before. Her name is Vanita. She was a murder victim."

There didn't seem to be enough drugs in the world to help her forget the sight of those bloody eyes floating before her, but she would certainly try. She grabbed four Cepts, thought better of it, and put one back. Lex would have Oozers. She'd ask him for one before she went home.

Home . . . It was all she wanted, and it would take forever to get there. If she was even safe there. The killer knew her, she couldn't stop thinking it like a scratched record skipping over and over again in her head. *He knows where I live, he knows where I live . . .*

They trudged back along the streets, not saying much, letting the icy air cool them down. Her water bottle was as empty of liquid as her body felt.

Finally Lex spoke. "So why come a murdered ghost kill other people? Kill hookers too?"

"Yeah. Ghosts . . . especially murder victims, they just hate. They get stuck in whatever pattern they were in when they died, they don't evolve or anything."

"So this dame doing the killings works with some dude. Kills for they eyes? She see without em?"

She sighed. Her sweaty bangs were turning into little icicles. "I don't know. I don't think so. Blind people become blind ghosts, and her murderer took her eyes, so I guess she needs them."

He nodded. They walked on. "You staying at mine?"

"I should go home."

"Ain't sure that's a good idea, with him knowin you and all. Maybe my place better, aye? Keep you safe."

"I don't have any of my stuff, and I have a lot to do tomorrow. I'll be fine," she said, but he was right, and she knew it. Her heart wouldn't stop jackrabbiting in her chest, fear and exertion and speed making her movements jerky. She wished her Cepts would kick in.

"How bout I come along?"

"No, thanks."

"Get your stuff then, an come back to mine. Ain't joking, Tulip."

His concern made her skin crawl. One minute he'd want her to stay at his place to keep her safe, the next he'd want to stay at hers, and before she knew it . . . ugh.

It wasn't that she didn't want to stay at his place, although she really wanted her own bed. It certainly wasn't that she didn't like the thought of having a warm body next to hers, tonight of all nights. She just couldn't stand the thought of needing it. She didn't want her life to be any of his business. Once people started thinking she was their business, they'd start wanting a say in what she did. Where she went, who she saw. What pills she took and how often. Addiction was a sensitive little plant; it needed privacy in which to grow. "Yeah, okay."

"Come get you, I will. You get all your needs, aye, and ring me up."

"Okay," she repeated.

She just hoped it would be as safe as he thought. They'd followed her without her noticing. Nothing said they couldn't do the same to Lex.

Chapter Twelve

The Church has trained you. The Church has put its trust
in you. The people have put their trust in you. It surrounds
you like an aura wherever you go; and you must never
forget it.

—*The Example Is You*,
the guidebook for Church employees

Terrible was waiting for her outside the door of her
building. The sight of him eased something in her chest,
made her smile. Such a shitty night she'd been having.
Her head still hurt and she couldn't stop seeing that
face, those eyes, picturing it coming for her . . . She
could do with just hanging out. Having a couple of
beers and relaxing. Maybe he'd even crash on her couch
and she could text Lex and tell him she wasn't coming
after all.

Then she saw the look on his face and knew he wasn't
there to listen to records and it would be a long time
before either of them got to crash anywhere.

She stopped, her bag falling from her slumped shoulders. "Another one?"

"'Bout an hour past."

An hour. Of course. Vanita and her Bindmate must
have left the Crematorium and headed straight for a new
victim to get Vanita some fresh eyes.

The pounding headache was back. "Where?" He
hesitated.

"Where?"

He jerked his head to the right. "Around yon corner."
Her head thumped. "Right by my place? Right here?"

People died on her street all the time. Hell, people died on every street in Downside all the time. It wasn't exactly the safest place in the world. But a ritual slaying right by her home . . . No shit they knew where she lived, who she was.

The eyeballs hid in an inert plastic bag in her purse. She should show them to him, tell him what happened.

But not now. Not here on the street, where anyone could see, not knowing what his reaction might be. After they'd looked at the body maybe he'd come up to her place for a while and she could show him then.

She grabbed a cigarette from her bag, tilted her head so he could light it from the roaring flame of his metal lighter. "Show me."

He led her around the corner and back to the small private parking lot behind her building. It didn't belong to her building—but fuck, the tiny room in her apartment where the washer and dryer sat overlooked it. The window ledge in that room was wide and smooth; sometimes she liked to sit on it and smoke a kesh and read. If she'd been home, would she have seen something, been able to do something?

The crowd around the body was larger this time, not just hookers but residents, some with pajama bottoms sticking out from beneath their heavy coats, some still dressed for a night out, all with the same expression on their faces: hostile, fearful, suspicious.

She recognized the girl. At least she thought she did, thought the broad nose and pointed chin were familiar. It was difficult to see anything beyond those gaping, bloody holes where her eyes should have been.

"Be the Cryin Man," someone said. "Ain't even think the Church can do nothing 'bout him. He too powerful, yay?"

"It's not the Cryin Man." Chess spoke without thinking as she knelt by the body, pushed the fur minijacket and vinyl blouse aside to see the burn mark on the chest. Blistered, just like the others. The poor thing had been alive, bound and gagged, when he'd done this to her.

"Who else it, then?" someone demanded. "Be the Cryin Man's symbol on her, you ain't say it's not."

"Gotta be the Cryin Man, everybody sayin—"

"It's not the Cryin Man," she said again, barely paying attention. Where was the girl's purse? It wasn't on the ground beside the body or anywhere nearby that Chess could see.

"You ain't know nothing," a man scoffed. "How I'm supposed to trust some junkie Churchwitch—"

The words sliced through her like razor-sharp fangs. Her face flooded with shame, so hot she imagined it steamed in the icy air.

At least it wasn't difficult to identify the speaker. All she had to do was look for the man with Terrible's fist locked around his neck.

"Ain't think I hear you right," Terrible said in a calm, quiet voice. "Wanna loud up?"

The man shook his head. His eyes bulged. He looked like a bug, with his thin fair hair standing in wisps off the top of his head and his hands clenching into tiny useless fists.

"You sure? You got else to say, you best say it now, instead of later. Now we got us watchers. Later might not be true, dig?"

The man dug. So did everyone else in the crowd. Watching them all step back might have amused her if she hadn't been so humiliated, and so sick at the sight of the dead girl before her. This one was her fault. She hadn't caught the bad guy, she'd let him get away, and this girl's blood was on her hands. Just like Brain's. Fuck, she needed a drink.

Terrible let go, dropping the man in a gangly heap, and crouched down beside her. "All just the same, aye?"

She nodded. "And I don't see her purse."

"Elitha, where her purse gone to? She have it when you found her?"

Elitha was definitely familiar. Chess had given her a cigarette on the corner just a few weeks back. "Ain't seen it," she said, blinking back tears. Her thumb drifted to her mouth and she bit the nail, looking for all the world like a little girl playing dress-up. "She gone and I ain't even can find her purse."

"Were you with her?" Chess asked.

"Were at the house, me. She ain't showed up there . . ."

Terrible took her arm and led her away from the crowd. "You sure now it ain't the Cryin Man? You find something?"

His eyes told her what he was thinking: he wasn't even going to dignify the "junkie Churchwitch" comment by mentioning it, wanted to get her mind off it. Maybe it was possible, maybe not, but she appreciated it anyway. If he'd tried to talk to her about it, she probably would have done something stupid like cry. By keeping his silence he allowed her to keep what little pride she had.

Luckily it also gave her a minute to think. She couldn't tell him about Vanita, not without coming up with a good reason why she knew. But she did know Remington wasn't the killer, and why. "I went into the spirit prison today. Remington is there. I saw him. It's not him."

"Fuck." He stood for a minute, staring at a point just over her head. She could see him reordering his ideas to fit the new information. "Bump wanting me to swing you by him, cool?"

"What, now?"

"Aye, if you got time."

She thought about it for a minute. She was so tired . . . Maybe Bump would give her some speed if she went.

The Pyles would be expecting her the next day, but at no set time, and hard as it was to believe, it was only one-thirty now. And maybe when she talked she'd think of a reason, an excuse . . . "Yeah, okay. Just let me get something from my place first."

The crowd around the hooker's body had mostly dispersed. A few stragglers still clumped together off to her right, as if waiting for her to rise. Or maybe they were just unwilling to leave until she'd been collected by whoever was coming to do that job, eager to witness her final indignity as she was loaded into the back of someone's truck like a piece of furniture abandoned on the curb.

As if on cue a van pulled up, its headlights bleaching the dead girl's skin and making her hair glow silver in their cruel sharp brightness. Chess watched, along with everyone else, while the girl's small, pale form left for her last ride.

The drive to Bump's place didn't take long—just about long enough to hear "Ace of Spades" all the way through—but it felt like forever. Whatever Bump wanted to discuss with her, it couldn't be good. Since their little deal regarding Chester Airport a few months back they'd barely said two words to each other, and even if they had . . . When a drug dealer summoned you it was never good news.

"You right? Know it must be a shake-up, seein them girls."

Her Cepts made a bitter, eye-watering mess between her teeth as she crunched them, left her tongue feeling gritty and dry after she washed them down. On top of the three she'd taken an hour and a half ago, and the Nips, she was pushing it, but she couldn't have given less of a shit at that particular moment. "What about you? You knew them. I didn't."

He hesitated, like he was trying to figure out how best to reply. "Aye. Sure wish we could end this."

He glanced at her, slowing the heavy car to a stop near the Market. They'd have to walk across it to get to Bump's place. "Got a thought for you. What you think iffen I say I hear Slobag got himself a problem just like this?"

Oh, shit. This was it, he knew, he'd somehow heard . . .

That's why he was taking her to Bump's place. They suspected her.

Which was only what she deserved. She *was* lying to them, and she *was* going behind their backs. They didn't know she'd agreed to sabotage Chester Airport for Lex or that she'd discussed their dead hookers with him. Didn't know she'd been wandering around his side of town earlier, that she got most of her drugs from him, that she was literally sleeping with the enemy. So why was her stomach aching, instead of twisting in fear?

"Chess?"

"I didn—Um, Slobag's been losing hookers?"

"Aye, what I'm told. Earlier some boy give me the rumor. Ain't wanted to say it out where any can hear, dig?"

"I—no, actually. Why don't you want people to know it's happening in Slobag's part of town?"

He pulled out his cigarettes, raised his eyebrows. Chess nodded and he lit two, handed her one. "Causen some still thinkin it is Slobag, an we ain't ready to tell them untrue. They worry less, aye, thinkin it's fighting instead of ghosts."

"Damn, Terrible. That's clever."

Dull color crept into his cheeks, visible even in the meager light shining through the windows. "Aye, well," he said. "Well. Point is, ain't just our side getting it."

"And this is why Bump wants to see me? Why would he want to talk to me about that?"

"Could be. He just say me bring you."

"So what do you think he wants?"

"Ain't sure." He blew out a thick stream of whitish smoke. It hit the windshield and curled away like the foam at the bottom of a waterfall. "You know Bump. Always wants to hear the knowledge straight from them got it, meaning you, aye. Maybe he got some plan figured up, wants the help from you."

He popped the door handle. Cold air shoved itself into the car. "C'mon. Best see what he's wanting."

The Market was still moving, but with the emptiness around the edges that signified a slowdown. The only crowd still visible was the one waiting to get into the pipe room, a snaking semi-formed line of shivering people who barely looked at one another. Chess could almost taste the smoke herself. Maybe after she found out what Bump wanted . . . She had thirty dollars or so on her. More than enough for a hard little lump of Dream and twenty minutes of oblivion on the curving sofas. Get those eyes out of her mind and give her a safe place to spend some time, too.

"So what's working on your Church case, that dude from the TV? Think they got it real?"

"I don't know." She dragged her gaze away from the lucky horde. "Could be, could be not. I'll just have to wait and see what else I can dig up."

"So them ghosts, meaning if they ghosts. Murdered, aye? Makes em mean up? More than others, dig."

"Yep. The ghost of a murder victim . . . They keep it, if you know what I mean. They stay locked where they were when they died." Hadn't she just had this conversation?

"Aye, some things ain't easy to move past. No difference how hard you hit, never leaves all the way. Like that? And they wants their fair evens and come back to get it."

She blinked, trying to soothe the stinging in her eyes. "Doesn't work that way, though."

"Naw. Ain't can change aught what's already done. Only can try and lose the memory, but ain't can lose it real. So them just keep thinkin on it. Like cars on blocks, don't go nowhere."

His eyes lowered, away from her face to his feet. Chess watched him reach up and rub the back of his neck, watched him pull another cigarette out of his pocket.

"Yeah," she said. "I think that's a lot what it's like for them. For everyone, really."

He blew smoke into the air, his expression changing. "Like this, aye. Wait and see. Only you know how Bump feeling when it comes to the waits. Ain't make him happy."

"Yeah, I get that about him."

He gave her a little grunt in acknowledgment as they started walking toward Bump's place. After a few steps he stopped, his scarred upper lip twisting.

"What?"

"Fuck. Hold it here, aye?"

"But—" she started, but he was already gone, running across the cement. At the far end of the Market a figure moved, spinning away from the gaggle of people hovering around a fire can. Ah. Somebody owed Bump money.

He'd told her to wait, and that's what she knew she should do. But she didn't. Instead she followed, nodding to Edsel as she passed his booth, moving as quickly as she could. Her bag thumped against her leg, reminding her she'd forgotten to show Terrible the eyeballs. Idiot. Well, before they went in to see Bump for whatever it was he wanted, she would.

Finding him wasn't hard. Once out of the Market she just followed the begging wails to the next street over.

Terrible's victim lay facedown on the pavement, with Terrible's heavy knee sunk into the middle of his back. Chess slipped into the shadows against the building on the corner. Along the street others did the same, random strangers on the street who knew what was happening and did not want to be involved, did not want their witnessing of the event to be taken as involvement. Terrible had his prey; nobody wanted to be next.

"Ain't enough money in it, Nestor," he said, rifling through the man's ragged wallet. He pulled out a few tattered bills and stuck them in his pocket. "Ain't good for you, dig? Bump wanting his money. Almost three months gone you had the owes."

Nestor squirmed like an upside-down bug, tried to kick his legs back but couldn't. "I just need a wee more time, just a wee more—"

"What kinda work you do?"

"Huh?"

Terrible stood, urging Nestor faceup on the cement, keeping his boot on Nestor's chest. "What kinda work you do, Nestor? You use your hands for work?"

"N—Aye, aye. In the factory, aye? Makin them clocks, the ones with the—"

Terrible snapped Nestor's leg with one heavy stomp. Nestor's shriek echoed off the walls, burrowed into Chess's brain.

Her heart pounded. She should leave. He wouldn't like her seeing this, she knew. But something held her there, plastered her against the cold brick, watching his body outlined in the phosphorescent glow of the lone streetlight.

Terrible knelt down and flicked open his switchblade, held it where Nestor's terror-wide eyes could focus on it. "Next time you ain't so lucky, aye? Two weeks. Two weeks, and Bump have it all. Or you pay more than lashers, if you dig."

Nestor nodded—Nestor's entire body seemed to nod, but that could have been convulsions. "Please . . ."

He winced when Terrible's beefy hand smacked him lightly on the cheek. "Naw, all done now. You get Bump's money, we ain't do this again. Real easy, dig? Ain't personal."

"How if I . . . how if I get some knowledge? Some knowledge Bump . . . might can use?"

"Like what?"

Nestor shook his head.

"Aw, shit. Don't make me get mad, Nestor, aye? Give me the knowledge, maybe Bump give you another week. Ain't give me the knowledge, you lose a week. This ain't some game."

Nestor whispered something, his sibilants harsh and whistling. Terrible nodded, stood up.

"You get it, we talk. No promising, dig? Still got two weeks, I come find you."

He stood up, turned. His eyes met hers.

Her first instinct was to back up farther, to slip around the corner. Too late for that, and honestly, what did it matter? It wasn't like she didn't know what he did for a living, hadn't seen the results of that living before.

So she just waited for him to join her, leaving Nestor crying on the pavement without a second glance and heading back toward the Market.

"I forgot to tell you," she said, her nervous voice loud in the silence. "Somebody left me a present today."

"Aye? What—aw, shit. You must joke."

"Nope." She handed him the bag. The outside felt sticky, even though she knew it wasn't. Like the eyeballs inside were trying to worm their way through the plastic and suck her fingers into their blind depths. "In my car, on the driver's seat. Outside the Church."

"And now we gots us another body outside your place. Damn, Chess. Why you ain't gave me a ring up?"

She shrugged, hoped it looked casual. "I figured I'd see you later anyway. I had to work tonight, I needed to get home and sleep."

"Ain't you think them eyeballs might be important? Like maybe you oughta stay off your place, somebody comin after you?"

"What the fuck was I supposed to do? I'm not stupid. I got the message, okay? But I still live there, and I needed to go home and sleep. For my actual job, you know, the thing I do that doesn't cause people to break in to my house or leave eyeballs in my car."

"That thing you ain't be able to do, you ignore shit like them eyeballs."

They were back in the Market now, winding their way through the last clumps of stragglers. She didn't bother to wonder why people got out of their way so fast; Terrible didn't look happy, and she imagined she didn't either.

"Look." She grabbed his arm, made him stop and face her. "Yeah, I probably should have told you about it earlier. But it's done now, right? I—I'm going to stay on the Church grounds tonight. I'll be fine."

She forced herself to meet his eyes when she gave him the lie, knowing he would believe her anyway. That he would trust her. Shit, she was a sleazeball. Bad enough that she lied about where she got her pills, how many she took. That was her business. But this . . .

He didn't look entirely pleased, but he nodded. "You call me, aye? Anything go on there. Church might be safe, but them have magic too, aye? Like them Lamaru got past yon spells, got in your place."

"Yeah, but they had Randy to tell them how."

"And you know them now ain't got the same? Just keep me straight if aught happen."

"Yeah, okay. Okay, don't look at me like that."

"Shit. Anybody try breakin in on you like to find themselves knifed up right, aye?"

She smiled. "Yep. Especially now I've got somebody teaching me how to fight."

"Figure you good enough now? Only I ain't want you takin my job."

"Yeah, I thought about it, but I figured I'd let you have it. You know, give you something to keep busy."

"Aye, thanks. Thanks for holdin me in yon thoughts."

They'd reached Bump's place now, at the edge of the Market where the wind whistled around the corners. Chess caught a whiff of the pipes, the thick, sweet honey scent carried in the frigid clear air. Without thinking she sucked it down, wished for one miserable minute she were there instead of standing in the cold.

Waiting to see Bump and find out what illegal task he had for her to do next.

Chapter Thirteen

Dangerous magic exists; it will tempt you. This is why a Church employee must be honorable first and foremost.
—*Careers in the Church: A Guide for Teens*,
by Praxis Turpin

Terrible reached up and knocked on the plain black door of Bump's house, while Chess steeled herself for the horror she knew awaited them within. Not Bump himself, but his dubious taste in interior design.

It had gotten worse. The first thing she saw, after following a nondescript little brunette down the vicious crimson hallway, was Bump seated on the scarlet velvet couch. Above his head floated a new painting she'd never seen before, of a nude woman—big surprise—with her legs spread obscenely wide and a happy smile on her garish face. Whether deliberately or not, Bump had positioned himself right below the center of the picture, so it appeared as though he'd fallen out of her and she was looking down, shocked and pleased to see what she'd birthed.

Even for Bump it seemed extreme. One quick glance was all Chess could stand, especially when her mind kept removing those cheerful eyes from the woman's image, kept replacing her grin with the silent dead visages of the hookers on the street. With Vanita's furious translucent face.

How many Cepts had she taken? Could she take a couple more? The jitters just weren't going away, despite her put-on bravery and the brief moment of levity outside the door. The thought of that murder happening right outside her bedroom, the memory of the Crematorium, the eyes . . . She had her notebook. She could probably afford to take two more. It wouldn't matter if her mind slowed down a bit, not when she could take careful notes to examine when she was better able to.

"Been awhile, Ladybird," Bump said, motioning with one pajama-clad arm for her to sit on the other couch. The pajamas were fur, of all things, a horrid hot pink fur with black zebra stripes. His thin reddish frizz stood up from the back of his head like dander.

Pajama-clad and uncombed he may have been, but he was still Bump. Against his leg rested a shining black cane with a gold handle, and heavy rings glittered on his fingers, casting tiny sparks of light on the walls.

Chess sat, ignoring the desire to lay down a cloth of some kind first, and waited for him to speak.

"Whyn't you take yon fuckin coat off, yay? Ain't cold in here. Stay awhile with Bump. Bump gots some things to fuckin chatter on, if you dig."

Fine. If he expected her to stick around, he could help her out. She shrugged the coat off and gave him a deliberate yawn.

"Always a fuckin deal with you, yay?" He stood up— the pajamas were even worse viewed full length—and oozed his way to the shiny black bar in the corner, returning with a little black lacquered box. "My private stash there, Ladybird. Hope you 'preciate it."

She certainly did. The box was ingeniously made, opening to reveal a mirrored bottom and slots to hold whatever accoutrements were necessary. Chess busied herself cutting a couple of lines while Bump talked.

"So what you got on for me? You got a find yet?"

"Not really. It's a ghost, but not the Cryin Man like everyone thinks. It's—he's still in a spirit prison. I saw him today. Other than that . . . Didn't Terrible tell you?"

Bump's eyebrows practically disappeared into his hair-line. "Yay, he give me what you see, ain't give me what you fuckin know. You dig me?"

"Show him them eyes, Chess."

Oh, right. For a half a second she'd actually managed to forget about them. She reached into her bag with tingling fingers while Terrible kept talking.

"Ain't caught up with Two-Eye Lou, Bump. Nobody seen him or heard aught, aye? Checked his place, ain't look like he been around."

Bump made a face. "Sneakin off, yay. Knows he wanted."

Terrible nodded. "Caught Nestor out there. Took this offen him." She glanced up to see Terrible slap the limp bills into Bump's outstretched hand. "He tryin to make a deal, dig, say he hear something about some ware-house up Ninetieth, but he ain't sure. Ask if he get the knowledge, maybe you deal. Could be something, aye?"

Bump shrugged, inspected both the bills and the eye-balls with equal lack of interest. "Somebody gave these you, Ladybird?"

She nodded. A long silence followed, broken only by the sound of the little gold straw clicking against the mirror and Chess's long, deep inhalation.

Oh . . . *damn*. Bump's private stash was something to be appreciated indeed. Her nose went numb, her sinuses went numb, the entire right side of her face went numb, while her heart gave a cheery leap and started pattering away in her chest. Instantly the atmosphere in the room changed. The red walls were cozy, Bump's furry jammies adorable, the vulgar picture on the wall—well, that was still vulgar, but it didn't bother her as much as it had.

The little smile that crossed Bump's face bothered her a lot more. He was planning something, oh yes, and she was already steeling herself. Not that she'd have much choice in the matter, but it made her feel a little better to pretend she would. To pretend she'd tell him to fuck off instead of agreeing to almost anything he wanted because she needed her drugs. And fuck, she didn't just need *those* now. She needed protection. Needed this sleazy drug-dealing pimp with his pornographic décor and his appalling pajamas. If she'd thought she was worth a shit, she'd really hate herself right about then. As it was . . . just another day in the fucking sewer.

"Fuckin eyes from Bump's girls?" He picked the bag up, inspecting it, poking at the eyeballs through the plastic. "What say? You think so?"

"I don't know. But they were in my car, so . . ."

"So guessin we fuckin need to get movin up, yay? You the expert here, Ladybird. So you fuckin run it down for Bump. What this ghost want? Why the killing?"

She caught Terrible's glance. No expression on his face gave her a clue, no hint to what he was thinking, but she wouldn't have bothered telling Bump about their talk anyway, even if it had mattered. "Ghosts kill, Bump. It's what they do."

"And you stop em, yay? Ain't that what you fuckin do? So why you ain't done it yet."

"It's been three days." Shit, now she was getting defensive. What a dickhead he was.

"Yay. Three days an awful long fuckin time. 'Specially now you got somebody tailin you, Ladybird. What them eyeballs mean, yay? They fuckin watchin you?"

She shrugged. Obviously that's what they meant; he wasn't asking for an answer, just acknowledgment.

"Maybe you next, what you think? Maybe use you as bait, yay? Put you in a ass-grazer, on the fuckin street?"

He couldn't possibly be serious. Trouble was, with Bump there was no way of knowing for sure.

"Naw. Ain't work." Terrible moved in his seat, his

eyes shadowed. "They know she is, they know she ain't a whore."

"Put a fuckin wig on she, yay? Cover that ink she got. Bet they ain't know she then. What you say, Ladybird? Maybe you bring in a few lash—"

"She ain't do it, Bump."

Bump wrinkled his nose like some fucking prissy schoolgirl. "Just askin, yay? Havin me a fuckin thought. Ain't like putting she in fuckin danger. You heard she just then. Beatin ghosts she fuckin job, dig. So why ain't we put she out, let she do it?"

"Ain't work," Terrible said. Something in the way he leaned forward on the couch made him look bigger, like an animal with its back up.

"Terrible thinkin it ain't," Bump corrected without looking at him. "But Bump got a more . . . friendly image of you, dig. Seem to me you the kinda ladybird like to get herself a choice, make she own decision, yay? See what kind of things she could do for herself, if she only willing, an listen with an open fuckin mind."

"Things I could do for myself?" She wasn't considering it, not really . . . but he did have a point. It was her job. Save the cold, and the disgusting suggestion that she might actually turn a trick or two, it wasn't a half-bad idea.

That was the problem with Bump. Despite the fact that he was practically a textbook melodrama villain— she expected him to grow a mustache to twirl any day— his ideas made sense.

Not to mention that if they did come after her, Vanita and her human . . . then Chess would be able to identify her. They would all be able to identify her. No more hiding knowledge because she couldn't think of a good reason to have it, because it was knowledge she picked up on the wrong side of town.

Identify, hell. Maybe she could *catch* her.

"Yay, you know. Keepin Bump's fuckin friendship. You know you my Churchwitch now, yay? Seems all everyone got that knowledge. Make life fuckin easier, yay? You ain't wanna lose that, dig. Ain't wanna be not Bump's fuckin friend. And maybe you get ahead in line, you visit the pipes. Maybe get your needs held out the pile for you, supplies get low. Aught like that, yay? So you never run out. If you dig me."

Oh, she dug all right. The threat couldn't have been more clear if he'd sculpted it from ice.

Not that it was necessary. They both knew all it took was one phone call to the Church and she'd be busted. No job. No home. Nothing. Nothing, or a long stint in some dryout prison and a lifetime of suspicion and misery. A lifetime without her pills, without the pipes, without . . . without everything.

Bump's eyes gleamed like a cheap gold watch hanging inside a fence's jacket. "Now she see," he said. "And long as we havin a chatter, we fuckin friends . . . Gotta meet set up, Bump do, with Slobag. You be there, yay? Maybe bring some fuckin magic with you on the night, yay, an help Bump out. Maybe get what you need, make Bump some fuckin magic. Hear a good witch even can make a man dead, got strong enough magic. That true, Ladybird?"

Terrible jerked in his seat. "Bump, she ain't—"

"No."

"What's that?"

Chess shoved her arms back into the sleeves of her coat. "I said no. No. I'm not building a death curse for you, I'm not—"

"Who say make a death curse? That ain't what Bump say, is it? Nay. Bump just ask a fuckin question, seem to me you might be fuckin polite and answer, 'specially now Bump gave you something, yay? Just wanting some knowledge. Maybe what goes in them fuckin curse bags, yay? Maybe wheres Bump can find out. Iffen you think you ain't fuckin good enough do the job you own self."

Was he *daring* her? She forced herself to focus through the dizzy Cept-and-speed haze in her brain, through the tiny part of her that wanted to take that dare. Not good enough? She was fucking good enough, she was *damn* good. If she wanted to she could—

No. She was *not* falling for that. "Death curses are unreliable, they can backfire, you don't want—"

"Aw, now, ain't down yourself so hard, Ladybird. Bettin shit backfire, it causen them what made it ain't know what they doin, yay? Ain't got the fuckin skills like you got. Ain't sayin you gotta do aught, dig. Just askin. Say maybe Bump gets, what, some hair offen Slobag head. Maybe it like insurance for Bump. For Bump and Terrible, yay. And all. Bump keep everyone fuckin safe, yay? What happen here iffen Bump ain't around? What if aught happen to Terrible? You ain't like that, Bump ain't think. So ain't so much of an ask, when you give it some fuckin thinking. See? Open your mind, an see if Bump ain't right in he thinks."

She shot a glance at Terrible, still sitting on the couch staring at his feet. His hands were clasped together, dangling between his knees, so tight his damaged, over-sized knuckles were white. Had he known about this? He might be mad, but he wasn't exactly pounding Bump into silence. He did owe Bump a lot more loyalty than he owed her. All she was to him was a friend, maybe. Bump was his boss. Bump had taken him off the streets when he was a child, given him a home, a job.

He could have warned her, though. She would have thought he'd at least do that. He should have at least done that. She'd just stood outside with him and felt like the world's biggest jerk for telling him a little nothing lie, and here he was letting Bump suggest she turn tricks and do murder, and he hadn't even let her in on what to expect. Didn't he even—whatever. Fine.

He wanted her to do this. He'd brought her here, and he was keeping his mouth shut. Obviously he'd made his choice about what was more important here. He'd argue about her wearing a short skirt on the street corner, but thought she'd be just fine to whip up a death curse. Did he even know her at all?

She caught a glimpse of her own reflection in the mirror at the bottom of the box; the remaining line broke her image like a pure white scar down the side of her face. Fuck that. She leaned down, sucked it up. The movement felt written in blood. "Yeah, okay."

Bump grinned, and in the tigerlike tooth display she saw he'd known all along she would do it. Known he had her.

"There's lots of spells you can do with someone's hair or nails or whatever," she said, in the probably vain hope of setting some sort of boundaries. "Minor stuff. If it's even any good, I mean. Some people don't really imprint themselves, if you know what I mean, and their hair isn't really useful. So I can't guarantee anything."

"Well that's real good, yay, real fuckin good indeed. Got belief in you, Ladybird, know you try an help your friend Bump. Give you payment, too. Whyn't you take the rest of that fuckin bag, for starts. And then Bump see what he can fix up for you. You come back on the morrow, maybe Bump have something for you. In the means, you start fuckin workin up what you can do, yay? We gonna get aught from both of em, so you do the thinkin."

"Both?"

"Yay, dig me. Slobag an that fuckin cunthound son he got, what he name?"

"Lex," Terrible said.

Chapter Fourteen

The wild psychopomp is dangerous and unpredictable. What they do is given to them by instinct, by energy and magic itself; their wisdom surpasses ours and is cruel and unfeeling when manipulated.

—*Psychopomps: The Key to Church Ritual and Mystery*, by Elder Brisson

Terrible swung on her the minute he closed his car door behind him, his heavy brow beetling over his deep-set eyes. "You ain't—"

"Did you know what he wanted?" Frost completely covered the windows of the Chevelle. It was like being in a spaceship hurtling through emptiness. She dug around in her bag to avoid looking at him, then focused on unscrewing the lid of her water bottle with slow deliberation.

He should have warned her. How could he do that to her, how could he put her in that position?

He wasn't answering. *Damn* him. "Terrible, did you know what he wanted?"

"Naw, it weren't—Shit, I ain't know he plan on that. He say it earlier, aye, but I had the thinkin he dropped it. He tole me weren't on, the bait, meaning. I tole him no way."

"But the other thing? The part where I use magic to kill people? You knew about that? You—you knew? And you didn't tell me?"

"He ain't said that, not ever. Not before. Chess—"

"Guess he just came up with that on the spur of the moment, huh. What a clever, original thinker he is."

"You ain't doin it real though, aye?"

"Why?"

He blinked. Frigid air blasted from the dashboard. Chess pulled her coat more tightly around her neck.

"Just . . . I ain't think you'd do it. This is killing, Chess. Bump ain't jokin, dig. He say maybe some other magic work, but he ain't . . . he ain't gonna ask you it, when it gets time. He ask for death. You know, aye?"

"Yeah, so?" His concern grated on her, like sandpaper rubbing her soul raw. She couldn't believe he hadn't warned her. Couldn't believe he'd let her walk into that blind. He could say all he wanted that he hadn't known, but he knew Bump. He had to know this kind of shit went on in Bump's fuzzy head. And he'd sat there with his hands tight and not said a fucking word.

It didn't matter that the more she thought about it the more she thought acting as bait was probably the best plan possible—which wasn't saying much. It didn't matter that he'd tried to stand up for her over that. What mattered was how he'd let her down. How he'd kept something from her.

And speaking of keeping things from her . . . Lex was Slobag's *son?* All this time and she'd assumed—hell, she'd assumed he didn't have parents, just like her. He'd never mentioned them, never said anything about any family except his sister, Blue, whom Chess hadn't met.

He wasn't just a soldier in Slobag's gang. Wasn't even just a higher-up soldier. He was heir to it. One day it would be his.

And he'd never told her. For almost four months now he'd kept it hidden.

Did Slobag know who she was? Did they *all* know who she was? If Terrible was getting rumors about Slobag's hookers being murdered . . . would he one day hear that Slobag's son was spending the occasional night with a Churchwitch? It wouldn't be hard to make the connection there.

Slobag could shop her, too, if he knew about it. Why not? Why not take away the one asset Bump had that he himself didn't? At least she assumed he didn't, or Lex wouldn't have asked for her help with the murders.

And sometime soon—shit, she hadn't even asked when—she'd be standing around with all of them. Bump and Slobag, Terrible and Lex. Every one of whom thought she owed them something.

Not to mention her mysterious friend, the one who'd left human body parts in her car outside her work and followed her through the dark streets.

How the fuck had she gotten herself into this one. Did she *want* to be killed?

The fact that she didn't have an immediate answer to that one chilled her even more effectively than the wind outside had done.

"I just . . . Look, Bump get ideas on the sometime, ain't mean they gotta be done, if you dig. Lemme talk to him."

She set the cap back on the bottle with a decisive snap, not bothering to screw it on, and turned to him. "What the fuck, Terrible?"

The wipers groaned across the glass, pushing slushy chunks of frost out of the way. Splotchy shadows swept across his face before clearing, leaving him pale in the streetlight's glow. "Ain't like it. Told him so."

"And you didn't bother to tell *me*, right? Just to let me know what to expect, to give me a—Fuck. Whatever."

"Ain't expected him to say. Ain't expected you to give him the aye iffen he did."

"So you're blaming *me* now?"

"Naw, I just—killin people, aye, it ain't—"

"You kill people all the time."

He clicked something on the dash. Hot air hit Chess's frozen skin as he shoved the car into gear and pulled away from the curb.

"Aye," he said finally. His hands clenched the steering wheel like it was a neck he could break. "Aye, I do. But you ain't me."

"What, you don't think I can handle it?"

"Ain't say that."

"So what are you saying?"

"Nothing. Ain't sayin nothing, dig? You make you a choice. Cool by me. Whatany you want."

"You're the one who took me there. Without even warning me. I don't know why you're so fucking upset about it now."

"Ain't upset. Like I just say, you do what you like, aye?"

"So why ask me if I'm really doing it to begin with?"

His eye twitched, but he didn't answer.

"Terrible?"

He switched the radio on, Motorhead so loud her seat vibrated. She snapped it back off. "Terrible."

He reached for the stereo knob. She caught his arm before he could reach it, and he slammed on the brakes.

The tires squealed on the street, the heavy front end of the car tipped down and sent her flying toward the dash.

His arm caught her before she hit. "What the fuck you want, Chess? Wanna have a little chatter? Fine by me, you chatter away, then."

His anger crawled over her skin, enough energy to make her tattoos tingle. She should have been scared, especially after watching him snap Nestor's leg on the street earlier. Maybe if she wasn't so high, she would have been. She didn't imagine most people saw him the way he looked now—his big body looming over her, his eyes narrow and dark with rage—and lived to tell about it.

But she wasn't scared. She fixed him with her eyes and said, "You set me up. You set me up, taking me there, just like Bump's little lapdog. So I don't know who the fuck you think you are to judge me for saying the only fucking thing I could. No, I don't plan to actually kill people. But I want to find out who's killing those girls. I want to keep my job. And I definitely want a fucking apology from you for doing that to me."

In response he stabbed the gas pedal. Chess fell back against her seat. She still hadn't screwed the cap on her bottle and water sloshed onto her coat.

Fine. He wanted to be like that, fine with her. This was his fault. There was no doubt in her mind she was right about that one, and that he knew it. And he had the nerve to get all fucking superior with her? To act like she'd done something wrong, in doing the only thing she could?

If he was really her friend, he would have helped her. Would have understood. Wouldn't even have asked, wouldn't have thought for a second that she was actually planning to build death curses. He knew what that entailed, knew they required a sacrifice to work—if they worked at all. If he was really her friend . . .

How pitiful was she? No, he, wasn't her friend. Back when everything went down at Chester Airport, she'd been the one who asked him if they could hang out sometime. She'd . . . she'd been the one who'd kissed him in that bar. She thought. Her memory of who started that one was pretty fuzzy. Everything after it she knew, with miserable, breathless clarity.

This whole stupid friendship thing was some dumb fantasy she'd made up in her head. Made up because she'd gotten weak. Because she'd been enough of a loser to think it might be nice not to be alone all the fucking time.

Because she'd been dumb enough to trust a man who

sold drugs, managed prostitutes, and beat and killed people for a living, a man people ran from if they saw him on the street. Not just trust him, *really* trust him.

Shame and disappointment made a lump in her throat that she couldn't get down. Hadn't she learned her lesson? No one was trustworthy. No one was safe. And that was Fact, and Truth.

"You know what?" She risked a glance at him, but he was staring through the windshield with his big jaw set. "Forget what I said. I really am going to do it."

The silence in the car deepened.

He pulled up outside her building a minute later. She didn't bother to say goodbye as she swung herself out of the car and slammed the door.

He didn't speak either. But when she got back into her apartment and peeked through the stained-glass window that made up the front wall, the Chevelle was still sitting on the curb, its engine rumble the only sound she could hear.

Lex always kept the blinds of his bedroom windows pulled down, blocking as much light as possible. A good thing for sleeping during the day, but not so helpful in the middle of the night.

Chess wasn't sure what woke her up, dragging her from sweaty, nervous sleep, until she heard the sound again.

Skritch. Squeak. Like nails against glass.

She started to roll over. Lex hadn't moved; his heavy, even breathing made calm background noise. She adjusted her T-shirt—odd to be sleeping there with clothes on—and tugged the blanket back over her shoulders. Just a tree branch, she figured. The wind had picked up by the time she'd calmed down enough to call Lex and have him come get her, whipping her hair across her face, stealing her breath when they emerged from the tunnel—

There weren't any trees outside his window.

Skritch. Skriiiitch.

She sat up, turned her head so fast it made her dizzy. Something was outside the window. On the fifth floor.

She reached for Lex, meaning to wake him up, make him go look, but stopped herself. That was the kind of thing boyfriends did, right? Boyfriends and husbands. Lex was neither. She wasn't going to ask him to fight her battles for her, much as she was tempted to. Especially not when the clock told her it was almost five in the morning.

Besides, she had a feeling that whatever lurked on the other side of that glass, he wouldn't be able to do anything about it.

She slipped out of bed, wishing she had more clothes on than just the shirt. Even a pair of socks might help. Realistically she knew whatever it was out there probably wouldn't be able to hurt her; ghosts couldn't float fifty feet off the ground, and nothing else would be able to come through the walls.

But something about being barefoot, about the cool air against her naked thighs, made her feel especially vulnerable. Somehow she was pretty sure whatever waited outside the window was probably not going to make her feel any safer.

She folded her arms over her chest, hugging herself tight. The cold floor numbed her bare feet by the time she reached the window.

What she saw when she yanked the blind down, hard and fast so it flipped back up with a whir, numbed the rest of her as effectively as an hour at the pipes.

An owl. No, not *an* owl. *The* owl. She would have known that, even if the chances of two Great Horned Owls showing up in Downside were about as good as her chances of becoming an Elder someday. Would have known it even if the owl before her hadn't held an eye-ball in its sharp, vicious beak.

Cold black eyes stared at her through the glass. The air left her body. Frozen, she stood, trapped by its bottom-less, empty gaze. The owl. The harbinger of death.

Who had just died? Whose fresh, dripping eye did the owl hold in its beak?

And who would be next? She thought she had a pretty good idea on that last one.

The owl flapped its wings at her, and the motion broke her trance.

"*Arcranda beliam dishager*," she whispered, pushing the words out with her power, feeling her magic slide through the glass and hit the warm, feathered body. Almost instantly the energy backlashed, bloody red and thick with the now-familiar clenching ache of sex magic. Her jaw set; she refused to react, refused to move, despite knowing the owl didn't give a shit either way. It was a tool, a pet, not a practitioner. But they were watching, she knew they were. From a rooftop, from the ground, from somewhere. They saw her. Bastards.

The owl flapped its wings again, leapt from the windowsill. Chess stood and watched it fall, watched it catch the wind and soar back up and away, over the crumbled roofs of Downside, until she could see it no more in the darkness.

Without thinking she climbed back into bed, and lay there staring at the ceiling until Lex woke up around noon.

Dead hookers. Four dead hookers now—not counting Slobag's—the streets had been alive in the morning with discussion of the second body found just before dawn, up by Seventieth. The hooker whose eye Chess had seen being munched by the owl outside Lex's window.

And Terrible hadn't called to tell her about it.

Thinking about dead hookers wasn't a pleasant way to spend the drive out to the Pyles' place, but it was better than any of the other topics she had to focus on at the moment. And it reminded her of the position she was in, made her feel sick for getting involved to begin with. Which kept her from checking her phone every few minutes like some stupid girl.

She pulled over a block back from the edge of the Pyles' white wall to empty her pillbox. Four Cepts. She'd have about six hours, she figured, before she had to get out of there. Not that she planned to stay that long, with the heartless white sky threatening snow and her mind focused on questions she wasn't sure she could answer. On questions she didn't *want* to answer.

Vanita had clearly decided to step up her game. Eyeballs in her car, two murders in one night. That was a lot. So . . . was it her fault? Had the little run-in with Vanita pissed her off even more, made her rush to build up some sort of eyeball stockpile?

She didn't know, but the thought made her pills stick in her throat.

She forced them down and drove on.

Against the white sky the house looked even more threatening, as though the gray slate roof and the branches like bare, bony fingers were the only things keeping it from attacking her. She hadn't had much time the night before to think about the ghosts she'd seen, about that axe rising toward the ceiling and slamming back down. Now the memory came back full force, and she shuddered as she stepped out of the car and handed her purse to one of the security guards.

"Merritt's not here?"

"Later."

Good thing she hadn't brought her pills. His search was alarmingly thorough. More than she'd expected it to be, if she thought about it, but she didn't say anything, not even when his hand brushed her breast a few more times than she thought strictly necessary.

There were more guards out as well. The one holding her purse—Taylor, his badge read—caught her curious stare.

"There was a break-in last night," he said. "We think."

"Oh?"

He shrugged and handed back her purse. "Have fun. You can go in the side."

"Actually, I'd like to interview some of you guys first, if that's okay."

"Mr. Pyle didn't say anything about—"

"And you can ask him if you want, but I have the authority to interview anyone and everyone on the premises. I'd like to start that now. If you can get me a list of all the guards' names, please? And if you know anyone who's specifically seen an entity, I'd like to talk to them first."

He hesitated. "I'll have to ask Mr. Pyle."

Asshole. She was not in the mood for this today, not one bit. "Fine. Can you just show me where the security office is before you do? It's cold out."

That he could apparently do, albeit without speaking.

The security office hid behind the garage, an unobtrusive shedlike building with one-way glass. It distorted her reflection as she walked past it, twisting her torso, squashing her face, and making her forehead bulge.

Bright fluorescents of the same type as in the hallway connecting the house and garage hung from the ceiling. Added to the winter light through the windows, the room looked almost like one of the ritual rooms in the Church, pale and clean, waiting.

Along one wall sat a long gray desk, its surface stacked with small monitors. Security cameras. Fuck, she hadn't even thought there might be outside cameras. Had they seen her? No, they couldn't have. They would have caught her if they had.

But one of the cameras was clearly trained on the back of the house. Arden's window was there, at the far end. So why hadn't anyone been watching? Why hadn't her presence been discovered until someone noticed the open bathroom window?

She glanced around the rest of the room, taking in the switchboard, the wheeled leather chairs, the smaller desk with its neat trays full of paper. A shelf half-full of radio receivers covered the thin slice of wall by the door. Beneath it was a gun rack prickly with rifles.

Taylor's back was turned while he called the house, presumably to discuss her requests. Quickly she traced the wire leading from the back-of-the-house monitor down beneath the desk, where the recorders were. It was probably too late, but just the same . . .

The disk came out with a quiet click. Chess, her ears pricked for any change in Taylor's voice behind her, tugged her nail file out of her bag and scraped a series of deep, quick slashes across the shiny surface. It probably didn't matter. But she felt a little better for having done it.

The disk was back in and she was leaning against the low, cool rim of the desk before Taylor turned around.

"Okay," he said, and the new coldness in his deep brown eyes told her he didn't like what he'd just heard. Interesting. "Mr. Pyle says welcome back, and to give you whatever you need."

"Those lists, please."

"Uh-huh. But tell me something first, Miss Putnam. You don't really think Mr. Pyle would fake a haunting in his own home, do you? Scare his wife and daughter like that, just for money he doesn't need?"

She didn't bat an eyelash. "I'm just here to help."

"Uh-huh."

Staredown was a game she'd learned to play very early in life, but it wasn't a very interesting one and she really didn't care enough to bother. "Are we going to have a problem?"

Just as she'd thought, he backed down. "No. I just want to make sure you know how I feel. Mr. Pyle's a good man. He's not some cheat."

"I'll take that under advisement."

"You should. Seeing as how I'm one of the only guards who's actually seen a ghost here."

"So tell me about it." She spun one of the chairs around and plunked herself down, grabbing her notebook and pen. At the same time she turned the knob on the small recorder in her bag.

"What did you see?"

"I was making the three A.M. rounds in Mr. Pyle's offices on the opposite end from the living areas. He leaves windows open there some nights, falls asleep at his desk or on his couch. He works hard, Mr. Pyle. So sometimes I have to go in there to wake him up, or close the windows and make sure everything's locked."

"Why? I mean, you guys keep the grounds here pretty closely watched, right? So why check inside too?"

His eyes narrowed. "We like to be thorough."

"Okay, just asking. Go on."

"On that night, Mr. Fletcher was here—you know who he is, right?"

When Chess shook her head he sighed and grabbed his own chair. "Oliver Fletcher is the producer of Mr. Pyle's show. He's Mr. Pyle's boss, basically. But they're good friends, too. Mr. Fletcher's the one gave Mr. Pyle his start, way back when Mr. Pyle was still just doing stand-up in little clubs. Mr. Fletcher scouted him, got him on one of the TV talk shows he produces, kept inviting him back. Then he cast him on *The Monastery*, and . . . I guess you know the rest."

She didn't, really, but she could guess. Roger Pyle became a big star, and Oliver Fletcher had a hit show, and they both made pots of money.

She wrote Oliver Fletcher's name on her pad. Might be worth a look into his financials, too, if he and Pyle were such *good friends*.

"Anyway, Mr. Fletcher was here and sometimes they'd stay up late, but not that night. I walked into the office, and . . . and it felt wrong in there, you know? It smelled funny." He paled a little. "I tried the light switch but it didn't work. I thought the overhead bulb was burned out and I should try the lamp. I didn't want to. It smelled so weird and it was really cold in there, and it just . . ."

He smoothed his hands over his arms, a gesture Chess recognized. The tiny hairs there stood on end. People never seemed to notice it consciously, but they always tried to soothe themselves when it happened. Either Taylor was telling the truth or he was a damn good actor.

"It just felt so creepy in there. And it never has before and the light wouldn't work. So I decided I was being stupid, I mean, getting freaked out because of a fu— freaking smell, when it was probably just the heating system in the house working out the kinks. So I took a couple more steps in and . . . and that's when I saw them."

"Them? More than one spirit?"

He nodded, but it looked like a reflex. He didn't look at her, didn't even seem to fully remember she was there. "A man. He was wearing kind of a . . . kind of a loose shirt, white or light-colored, and pants. But I couldn't see all of the pants, you know, he kind of . . . turned into mist around the knees, and the light came through the windows around him. But he had an axe."

"An axe?" A chill crept its way up her spine, interrupting the cozy warmth of her pills.

"An axe. A big one. And he . . . in his other hand was . . ." Taylor shuddered. "A head. Someone else's head, a woman's head. He held it by the hair, it was all tangled and knotted . . . and I think she was behind him, her body, with no head. It looked like a woman's headless body behind him. Reaching for him.

"I ran. I turned and ran, all the way through the living room, into the walkway, and I kept running until I got out here, and I slammed the door shut and I . . . I waited for the man with the axe to come get me."

He turned to her now, his eyes wide. "So you see, I know they're real. I know Mr. Pyle isn't lying. That thing saw me. It was coming for me. I know it was."

Chapter Fifteen

A good Debunker is ready for anything, never surprised, never caught off guard.

—*Careers in the Church: A Guide for Teens*,
by Praxis Turpin

The security room door opened. Taylor leapt out of his seat, his broad face flushed. For a second he looked crazed, like he was about to pick up an axe himself, then his color normalized and he broke into a grin.

"Mr. Fletcher! What a pleasure to see you, sir."

So this was Oliver Fletcher. Tall, slim, with striking salt-and-pepper hair swept back from a high, smooth forehead. Success and power wafted from him like expensive cologne, and he knew it. The smile he turned on her had the hint of cool appraisal men gave when they were trying to determine just how much they'd impressed her.

Her lip wanted to curl at the sight of it. Instead, she forced a bright smile. Best not to make an enemy of him quite yet.

"Great to see you, too, Taylor," he said, but he didn't take his eyes off her. "And who is your lovely guest?"

Taylor introduced her, while her cheeks started to ache from the stiffening smile.

Fletcher's face darkened. "Ah. Roger's ghosts. Such a terrible shame. He builds his dream house, and this happens."

"Have you seen the entities, Mr. Fletcher?"

"Me? No. No, I haven't. But I can assure you if Roger says they're here, they're here. Such an honest man, Roger is. He'd give you the shirt off his back if he thought it would help you."

Was it her imagination, or was there a note of contempt in Fletcher's voice?

Taylor certainly didn't seem to think so. His gaze fixed on Fletcher as though the man had just announced the sun did in fact rise and set upon his order.

"He seems like a very nice man," she said, hoping to keep him talking.

"He is. Always has been. A shame, though. It's so easy for people to take advantage of a man like that. So naïve . . . I've tried to tell him, but it's no use. He's determined to trust people." Fletcher gave a little laugh. "What can you do with people like that?"

"Cast them in your TV shows?"

He laughed, but she caught the glint in his eyes. Damn, that was a mistake. Fletcher liked his women pretty and empty, vessels for whatever he wanted to fill them with. And she had a pretty good idea what that might be.

In fact, she knew it. He turned to say something to Taylor and, in the sleek dark back of his head, she realized she'd seen him before.

The night before, in fact. His had been the head buried between Kym Pyle's legs on the couch.

Taylor trotted off somewhere at Fletcher's command, leaving her alone with him. Good. Maybe he could tell her more about the Pyles—without the hero worship of the security staff.

He settled himself in Taylor's abandoned chair and pulled a sleek gold cigarette case out of his pocket. His eyebrows rose. "Do you mind?"

Excellent. She shook her head, her smile becoming genuine as she pulled out her own pack and let him light her. She rarely got to smoke at work.

"So, Mr. Fletcher, do you come out to visit the Pyles often?"

"Not as often as I'd like. And before you ask, no, I've never seen anything out of the ordinary here."

"But you're so sure Mr. Pyle is telling the truth."

"I know Roger. He wouldn't lie."

She sensed an opening. "Kym? Arden?"

"Arden is a troubled young lady, but don't you think she lacks the sophistication to pull off something like this? Roger's told me some of the things he's seen, and Kym has seen. It sounds quite terrifying."

"And Kym?"

"Kym lacks the intelligence."

"You don't think much of her?"

"I didn't say that. Kym is a beautiful woman."

Chess pretended that answered her question. "Do you think there's someone else, perhaps? Someone who might have the sophistication and the intelligence?"

"Why don't you tell me, Miss Putnam. Have you honestly ever seen a fake haunting on the level of what is apparently happening here? Do you think anyone is clever enough to stage such a thing?"

"I really couldn't say."

He stood up, his flat smile reflecting a satisfaction that rang alarms in Chess's gut. "Well, please do say, if you find that person. I'd like to hire him."

Two hours later Chess sat once again in the orange and ivory living room, before a cheerful fire, and checked her notes. After she'd had a few quick words with the Pyles she could leave, and not a moment too soon. She wasn't itching yet, but it would take almost an hour to get home and she wanted to leave herself some room.

As long as she was checking her notes, she might as well check her phone. No calls. No texts. Nothing. She'd spoken to Lex that morning, but . . .

She closed her eyes, shook the thought from her head. This wasn't the time to focus on anything but work, especially now her mind was clear.

Two other guards had seen ghosts. All of the descriptions were similar and matched what she'd witnessed herself. The smell—it still seemed to cling to her nose when she thought of it—the man in the loose shirt, another man, the woman she'd seen in the bathroom mirror.

A murderer and two victims. Only one man—she guessed it was the son—was still unaccounted for, unless he was the figure Roger had seen in the guest bedroom.

Then there was Oliver Fletcher. Interesting. Obviously a friend of Roger's and an admirer of his talent. Just as obviously contemptuous of him and his family, no matter how many sex parties he attended at their house. She wondered if he'd flown in specifically for this one or if he had some other reason to be there. He and Roger worked together on the TV show. Was he producing the film as well?

She'd ask Roger Pyle. Who was just walking into the room, a big grin on his cheerful face. She checked his eyes. A little dilated, nothing big. Come to think of it, she hadn't found any drugs in the Pyles' room. Maybe he kept them in the office? Shit, she was going to have to come back with her Hand, put them all to sleep, and get into that room. Especially since another significant episode had occurred there.

This week was never going to end. Dead hookers at home, a cavernous house full of miserable people here, and not an answer in sight.

It could have been worse, yes. She knew that from experience. But the thought didn't seem to help her the way it usually did.

"How are things going?" Roger asked. "Is everyone being helpful? They're giving you everything you need?"

She nodded. "Everyone's been great."

He visibly relaxed. "Excellent. Excellent. Please let me know if there's anything else I can do."

"Actually, I was wondering something. Most of the staff members who've witnessed the entities report a particular smell. But you didn't mention it when you told me your experiences. Was there an odor that you recall?"

Roger's forehead creased. "Not . . . No, I don't think so. I know I felt a little odd, but I assumed that was just because I'd drunk too much coffee. You know, caffeine makes me jumpy sometimes, a little fuzzy. But I didn't notice a scent or anything."

"Was that every time, or just that first time? The night of the attack in your bedroom, for example? You hadn't been drinking coffee then."

"No, no I guess I hadn't. I don't . . . I'm sorry, Miss Putnam, it was just so terrifying, I don't remember if I smelled anything or not. I was so focused on Kym and her injuries."

She nodded, smiled to let him know she understood. "Of course."

"Have you read the articles? About the murders, I mean." Roger shuddered. "I just don't understand how someone could do something like that. And to think it happened here, on this land. Awful. No wonder they've come back."

"Well, it isn't always a matter of—"

"Do you think if we discover who killed them, they'll go away? I wondered about that. Like in old books, you know, where they can let go of the trauma because the truth is known. Does that happen?"

She couldn't help but smile. He looked so hopeful. "I'm afraid not, Mr. Pyle. It's been tried, but we've learned it really makes no difference. Even if we discover the truth, the dead don't feel that knowledge. It just doesn't affect them or get through to them, so they can't move on. The ones who are trapped by it, I mean."

And that was conversation number three on that subject. Surely that wasn't a coincidence? What was she trying to tell herself there, what was she missing?

"Have you been to the City? What's it like?"

Her smile became fixed. "It's very peaceful."

Terrifying was more like it. Dark and cold and full of spirits. The remnants of life, moving silently through the cavernous space. It was emptiness.

Apparently she was the only one who felt that way. No one else seemed to have a problem with the City. But for her it was . . . a nightmare. Someplace so awful it was worth staying alive just to avoid it.

She changed the subject. "I met Oliver Fletcher. In the security office."

"Oliver? That's great. He's an interesting man, Oliver. Helped me . . . Well, I guess he's been the best friend I ever had, really. I owe my whole career to him."

"Now, darling, don't be so modest. You got where you are by hard work." Kym Pyle knew how to make an entrance, Chess had to give her that. Today she wore a snug black sweater with a deep V neck and a pair of red cigarette pants, and her blonde hair was swept up into a smooth knot on the back of her neck.

She ran crimson fingernails through Roger's hair, giving him a smile much warmer than anything Chess would have expected to see. Perhaps she'd worked off all her tension at the party.

Or perhaps the Pyles had decided it would be less suspicious if Kym didn't act quite so much like a dominatrix who'd had a bad day.

Kym turned to her, the smile fading. "Miss Putnam. I thought you'd left over an hour ago, didn't anyone tell you?"

"Tell me?"

"The snow. Haven't you seen? It's an absolute storm out there. I thought one of the staff had let you know—"

Chess leapt from her seat, Kym's voice fading to a drone in the background. Thick orange curtains covered the broad windows; Chess yanked them apart and gasped. It wasn't just snow. It was a blizzard, huge fat flakes obscuring everything.

Oh fuck. Oh fuck oh fuck oh fuck—

"I should go." She snatched up her bag and yanked the zipper open. "I'm sorry, but I—"

"You can't go," Kym said. "It's terrible out there. The roads—"

"But if I don't try now, who knows when I'll be able to get out of here?" Keys, where were her keys? The security room, on the hook. She'd relinquished them when they parked her car.

"But I don't think you'll be able to get out of here *now*." Kym settled into a chair. "Arden says it's been snowing for over an hour. I'm so sorry. I was napping, and I guess with the curtains closed . . . I can't believe no one warned you. Roger, I'm going to have another talk with the security staff, they're not being very attentive. What do we pay them for?"

"No, I'm—I'm sure it will be fine, I mean, I've driven in snow before, so—"

"They don't salt the roads out here," Roger said. "The plows will be along eventually, but not until after it stops."

"I'm sorry." Chess slung her bag over her shoulder, blinking back tears. Oh shit oh fuck how had she let this happen? "I really need to at least try, I can't impose—"

"It's no imposition, don't be silly. You must stay here, Miss Putnam. Have dinner with us, stay the night. We have plenty of room. It's so miserable out there, you can't drive in that."

"I'm just going to have a look," she managed, before escaping from the room and throwing herself down the long bright walkway.

It was impossible. Snow fell fast and thick, clinging to her eyelashes, coating her clothing. Three or four inches of it already covered the ground; she couldn't make out the wall at the edge of the property. Everything was white. No landmarks, nothing.

Nothing to look at. Nothing in her pillbox. Her hands shook as she raised them to her face, jammed her fist against her mouth.

How long did she have? Two hours, maybe three, before it started, and another couple of hours before it got really bad? There were a few hard candies in her bag, the sugar would help for a little while, but . . . a whole night?

Her eyes stung and she swiped at them, trying to will her heart to slow down. It was okay. It would be okay. The snow would stop in a few hours. It could stop any minute, right? And it was early evening. People would be commuting, the plows would come through, she could get out.

Surely the Pyles had a small plow or something, living out here. Maybe one of the security guys—maybe Merritt—would help her get out. If she could just hold on for a little while, an hour, two, she'd be okay. She'd planned on staying until six or so anyway, right?

Right. So she would be fine. All she had to do was wait it out, just hang out for a little longer, and she could go home and get her pills.

Just a little longer.

Chapter Sixteen

So much fear and misery, so much anger, made human-
kind vulnerable to the dead, for they ceased to remember
the danger posed by the unseen.
  But the unseen never forgets. It never stops looking for
its chance to destroy.
  —*The Book of Truth*, Origins, Article 459

She had to admit it was interesting. Interesting in the
way a man might find his last few hours before facing
the firing squad interesting, sure, but still interesting.

She'd never had a chance to spend this much time with
her investigation subjects before. She'd certainly never
spent a night in one of their homes.

Damn shame, then, that in another couple of hours
she wasn't going to be good for anything but hugging the
toilet bowl and wishing she were dead. And trying
desperately to figure out how she was going to leave in
the morning without anyone noticing she could barely
stand.

She wiped her damp forehead with the back of her
hand and tried to focus on the plate in front of her.
Outside the tall dining room windows, snow swirled in
the empty sky. Inside, voices chattered around her,
discussing empty things. Shopping. Mutual friends. If
she'd cared about their world at all, it would have been
fascinating. As it was, the only thing she cared about
was keeping herself from scratching her arms raw.

The itch burned like fire on her palms, on her calves
and the sensitive skin of her wrists. Her stomach hadn't
joined the party yet, but it was only a matter of time.

Servants cleared the table silently, removing Chess's barely-touched chicken and replacing it with some sort of chocolate confection. Chess grabbed her fork. Sugar. Sugar would help a little. It might help enough for her to get back upstairs without anyone noticing something was wrong.

"So, Miss Putnam, you're staying here tonight?" Oliver smiled at her from around a forkful of food.

She nodded.

He turned to Roger. "Why haven't you given her my room?"

"Well . . . because you're in it?"

"But my room is the nicest. Please, I insist."

"Thanks, Mr. Fletcher, but it's fine."

"No, you must have mine."

"I'm really happy with the one I have."

"You can't be." His brows drew together as if he was an infant and she'd stolen his pacifier. "Mine is the nicest, you must have mine."

"Oliver, I think you're making her uncomfortable," Roger said quietly.

Chess seized on it. "Yes, please, Mr. Fletcher, don't make me feel guiltier than I already do. I like my room and I wouldn't feel right about taking yours. Please."

Fletcher opened his mouth, his face red. Chess stared back as coolly as possible. It was nice of him to offer, but really, why the insistence? It wasn't like she cared. She wouldn't be sleeping in there. She could be about to spend the night in a dungeon for all it mattered.

"Arden," Kym said, dipping her fork into the puddle of chocolate sauce around the edge of her plate and slipping it into her mouth, "don't eat too much of this. You've gained enough weight as it is."

Arden scooped up a huge mouthful and shoveled it in. "Arden! What did I just say?"

"I don't care!"

"If you don't care, I certainly do."

"Let her enjoy her dessert," Oliver said. He leaned back and put an arm over his chair, the pose obviously calculated to show off the muscular chest beneath his casual white shirt. He winked at Arden, who smiled back.

"See? Oliver likes me the way I am."

"Oliver isn't your mother."

"I wish he was."

Their voices scraped across her skin like claws. Why wouldn't they just shut up?

The discussion deepened, turning into a fight. Every muscle in Chess's body cringed. She shouldn't be here for this, it was like they'd forgotten she was even in the room. *Was* she in the room? Why was she here?

Her hand trembled on her fork as she scooped up more dessert. Some kind of pie, covered with whipped cream. The sort of thing she never ate, cloyingly sweet, coating her tongue with stickiness. It was like swallowing lard.

Almost exactly like it, in fact.

That was a memory she didn't want to revisit. None of her memories were ones she wanted to revisit. Too bad. They were all coming, she knew that, hovering like the ghosts that might or might not be haunting the Pyle house, waiting until she was at her most vulnerable before attacking.

Arden's screams turned incoherent; every one was like fingernails scraping Chess's brain. Her footsteps as she ran out of the room vibrated up from the floor and made Chess's legs tremble.

Blessed silence fell. Blessed to Chess at least. The others looked embarrassed. "I'll go talk to her," Oliver said, dropping his napkin with careful negligence onto the snow-white tablecloth.

"No," Kym said. "Nobody can talk to that girl. I just don't know what we're going to do with her. There's a Church-run school I read about, outside Arcadia. They'll straighten her out. Miss Putnam, don't you think a Church education is best?"

"What? Oh, um, yes."

"Do you think they'll be able to help Arden?" Her steely gaze trapped Chess in her chair like a bug under glass.

"Nothing's wrong with Arden but typical teenage growing pains," Oliver said. "The offer to let her come stay with me is still open, you know."

"We can't impose on you like that," Kym said. Chess glanced at Roger, who was still sitting in his chair, hardly moving. Stoned again? Where did he keep his drugs? Maybe she could sneak into the office and find them. She'd pulled her transmitter out from under the carpet already, she could lay it out by the office door, maybe there would be something in there.

And if she got caught? Fuck it. She didn't care, not now. She needed her pills. She needed something, anything. Even some decent cold medicine might help. Just . . . just anything. She wiped her forehead again and stood up, her fork clattering against her plate.

"I'm sorry. The meal was lovely, thank you, but I'm—I'm going to leave you to your evening, if that's okay."

"That's not necessary." Roger spoke for the first time. "Really. We were going to watch a movie, Oliver's newest. It hasn't been released yet. There should be *some* perk for having to spend the night in a haunted house, right?"

Her smile felt more like a grimace. "Oh, no, I couldn't intrude. I'll just . . . I'll just go ahead now. Thank you so much, though."

"Are you sure?"

She nodded. If he didn't stop talking in the next minute, she was going to turn and run for it.

"Just ring the buzzer if you need anything," Kym said. "And the blue button will put you through to security."

"And if you see a ghost," Oliver said, "well, I guess you know what to do, don't you?"

His lips parted; Chess thought it should have been a smile. It looked more like he was getting ready to eat her.

She fled.

The office door was locked. With trembling hands she picked it, her mouth flooded with saliva. He had to keep them in there. Had to. Where else would they be?

The lock gave and she slipped through the door into the darkness. True darkness; the window shades were pulled tight, blocking what little light might have come through with the storm raging outside. Wind howled around the corners of the house. It hadn't been audible in the dining room, but here it was, the wild anger of the skies making its presence known. Chess shivered beneath her sweaty skin and headed for the desk.

Nothing. Papers, sure, lots of papers. Ordinarily they would have interested her, but as it was she barely spared them a glance. What difference did they make? What difference did the outcome of this fucking case make? She needed her pills. That was what mattered.

A sob escaped her throat when she got to the last drawer. Still nothing. No little baggies filled with multi-colored promises, no envelopes, no coin purses, no . . . fuck, no pills, no drugs.

Behind her was a liquor cabinet, stocked with shining bottles and crystal glasses. On top of it sat a small TV and disk player. Chess made her way toward it on legs just starting to feel rubbery.

Her panic wasn't helping. Physically she wasn't that bad yet. Itchy, sweaty, a little shaky. Her head hurt. Nothing she couldn't handle in itself. It was knowing it was going to get worse, waiting for it to get worse . . .

She opened the cabinet, started shifting bottles. Maybe Pyle hid his stash behind them. A bar was a reasonable place, right?

Some part of her watched herself, sickened at the very idea that she was on her knees hunting for drugs to steal from a subject's house. The rest of her didn't give a shit. None of her was surprised. This was what she was, after all. A junkie Churchwitch. Nothing. Nobody.

A filing cabinet yielded nothing. Some financial records she barely glanced at, and a few photographs of Kym dressed up in some sort of naughty Goody outfit.

Bookshelves held only books. No secret panels hidden in the walls, no safes sheltered behind tacky paintings. The room was clean.

So where the fuck did he keep them? Not in the bedroom. Not in his office. Where? For fuck's sake, where? She knew he had them. He had to have them, she'd seen it in his eyes. So where did he keep his fucking drugs?

Tears poured down her face. Nothing here, nothing anywhere. Her pills were at home. The snow piled up outside. She was trapped. And there wasn't even an arm or leg she could chew off to get herself free.

When the smell started she wasn't quite sure. She didn't notice it until it was the only thing to notice, so strong it was almost a solid thing she could touch. With a sinking feeling that had nothing to do with her pills, she stood up and saw the ghost.

His back was to her—both of their backs were to her. The same tableau Taylor had described earlier in the security office. The man with the axe, holding something in his left hand that could have been a clump of dirt if not for the ragged skin at the bottom. The neck, where he'd severed it.

Behind him the other figure stood, gnarled hands reaching out. The flowing gown blew against its body, identified it as female.

They stood between her and the door. Normally she might have tried to run for it, but she didn't think her legs would carry her fast enough, steady enough.

Her stomach lurched. She had no idea if it was the smell or the withdrawal or the ghosts themselves. Her head pounded, as if her brain was swollen too big for her skull and was going to break free at any second.

The ghosts moved. The man lifted the axe, swung it over his shoulder. He turned his head. Toward the desk.

Toward Chess.

The edge of the liquor cabinet hit the backs of her thighs hard. She barely felt it. Not daring to take her eyes off him she dug in her bag, finding the graveyard dirt and clenching it in her fist. It might work. Would work if she could get any power behind it, if she had any to use. She felt like a shorted electrical cord; sparks sputtered beneath her skin but nothing could conduct.

The man lifted his hand, displaying the severed head. Showing her. He saw her. Not like the night in the bathroom. *He saw her.* He knew she was there. His axe might not be able to hurt her, but a letter opener sat on the desk, sharp edge gleaming in the horrid greenish light the ghosts projected. If she saw it, he would.

She pictured it, like a real-life horror film. Saw him pick up the letter opener, his body gliding through the desk like it wasn't even there, and bring it up to strike, saw herself try to raise her arms. Saw the opener plunged into her chest, blood spurting from the wound, changing color as it passed through his translucent form.

Finally the image galvanized her. The ghost started to

move, the woman following like some bizarre heeling dog. She had to act now, now, *now*—

The dirt flew from her hand, dusting itself over the figures.

"Arcranda beliam dishager!"

The generic banishing words, forced out through her constricted throat, felt like nothing but syllables. No power, nothing behind them. The ghost didn't falter. He took another slow step in her direction.

She tried again, struggling to focus, to find that well of power deep inside herself. She knew this, she could do it, she'd done it hundreds of times, it was her fucking *job*—

"Arcranda beliam dishager!"

Still nothing. She didn't feel weak, it felt like it should have worked, but what the fuck did she know? She could barely feel anything at all except her stomach twisting in her belly.

No choice, then. She ran, the floor spongy and uneven beneath her feet. Her hands slipped on the doorknob; she glanced back and saw the ghost's head turning, watching her. From this angle she could clearly see the head he held in his hand, the face she'd seen behind her in the bathroom mirror.

A scream tried to fight from her throat. She held it back, gritting her teeth so hard they hurt. The doorknob gave.

She flung herself forward, falling on the floor. The ghosts were still in the office, moving again, as though they were coming for her . . .

Kym's voice filtered from the living room. Chess managed to get up, giving the ghosts one last look before she closed the door on them. Her hands, her entire body, felt like a wrung-out washcloth.

The door wouldn't stop them. She had to move. Had to get up those stairs as fast as she could, had to get to the room they'd given her and lock the door so she could fall apart in private. Fuck the Pyles, they could fend for themselves, they hadn't had any problems in the living room yet, right?

But they weren't coming through the door. Why weren't they coming through the door? That wasn't right, not at all.

Chess waited, hidden in the corner, staring at the door until it became nothing but a black outline against the pale walls, until her eyes burned and the door swelled in her vision. An optical illusion. No ghosts. Somewhere deep down she knew that was important, knew it meant something, but she couldn't remember what. All she could do was dread the coming night.

She slipped around the corner, chanced a peek into the living room. One of the servants was setting up a projector; a neat little thing, sleek and stylish and obviously very expensive. Nothing but the best for the Pyles. At least it would keep them busy; hopefully they wouldn't decide to check on her.

Every step felt like a mountain she had to climb, but thankfully no one saw her. The walls tilted, the floor spun. She couldn't breathe. Her shirt stuck to her chest by the time she got to the top.

Which room had they given her? There were so many doors, so many, and she couldn't remember if hers was the second on the right or the third. Did it matter? How many doors were there?

She stumbled on numb feet across the hall and opened the first one she saw. If she was wrong, she'd be wrong. So what.

Arden Pyle knelt before the gleaming white toilet of a small bathroom, one hand holding her pale, sweaty hair off her face. Throwing up. A nice preview of what Chess's night would be. She was tempted for one confused, bizarre moment to ask the girl to move over.

Arden's mouth fell open. She turned her guilty face down, then back up, meeting Chess's eyes. A small purplish bruise peeked out from the open neckline of her bathrobe, like a hickey. "Don't tell," she said. "I just . . . Don't tell my mom, okay?"

Chess nodded dumbly and turned away, pulling the door closed. Bulimia. Not a surprise, really. Also none of her business. And not something she was even remotely capable of lecturing about. What was she supposed to say? Try downers instead, they suppress the appetite? Life advice was definitely not her forte.

Her room was the next one to the left. She flung herself on the bed and waited to die.

Not dead yet. The numbers on the clock were fuzzy, glowing red in the darkness. She couldn't read them. Couldn't focus on them. Too bright. Hurt her eyes.

A weight sat on her; she sweated beneath it. The blankets. She vaguely remembered pulling them over her during the last bout of shivering. Her jaw ached. Her arms and legs ached. Her stomach had disappeared, leaving behind a fiery pit.

A fiery pit that demanded attention. She threw the covers off. Or rather she tried to throw the covers off. Her arms refused to throw. Instead all she managed to do was push feebly at the blanket, like a newborn.

The next cramp came. She fell off the bed in a sweaty, painful heap. The bathroom? Where was the bathroom? It was so dark. The room wouldn't stop moving, she couldn't make it stop, a roller-coaster ride she couldn't get off of. Helpless. Hopeless. Beneath her hands and knees the carpet rubbed like straw, cutting her, tearing into her. She'd be slick with blood by the time she made it to the bathroom. If she made it.

Her mouth filled with saliva, acrid and bitter. She couldn't swallow it. Couldn't spit it out on the carpet.

So she held it there, warm and disgusting as a mouthful of urine, and tried to crawl to the bathroom.

Too weak. She fell, her skin shrieking when it rubbed against the carpet. It was so cold in there, so fucking cold, she couldn't take it, she needed her pills, oh fuck . . .

Try again. Pain shot through her body, bending her double. Her stomach again. Itchy. Scratch the itch, make the itch stop. Push the wet, ropy strands of hair off her face and scratch her neck, her legs, her arms. Everywhere itchy. Wouldn't stop.

She couldn't hold back the sobs anymore. Her mouth opened and they came out, dribbling onto the rug along with her spit. Things crawled beneath her skin. She wasn't Chess anymore. Couldn't think of herself by name, couldn't think of herself as a person. There was only pain and cold and shaking, only the burning need she couldn't get away from, looming over her like a dark entity in the room.

She'd eaten that dessert, that fatty, greasy dessert. She saw it again, the plate full of whipped cream and chocolate, and she couldn't hold it any longer.

The bathroom door was closed. She fumbled at the knob while the contents of her stomach forced their way up, threw herself at the toilet and missed. She puked on the floor, on her hands. Her knees hit the tile. One more note of pain to add to the symphony.

The toilet glowed white beside her. She climbed her hands up it, rested her head against the cold porcelain. Too hot now, her whole body, hot and swollen like she would burst open in a stiff breeze.

Her hands traveled down her legs, scratching, tearing at her skin. Her pills. She needed her pills, oh fuck, oh fuck, she needed them so bad, she couldn't *do* this.

Razors? Were there razors? She should have taken Arden's from her closet. Should have taken it, and she could have slit her throat. The City didn't scare her, not now. Not when this was life, this pain, this need, this desperate horrible shaking and cramping and spit pouring from her mouth and tears from her eyes and she needed to use the toilet for something else now, something unpleasant . . .

It lasted forever, acid falling from her. All the while she scratched. Her hands clenched into talons, she couldn't unbend her fingers, they hurt, every muscle in her body cramped, and she was going to fall off the toilet, and wetness under her nails told the tiny rational part of her that she'd broken her skin with the scratching and she was bleeding.

Blood. Her blood was so empty. She needed her pills. Why hadn't she brought more pills? She could have hidden them. It was gross but she could have done it. Why not, why pretend she had any fucking self-respect at all? Was self-respect worth this pain?

Vomit splattered the floor in front of the toilet. Good thing she'd taken her jeans off when they started hurting her skin. What difference did it make? They'd find her in the morning, they'd come and find her and call an ambulance and maybe it would get there, maybe they would take her somewhere, and everyone would know. Everyone would know how filthy she was, how weak and desperate, because she thought she was too good to use a woman's best hiding place.

That was what one of her foster mothers had called it. Chess saw the woman again, her thin body bare as she showed Chess exactly how many things she could hide there, how little Chessie could hide things for her too and then take the bus across town and let the nice men take the things out, and they would give her some candy, and some money for Mrs. Foster Mother. Saw her, saw the endless parade of them all, leering at her, yelling at her, telling her how worthless she was and how she was only good for one thing, calling her names, felt their punches and their invading fingers like they were there in the room with her. And all the while she screamed in her head and saw the mess she'd made, and shame and despair overwhelmed her.

Toilet paper. Find the toilet paper. Wipe her mouth . . . wipe her legs. Wipe away the memories. Wipe the floor. She couldn't do it well, but she could do something, couldn't she? To prove she wasn't as bad as they said, she wasn't worthless, she was . . . Tears ran down her face, spattered her hands. She *was* worthless, they were right.

Hot again, burning hot. Delirious. She thought she saw something pale in the room, something moving past the open bathroom doorway . . .

Her shoulder crashed into the floor as another cramp, worse than the others, seized her, drove her out of her body, out of consciousness. She wanted to scream. Wanted to keep screaming until she passed out again and stayed out.

The cabinet was next to her face. It took her four tries to grasp the handle and pull the door open. Its rough edge hit her thigh, scraping her bare skin. Felt good. Scratching the itch. She did it again, until her arm hurt and she dropped the handle while her hand cramped up again.

Too dark to see in there. Razor blades? Drain cleaner? Anything. She couldn't do this anymore. She couldn't feel this anymore. The worst spirit hell, the darkest prison pit in the city, couldn't feel like this. Even what she'd seen in Prison Ten wasn't this bad. There was respite there.

This was punishment for all her trespasses, wasn't she paying for them now? Surely when the psychopomp— *her* psychopomp, the one coming to get her—picked her soul up on its feathered back and flew her underground, it would know that, feel that?

"I've paid," she moaned, and the sound of her own voice scared her. "I've paid enough."

She brushed her hand over the cabinet floor. Nothing under there. Not even a fucking washcloth she could shove down her throat. Suffocation wouldn't be that bad, right? It wouldn't be so terrible.

Her legs kicked at nothing. They wouldn't stop moving. She threw up again, barely able to lift her head to move it out of the way. Her head hurt. Hurt so bad. Like someone slamming a hammer into it, over and over, beating her with it, everywhere. Her vision was red with the blood in her brain.

Another flash of white passed the doorway. A shape, vaguely human, looming there. So big. Almost as big as . . .

The shape turned into nothing but a blur. Had to stop crying. Should stop crying. What difference did it make? Good that a ghost was there. It would kill her. It would put an end to this, oh fuck, she couldn't wait, end this now . . .

Her arms shook under her weight. She crawled out of the bathroom. Find the ghost. She'd find it, and she'd— there were heavy things, right? It could crack her skull open. That would be quick. End the pain.

She collapsed and crawled on her belly to the bed. The ghost stood in the corner, not moving. Did it see her? Was she even there?

She didn't have her knife. Hadn't brought it. Hadn't brought anything, hadn't brought her pills, oh shit, her pills, she needed them so bad, she couldn't live without them, she couldn't take this anymore . . .

It took hours to open her bag. The ghost stayed by the window. Through the window only blackness. The snow had stopped. Fucking lot of good it did her, she couldn't drive like this, couldn't get out of this room, walk down the stairs, much less steer a car. She wouldn't even be able to get her feet into her shoes, her toes were cramped, bunched up at the ends of her feet like dead mice.

Something small and cool fitted itself into the palm of her hand. Her phone. The outside world. Someone she could call.

Someone she wanted . . . *needed*. The thought cleared her head, as much as it could be cleared, and she clutched the phone as if it was a full pillbox.

The ghost didn't move. Didn't even look at her. Why? Why wasn't it moving?

Her fingers hurt. She dropped the phone. She couldn't hold it, not in her claw of a hand.

Crying again, crying and putting her fingers in her mouth, her disgusting fingers, but she didn't have a choice. She gagged, gagged again. Bit down on her fingers and forced her wrist up and away. Had to unbend her fingers. Had to use them.

The ghost disappeared. Good. She'd need to open the window. If he answered. If he came. Oh please . . .

The phone didn't want to open. She worked it with her bleeding, slimy fingers, poked at it with her teeth. Got it. Dropped it when another cramp turned her body into a crooked plank on the floor. Picked it up again. Pressed the button.

Please . . . please . . . please . . .

He answered. Asked questions. She tried to reply, tried to make sense. Tried to tell him how to get in.

And waited, unmoving, on the floor by the bed.

Chapter Seventeen

For a human to work with a ghost is a grievous error, a crime against humanity so severe it cannot be fully expressed. For above all acts it is one with no gain; nothing good can come of it.
— *The Book of Truth*, Rules, Article 178

Somewhere by the ceiling she hovered, looking down at herself, a tiny bedraggled figure huddled against the wall, shivering. She'd given up trying to climb back onto the bed. Given up on the idea of forcing her jeans back on her bleeding, oversensitive legs. Given up on everything. She was gone. She was lost in the pain.

Monsters clawed at her from the inside, biting her guts with sharp teeth. Her heart pumped gasoline through her veins. The small trash can in her arms was hot from her skin and full of bile. Her legs wouldn't stop moving, every scrape against the carpet making her want to scream.

A black shape appeared in the window. First a head, then shoulders. Fingers closed around the bottom of the pane and lifted. Chess slammed back into her body.

Her head lolled sideways. "Hi," she wanted to say, but what came out was "Please."

Didn't seem to matter. She didn't think he'd heard her.

He slid himself through the window, reached back, and yanked the ladder into the room. What was he doing? Why was he taking so long?

He wasn't going to help her. She knew it now. He'd come to laugh at her. To taunt her. She'd thought . . .

she'd thought it was okay, that he cared enough to help her, she'd been wrong, fuck, so wrong.

He barely glanced at her, stepping over her restless legs to the bathroom. Light burned her eyes. She closed them and turned away. Did he have to look at her?

Water running. Big hands on her head, on her arms. He pressed something cool against her forehead, wiped her face clean. It felt good. It felt amazing. "Chess. C'mon, Chess. You keep aught down?"

Her answer was a sob. Now that he was there, now that she knew he would help her, all she could do was cry.

"Gimme that now." The trash can left her arms. "All be right, aye? Hang on."

"I can't." She fell forward. His broad chest caught her, so hard, so strong, and she huddled against it. Tried to climb into it, to become part of him and never have to be alone again. Cold still clung to his coat, it must have been freezing out there. "I can't, shit I'm sorry, thank you, please help me, please help me thank you so much . . . please Terrible I'm so sorry . . ."

He gripped her shoulders and set her back against the wall. For some reason this made her feel even worse. She really was disgusting, wasn't she? He couldn't even bear to look at her. Good thing she hadn't called Lex, then. It hadn't even occurred to her.

Another cramp hit and wiped the thought from her mind. She bit her lip and tasted blood. Her stomach roiled again; she lunged for the trash can and threw up. Kept throwing up, then fell to the floor. No strength left to hold herself up. Her hands clawed the carpet.

Terrible picked her up, set her against the wall again. "Cool, Chess. Let's get you right up, aye? Gimme your arm."

"Wha—no, no. No needles, please, no needles . . ."

"No choice, baby. C'mon. You ain't keep aught down,

you ain't swallow no pills. True thing, Chessiebomb. Lemme do this."

"I can't."

"Aye, you can. C'mon. Left me some footprints in that snow outside like an arrow, dig? Ain't got much time afore somebody sees, them security keep the schedule you say."

Air swirled around her body when he scooped her up and carried her into the bathroom, setting her on the cold tile. She kept her eyes closed. Too bright in there, the white tiles and the white lights like some garish institution. She could only imagine what it looked like in there, despite her pitiful efforts to clean it up. She didn't want to see. She hated that he could, that he saw the mess, saw her in her bra and panties like a corpse waiting to be disposed of. So weak, so fucking weak . . .

The rubber catheter, slightly sticky. The faint ache in her arm when he pulled it tight, the flat sound of it snapping. The sharp scent of alcohol, cold on her skin. She swallowed, swallowed again. Her feet hit the floor, fast, pattering like a drumroll. It was coming. Oh fuck it was coming, the needle made her sick but relief was coming and she didn't care anymore, didn't care . . .

"You make a fist?" His fingers closed over hers, helping her. "Fist up, baby, c'mon. Make a fist for me, aye?"

She tried, fighting against the searing pain. Worked it as tight as she could, released it, did it again. His light smack on her inner arm made her want to scream, but she gritted her teeth and kept flexing her hand, kept doing it . . .

It didn't hurt. Not like it had when she'd done it herself. She felt the needle pinch, felt it sit for a second, felt Terrible's hands move. Felt the catheter unsnap.

Felt . . . *fuck*. Oh, yeah. Oh fuck yeah . . .

Still humiliating. Still horrid. But it didn't matter so much now, did it. No. No, because her muscles were relaxing and tears of gratitude pricked her eyes and her stomach cooled and settled. Her headache disappeared.

"Thank you," she whispered. Lights danced behind her eyelids, beautiful lights, peaceful lights. "Thank you . . ."

The trash can appeared under her chin before she realized she needed it, before she threw up again and felt absolutely nothing while doing it. Amazing. That's what it was. Cool damp fabric wiped at her mouth, at her face, soothing her sweaty skin, and she sighed and tilted her head back so he could get her neck and chest, too.

Wanting him to move it farther down, to wipe away the sweat and blood and tears like he'd wiped away the misery, and make her clean and whole again.

Her eyes flew open. Terrible. She'd called Terrible. When he hated her. When he'd betrayed her, sold her out to Bump, put her in the position he'd put her in.

But seeing him crouching beside her, his eyes scanning her face, she couldn't seem to find the anger. Maybe she was too high. Now that was a glorious thought. High again, peaceful again. The ugly memories receded, the angry accusing voices disappeared. All of them, and nothing mattered anymore. Not even how pissed she was.

"Aye," he said. He reached out with the cloth again, then seemed to think better of it and handed it to her instead. She wiped her sticky fingers on it while he continued, "I gotta get gone. Had to park a good way off, dig, road still ain't clear closer up."

"Oh."

He reached into his pocket, pulled out a little bag. Cepts, a dozen or so. He was forgiven.

"These get you home on the morrow, aye?"

"Aye—yeah. Thanks."

"You right now?"

She nodded, wiping her eyes with her hands so she didn't have to look at him. She might have forgiven him, but it didn't seem he'd forgiven her.

Or maybe he had and it was simply that she was huddled on a bathroom floor, a few feet away from the mess she'd made earlier, with her soaking wet hair clinging to her skull and her entire body streaked with blood and coated with sweat and vomit. Yeah. Not exactly her most alluring moment.

"Cool. I . . . cool. Chess, gimme a call you get back, aye? Got . . . got some stuff Bump wants done, gotta have a chatter on."

Fuck. One thing she could say for heavy torturous withdrawal, at least she hadn't had to worry about what Bump wanted her to do. Or think about what had happened in the car.

But she just nodded, as if the subject didn't make a heavy weight thud into her chest. "Fine."

For a second she thought he was going to say something else. His mouth opened, his head tilted to the side. Then he picked up the spent needle and catheter and shoved them into his pocket. "Right. On morrow then."

She watched him cross the room, watched him push the ladder back out the window and slip over the sill, disappearing into the night. Gone.

Gone, like the ghosts who'd ignored her earlier. Strange, that. She'd think about it later. Right now all she wanted to do was sit and feel good, sit and relax.

And clean up the filthy bathroom before morning.

She stuck a fresh-rolled kesh between her lips and fired it up. Almost five o'clock, back at her apartment, and she had nothing to do and nowhere to be. The free time felt odd. She kept expecting someone to knock at her door and drag her out into the cold.

Nobody did, though. Good. The last thing she wanted

to do was think about hookers, or Bump, or Lex. Or, especially, Terrible. Instead, she sucked the hot, harsh smoke deep into her lungs and started flipping through Fletcher's financial records, at least those the Church had been able to access on such short notice, rifling through the details of his accounts with cool calculation. Just the way she knew he would do were their positions reversed.

What would it be like, to have that kind of wealth? Money had never meant much to Chess beyond how much oblivion it could buy, but it was difficult, looking at credit card records showing more money spent on shoes than she spent on food in half a year, not to feel something. Some twinge of envy, some pang of despair. The world was full of men like Oliver Fletcher, men for whom everything came easy. What they did or how they lived interested her not at all, but their peace of mind . . . that, she envied. And it looked like Oliver could afford an awful lot of peace of mind—at least until she looked more closely.

The kesh burned down nice and slow while she took notes, her occasional drag the only sound in the room save the scratching of her pen on the paper. A lot of money moved into the accounts, but if she wasn't mistaken, almost as much moved out. Lease payments on seven cars. Mortgages on three homes. Fuel for a private jet. Designer clothing bills that Chess had to read four times to make sure she was seeing them correctly through her increasingly blurry eyes. Payments to management companies, publicity firms, costumers, special-effects companies . . .

And bank transfers to a separate account. Always the same account number. No name listed. Thousands of dollars at a time.

She made a note of it, checked three times to make sure she'd copied it correctly. Tomorrow she'd put in a request for those records as well, to see who owned the account. It might be important, it might not, but something about Fletcher, the memory of his smirk the night before, made her itch to find some dirt on him. An abuse of her position, perhaps, but who knew. He was certainly one of the best suspects she had.

Not that she had many. She hadn't even had a chance to talk to Merritt again, to get his impressions of the family. She hadn't gotten anything from Roger Pyle indicating he had any reason at all to fake a haunting; hell, she hadn't yet managed to find any real hard evidence the thing was fake, although she knew in her gut that it was.

She took another drag, tapped off the ash into the plastic ashtray on the floor.

Maybe she'd take a nap, put on a record and snooze here on the couch. She hated to waste a good high sleeping, but she hadn't slept much of late. Of course, having eyeballs left in her car and being followed all over the city didn't exactly promote sweet dreams, even without the withdrawal, and the fighting with people she—people she liked, and worrying about death curses and being caught.

Someone could be watching her now. She'd tacked a blanket to the ceiling in front of the stained-glass window, a cheap and shabby attempt to keep prying eyes out—the analogy made her giggle a little—but still . . .

Paranoid. That's all she was. Paranoid, and the words on the pages in front of her were starting to swim. She stuck them back in the file and closed it. No more reading. Time for some music, or maybe more episodes of Pyle's TV show, which actually wasn't half bad. She hadn't finished the first disc.

And she still hadn't watched the disks she'd copied at the Pyle house. Now might be a good time.

The disk started playing as soon as she shoved it into

the machine, but she grabbed a bottle of water for her cottonmouth before sitting back down. The kesh was almost cashed; she pinched it between her fingers and settled herself cross-legged on the sagging cushions.

The Pyle room. Kym, naked, her wrists tied together, a wicked smile on her face. Oh, shit. Was that all these disks were? Roger and Kym's private porn collection? Chess was in for a long couple of hours if that was the case. She had about as much desire to watch that as she did to tattoo Lex's name on her ass.

Yes, they were. The next disk was the same, and the next. Is this what being in a relationship did to people, bored them with each other to the point that they had to dress up as shepherds and milkmaids, as witches and Elders, as schoolgirls and teachers, anything to pretend they weren't fucking the same person they'd fucked last time?

And these were people who were supposed to like each other—*love* each other. Who'd legally committed to loving each other, had been bound by blood and magic in the Church. Now they were trapped forever, with someone they knew so well that all they had left was boredom. Nobody could really know another person and want them, love them.

Hell, the only reason Lex had stuck around this long, the only reason, aside from the free drugs, that she allowed it, was because they didn't see each other very often and didn't care about each other very much.

And she was smart to handle it that way, to keep that distance; hell, didn't this video, and all the others, prove it? Smart to avoid being with anyone she might actually really feel something for, who might actually really feel something for her. Smart to avoid getting involved with people she knew she could—

Her thought stopped right there as the scene before her changed, a different setup, a new act. Her bleary eyes focused, her mouth fell open, her stomach gave a mighty lurch, and her fingers fumbled for the phone.

Kym Pyle, tied to a wicked-looking iron rack in a room Chess didn't recognize. Her skin was painted or dusted with some sort of whitish powder, so she glowed in the dim light, and black circles were painted around her eyes. She struggled against the chains holding her, bared her teeth, her naked body twisting as Roger approached, tossed what looked like dirt at her to quiet her.

As if she were a ghost.

Ricantha to control and create ghosts. A sigil to lock the soul in the body and althea to keep it from joining its own psychopomp. An owl to hold it after release and carry it where it was needed. Perhaps a mild electrical setup, to force the spirit into solid form?

Chess couldn't stop staring at the screen, her own eyes wide and so dry they clicked when she blinked.

Terrible said a whore's purse was like her own soul, the only private thing she had. Something with that much energy was a totem, a placeholder to connect a soul to the world above the City.

She'd been so stupid, so fucking stupid. So focused on eyes and her own precious ass that she'd missed the most blatant clue, the most obvious fucking thing.

As she'd kept saying, ghosts got stuck where they were when they died. They didn't move on.

What did a hooker do? She had sex. She had sex for money.

So if you were the ghost of a murdered prostitute and you wanted to run a whorehouse, what was the most logical thing to do?

Fill it with ghost whores.

The scene on the disk changed, but she wasn't paying attention anymore. She was hitting Terrible's button on her autodial, trying to stop her hands from shaking.

Could she have prevented this if she'd paid better attention?

She'd handled this all wrong, right from the beginning. Getting involved with Lex and wasting so much time spinning her drugged-up wheels worrying about being watched and being caught and keeping herself from exposing anything she didn't want exposed.

And speaking of exposure . . . She snapped the phone shut. She hadn't talked to him since he'd left the Pyle house. Hadn't really talked to him since that stupid argument. What was she supposed to do now, call him up, tell him what she knew, let it end there?

No. She was just high enough, just excited enough, to decide she had to do this in person. To decide she deserved to see his reaction in person, she deserved to— well, she wanted to see him, and with her head half in the clouds she felt confident enough to do so. After all, she did owe him something, right?

Time to pay it back.

Chapter Eighteen

You are of course encouraged to speak to children, to answer their questions with the kind of Truth appropriate to their age and situation. Never forget they are not yet mature; they are children.
—*The Example Is You*, the guidebook for Church employees

Twenty minutes later she stood in the hall outside his place, her stomach bouncing with cheerful butterflies and a twelve-pack of beer weighing down her left hand. The thick steel door gave a flat thud under her knuckles.

No answer. Okay. Well, where was he? It had never occurred to her he might not be home.

She knocked again, shifting her weight from foot to foot. What if . . . what if he was inside, and knew it was her, but wasn't answering? Didn't want to see her?

No. She wouldn't believe that. She had to talk to him, she had to tell him, and he had to be home to listen because she was right and it was important.

She had to be right. It was the only answer that fit, but . . . damn it was a fucked-up theory, wasn't it? Who the hell would pay to fuck a ghost?

The twelve-pack in her left hand grew heavy. One more knock, one more minute waiting while she switched the twelve-pack from her left hand to her right.

Terrible opened the door midswitch. His face gave her nothing. Shit.

"Hey, Chess." Pause. "You right?"

"Yeah, right up, um—here, I brought you—" What

was she doing? She held the beer out to him, stopped. She'd brought him beer, was she an idiot? She'd come to tell him something horrible and she'd—Oh, screw it.

"I figured it out," she said. "What the ghosts are doing, the killers. I know what they're doing with the hookers."

Well, at least now he looked interested. "Aye?"

"Yeah, they—they're fucking them, Terrible. They're—they're killing the girls, and they're trapping them and fucking them. A whorehouse of ghosts. I can't believe I missed it, that I didn't figure it out before. But that's what they're doing, I know it. I know it."

He was silent for so long she thought maybe he wasn't going to reply at all, maybe he was just going to turn around and shut the door in her face. "Terrible?"

"Aye. Just . . . you sure?"

"Pretty sure, yeah. I mean, it makes sense, doesn't it? And the sigil—there was one at the Church, an older one not quite the same, it keeps the soul from leaving the body. Not like before, with the thief, it's not a dark rune, it doesn't power or feed anything. It . . . Fuck, just trust me. I'm right. I know I'm right."

"Ain't doubting, dig, just . . . what about Little Tag? The men, meaning? Figure them . . . them bein used too?"

Ha, she was ready for this. "Sacrifices. Blood and energy sacrifices to start the spell, most likely. Sex magic like what I felt . . . Ghosts can't cast it. It needs the kind of power you get by stealing someone's life to start. They probably used their—did, um, were the men missing their—any parts?"

"Aye. Missin all sorts, dig. And . . . aye, them too. Ain't had the thought before, them so cut up elsewhere. Lots missing, feet an insides an—lots missing, dig."

"It had to be to start the spell." Sexual organs, organs of regeneration, carried so much energy even after death.

And that would help explain the darkness in that magic, the horrible itchy tickle of insanity beneath it. Men had died for that spell, tainting the magic irreparably just as it tainted the spell's creators.

Terrible shifted on his feet. "Why? Human workin with the ghost too, aye? Why's he into it?"

Ooh, motive, right. She'd been focused so hard on the girls, and right now her brain seemed to be floating a good three or four feet above her skull. "If they're Bindmates . . ."

"Doin whatever keeps the ghost happy, aye. Maybe makin lashers too, you think?"

That cardboard was really starting to dig into her hand now. Much as she hated to interrupt their thought process there, and especially as much as she hated to remind him why she'd bought the beer, her fingers were numb.

"I wanted to give you this." She thrust the beer at him.

He looked puzzled. Oh, shit, he was going to make her say it, wasn't he?

"For helping me, you know. The other night. I mean, I know it was really cold and late and . . . I just wanted to say thanks. A lot. Thanks a lot."

He'd invite her in now, and they'd keep talking. Maybe they'd have a beer or something, or he'd get them some food—ooh, food would be good—and she could tell him what she'd figured out and prove she wasn't useless.

Then she noticed he was dressed to go out, with his jacket on and his keys in his hand.

"You ain't need to buy me nothin," he said. "No problem, aye?"

"But I want to. I—Just take it, okay?"

Was he still mad at her? She'd apologized that night, but even she wasn't sure what she'd been apologizing for in that state of mind. And he looked so surprised to see her, like he didn't even know what to do with her. Sure, she'd only been to his place a few times, and never without calling first or having him invite her back there, but it wasn't like him to leave her standing in his doorway. Especially not when they had things to discuss, important things.

"Terrible? Can you please take this? It's kind of heavy."

"Oh. Oh, aye." He took the pack from her hand. Chess clenched her fist and released it, trying to get her circulation back. Deep ridges cut into the insides of her fingers. "Thanks."

She nodded. "So where you going?"

"Gotta do somethin."

Shit, he really was mad at her. Something was wrong, and she couldn't imagine what else it could be. Either something about her theory bugged him, or he was mad at her.

There was a third possibility, too, of course. He'd seen her the night before covered in puke, with her bare legs scratched raw while she huddled on the floor in an agonized withdrawal haze. Could be he was simply disgusted by her. Could she blame him?

No, she couldn't. But that didn't make her feel any better.

"Um, can I come? I just . . . I thought we could talk about some stuff. About this, you know. And where they might be, since we know what's going on we can plan . . ."

He hesitated. "Ain't really like that, meaning, just somethin I gotta get done, dig?"

"I could just come along for the ride, or whatever." Her face burned. No point in pushing it. He obviously didn't want her to go. He'd heard what she had to say, and didn't seem to want to discuss it further, so she guessed he just didn't want anything to do with her.

Her shoulders sagged. Maybe she'd call Lex, tell him about the ghost hookers. He'd want to see her, anyway, even if it was just to try and get her naked. Which was fine, really. Why not? "Okay, well . . . um, call me—"

"Chess, hey. Whyn't you come along, then, aye? Be . . . be cool to have some company."

Sitting in his car listening to Nine Pound Hammer and smoking a cigarette, it felt as though the events of the night before hadn't really happened. Hell, it felt like none of the events of the past week had happened, especially since her body felt wrapped in warm cotton and her mind was calm.

Terrible took a deep breath, his gaze fixed on the road. "I ain't . . . Shit. Ain't should have took you to see Bump, and not give you the knowledge what he wanted, Chess. I mean, he ain't tell me sure, but . . . thought maybe he had the idea. Some idea. Should've said, but I had the thinking maybe you ain't come if I tell you, an Bump wanted you, aye? Got mad, but not on you, dig. Weren't you."

Surprise made her breath stick in her throat. It took her a few seconds to even register the words, seconds when she felt him glancing at her out of the corner of his eye, waiting for her response. "I'm sorry too. I didn't mean to say some of that stuff. I mean, I said it, but I didn't mean it. I didn't."

His shoulders relaxed; she hadn't realized how tense he looked before. She probably would have been tense, too, if it had been physically possible. The rush was over, sure, but she still felt relaxed, calmer than she'd been in days. "Aye, no worryin then."

They sat in silence for a minute, but a comfortable one. An easier one.

"Terrible?"

"Aye."

"Do you think we'll find them fast? The house?"

He shrugged. "Ain't can say. Hoping so. Leastaways now we got the knowledge what we lookin for, aye? How'd you catch it?"

"Oh." Okay, this was awkward. "I was reviewing some evidence for work. I thought it was evidence, anyway, but it was, ah, some homemade videos, and they'd made the woman up to look like a ghost . . ."

He grinned. "Ain't what you was expecting, aye? For evidence."

"No, No, it definitely wasn't what I expected."

"Guessin Church work more fun than I thought."

She laughed.

"Maybe I oughta sign me up, what you say? Think I fit in right, aye? Ain't even notice me in the crowd. Like invisible."

"I don't think you could be invisible anywhere," she said, and heat rushed to her face. She hadn't meant it like that, hadn't meant anything at all.

He switched lanes, sliding the big car to the left. Cleared his throat. "So you straight on wanting to do it? Hit the street, I mean? Maybe it ain't worth it, with what you figured up . . ."

A change of subject was a good idea, but it would have been nice if he'd picked a different one. "No, it's not a bad idea, really. I don't think it will work, but I guess it's worth a try."

It won't work because they're following me everywhere, she thought, but couldn't tell him. She'd have to lie about where they'd seen her—where she'd seen them—and she didn't want to. Didn't want him pressing her about a place to stay, either, not when she could use Lex's place. Didn't even want to think about any of it, just for a few minutes.

"Naw, neither me. You seen em again? Got any more eyes in yon car?"

"No. But that doesn't mean they're not out there, that they won't recognize me, you know? Think if I tell Bump that, he'll listen?"

"Ain't everybody listen to you?"

Her surprised bark of laughter embarrassed her, too loud in the enclosed space. Her high was definitely fading, but the cheeriness wasn't. She felt pretty good, in fact, for the first time in a while.

They were out of Downside now, heading along the highway toward Cross Town. She didn't ask where they were going. She just looked out the window at the white sky spread over the city like a shifting ocean of clouds. "So it's been a couple of days since any girls were attacked. You think having them at Red Berta's house is working? Are they still at Red Berta's?"

"Aye. Still there, an she pissed up right on it too. 'Nother reason be good get this all solved. She loud, Red Berta, aye?"

She pulled out her cigarettes, lit one up. "At least it's keeping them safe."

"Aye, she know. She ain't a bad one, Red Berta. Just like things the way she like, dig. Ain't guess havin them girls in she house easy, screechin and fighting the way them do. Like birds, the way them screech."

"Like psychopomps do," she said without thinking, "when they claim a soul."

The words hung in the air between them for a few minutes while he pulled off the highway and started navigating the wide streets of Cross Town.

It wasn't a wealthy suburb, but it had aspirations. The newer homes being built were larger, with bigger yards. More space. As the memories of the horror of Haunted Week started fading from the collective consciousness, people were more willing to spread out; it was becoming irritating rather than comforting to have your neighbors close enough to hear your shower run.

What did Terrible have to do out here? She opened her mouth to ask, but he cut her off.

"We ain't stayin long," he told her, sliding the car up in front of a nondescript pale blue house, bigger than some on the street but not the biggest.

"Where are we?"

"Friend of mine," he said. "Gotta drop off something."

That was a surprise. He had friends? And friends outside Downside. She wanted to ask about it, but something in the set of his wide shoulders, the oddly subdued quality of his silence, made her hold her tongue. Instead she just followed him to the door, her coat tight around her, waited while he knocked and footsteps sounded from within.

The door flew open. A young girl leapt out of the warmth and light behind it. Startled, Chess stepped back, but Terrible was ready. He picked the child up, let her wrap her thin arms around his neck.

"Uncle Terry! What did you bring me?"

Uncle Terry? What? He didn't have any family, didn't even know for sure how old he was, when his birthday was. So not only did he now have friends in Cross Town, he had friends so close their daughter called him "Uncle"?

What else did she not know about him? Her stomach gave a funny little twist.

"Maybe I got something for you, little cat. But I ain't stayin long, just gettin a quick chatter with your mom, aye?"

Chess followed the little girl's pouting face deeper into the house, feeling with every step that she was moving away from the familiar. It had been so long since she'd been in a house like this as a guest—had she *ever* been in

a house like this as a guest?—and not a Church repre-
sentative, starting an investigation.

A petite woman with dark wavy hair like the girl's
examined Chess from her feet to the top of her head
before giving her an unwilling smile.

"I'm Felice," she said.

"Chess."

"Uncle Terry brought her with him," the girl said as
Terrible lowered her to the floor. She looked about seven,
that awkward period when a child has left babyhood
behind but the blossoming of puberty is still years away.
Tall for her age, with long skinny arms and coltish legs,
and a grin that seemed to fill her entire face. The effect
was charming, as if her happiness was too big to be
confined.

"Yes, Katie, I see that."

"Are you Uncle Terry's friend? Do you work with
him?"

What should she say? Why was Terrible here?
Was this woman a steady customer? A local dealer?
What?

No. He'd said they were friends, and it looked like
that was all it was. He wouldn't have felt the need to
hide it from her if there was a business connection. Chess
decided to be honest.

"No, I work for the Church. I'm a Debunker."

Felice's eyebrows disappeared into her hair. The little
girl's mouth fell open. "You catch ghosts?"

"Sometimes. Mostly people don't have ghosts, though.
They're just pretending."

"Daddy says that's lying," Katie told her. "He says it's
very bad to lie."

"He's right," Felice said. "Katie, honey, why don't
you go and watch TV or something? Mommy needs to
talk to Uncle Terry for a minute in private, okay?"

"I want to stay."

"Well, I want you to go watch TV, and I'm the mommy. So go on, now."

"Aye, go 'head, little cat. Here, you take that, aye? An tell me what it's for." Terrible slipped the girl a twenty.

Her grin grew even wider as she recited, "A dollar is for me. The rest is for my kitty bank to hold until I'm a grown-up."

"Good girl."

She gave him a kiss on the cheek, shot a glare at her mother, and started walking away slowly, like she hoped they'd forget about her and she could stay.

The atmosphere in the room changed, subtly, but enough for Chess to feel it. Tension crept over her skin. Should she leave, too?

Terrible raised his eyebrows, lifted his shoulders almost imperceptibly. Up to her; she could stay if she wanted, she could go in the other room if she wanted.

Somehow staying didn't feel like a great idea, though. "Katie, can I come with you?"

Katie nodded, the eager expression on her face warning Chess to prepare for interrogation. Once a year or so the Church sent Debunkers and Enforcers to local schools to discuss their work, a way of reminding the children the Church was always there. She had a feeling this was going to be like one of those endless question-and-answer sessions.

She wasn't far wrong. Katie asked about work, asked her to tell a scary story, asked if Chess knew any liars in her neighborhood, asked if she'd been to the City, asked how many ghosts she'd seen, asked to see her tattoos. All the while the low rumble of Terrible's voice came from the kitchen, sometimes louder, sometimes quieter.

"I'd be afraid to get a tattoo," Katie said. "Mommy says they hurt. Uncle Terry has a lot of them, but he's a man."

"They don't really hurt. It's just a little sting, it's not

bad." Not entirely true, but she wasn't permitted to talk about the ritual anyway, the chanting in the pale room while the tattoo gun buzzed and herbs burned in the corners and energy beat against her skin.

"That's what Mommy said about the dentist. But it did hurt. Even after they gave me that gas that's supposed to make it not hurt. Do you know that gas? It made me feel funny, like my head was too light."

Chess nodded. "I can't have the gas. I'm allergic to it."

"Really? Like it makes you sneeze?"

"No, it makes me feel sick, and my head hurts really bad . . ." She stopped. She'd forgotten all about that, her first visit to the dentist, shortly after starting her training. She'd felt like she couldn't breathe, like she was going to die . . .

Like she'd felt at the Pyle house when that horrible smell came.

Shit, was it really that simple?

Of course it was. The gas disoriented people, made them a little high. Just high enough that they wouldn't notice the beam of a projector, or the clicking as it was turned on. Just high enough that their heart would be beating faster and their fear response elevated. High enough that their reaction might be taken as fear, would *be* fear, when their consciousness suddenly altered itself.

Dental gas had a vague but distinctive odor, sort of sickly sweet, she remembered. The kind of smell that would need to be masked with something else, something strong enough to hide it completely. Like the stench of rotting flesh.

"Chess? Are you okay?"

Chess looked back at the girl. Katie's big dark eyes were wide with concern, and a bit of fear.

"I'm fine," she said. "Just thinking about something. But could I use your bathroom?"

Once there she grabbed her Cepts, stuck a couple in her mouth, and washed them down. So it was a fake haunting at the Pyle house, it had to be. That made sense. That's why the ghosts hadn't attacked her two nights before, why they hadn't come through the door. That's why she'd felt so sick, so much worse than she ever had, even when she'd faced the Dreamthief.

But unless the gas had been set up specifically for her benefit, its presence also exonerated at least one of the Pyles. Had Kym arranged the whole thing to terrify Roger—to get him to sell the house and move them all back to L.A., maybe? Or some other reason? Or had Roger done it, to scare his wife and daughter? Arden could have done it, she supposed, despite Oliver Fletcher's denigration of her, but the idea that a four-teen-year-old girl would be able to get hold of a large quantity of gas was a bit far-fetched. Far-fetched, but not impossible.

And she'd almost missed it. She planned to go back to the Pyles' the next day anyway—another rule of Debunking, never go on a set schedule, always throw them off if you can—but the visit took on new signifi-cance now. She needed to check the plumbing, check the utility room. Was there some kind of timer? The memory of blood rising in the sink came back to her; the gas could be pumped up from the pipes, spreading into the bedroom from there. The office had a bathroom, too, didn't it?

And speaking of bathrooms, they were going to wonder what happened to her if she didn't leave this one. She rinsed her hands and left, so deep in thought she didn't realize someone else was in the living room until she sat down.

Katie's father, she guessed, and her younger brother. Two more dark heads bent over a book next to Katie's. The boy looked up and smiled. Chess expected to see the same wide-open grin as the one on Katie's face, but this was different; he must have inherited it from his father. Yes, he had. They were almost identical.

So Katie looked like her mother . . . no. No, she didn't. Chess knew that smile, knew whose it was. She'd seen it before, dozens of times.

She felt like she was interrupting, intruding on something she didn't understand. She felt awful. Too many revelations, too much in her head for such a short time. She should have taken more pills.

So it was a relief when Terrible came out of the kitchen, despite the glower on his face. He barely said a word on the long drive back to her place. And Chess had no idea what to say to him, so she watched the snow fall, flakes diving into the windshield like tiny kamikaze ghosts.

It wasn't until he parked near her building that she came up with something to say. Whether it was the right thing or not she didn't know, but she had to try. Couldn't let it go, even though she knew she should.

Feeling a little like she was jumping off a cliff, she turned to him. "Terrible, why don't you come up for a beer? And you can tell me about your daughter."

Chapter Nineteen

This was when the Truth finally came out; this was the moment when the eyes of humanity saw it.
—*The Book of Truth*, Origins, Article 1520

Standing beside the utility shed on top of her building, sheltered by its small roof, was like standing in the mouth of a cave, watching the silent snow fall a foot away. Without the wind, the air around them felt almost warm, the curious warmth that always seems to exist when it's snowing, as though the snowfall provides insulation.

And like people in a cave, they were hidden. Hidden from the eyes of Downside by the sheer height of Chess's building. From their viewpoint they could see the entire city, blurred and softened by flurries and thick smoke pouring from chimneys, but they might as well have been invisible themselves, tucked in the shadows. At least she hoped so.

The roof was her idea. Inside he'd seemed restless, caged, and his unease made the walls shrink around her as well. So up they'd come, with the twelve-pack she'd bought him earlier and a bottle of bourbon he'd pulled from his trunk, and they leaned against the shed and stared out at the dusky sky together.

"Knew it ain't work," he said, breaking the silence. "Felice, meaning. Rich girl, thought she were daring comin down here. You know. Liked her, though. Me an her, we saw each other maybe five, six months, she came up pregnant. Only find out causen I run into her one day—she quit on my calls, dig, when she found out. Ain't wanted to tell me. Ain't wanted me involved. Can't say as I blame her. My life ain't nothin for a kid. Ain't even got a name to give her, aye?"

Chess didn't answer, afraid that if she spoke, he would stop.

"So finally we agreed ourselves a deal. She already seein Bill—seein him the whole time, but knew the baby weren't his, if you dig—an he wanted to marry her. I kick in some lashers every month, I see Katie when I can. Ain't such a bad deal. Least I get to see her. To know her, dig?"

"She doesn't know?"

He shook his head, took a long drink from the now half-empty bottle in his hand. "For the best, aye. Nobody know cepting Bump. Nobody else."

"Thanks."

He glanced at her, nodded.

"She's really pretty, Terrible. And smart."

"Ain't she? Go to college one day and all. Ain't get that from me. Tall, though, like me."

"She has your eyes. And your smile."

In the glow from his lighter flame she saw him flush slightly, but he didn't reply.

Chess leaned forward so he could light one for her as well. "You ever think about having another one?"

"Naw. Had em cut me, dig. Right after I found out. Only reason any dame want a baby off me is money. Got lucky with Felice. Ain't takin chances on having luck again."

"Me either," she said, watching her exhaled smoke mix with the snow.

"What?"

"I'm not . . . I can't have children."

"Thought no Church dames could, aye?"

"Well, no, not exactly. The Debunkers and Liaisers aren't allowed to—anyone who works with ghosts or has a more dangerous job can't. The Goodys can, and some of the material employees. They really like pregnant women in those jobs, give them a bonus and everything, because of the extra power they have when they make charms or ritual tools or whatever."

She took a deep breath. It felt weird to be telling him this, to be telling anyone this, but she owed him. She had a secret of his now, one so big it was pushing one of hers out to make room.

"So yeah, they would have given me an IUD, when I got hired, but they didn't need to. I had . . . um, when I was thirteen I got pregnant. One of my foster brothers, I don't remember which one. He . . . you know, no surprise or anything, they all did, but he got me pregnant, so they took me to this doctor. They said he was a doctor. And he did it wrong, he cut me or something and I almost died. So . . . I'm too scarred or something. Too damaged."

"Shit, Chess." He settled himself on the little ridge on the wall and folded his arms.

Tension she hadn't known she was carrying left her. Anyone else might have made a big deal about that story, would have wanted her to talk about it, to dredge it all up in her mind again and relive it under the misguided idea that she could somehow banish it by exposing it. Or they might have smothered her with horrified sympathy until she wanted to start crying just to make them shut up, or looked at her with big cow eyes like she was nothing more than an experience, her humanity gone and replaced by a collection of bad memories.

But he did none of those things, simply stood next to her, smoking. Accepting what had happened, accepting her for telling him. He killed a beer and opened fresh ones for both of them, chasing his slugs of bourbon. When he handed hers to her, the neckline of his bowling shirt gaped open a bit, and pink neon from the sign across the street highlighted the tiny script tattooed around the base of his neck, just above the top of his black undershirt. She'd never actually read it.

Chess set her beer down and stood in front of him, angling herself between his long sprawled legs so she could open his collar all the way. Daring herself to read it, to stand this close to him.

Ego vos mergam, nec merger a vobis. I sink you, that I will not be sunk by you.

When she looked up he was watching her, his face immobile. The half-healed wound under his eye made a dark slash on his cheekbone, blending in with the scar above his lip, the bent and crooked nose, the simian brow. Funny, she couldn't remember the last time she'd noticed any of those things, really *seen* them, whereas once they'd been all she could see.

"What does it say?"

He shrugged. His gaze transferred from her to a point just beyond. "Only know it Englished, dig. Ain't pronounce the Latin."

She could—Latin was a required Church subject—but she didn't tell him that. Instead she repeated, "What does it say?"

Pause. Beneath her fingertip his pulse kicked steadily. She glanced at it, watching it move. He trusted her to touch it. Trusted her to touch him. To stand this close. Trusted her with his biggest secret. What would he do if she put her mouth over that vein, gave that soft skin a gentle nibble? Would he trust her still, would he let her?

"Says you try and fuck with me, you get fucked," he said finally. His eyes came back to hers. "Says I get you first."

He smelled good. Tobacco and pomade, bourbon and beer mixed with something she couldn't define, and the scent of smoke in the air and the snow itself, faintly metallic but pure at the same time. For a second Chess saw the two of them as if she wasn't in her body, saw them leaning against the little shed, their bodies almost touching, two black silhouettes against the dusky sky.

She wanted to . . . wanted to show him something. Wanted to say something. That she was glad they were friends again and she appreciated what he'd done for her, how he'd trusted her, and that she trusted him, too. How important keeping his secret was to her.

But there didn't seem to be words for that, at least not ones she wouldn't stumble over, so she leaned forward and kissed him.

She'd intended it to be brief, just a peck, really, but once she got there she didn't know how to pull away. Didn't know how, and when his chest hitched under her palms, when he responded, she realized she didn't want to. She wanted to stay. She wanted to kiss him.

Something clanked. He'd dropped his beer, and his warm, hard hands slid across her cheeks, cupping them as if he was reassuring himself she was really there. His fingers pushed through her hair and down to touch her neck, down farther still until her coat tightened around her, pulled taut by his fists. His lips against hers sent shivers down her spine, out through her limbs, heat welling up inside her, and the only way to get rid of it was to give it back to him the same way—like a secret. Like trust.

Somewhere in the back of her mind she thought if she kept kissing him, she'd get more secrets, get answers to questions she didn't know she had, and it excited and scared her in equal measure, made her dizzy.

Like playing with forbidden spells early in her training, like the rush of a line of speed she wanted just a little too much, she wanted this. Wanted to take from him and give back, too. Wanted to *share* something. She let her fingers move up, across the hard bone of his jaw to the short rough hair of his wide sideburns scratchy-soft against her skin.

His mouth eased hers open so his tongue could slip inside and she welcomed it, tasting bourbon and smoke and something more she didn't bother to try and define. His big hands moved again, finding her hips, engulfing them, his fingers splayed apart just above her bottom. She felt every one of them through her jeans like a separate brand, like electrical wires sending mild, delicious shocks through her.

That wasn't enough contact. She wanted to feel his skin. Wanted to press herself against him and let his big chest shelter her, wanted his hands on her, his body on hers, inside hers. Hunger overwhelmed her, a desperation she'd never felt before, never known she could feel about something non-narcotic. It grabbed hold of her and shook her from the inside, making her breath come faster and her grip on him tighten. More, she wanted more of this, more of him. *Needed* more. Her entire body felt feverish, oversensitive, an exposed nerve begging to be soothed.

His pulse throbbed beneath her palms, as fast as her own heartbeat. She slid her hands down, finding the hem of his shirt and snaking back up under it, searching for bare flesh. The image of his naked chest as she'd seen it once, months before, filled her mind. Her fingers itched to touch it, to roam across that wide expanse and memorize it by feel.

His skin shivered under her hands when she stroked the hard muscles of his abdomen, flattening her palms to try and feel as much of him as she could. To feel all of him, everything. She slid her hands higher, finding the thick hair on his chest, curling her fingers into it. He made a sound then, so soft she barely heard it, but felt it in every pore and muscle of her body.

What was more than just a kiss became more even than that. His hands moved again, one sliding over her bottom and yanking her closer, the other tangling in her hair, twisting it. He leaned forward, kissed her harder, deeper, until her head started to spin and her breath came in short, desperate gasps and she was lost, overwhelmed.

She found his heavy belt buckle and yanked at it, moved toward the button fly of his jeans with no conscious thought save trying to satisfy this craving—this craving she tried to pretend was new but wasn't. Through the thick fabric she felt him, burning hot and ready. He gasped, and her pulse kicked and the answering heat between her thighs practically screamed—

He squeezed her hips, hard. Too hard, and it took her a second to realize he wasn't squeezing. He was pushing. Pushing her away.

Like an idiot she stood there, her hands still playing with his shirt, before the realization that something was wrong finally penetrated the sweet hazy fog in her brain.

"What's this, Chess?" His voice was so rough and low she wouldn't have known it was him if she hadn't watched his lips move. "You feelin sorry for me?"

What was he talking about? Why was he talking at all? Confused, she just stared at him, trying to find the words to ask but unable to come up with any.

"Shit." He straightened up, stepped away from her. His fingers went into his pocket and pulled out a cigarette. In the dim snowy light it looked like they were shaking. "You ain't need to do that, dig?"

Oh. Shit was right. She'd made an ass out of herself. Again.

Her own hands were none too steady when she picked

up her beer and drank half of it off. "I'm sorry. I didn't mean to, I—"

He flinched. "Aye, well. Don't want you doing aught to pretend you ain't recall on the morn."

She gasped. She couldn't help it. He might as well have spat in her face.

"Aye, I knew."

She had pretended she didn't remember. Had lied to him, three months before, after that night in the bar. Pretended she didn't remember him holding her, lifting her up, bracing her against the wall while their lips fused together.

Yeah, she'd been fucked up that night, thanks to an illegal—and extremely potent—pill she'd found. But not that fucked up. Not so fucked up she didn't know what she was doing, or that she couldn't replay the whole thing in her head still, relive it in detail.

What the fuck was wrong with her? Why did she keep doing this?

It was easy to be wanted by a man when he'd never seen the bad parts. And she had so many of them, so much to hide. So many, it was amazing anyone who'd known her more than a few days still wanted to be with her at all.

Terrible knew more about her than anyone else did. And he was rejecting her. And she deserved it.

"I'm sorry," she said again.

Clutching her beer, she turned away from him, walked out into the snow. Minutes before, Downside had looked almost pretty, almost romantic, with snow covering the filth. Now she sensed it all hiding beneath the surface, the dirt and grime, the broken needles and used condoms and rats and garbage. Felt the hostile eyes of the city on her like they all knew who she was and what she did. Imagined she saw the murderers moving like phantoms between the cold buildings, plotting against her, watching her.

Tears slid down her cheeks. She swiped at them, pretending to push her hair back.

"Aw, fuck." The soft air around them, the distance she'd put between them, muted his voice, muted the gentle slosh as he lifted the bottle again. "Now you got the thought I ain't want you, aye?"

What the fuck? What was she supposed to think? Hadn't he just told her he didn't want her? She opened her mouth to ask, shut it again. No point.

Silence turned the air cold.

"Shit. I want you, Chess. Make no mistake on that one, dig? Want you bad. So bad I ain't even can think of any else sometimes, 'cept getting you under me. Ain't give a fuck what pills you swallow get you through the day or what happens you ain't got em, aye? Still want you."

She didn't move. Waiting. Not sure how to react. Not sure how she felt, if she could even believe him. He'd *had* her, there. She'd been at his fucking buttons, hadn't she, like a starving victim about to tear into a banquet? In another few seconds she would have had her hand down his pants while her other hand shoved her own clothes out of the way, would have begged him to take her up against that wall in the cold.

And he knew it. She knew he did. Only someone who knew nothing about women would have failed to notice how her fingers dug into his skin, how her breath came so fast. And he definitely knew about women. So if he wanted her . . . this was kind of a fucked-up way to show it.

"But I ain't . . . ain't think I can take it, wakin up next to you on the morn, have you fake like nothing happened. Or tell me you made yourself a mistake. Or say, aye, thanks, maybe try that again on the sometime. I know how you run it, keepin it cool and no repeats, and I dig it, aye? Got your reasons. So I figure . . ."

His lighter clicked, snapped shut. Pause. She could

picture him standing against the wall, staring down at his feet with his hand on the back of his neck like he did when he was thinking or upset, or when he was about to say something he thought made him seem vulnerable.

"I figure you really wanted me you'd say. Like now, maybe, if you dig. I'll fuckin carry you down your place on a run, you tell me aye, get you on your back afore the next word comes out your mouth. But you oughta have yourself certain, causen I ain't looking for charity, an I ain't letting you go after. Once . . . once ain't enough for me, dig?"

Fresh tears stung her eyes. She had no idea what to do, absolutely none. Every sentence that came to her mind seemed wrong, every action precipitous, and all she felt—aside from the throbbing below her waist and the odd, light sensation in her stomach—was an emotion so familiar she couldn't possibly mistake it.

Fear.

He terrified her.

He terrified her, because when she'd kissed him, when she'd gotten so desperate for him so fast, so fucking fast, she'd still been there, too. Hadn't lost herself. Hadn't been looking to use him like a machine calibrated to give her orgasms so she could forget who she was for a few minutes. Had been acutely aware she was kissing *Terrible*, that it was *his* body against hers, *his* hands on her hips, *his* lips making her blood sing.

She'd still been there. *She'd* wanted him, herself, Chess, not just her body. That desire, that crazy, intense need . . . that hadn't been only physical. What did that mean?

She heard him behind her, smoking his cigarette, opening another beer. Waiting. Melted snow mixed with the tears on her face and dampened her hair. Maybe that was the problem. Maybe she was frozen, that's why she couldn't move.

"Well," he said. "Well. So now you know."

Why weren't her feet moving? What the hell was she so scared of? She wanted to go to him, could picture herself going to him, taking him to her place, to the bed she'd never allowed even Lex into. Pictured again his chest bared, her fingers sliding across it, over his stomach and farther down.

The images wouldn't stop. She saw his mouth on her breasts, his hand between her legs, and her entire body clenched so violently she thought she might fall. Oh, she wanted him. Had wanted him for months, probably at least as badly as he wanted her. She couldn't deny that anymore.

She just . . . couldn't go to him. Her feet literally refused to move. As though they knew what kind of person she was and were punishing her by ignoring her orders. Her mouth refused to open, to utter that one small word that was all he needed to hear. Her body was taking its revenge on her, and what a time it picked.

Glass clinked against glass behind her. Terrible coughed, gave a small sniffle. "Think I'm done talkin just now, all the same to you." Pause. "G'night, Chess."

She stayed out there, staring into the snow, until the Chevelle's engine noise faded into the distance. He was gone, and she was alone up there, alone and apart from the city so peaceful under its secure snowy blanket.

The buildings spreading from the edge of her roof were full of people, full of lives. Inside them lovers huddled together against the cold, inside them families laughed or fought or whatever it was families did together. And here she stood, invisible. Trapped.

Alone. And for the first time she could remember . . . alone didn't feel very good.

And that was the scariest thing of all.

Chapter Twenty

She woke up the next morning at Lex's place, with her head fuzzy from an Oozer dream and no clear idea of how she got there.

She sat up, pushing off the heavy blankets, then fell back when memory thumped her in the head. And the chest. And the stomach.

Terrible. His hands on her hips, his mouth on hers. His voice rolling over her skin.

And she'd run. Stood on that roof until she couldn't feel her hands and feet anymore, then gone straight to her car, straight over here, and used Lex like any other drug. And when that hadn't worked, she'd found one that would.

Too bad she wouldn't be able to do that forever. She had to work today. The Pyle case was almost wrapped up, or it would be once she found the proof, which shouldn't be hard now that she knew exactly what to look for.

Lex rolled over on the bed next to her, the white sheets sliding down his bare chest. He did have a nice chest. "Hey, Tulip," he mumbled. "Figured you ain't be waking for hours, aye? Tired yourself pretty well out last night, you did."

"Apparently not," she said, blushing.

"Nay? Tired *me* out. C'mon back here, help me wake up." His hand ran up her bare back, over her shoulder, and down her arm. She shivered when he took her hand, moved it so she could feel him hard beneath the sheet.

She took it back, though. "Looks to me like you're already awake."

"Then help me get back to sleep. Seems to me it's all your fault, dig? I was tucked up here like a good boy, aye, till you come raging in and practically tore my clothes off with them teeth of yours. Ain't complaining, me, but seems you'd help a guy out, seein as how I recall at least five times you—"

"I have to get to work."

"Guarantee you a couple more . . ."

She smiled over her shoulder at him. His spiky hair was flattened on one side; it gave him an endearingly drunken look. "I can't. I need to take a shower."

"I come along, me."

"Nope." She pushed the covers off all the way, reached for her bag, and dug out her pillbox. "But if you're nice maybe I'll come back tonight."

"At least twice, aye? Only I may be too tired out for more. Still trying to recover and all."

Chess rolled her eyes, tossed a couple of Cepts into her mouth, and grabbed the water bottle.

"Meaning to ask, where'd all them scratches come from? Lookin like you had yourself a knife fight with a dwarf, aye?"

She glanced down, swallowing the pills. Her legs did look awful. She hadn't really looked at them—had avoided looking at them—until now, aside from smearing them with antibiotic cream twice a day. Even then she hadn't *looked*, just rubbed the cream on and checked them quickly for excessive redness.

In the cool light from the window they looked angry,

as if her soul had tried to claw its way out of her body
and failed. Or perhaps it hadn't failed. She felt particularly empty this morning. Maybe that's what was
missing.

She almost hoped it was.

"Oh. I just . . . caught a rash at the Pyle house. No big
deal." Her jeans were across the room where she'd
thrown them the night before. She felt Lex's eyes on her
while she went to get them and yanked them on.

"Some rash."

His phone rang, and he answered it in Cantonese
while Chess found her shirt between the cushions of the
little couch, slipped it over her head, and started hunting
for her bra and panties.

The panties were behind the TV. The bra was still
missing when Lex hung up the phone.

"Well, well," he said. "Looks like I see you later after-
every, aye? Tonight be the night."

"For what?" She fished the bra out from under the
bed, separating it from Lex's boxers and tossing it onto
the couch with the panties.

"Meeting Bump. Hear you gonna be there, too. Cozy
little group we make, aye?"

She'd known this was coming, so why was she
surprised? Maybe because she'd been hoping it was just
a bad dream. The mere thought of sitting in a room with
both Terrible and Lex sent cold shivers all the way down
to her toes.

"Lex . . . you can't know me, you know? I mean it.
You can't even—Does your father know? About me?"

His eyes narrowed. "My *father*?"

"What? Oh—" Right. She hadn't mentioned it, had
she? "Bump told me. Why didn't *you* tell me?"

"It matter?"

"No, not really. I just don't know why you never
mentioned it."

"Never come up, aye? Man's gotta have secrets, Tulip. You want me knowing all about you?"

Ugh. She didn't even want to think about that. Opening up to Lex? "No."

"Aye, ain't figured you would. Come on back here to bed now. Getting cold."

"Bump called you a cunthound."

He snorted, his mouth stretching into a grin. "Bump gots him a way with words, he do. Ain't sure 'hound' quite the right one, but ain't matter, guessing."

Chess was fairly certain "hound" was *exactly* the right word, but there wasn't much point in discussing it. Wasn't much time, either. She wanted to get moving. "So does he know about me? Slobag, I mean. Your father. Does he?"

"Coursen he do."

"Fuck! Why?"

"Hey now, ain't be like that. He knows, is all. He's the one had me come to you back in the start, recall? Knows where his pills is going. Ain't no fear. He ain't a chatterer, him. Knows we want to keep you helping us, we gots to keep it all on the silent."

"But does he know, I mean . . ."

"His house, ain't it? You thinkin anybody come in here he ain't know about?"

Her Cepts were kicking in, spreading pleasant warmth through her body, but it didn't stop the headache's threat. She washed down another one, glaring at Lex over the top of her water bottle. "I don't know why you can't get your own place, like a normal person your age."

"You ain't never cared afore. Little late now, aye?"

"Terrible doesn't live with Bump."

"Maybe you oughta start fucking Terrible, then, you so bothered. Shit, Tulip, what's the junters for? I live here. Always have. Why you gotta be so serious all the time?"

She couldn't come up with a reply at first, focused on keeping her face immobile. His words called up a whole album's worth of mental pictures, and that was the last thing she needed right then. Finally she said, "Just promise me, please. You've never seen me before. You don't know me, okay? No winking or flirting or anything?"

"Aw, now what kinda cunthound I be, I ignore one as sweet as yours right there across from me?"

In spite of herself, she laughed. "Okay, yeah. I guess you've got a point there. Just promise you won't go too crazy. Please?"

"What I get iffen I do?"

"My eternal gratitude?"

"Gonna have to do better than that."

"Um . . . knowing I won't get killed for seeing you?"

"Was thinking something more in the physical way, dig." He sat up, letting the sheet fall still farther down his body. "You ain't really think Terrible kill you?"

She shrugged. No, he probably wouldn't. But she didn't want to find out. "Don't know."

"Nay, Tulip, ain't gonna happen. You on the worried side way too much for health. Now you gonna come over here, wish me a proper good morning, or what?"

The clock read 12:47. She was late. Not that anyone was expecting her, but it was a later start than she'd wanted to get.

What the hell. Another fifteen minutes wouldn't make much difference, right? And she could try and make him promise some more that he wouldn't do anything to fuck with her at that meeting, or drop some of those little hints he thought were so clever and impossible to catch but which were neither.

So she sighed and pulled her shirt back over her head. "Good morning," she said.

*   *   *

She hated the gas mask.

It wasn't so bad as gas masks went, really. Once at Terrible's place she'd thumbed through one of his books, a history of the Second World War. The masked men in those photos had resembled insects, with their round blunt mandibles rising from the mist of gas around them. Just thinking of wearing something like that was enough to speed her heart rate.

The small Church mask was different, more like a surgical mask, fairly light and comfortable. Claustrophobic tingles still ran up her spine when she slipped it on, then bent down to shove a towel into the crack under the Pyles' bedroom door.

Telling the Pyles she was about to do dangerous magic had convinced them to brave the brittle cold, at least for a few hours. Hopefully she wouldn't need that long, especially as what she had planned had very little to do with actual magic.

Plastic rustled as she opened the bag of green wood chips she'd picked up at the Church earlier. Another bag held her largest firedish, which she set on the floor just outside the bathroom before dumping in the chips. They took a minute to catch, but when they did, white smoke rose in a thick column. Excellent. In a few minutes the room would start to fill, and she could head into the bathroom.

Time to test her theory.

She switched on her electric meter, let the leads dangle from her belt, and headed for the bathroom.

The meter gave a gentle beep when she crossed the threshold. Good. Whatever the device was—the device she assumed had triggered the receiver on her belt the other night while the Pyles were having their little party—it was on. Nothing to do now but wait.

Too bad the smoldering wood and the smoke gave off too much heat to use the infrared lens. As it was, all she could do was sit, her eyes darting around the room, waiting for the telltale disturbance in the white haze.

It came. Without a sound, without any indication at all save the sudden movement in the corner. From the cupboard where the cleaning supplies were kept.

Chess moved carefully in that direction, shining her flashlight into the wavering smoke. Easy enough to track it once she knew where it came from. Easy enough to find the tiny hole in the ceiling of the cabinet, to place her fingers over it and feel the cold stream of gas dampening her fingers.

She grabbed a wrench with her free hand and crossed to the sinks, waiting. She might not hear the click, especially not over the faint snap of the woodfire, but she'd see the results. Her camera bumped gently against her chest as she moved.

Without the dizzying, sickening influence of the gas, she saw the ghost for what it was. An image superimposed on clouds of smoke, the light from the hologram projector clearly visible as a widening beam descending from the ceiling. She tilted her head back, found the tiny hole before the image disappeared, and marked it with her eyes.

In the little cupboard a stepstool rested against the back wall. She grabbed it, unfolded it, stood on it to inspect the hole further and take some pictures. Once she'd proved who the guilty party was, she'd open the ceiling to get at the projector. That would be fun.

Was this the daytime show or the nighttime one? She glanced toward the bedroom, curious to see how the trickster managed to darken the room, but was disappointed. Instead, the sink started burbling, and drugged roaches lumbered out of the drain. She yanked on a pair of gloves and grabbed the wrench.

Some parts of her job she loved. Some she did not. This was definitely a case of "did not." Thick red liquid oozed out of the pipe when she loosened the bolt. Again, she'd need to rip off the tiles and open the wall to know for sure, but it seemed elementary once she thought about it. A simple toggle switch or sensor set in the floor. A pump behind the wall. Anyone with basic electrical and plumbing knowledge could have set it all up.

Probably a timer somewhere, too, to vary the effects. The image of the man, for example. Chess hadn't seen that the first day. Of course that could have been because of the light streaming in through the window. It didn't really matter.

She tightened the bolt back up, opened the window to clear the smoke, and started cleaning up the crimson mess on the tiles, scooping some of it into an inert plastic jar to be analyzed. Being thankful for an allergy never crossed her mind before, but she was certainly glad now. Who knew how long it might have taken her to solve this one if it hadn't been for her reaction to the gas?

It was clever. But even clever only got so far, especially without luck, and sooner or later everyone's luck ran out.

She shivered as she wrung out the paper towels and tossed them onto the smoldering wood. Everyone's luck ran out, indeed. She just hoped hers wasn't about to.

Chapter Twenty-one

Yeah. Her luck lasted just as long as it took to walk down the hall and run into Oliver Fletcher, and to give in to his insistence that she "meet" with him in Roger's office.

She looked at the pictures in her hand again, shuffling through them as if she could erase the images by rubbing them against one another. Herself sitting on her living room couch, smoking a kesh. Bumping up off her hairpin, hunched over the wheel of her car. On the street with Terrible, his body a huge shadow next to her, tossing pills into her mouth. And again. And again.

Fuck. Oh fuck oh fuck oh fuck oh fuck.

She took a deep breath, tried to steady her voice as she tossed the pictures back on the desk toward Oliver Fletcher. Goodbye, new car. Goodbye, bedroom heater. Goodbye, last vestiges of integrity. "What do you want me to do?"

"I think that should be obvious. I have these pictures, and I think they'd be of great interest to your emp—"

"Yeah, I understand. I'm asking what you want me to do. Lie and say it's a real haunting? Or blame it on someone else?"

Fletcher leaned forward, all business now. "What do you think is best?"

"Are you serious?"

"Of course. You're the one with the experience here. What do you recommend? If you say it's real, what proof do you need to provide, what documentation?"

Yeah, like she was going to give out that information so he could pull this shit again. Start himself a little cottage business cheating the Church. "It varies."

"Whatever you need, I can provide. I think it's obvious I have the ability."

"Yeah."

"You have to admit, this was much better than the average fake haunting."

Was he fucking kidding? "What do you want, a pat on the back? I don't go to your movies, Mr. Fletcher. Don't expect me to applaud, okay?"

"There's no need to be so rude."

"Oh, for fuck's sake." She grabbed her bag, fished out her smokes. He had a lighter ready before she even got the butt into her mouth, like they were on some kind of date or something.

She let him light her anyway, though. "So, why? Why do this?"

"Why? I—" He shook his head, reached for the glass to his right. She hadn't noticed it before; now she smelled the whiskey inside. "I should think that would be obvious. Roger Pyle wants to leave the show and go on to movies—and not my movies. He's my biggest star, and I need him to get my next script off the ground. I need him out of here and back where he belongs. He owes his entire fucking career to me, he owes me that much. And—but never mind that. How did you not figure that out? You found out how I'd faked it—nice trick, by the way, with the smoke in the bathroom—but my obvious motive went completely undetected."

"Not completely undetected. I was pretty sure it was you." Something about that bothered her, now that she was thinking of it. It seemed a little too easy, a little—

"But you had no proof it was me. In fact, you still don't."

"I can get it."

He shook his head, smiling. "I doubt it. Ah, the arrogance of youth. I was like you, you know. Despite my failings, I was so certain I could do no wrong."

She couldn't resist. "As opposed to now."

His lips quirked. "The difference is now I know that what I'm doing is wrong. I'm just determined not to get caught."

"Which is why you're blackmailing me."

"Wouldn't you do the same, if you were me? Really, you do open yourself up for that sort of thing. If I was able to find evidence of your drug use—it's more of an addiction, isn't it, than just 'use'?—simply by following you home, I can't believe no one else would be able to. You should be more careful."

"Yeah, I'll keep that in mind." She would, too. "Have you sent those pictures to anyone else?"

"What? Oh, no. They're all here, with the memory chip. I'll be keeping that. I'm sure you understand."

Yeah, she understood. But she didn't like it. She didn't trust him. Who was to say he wouldn't decide a few years down the line that he needed a little Church-related favor? She was already at Bump's and Lex's beck and call. She didn't need another blackmail buddy holding something over her head.

He must have seen her give in, because that irritating smile widened ever so slightly and he gathered the pictures back into a neat little stack. "Let me know what kind of evidence you need, and how you'd like to handle this. I'll go along with whatever you decide. Here."

A business card sat between his index and middle

fingers, as though he couldn't be bothered to hold the thing properly. "That's my card, with my cell number on it. To prove my trustworthiness. A lot of people would pay a lot of money for that number. As long as you keep my secrets, I'll keep yours. Fair enough?"

The card stock was so stiff and sharp she could have cut lines with it, and the cell number did indeed sprawl across the back, written in thick black ink.

"Just give me a call," he said, and turned back to the papers on Roger Pyle's desk. Dismissing her.

Which was no more than she deserved.

Slobag hadn't wanted to come too far into Bump's territory, and Bump hadn't wanted Slobag to see where he lived anyway, so the meeting was being held on the Aceria Bridge, so far west it was almost in Cross Town. From where Chess stood, dead in the middle, she saw the orange glow Downside's fires cast on the fog and smoke, saw the orderly lights of Cross Town, even the houses on the hills of Northside. It was so quiet, so still. Like being somewhere else entirely.

Somewhere she wasn't being blackmailed, somewhere she wasn't scared shitless she was about to get busted hardcore when Lex "accidentally" let something slip. Somewhere she couldn't feel Terrible's eyes on her, somewhere she hadn't fucked everything up between them. Again.

It was cold despite the roaring fire built in a fire can off to the left, and Chess was glad. It gave her an excuse to huddle into her coat, into herself, propped against the railing with her head down.

Beneath them the icy waters of the Eternity River raged, swollen from the snow that had melted during the day, so strong and hard that the bridge vibrated. For a moment Chess imagined it breaking, pictured them all falling, swallowed by the black current. Would it hurt?

Or would the water numb her so she didn't even feel when her lungs stopped working, when her—

"You all set, Ladybird? Gonna get what you fuckin need of they?" Bump's gold-circled eyes peered at her from beneath his raggedy wide-brimmed purple hat, its gold buckle catching the firelight and throwing it back. He looked far from the Bump she'd seen in ridiculous pajamas the other night; this was street Bump, power resting on his shoulders as casually as the dingy white fur cape he wore. Beneath the cape she saw at least three shirts, slashed in places so the fabric beneath them could peek out, and his bottle-green velvet trousers tucked into heavy fur boots actually looked clean.

He'd painted his fingernails black. The diamond and gemstone rings covering his knuckles clanked when he moved. His gold-tipped cane sparkled and thumped against the pitted cement road when he walked, adding to the dissonant symphony.

"What?"

"Get what you need, make me some spells, yay? Figure Lex be easy, you run them sweet fingers through he hair no fuckin problem. Maybe you smile pretty make he think he got a chance. Slobag, you let Bump handle. Bump gots a fuckin plan."

"But I thought—" She glanced at Terrible, but his face was impassive and his eyes hidden behind sunglasses, flames reflected in the dark lenses. Empty-eyed, fire where his eyes should be. She shuddered, and not just from the image. Beyond greeting her he hadn't spoken at all. "I thought you'd changed your mind, you didn't mention it again, and I thought you were going to get whatever you needed."

"When Bump said that? Ain't recall fuckin saying it. You got a memory Bump ain't got, Ladybird? Them pills messin with your fuckin mind, yay? Never said that."

She bit her tongue and took a deep breath before replying. Dickhead. "They're going to know what I'm doing. They'll know what I am."

"Just do it, yay? You get what you fuckin need. Insurance, yay? Something Bump got for if there's a fuckin need any else time."

She guessed it didn't really matter. He'd come to her for whatever spells he wanted, and she'd fake it, make them ineffective anyway. So she just nodded. "Fine."

"That's good. That's real fuckin good. Ain't gonna be here long this night, yay? Fuckin cold. Bump ain't like the cold."

Another nod. Another glance at Terrible. She'd hoped to have a chance to talk to him alone, but Bump hovered around her like a vulture waiting for its prey to die. Somehow she didn't think Terrible would appreciate Bump overhearing their conversation, even if she didn't mind. Which she did.

Wasn't like she knew what to say, anyway.

Not for the first time she wished desperately she'd never kissed him to begin with. If she hadn't started it, he wouldn't have ended it, and she wouldn't have to worry about any of it. Could have gone on ignoring the undercurrents in their friendship, ignoring the memories.

Why was she so determined always to do the exact wrong thing?

She sighed and huddled farther back into her coat, then thought better of it and reached for her pillbox. Bump wanted her to cozy up to Lex? In front of Terrible? Yeah, great idea. Numb was the only way to get through this.

Three more Cepts would help. She swallowed them and lit a cigarette.

She'd smoked it about halfway when headlights swept across the bridge, bleaching color from everything in their path, and then died. Slobag had arrived.

Her first thought was that he could have been a carbon copy of Bump. Same hat, only in red. His matching cape was covered in tiny gold bells. Both his shirts and blue brocade pants were slashed. But he didn't carry off the look with the same insouciance as Bump. It looked costumey on him, and she knew from the way he moved that unlike Bump he wore the clothes for flash, because it was expected, not because he really enjoyed wearing them.

Her second thought was how much he looked like Lex. There was no denying the resemblance there, none at all, although Slobag wasn't as tall as his son, didn't have the same lazy sense of entitlement.

Said entitled son stood just behind his father, the black spikes of his hair shining like onyx. His gaze scanned the bridge, found her, passed over her. The breath she didn't realize she was holding left in a sigh.

Chess stayed put while the men greeted each other, but when they neared the spot where she stood—Bump with his usual gliding walk, Slobag stepping as though he was afraid the road would stick to his shoes—she saw there was no point in trying to be unobtrusive. Slobag's eyes caught her, scanned her ruthlessly. She could read the message in them, and it wasn't cheerful. A mix between dislike because of her Church position and dislike because of whatever positions she got into with his son and heir, she imagined. His gaze felt like hard fingers on her skin.

"That's Chess." Bump waved his beringed hand in her direction. "Helping we out, yay?"

Lex grabbed her hand, lifted it to his lips. She refused to look at him, especially not when his tongue darted out and dove between her middle and third fingers. "You a helpful kind of girl, then?"

She snatched her hand back and folded her arms tight over her chest. Her face warmed; she kept her gaze focused on the bridge railing.

Lex laughed. "Aw, now, no reason to be like that, aye? Ain't gonna hurt you, girl. Unless that's what you lookin for, dig. I'm real good at givin the dames what they want."

Bastard. Sure, he was right. It would look odd if he totally ignored her. And she needed him not to; if Bump saw her refuse to even attempt to do what he wanted, he wouldn't be happy at all. But now she realized he planned to go as far as he could with this little act. She was the weakness in this gathering, the loose brick in the façade.

Or maybe not. She glanced at Terrible. His expression hadn't changed, but the dull color he couldn't control was creeping up his neck.

"You ain't sayin no, noticing," Lex continued.

With effort she kept her voice under control. "No."

"And lookie there, she said herself a word. It always this hard gettin you to talk?"

The words were a sneaky reference to their initial meeting, when he'd had her kidnapped, held her in a room until she started to withdraw, then taunted her with a bag full of Cepts until she agreed to talk to him.

"I've got another couple of words for you."

"Aye? Betting you do. Maybe later you tell me, what you say?"

She glared at him. His eyes sparkled back. Like this was all some kind of game.

Of course, to him it was. He wasn't the one in danger here.

When had being an addict gotten so fucking hard? So exhausting? It had been so easy for so long; she had a steady supply, she kept to herself, nobody bothered her. Now she was constantly up to her ears in intrigue and complications, being torn in every direction but her own, all thanks to her need for those pills.

She closed her eyes, shook her head. It didn't matter. She wasn't going to change anything, was she? No. So unless she planned to, she should shut the fuck up and focus on getting through this without getting killed.

Slobag cleared his throat. He'd taken a spot by a crumbling iron pillar, adjusting the layers of his clothing with finicky fingers.

Lex left her, swaggering to his father's side. Bump and Terrible stood on either side of Chess. They were ready to start.

Or they would be, when someone finally spoke. As it was, they all stared at each other, waiting.

The silence started to get on her nerves. Or perhaps it was Lex, who caught her eye and winked. Either way, she was edgy even with the extra pills, and uncomfortable against the railing. She didn't dare move, though, not even when the wind made her hair tickle her face or she thought, with a sudden sickening thud, that her murderous eye-stealing friends could very well be out there watching. Getting ready to attack.

Slobag lost. "You asked us to come."

The words explained one thing Chess had always wondered about Lex, anyway. His words were Downspeech, but his accent never had been. Slobag's wasn't either. Interesting.

"Yay." Bump leaned back, not bothering to hide his triumphant smile. "Sure did. Looks like we got a ghost, yay? Going after we fuckin whores. Bump hears you got a problem like it over your side. True?"

Slobag nodded.

"Ain't Bump, yay? Ain't going after you fuckin girls, none. Chess here got the notion some ghost using they eyeballs to see, takin they souls and makin them fuckin whores or ought, maybe she oughta fuckin chatter it so's you dig it."

Lex blew smoke out hard; the wind caught it and

carried it right into her face. "Aye, let's us hear what she say. You talk now, Churchwitch?"

With all eyes on her, glaring at him would only make her vulnerable. So she looked up instead, to a point right over his head, and quickly outlined what she thought—what she was sure—was happening.

Silence followed, broken only by the occasional shuffling of feet and the snap of Terrible's lighter.

"Yay, some fucked up," Bump said. He adjusted his grip on the cane; his rings clacked and sparkled. "What say, Ladybird? Think now we know what the fuck we look for, you find it? What you need, get it fuckin found?"

"I can banish them when we find them, yeah, but I don't know how to find them."

"We know they ain't up here, dig, no fuckin happening in Bump's territory Bump ain't got the knowledge of." This last was spoken with a satisfied glance at Slobag. "But maybe Slobag here ain't can fuckin say the same, yay? What you say, Slobag? They by your fuckin side? Maybe you have you a fuckin study on it. Maybe you head on there, Ladybird. Have you a lookie round, see what you fuckin see."

Now he wanted her to go over there and spy. Of course. For fuck's sake, did he not understand she had an actual job?

She nodded. Time to discuss it with him after this stupid meeting was over.

"Yay, that work itself out real fuckin fine." Bump stood up. "Ladybird come around, you take she safe, yay? Maybe best to pass the word, gonna fuckin send she down there."

Slobag nodded, glanced at Terrible. Bump laughed, an oily chuckle that Chess practically felt settle on her skin.

"Ain't no worries on Terrible, dig. Figure you fuckin guys ain't takin he out noways."

That successfully put an end to the meeting. Lex gave her fingers another tongue bath, and he and his father left. Chess did not watch them go. She was too busy lighting a cigarette, ducking down by the pillar out of the wind to bump up, anything to avoid getting into the discussion she knew she was about to have.

Make that *discussions*. First Bump wanted to instruct her on exactly what kind of information he wanted her to gather—she took notes—and to remind her he still wanted Lex's hair.

Then he left. Left her alone with Terrible.

She inhaled deep, wishing it was courage instead of speed, and watched him reach into his jacket pocket and pull out a small recorder. He glanced at her as he opened it, removed the chip, and placed both back in his pocket.

"You right, Chess?"

"Yeah, I just . . . so that was Slobag."

Terrible shrugged, but she felt his gaze on her. "Ain't so much, aye?"

"No, I guess not." The speed hit; her teeth felt like she'd rubbed them with aluminum foil.

"C'mon. Gotta get on out. I got some places needing to go. Ain't you got work?"

"Yeah, I've got a couple of things I could do, sure. But . . . I want to talk to you, for a minute. If that's okay."

What was she doing? He was going to let her off the hook! Was she insane?

She didn't feel insane. A little foggy, maybe, from the extra Cepts, and a little chatty from the speed numbing her nose and the back of her throat. But not insane.

She owed him this. As much as she would have loved to hide from it and pretend it had never happened, it had. And something about those words she'd heard, about him saying them, made her feel strong enough to give him something back.

He rubbed the back of his neck, stalling, then shoved his hands into his pockets, his eyes resolutely cast down. "You ain't need to say, Chess. It's cool, dig? Ain't a problem this side."

"But it's not, I mean, I feel like—"

He nodded, turning the gesture into a barrier against her words. "Aye. I dig it, no problem. I see you around sometime, then. Go an get in yon car, aye?"

"No, wait. Please." This was easier. He'd turned to go. She could talk to his back. The words came so much more readily when he wasn't looking at her. When she didn't know that behind the impenetrable lenses of his sunglasses his gaze was fixed on her face, watching her every move.

Her parched throat ached. She grabbed her water and gulped some, nearly choking in her haste. "It's not . . . it's not what you're thinking. It's not. It's . . ."

Shit, this was hard. How did you tell someone the truth when you weren't even sure what that was? When you'd never told it before, not like this? Her hands trembled as she screwed the cap back on her water bottle.

"It's not you, it's not that I don't . . . I just don't think I'm ready for that. I don't think I'd be good at it." Shit, she couldn't seem to get her throat and mouth to work properly. All her fear had formed itself into a horrid lump there, caked with speed behind her tonsils.

"I think I need some time. If that's okay. I mean, I don't expect you to sit around and wait for me. But I don't want you to think it's you, that I don't want . . . That's not it. And I don't—I don't want us to not hang out or anything. I want to. Um, I want *us* to. I just . . . need time."

The words hung in the air between them for so long Chess could practically hear their death rattle. Oh, shit, she'd done that wrong, hadn't she? She'd said that wrong, he didn't understand what she meant. She'd thought he would know, that he'd be able to read between the lines and understand, but what if he hadn't? Should she say more? But how much more?

Then he nodded. "Aye, cool. No worrying."

The cold hand wrapping itself around her chest eased its grip. Panic still hovered over her, battering at the edges of her high, trying to find a way in, but not as much as it had a few minutes ago.

Of course, she had no idea where they would go from there.

"You headin back your place now?"

"Don't know. You want to come over?" The words came out before she had a chance to think about it. Maybe that wasn't such a good idea. Having him in her place, just the two of them getting a buzz going . . . yeah. Maybe it wasn't a good idea at all.

"Thinkin on heading for Trickster's. New band playin, they ain't bad neither. Come along, if you're wanting."

She nodded, took the few steps that brought her to his side. Trickster's was probably a much better idea, because even just standing here next to him made her stomach flip a little. She couldn't stop looking at his Adam's apple, for some reason; the skin over it was so delicate, would be so sensitive under her lips.

"I follow you back your place, aye, leave yon car."

Her shoulder brushed against his arm as they walked. The contact sent a little shiver through her that had nothing to do with the cold wind. Shit, what had she done? What was she supposed to be doing? She'd just made a huge mistake, hadn't she. If the last week or so had taught her anything, it should have been that she and relationships of any kind didn't mix, that she'd been right to be alone for so long.

But that loneliness didn't seem like a peaceful retreat anymore. It just seemed lonely. And she knew, trusted without a doubt, that he wouldn't push her into anything. Would never have said anything if she hadn't forced his hand, would leave it up to her to decide what the next move was and when it would be made. And if she was turned on just being around him, well, that wasn't really new, was it. Even if she wanted to pretend it was.

He put his hand on the small of her back when they reached the end of the bridge, helping her across the gravel and loose chunks of cement there. The heat in her blood intensified. Shit, she really needed to stop focusing on this. Arousal was like misery; once she let herself feel it, it refused to stop, pouring into her like whiskey and filling her up. She was still scared, still not ready, but surely it would be okay just to kiss him? To be friends who kissed?

Just one kiss. Just to feel those hands on her again, to taste his skin. It didn't even have to last that long. She just wanted to touch him. To be close to him. She could kiss him, slide her palms up his chest, under his shirt. He'd hold her tight in those arms that felt strong enough to keep her together, and she could kiss his throat, scrape her teeth over it, dig them in and bite, tear that skin with her teeth so his blood pumped over her, *reach up and dig her nails into his eyes and yank them out and—*

She caught the scream before it escaped, threw herself away from him and fell to the cold ground.

"No! No, stay away from me!" She swatted at the hand he offered, scrambled away across the pavement. "They're here, Terrible, shit they're here I feel them—"

His fist closed around her arm, yanked her up from the street and pulled her close. She shuddered, resisted the urge to bury her face in his chest and inhale him like a line of speed. Grabbing her knife was probably a better idea; his other hand already held his gun ready, his gaze shifting over the trees at the edge of the road, the banks of the river.

"How close? You got em strong, or they still off?"

"I don't know." Air forced its way into her chest; she had to remind herself to breathe. How much of what she felt was sex magic, and how much was just plain sex? The bloodlust, that wasn't her, and it was strong, but how strong? No way to tell. It was too connected to everything else, to the need pounding through her.

"What you have us do? We wait for em, dig, maybe take em out? Got it in you, without all yon herbs and shit?"

She nodded, barely trusting her voice. "Let's do it."

His arm tightened around her, then loosened again, so quickly she would have thought she imagined it if she hadn't been so sensitive. Together they moved into about the same position she'd been in at the Crematorium with Lex, almost back-to-back, waiting. Watching. The river's voice lifted over the banks, a low hum in her ears. Wind shuffled the branches of the trees, adding to the white noise, and over it all was the sound of her breath in her chest, the sound of her blood in her ears. She tensed and waited for the magic to get stronger. Waited for Vanita and her mate to get closer.

Minutes passed. Her muscles started to creak with tension. Shadows in the trees moved, formed shapes that made her breath catch but disappeared when she tried to focus on them.

Nothing. Nothing there, and the energy was fading. At first Chess thought she was imagining it, that it was nothing more than wishful thinking, but no. It was definitely fading.

Terrible—had he felt the energy as well?—relaxed when she did. "Ain't comin, aye? Figure they seen us ready?"

"I guess."

His head tilted. "Like an alarm you got. They ain't sneakin up on *you*, aye?"

"Guess not."

It wasn't until she was in the car, with the Chevelle's headlights in her rearview, that it occurred to her to wonder if that was a good thing. If they couldn't sneak up on her, but they definitely wanted her out of the way . . .

What would they try next?

Chapter Twenty-two

And the Church sealed the cemeteries, the mortuaries, and places where the dead were stored. These are places of darkness, where no one living belongs.
—*The Book of Truth*, Origins, Article 1631

Lex seemed edgy, grumpy, and tired and not in the mood to be reassuring. Not that he ever was. Their relationship—such as it was—was short on such things, and long on jokes and admittedly great sex. So why, then, did she want nothing more at that moment than to head back to his place and crawl under the blankets? To seek some sort of reassurance, some sort of . . . something, that she knew probably wasn't there? It was like digging for gold in a garbage pile. And if that little analogy didn't tell her something, she didn't know what could.

She was going to have to end it. She'd always known it would have to end eventually, but now, after everything that had happened and the decision she'd made . . . Yeah, she was going to have to end it with him. Soon.

"Too cold out this night," he said, holding the edges of his leather jacket together against the wind. On his forehead and neck the sigils she'd drawn before they entered seemed to move with the shadows crossing his face.

"You could zip it up, you know."

"Nay. Make me look like a pussy, aye?"

She rolled her eyes. "Because you look so much cooler clutching it like that. Besides, it's not like anybody can see us. Nobody's around."

This was perfectly true. From the Remington file Chess had copied the address of the old cemetery in which Vanita had been buried, the plot and row numbers stark black on the white page of her notebook. She'd used her master key to enter, opening the gate with its huge protective sigils and warning signs. Citizens were not allowed in the cemetery, in any cemeteries; she'd brought Lex along because Graveyard Twenty-three—formerly known as Oak Hill Cemetery—was in Slobag's territory, a few blocks in, and because she'd wanted company. Banishing ghosts was her job. That didn't mean she wasn't still scared.

And the atmosphere in Graveyard Twenty-three did nothing to calm her. Broken tombstones littered the frozen, churned-up earth; dead vegetation tangled over them, along the messy rows between them, stiff, bare branches like spindly arms straining to grab her as she walked past. Trying to pull her down, to suck her under the earth.

She hunched her shoulders to hide her nerves and kept walking. Vanita had been buried near the center, Plot Fifteen, Row Thirty-eight, and if Chess counted correctly they were at Row Thirty now. *If* she had to, she'd brush aside the dead bushes engulfing the row signs and check. If she had to; she didn't want to. Didn't want to touch anything, certainly did not want to be here at night.

"Much farther on?" Lex blew on his hands. "No, couple of rows."

"Mighty creepy here, Tulip. Ain't see how you do this for work."

"I usually come during the day to get the dirt. And they're usually better maintained. The Church keeps them mowed and everything."

Twenty-three was in Downside, after all, so like everything else it was neglected and broken and filthy.

Like her.

"Why come this one ain't?"

She shrugged. "Maybe the guy who's supposed to do it isn't doing it. I don't know. It's not my department, I don't really know how they handle it."

Beneath her coat and sweater her skin heated, her tattoos tingling. No surprise there. The place was packed with residual energy, bottled up by the elaborate wards inside the fence and the sigils and runes on it. No one was permitted to live within a hundred feet of a cemetery, but the Church didn't neglect its responsibility anyway. To keep ghosts contained was the reason for its existence; to keep them contained, and to provide the people under its rule and care with a road map, a moral code by which to live and thus guarantee they made it into the City themselves. Guarantee that they didn't end up in a spirit prison, guarantee they didn't end up somewhere worse.

But it wasn't . . . She stopped. It wasn't just ghost energy making her heart speed up. It was sex magic, slithering like dry leaves up her spine, over her ribcage and breasts, down into her jeans. Vanita and her Bindmate. This was definitely the place, and she was definitely going to have a hard time not getting overwhelmed.

"Lex."

"Aye?"

"I think you should wait here. There's some—some magic here, I don't think you want—"

"Aw, now, Tulip, you know I ain't feel that shit, not ever, aye? Ain't gonna get me, no worryin."

"No, I—" She hadn't meant it for his sake. She'd meant it for hers.

Sex magic to raise Vanita, sex magic to power her, hell, sex magic to get off with her. All here.

And now Chess was trapped in it, feeling it wrap its sticky, musky fingers around her, press them farther into her, and she couldn't escape. Not if she wanted to get this done.

"I just think maybe you should stay here."

"Some magic thing I ain't can help with, you saying?"

"N—Yes. Yeah, you're blocking the energy. Stay here, okay. Just keep an eye on me."

"Here" was a half-rotted stump next to a crumbling mausoleum. It had been beautiful once—the mausoleum, that is, although the tree had undoubtedly been lovely too. The angel on top of the building had not been destroyed during Haunted Week; most graveyard statues were intact, simply because people had been afraid to enter cemeteries when it happened, and the Church sealed them up as it took over.

Chess had seen images of angels before, of course. The Archives were full of them. But something about this one, its stone head bowed as if under a terrible weight of sadness, its wings half unfurled, its hands pressed together, made something in her chest ache. So peaceful. What had it felt like, to have faith like that? To believe that death brought something better, brought peace and unity with something greater than oneself?

Of course, most people thought that now. The City didn't scare everyone; Chess was the only person she knew who found it dreadful. People seemed to like knowing they would live on.

But . . . the symbols of the old religions were so beautiful, so majestic in their power and grace. Someone, somewhere, had put that angel there because they really believed in it. She reached out and touched the icy stone of the disintegrating wall. It vibed under her hand, so old. Full of power, like the earth below her—

Right. Like the earth. Time to get moving. What was she doing, standing there staring at some statue?

"You right, Tulip? Lookin kinda pale, you is. Want me to dig the dirt?"

"I'm fine." Nothing a couple more Cepts wouldn't fix, anyway, or actually . . . She had a Panda, a nice little low, just a tad heavier than Cepts. Sleep wasn't the goal here, just keeping her head straight until she got the job done. She forced herself to chew it up; the faster it entered her bloodstream the better, given how that stupid sex magic had her heart pumping doubletime. "You can't, anyway. I have to do it, there's some ritual stuff I have to do. Wait here."

Vanita's grave was about halfway down the row, right where it was supposed to be. Chess inspected the brown needles of grass covering it, found no disturbances. Good.

No angels peered out from the headstone here. It was simply a plaque set into the ground, overgrown with dry ivy. Chess walked around the edge of the plot to push it aside, checking to be sure she had the right one. She did. VANITA TAILOR.

"*Aklamadii paratium revatska,*" she whispered, and stepped onto the grave itself.

Sex energy roared up her leg, finding every empty space she had and filling it, swelling into her, over her. She had too many empty places; everything was empty; it overwhelmed her.

Sweat beaded on her forehead as she knelt. Her tattoos tingled and burned, the sigils on her forehead and throat felt like they'd been scratched into her skin with spent matches.

The frozen earth resisted the spade, made it torturously slow to dig. Torturous especially because even as the Panda hit and her muscles relaxed a bit, it wasn't enough. Her skin still crawled, her blood still raced, her body beneath her clothes was damp everywhere. At this rate she'd be here until morning, damn it.

The best depth for gathering graveyard dirt was two feet, no one knew why. She wasn't sure she'd make it.

With every meager scoop of dirt she upturned, the energy strengthened; with every scoop of dirt her muscles tingled more, it grew harder to sit still, she was more and more aware of Lex sitting fifteen feet away, naked under his clothes. It didn't matter that she was sweating in earnest now, that her hair stuck to her forehead and her mouth was dry. Whoever Vanita's Bind-mate was, he was good. Powerful.

"Shaska leptika antida."

Now for the fun part. If by "fun" you meant "awful."

With her fingers she scraped at the dirt in the hole, scooping it into the inert plastic bag she'd brought along. Hard particles of it caught under her fingernails, dug into the ridges of her palm. It was icy, frozen, but it felt good against her heated skin.

The bag bulged by her side. She lifted her hand over its gaping mouth, grabbed her knife.

"Asteru antida, with blood I power. With blood I bind."

Air filled her lungs, fuller, deeper, until she felt ready to burst. She held it, focused on it, on the life and power in her veins, trying to separate as much as possible from the crawling sex energy threatening to make her go mad.

"With blood I bind," she said again, and sliced into her left pinkie.

Her blood hit the dirt. The energy backlash knocked her over, sex and darkness so strong she bit back a scream. At least she thought she did, thought she'd managed to keep silent, until Lex's face appeared and she was too lost to fight it.

She grabbed the back of his neck and yanked his mouth down to hers.

He tried to pull away, but she tightened her grip. Now. *Nownownow* . . . Without breaking the kiss she shifted her weight, pulled herself to her knees so she could press herself against him.

His car was outside the gates, but it would take at least
five minutes to get out of the cemetery. Too far. Too
long to walk. It was freezing outside but her blood
pumped hot enough for it not to matter.

"Tulip, what's all this—"

"Take your pants off."

"The car ain't far down, we—"

"No." She slid her clean hand around to his front
despite the awkward angle, and gripped him. Hard.

His hand slid over her bottom, dipped between her
legs, caressed her thigh, and she gasped against his
mouth and pressed closer to him.

"Awful cold out, Tulip." But she knew he wasn't
going to say no. He could barely get the words out as it
was, and he was growing against her palm with every
second. Good thing, too, because the energy kept building. Damn it, this is why she avoided sex magic. She
could hardly breathe. She didn't particularly want to do
this here, in the cold, in a graveyard for fuck's sake, but
if he didn't get those fucking pants off soon, she was
going to overload.

"That's not what you said the other night." His throat
was warm; she bit it, moved her hand.

His palm slid up under her shirt, bunching her coat,
exposing a thin slice of her belly to the frigid air. She
barely noticed. His fingers slipped under her bra and
danced over her nipple, making her moan low in the
back of her throat.

"Ain't know what's got into you, I ain't." His breath
hit her neck, the tender hollow of her collarbone, sending a violent shiver through her entire body. "First two
nights back you race in an throw me around, now
this . . ."

"You complaining?"

"Fuck no."

She found the button fly of his jeans and ripped it

open, reached for her own and did the same. "Good. Come on, it's not that cold—"

"Ain't what *you* said the other night, Tulip," he murmured, but his hand left her breast to slip down into her panties, and her head fell back so his lips could press to the base of her neck. Together they tumbled onto the carpet of dead leaves, onto the ground that should have felt harder than it did. Would have felt harder, if she hadn't been so close to exploding already.

Just as she started pushing his jeans down and his fingers started moving in earnest she heard it, a low choked sound over the roaring of her blood and their gasps in the still air. She cranked her neck up, seeing everything upside down, trying to track the noise . . . and her eyes met Terrible's.

She froze like a trapped animal, her already pounding heart threatening to leap right out of her chest. What— oh fuck, how long had he been there? Why was he there, how did he know where—

Right. She knew. Knew without having to hear him say it, knew before the thought had even formed in her mind. He'd gotten a phone call, maybe, from someone who didn't give their name. A text or a note. They couldn't get close to her, she felt them, so they'd found another way to take her out.

Gotcha.

Chapter Twenty-three

Secrets are never to be recommended, not amongst families or those you love. Again, we look to the Church for advice, and the Church tells us Truth is always best.
—*Families and Truth*, a Church pamphlet by Elder Barrett

She yanked herself away from Lex, rolling to her right and lurching to her feet. Dried leaves and blades of grass clung to her coat, tangled in her hair. Her jeans gaped open. It seemed to take hours to fix them, while Terrible's gaze burned holes in the top of her head. Fuck, what was he thinking? Was he mad at—stupid fucking question. Of course he was mad. She could feel it all the way over here.

The top button finally slipped into its hole and she looked up. Right into his eyes.

Or what should have been his eyes. She saw only black holes, deep and empty. He looked bigger somehow, big enough to spill over the graves, over the fence. Big enough to fill the world.

"The other night?" he asked, his voice pitched so low she felt the words more than she heard them. "Ain't what you said the other night? *Tulip?*"

Her mouth opened. Nothing came out. For a second she saw herself as she must look, flushed and disheveled. Filthy. Sleazy.

"How long, Chess?"

"Terrible . . ." Shit, was she crying?

Lex moved through the ivory-pearl moonlight and

stopped halfway between them. "C'mon now, Terrible, ain't nothin you needing to get yourself all—"

Terrible leapt forward. His fist caught the light for a second, the image imprinting itself into her eyes like a photographic negative, then swooped down so fast it whistled. The blow caught Lex at a downward angle; she heard something snap beneath the dull thud of flesh against flesh. Lex hit the ground like a hanging victim cut from the noose.

"Since Chester, aye?" His breath rasped in the air between them, fast and faster. "*Tulip?* Since . . ."

She moved before she thought about it, before she saw him lift his foot from the ground. He'd kill Lex if he could, if she didn't stop him. Kill him here, now. She heard it in his voice like a spool of cord about to unravel.

It worked, but not the way she thought it would. The second she touched him he jumped back, almost falling in his haste to get away from her. To keep her skin from making contact with his. His hands balled into fists, his arms rotating in their sockets like machine parts that could not stop moving.

He wanted to hit her. She saw it in his eyes, in the rapid movement of his chest, and knew he was barely able to restrain himself. For the first time in months, fear of him made her throat tight and her chest cold, fear of him and what he might do to her. Hurting a man who solved all his problems with violence probably wasn't the best idea she'd ever had in her life. She could sense his control stretched to its limit in the air between them.

She didn't have to ask how he'd made the connection between "tulip" and Chester, either. Lex had left her a note one day, a drawing of a little tulip. Terrible had seen it. He hadn't asked about it, hadn't commented, but she should have known he'd keep it stored in that fucking head of his.

"Terrible," she said again, but he shook his head. He

backed away, stumbled over a headstone but righted himself.

"Terrible, please just listen. Please." Something warm hit her bare hand and she realized it was a tear. "It's not—I know how it looks, but I didn't mean to—"

"Two nights past. He say two nights past, aye? Two nights—you seen him? That night you seen him, after I—you went from—"

Shame exploded in her chest. He'd heard that. He'd heard all of it. Seen all of it, knew what she'd done. She almost wished he would hit her, just hit her and get it over with. Maybe if he hit her he'd feel better. Maybe if he hit her she would too.

"For *months*," he spat. The fury in his voice raked over her exposed skin. "Fucking months, Chess. An you *need time*."

"But it's not like how—I don't care about him, I don't even like him that much—"

"Got a fucked-up way of not likin him, aye? Why the—aw. Aw, naw, naw, you ain't . . ." His hand raised, went to his mouth, started to sneak around to the back of his neck, then stopped. "You ain't buyin as much off Bump the last months. Since Chester. Figured you was cutting back, we did, but you ain't looked cut back on the other night, aye?"

She didn't answer. Couldn't answer. Her entire body shook; she wrapped her arms around herself to try and still it but it didn't help. She knew what he was thinking. Knew what he would say next.

"You fucking him for drugs? Being some fucking spy or aught like it, fucking him for *drugs*? He made you—like a fucking—"

He lunged for Lex's still form. Chess leapt forward, caught him and wrapped her arms around his neck, his chest. It was like trying to tackle a building. Heat radiated from him; she wanted to curl herself into it, to pretend none of this had ever happened. To beg him to take her home and forget it all. She wasn't scared of that now, not when she was about to lose everything. Had been unutterably stupid to be scared at all, what was wrong with her?

Her hands fisted his jacket as she pressed her face to his chest. He didn't touch her in return, stood unmoving, his body tense. "It's not like that," she managed. "I'm not . . . it's not like I'm . . . I'm not a whore. I'm not. That's not what . . . please, please . . ."

She didn't bother to finish. She was crying too hard to finish anyway, couldn't even bring herself to complete the lie. No, she wasn't whoring herself to Lex for drugs. Technically.

But the drugs were payment for her false loyalty, weren't they? For her betrayal. And she kept seeing him, kept spending the night with him, because he gave them to her. It might not have been the only reason, but it was one of them. She thought she was going to be sick. The one thing she'd sworn she would never do, the one place she'd always said she had too much self-respect to go, and here she was. She'd done it.

And she hadn't even noticed.

More gently than she would have expected, his hands found hers and disentangled them from his jacket. He pushed her away, his gaze focused on the ground. He wouldn't even look at her. She was glad. She didn't want him to see her like this.

"Naw," he said. "Naw, Chess, you ain't a whore. A whore's honest."

He turned and left. She watched him scale the fence, his broad back pausing for a second on top of it before dropping over the other side, leaving only darkness in its place.

Two hours later the cold shower had numbed her body enough that she felt ready to emerge from it. She didn't bother to towel off, trailing water across the floor and into the living room to get her pillbox.

She had an Oozer in there. That might work. Another Panda, too, although it wasn't like the one she'd taken at the graveyard had helped that damn much. But if she combined all of them, it might be enough to kick the memories out of her head and give her some peace.

How long, Chess?

Of course, there was always the lone Valtruin. That would do the job. But it also might cheer her up too much, make her do something stupid like go look for him. That would be a mistake. He'd managed to hold himself back before—except poor Lex, whose face had swollen almost twice its size by the time she dropped him off—but now? After having a few hours to think about it, after telling Bump? Her blood ran cold.

She didn't want to find him, no. She didn't really want to sit here and wait for him to show up, either. The dingy ivory walls of her apartment seemed to breathe around her, getting closer with every exhalation. Her books stared at her, accusing her. She couldn't stay here. Didn't want to stay here.

But she had no place to go. The image of the pipe room flashed in her mind. That's what she wanted. Wanted to descend the grubby stairs into the dim, high-ceilinged room full of couches, wanted to stake one out and suck the pipe until she couldn't remember her own name anymore.

But she couldn't. Bump might find out she was there. Terrible might be there, making his rounds or looking for people who owed. And she couldn't go to Slobag's. The thought of being even close to that part of town made her want to be sick. No pipes. Not tonight. Maybe not for weeks.

Her phone rang and she stared at it like it was a knife killer on her couch. Lex? Terrible?

Merritt Hale.

"I wondered if you wanted to get a drink? I know it's late, but my shift just ended, so—"

"Yes," she said, hoping he didn't hear the urgency in her voice. That was what she needed—to go out. To be out of her apartment, out of her head, surrounded by people. "Where? I'll come meet you."

He told her. A bar in Northside, about twenty minutes away but far enough out of Downside that she didn't have to worry. Perfect.

She dried her hair, threw some clean clothes on, and slapped on some makeup to try and hide the redness in her eyes, the splotchiness of her skin.

All that could be covered up. What was inside . . .

A whore's honest.

She grabbed her keys and slammed the door behind her, wishing her pills would kick in faster, wishing she could slam the door on the entire night and start over. Slam the door on her entire life and start over.

As it was . . . she'd just have to see how drunk she could get. She had a feeling it wouldn't be enough.

It was one of those middle-class chain bars, the kind with decorations carefully calculated to look "rustic" on the walls and an antiqued Book of Truth displayed under glass by the front to give the impression the place had been there since BT. It hadn't. She practically smelled construction dust when she walked in the door.

What was Merritt doing in a place like this? Beneath the newness it smelled of investment banking and snobbery. She hated it. Felt totally out of place. And the music blaring from the speaker didn't help, a steady collection of easy-listening bullshit that made her hair stand on end.

But the leather on the bar stools wasn't ripped and rough, and they actually offered more than just one brand of beer, which was a nice change from most places in Downside. She ordered a beer anyway, with a shot of vodka on the side, and told the bartender to keep them coming. She was going to drown out that fucking voice if it was the last thing she ever did.

Maybe it would be. Wasn't that a nice thought?

"You okay, Chess?" Merritt sipped his own drink—it looked like a whiskey and ginger—and furrowed his brow.

"I'm great." She sucked back her third shot and upended the glass on the bar. "Why?"

"Just wondering."

"I'm great," she said again. *A whore's honest.* Damn it! Not drunk enough yet.

They sat in silence for a minute. It might have been awkward if she'd been paying the slightest bit of attention.

"So how's the case going? I mean, do you think you're ready to banish the ghosts?"

Where was the fucking bartender? "Chess?"

"What? Oh. The case. Yeah. I'm still working on it." She glanced at him, sitting next to her with his fingers rubbing condensation off his glass. Right. She'd have to pretend she was still working the case, maybe even ask some questions, not just try and sink herself in an ocean of booze. "Have you seen anything there yet? Any ghosts? What do *you* think is happening?"

"Haven't seen anything, no. But the Pyles are starting to lose it, I think. I sure hope you find an answer soon, you know? Because if they decide to move, I need to let my landlord know I'm going."

"So you'd stay with them?"

"Yeah, absolutely. I get to go with them on their trips back to Hollywood, too, which is really cool. I'd like to live there."

She nodded. Getting the fuck out of Triumph City was an idea she could totally get behind at that moment. "How often is Oliver Fletcher around? What do you think of him?"

His eyes narrowed. "Why?"

"Hey, you brought it up."

"I didn't bring up Fletcher."

"No, but he's their friend, right? You don't want to tell me, don't tell me. I just figured as long as you wanted to talk about it, maybe you could help me out and tell me a little about him."

"He's a good person, Chess. They're all good people. They're not, like, scammers or thieves or anything. I know you have a job to do, but really, you should just go do your banishing or whatever and let them have some peace."

"Did you want to have a drink or lecture me?"

"Maybe both."

She rolled her eyes. "I'm good at my job, Merritt. I know what I'm doing."

"I'm sure you do, I just wish this could all get settled. It's making Arden sick, you know. And that kid has enough problems."

Arden . . . She'd seen Arden, hadn't she? The memory was fuzzy, ruined by the more overwhelming memory of pain and desperation, but she was almost sure of it. Arden throwing up, Arden's pale, guilty face. Arden with a hickey or something on her neck.

"Like what?"

He shifted on his seat, his brow furrowing. She grabbed her cigarettes and offered him one, hoping it would loosen him up.

He took it. "She didn't want to move here, for one thing. Bitches about it all the time. And I think she has a hard time dealing with her mother. I mean, you've seen Kym. It can't be easy to be kind of a chubby kid and have that in front of you all the time. It's just—Damn, look at the size of that guy!"

"What? Where?" Chess spun on her seat so fast she almost lost her balance. How had he found her, had he followed her or something?

Merritt looked at her strangely. "Over there, by the bathroom."

"What—oh." Not Terrible. Nowhere near as big, either. Terrible filled a room, the mere fact of his presence squeezing everyone else into smaller packages. The guy Merritt pointed out was just a guy.

Finally the bartender set another shot in front of her. She threw it back and motioned for another.

"Hey, you want to get out of here?"

"What?" Her throat burned, but finally it seemed to be working. She listened for Terrible's voice in her head and didn't hear it.

Of course, she also couldn't feel her extremities. But life was full of tradeoffs, right?

"Do you want to get out of here? My place isn't far. We might be able to talk better there. I want to—talk about the case. About the Pyles, I mean."

Hmm. Something he didn't want to discuss in public? Could be interesting, not that it mattered. At least it could be interesting if she was able to stay awake long enough. Hot on the heels of being drunk enough not to think of Terrible was being too drunk to think of anything at all, and appealing as that was, she wasn't at home where she could just pass out.

"Yeah. Just hang on. I want to go to the bathroom first."

The bathroom was bigger and nicer than she'd expected, but she didn't pay much attention. One wall was entirely made of mirrors, and the last thing she wanted to do was look at herself.

Instead she ducked into a stall and cut herself a thick

line on top of the toilet paper dispenser. That would be enough, she figured. Enough to keep her blessedly zoned out but still able to take notes if necessary.

Her face was already numb, but she felt the speed hit anyway. Good. Better than good. Her sluggish heart sped in her chest and the world started to sparkle, just a bit, just enough to drive her misery from her head.

For the moment, anyway.

His place was bigger than she'd expected, nicer, with a clean but bare kitchen and furniture that matched. Working for the Pyles must pay more than she'd thought.

He settled her on the couch and brought her a beer while she waited for the room to stop spinning. Fuck, she was drunk. Monumentally drunk. So drunk that her skin felt rubbery all over and her limbs heavy.

"I think it's Kym," he said, startling her.

"Kym Pyle? Faking a haunting?"

"If anyone's faking it—and I'm not convinced some-one is—it's her." He sipped his own beer. "She hates it here. She wants to go back to Hollywood. Bitches about it all the time."

"But she was injured." The words came out before she thought of them. Shit! Kym *had* been injured. She hadn't faked those scratches on her back. And Oliver Fletcher hadn't even been in town when that happened.

So who had been in the Pyle bedroom that night? Who had slashed at that pale skin in the dark?

Pale skin in the dark . . . like her own belly, as she'd fumbled with her buttons in the cemetery under Terrible's furious gaze.

Fuck. Why couldn't she get away from him?

"Lots of people injure themselves, Chessie. You know that."

Huh, he had no idea. She nodded. "So you think Kym set the whole thing up to get Roger to move?"

"It makes sense, doesn't it?"

"I guess so."

Merritt's hand found her thigh. So that was it. He might want to talk about the case, but he wasn't really interested in her thoughts. He'd brought her here for a different reason. Well, whatever.

She set her beer down and reached for him. Let him kiss her. Let his hands roam over her half-numb body. Her own movements were clumsy, indifferent, but he didn't seem to notice or care.

Then again, his technique didn't seem to have improved since he was seventeen. Or perhaps she'd just gotten used to more skilled hands on her body, more skilled lips against hers. His tongue probed and poked at her mouth, his head unmoving. Her chest ached.

He unbuttoned her jeans and yanked them off. His hand dug between her legs as though he was trying to reshape her, jabbing into her. It hurt, what of it she could actually feel, but she didn't care enough to stop him.

His own jeans were next. He dragged her over him before she was anywhere near ready, braced her hip with one hand while he fiddled around with a condom with the other. His lips traveled across her chest, over her neck, too softly for it to feel like anything. Where his hand had been rough and clumsy the rest of him was too slow, passionless, so she was bored and frustrated long before anything started to happen; and when it did start to happen, her boredom was not relieved.

She started moving automatically, her head a million miles away, dissociating from her body. A trick she'd learned over the years, one she hadn't had to use in a long time. It came back to her as naturally and easily as her magic did.

Oliver Fletcher claimed to be solely responsible for the

Pyle haunting, but there was no way he could have injured Kym. So who?

Merritt gasped and whispered something beneath her. She ignored him. It didn't matter anyway. She was essentially done with the Pyles. She'd start putting together the paperwork to report a real haunting in the morning—or whenever she managed to wake up tomorrow—and by the end of the week it would all be over with.

She sped up her movements, bored, wanting this to end, wanting to take her punishment and be done with it.

He tried to kiss her and she moved away, buried her face in his neck instead. He rubbed her back as if he was soothing a toddler. It annoyed her but she said nothing. He wanted her, at least. Didn't look at her with anger and disappointment. Didn't see her as a chance to put one over on his enemy. He may not have been any good at it, but at least he wanted her. She was worth something to him, even if it was nothing more than a few minutes of cheap thrills.

Her head swam. Too much booze, too many pills, too much movement. Blackness crept in around the edges of her vision. She fought it with what little energy she had left. She didn't want to sleep here. Wanted to go home. There was no way in hell she was okay to drive, but she had more speed, she could snort herself sober and make it if she was careful. Merritt's place smelled funny and small, and she wanted to leave.

His fingers curled around her hips, dug into them, and the pain drew her attention back to him as he finished. She barely managed to keep herself from sighing with relief. He was done. He was done, and she could go home, and maybe—maybe—she could figure out a way to fix things.

Or she could just pass out, which seemed more likely.

Either way, she couldn't help being a little grateful to him. He'd gotten her out of the house, gotten her drunk, given her a few minutes of peace.

It wasn't much, but sometimes it was enough.

Chapter Twenty-four

> Magic is neither benevolent nor malevolent; it is not good
> or evil. The motives of the practitioner are important, but
> that does not mean magic is safe if your heart is pure.
> Quite the opposite can be True . . .
> —*The Book of Truth*, Rules, Article 980

An hour and a half later she left her car in the lot by
her building and trudged toward the steps. Her thighs
ached. Everything ached. Her mouth felt fuzzy, her teeth
sharp and rough in her mouth. The half-gallon of water
she'd forced herself to drink sloshed around in her stomach; she had to fight to keep it down. At least it was still
dark. She didn't think she could face the sun.

Terrible waited on the steps. Chess stopped short, her
mouth open like an unhinged door.

His gaze took her in head to foot, her messy hair and
smeared makeup, her rumpled clothing and unsteady
footsteps. She felt his judgment and wanted to hide,
wanted to curl up into a ball on the pavement and wail
until he went away.

"Hi," she managed.

His hands dug into his pockets; he glanced around. A
few buildings down, a small crowd of teenagers passed
a kesh between themselves on the steps, their laughter
blasphemous in the silence.

"Terrible, please . . . just let me explain."

He shook his head. "You say anything to him?"

"What? I—"

"About . . . where I take you, on the other day. You tell Slobag about it?"

Katie. She shook her head so fast she felt her brain jostle in her skull. "No! No. I promise. I didn't—it wasn't like that, I didn't—"

"You tell him and I kill you," he said, his voice so rough it was almost unrecognizable. "Dig me? Ain't lyin."

"I didn't. I would never—"

"Ain't interested in what you never. Just had to say it. Just so you got the knowledge."

The sob burbled up out of her mouth before she could stop it, rising through the heavy, thick oppression of her high. "Please, can't we talk? Can't I just explain?"

He stared at her for a minute, like he'd never seen her before. Maybe he hadn't.

The pain in her chest was fucking unbearable. She thought she'd need to cut out her heart to make it stop hurting.

He turned to leave, and she thought of something. Something she did need to know. "Terrible. Did you—did you tell Bump?"

He stopped, but didn't turn around. Shook his head.

Hot, fat tears rolled down her face, down her neck, washing away the last vestiges of Merritt's unschooled mouth.

"Thanks," she said.

"Ain't done it for you." He glanced back at her, every bump and line on his craggy profile sharp in the street-light's glow. "Think I want Bump knowing how I fucked up? Tellin him you was worth trust? Him knowing how I—" He shook his head. "Ain't done it for you."

"I wasn't lying." She just wanted to keep him talking. Like if she could talk to him enough, she could convince him to trust her again, to be her friend again. To want her again. She wasn't scared anymore. Being with him wouldn't be scary. Being without him, being alone again . . . That made her booze-diluted blood run cold. "On the bridge. I wasn't lying."

"Fuck, Chess. I ain't as smart as you, but I know when I'm bein used, aye?"

"Terrible, you're not stu—"

"Naw. We get your help, if we find us this ghost house. Figure you can work that one, seeing as how it's helpin yon boyfriend too. Othersides that . . . ain't want to see you. You and me, it's done, dig? Nothing there."

He was gone before she could think of a reply.

She woke up with the sheets tangled around her like a snake, sweaty and shivering on her rumpled bed, feeling like she'd been fighting instead of sleeping. Her head ached. Her muscles ached. She felt dirty and tired and old, so old, like she'd been alive a hundred years instead of twenty-four. Like everything good that would ever happen to her had already happened, and all she had to look forward to now was death.

Without getting up she chopped out a line on the scarred tabletop next to the bed and sucked it up, wishing she could numb her brain as effectively as her nostrils and sinuses. As it was she would settle for the false calm of her pills, four little white friends to soothe her.

She stared at the water stains swooping across her dingy ceiling until her stomach settled and fog descended on her brain. Then she got up. Showered, washing the smell of Merritt's skin off her body. Dressed. Pretended it was a normal day, just like any other. Pretended she hadn't been busted, hadn't fucked over people she cared about, hadn't undone everything that might have been good for her along with her buttons the night before with Lex.

She had work to do. A haunting to lie about, a case to close.

Elder Griffin had given it to her personally. And she was about to let him down the way she'd let down everyone else who trusted her. Okay, the one other person who'd trusted her.

She stared at herself in the mirror, grateful for the false sparkle speed lent her eyes. She still had a job to do. Even if it was a lie, she still had that. Time to get it over with. Fill out the forms and turn them in so she could go back home and hide in bed for the rest of the day. Or the rest of the week.

Or the rest of her life.

Her car screamed at her as she floored it to Church, redlining the battered engine, rattling the windows. It had started snowing again, dusting the roads with white, making them slippery and treacherous. She didn't slow down. Maybe she'd wreck, just lose control and blast into a wall, and it would be over.

No such luck. Instead she made it to Church in record time, fishtailing into the lot and dumping the car at an angle across two spaces.

Despite the cold, sweat trickled down her back, thin acrid speed sweat, by the time she got inside. The wind made her face feel like a peeled tomato, as if it would bleed if she touched it.

Chess stopped in the wide hall, her heart pounding, as the reality of her situation overcame her. She was about to lie to the Church. Not the way she lied every day, pretending she was just like everyone else. A real lie. A lie that would cost them money. She wanted to scream, to rage around the airy space and throw benches and punch holes in the walls.

She was sick of this. Sick of being nothing more than a piece of someone else's puzzle, a stick of furniture to move wherever it suited someone else's needs. She was here, and she was stronger than this, harder than this. They could make her hate herself, make her doubt herself, but they couldn't take away her deepest instinct. Not just the need to survive, but the need to survive long enough and strong enough to tell them to go fuck themselves. She'd play Fletcher's game, but she would never let this happen again.

So she opened the door of Elder Griffin's office and marched inside to report the haunting with her head high.

Only to find him slumped at his desk, his hair sticking up and circles under his eyes that had nothing to do with Church ceremony.

"Cesaria," he said. "How fare thee?"

What was going on with him? He looked worse every time she saw him, as though something was eating him from the inside.

"Very well, sir," she managed finally.

"I assume you're here about Oliver Fletcher," he said. "I saw you requested his records. I . . . I cannot apologize enough. We thought since his involvement was peripheral . . ."

He sighed, shook his head. "I didn't agree with keeping it from you. I told them you would figure it out, that you were better than they thought. How they could have so little trust in you, when we have seen the fact and truth of your skill before, is a matter of extreme disappointment to me. But you . . . you have not disappointed me. Sit down, then."

Oliver Fletcher? Why on earth was he talking about Oliver Fletcher?

She plunked herself down in the cushy ivory chair opposite him, grateful for the chance to sit. Her legs didn't want to support her. They wanted to jiggle and shake, to work off the nervous energy that welled in her the minute she stopped moving, but they did not feel up to keeping her body off the floor at that moment.

"I did request his records, yes," she said. Her brain

whirred and clicked in her head while she tried to look as if she knew what he was talking about.

The Elder nodded. "'Twas not my decision."

"Whose decision was it?"

"I knew you would ask to see them," he continued, as if she hadn't spoken. Damn. She'd been hoping for more of a clue.

A pen flashed between his fingers, catching the soft bluish glow from the desk lamp and flashing it back at her with every nervous twirl he gave it. "I told them . . . And then you showed me that sigil. Did not trust me enough to tell me where you'd seen it, but I deserved that, did I not? For keeping it from you."

She opened her mouth, snapped it shut again. He couldn't mean the sigil she'd found on the dead hookers, could he? What the hell was going on?

"Which of the Pyles had that carved into their skin, Cesaria? Or was it Oliver himself? He was so proud of that one. Such an advanced design for a third-year student. We were all impressed. Jealous, if the truth be told, those of us in the upper classes. He had the kind of style we all wanted, effortless, so powerful for one his age. One day we might have made Elders, if we worked hard, devoted ourselves. But he had Grand Elder written all over him. We all knew it. All he had to do was reach out his hand and grasp it."

What in the world could Oliver Fletcher, film producer, have to do with some murdered prostitutes in Downside? Why hadn't anyone mentioned his Church education to her? It wasn't in the file she'd been given. He'd invented that sigil?

She was so busy trying to fit together pieces that didn't seem to be part of the same puzzle, she missed what he said next. *Fuck! Pay more attention, moron.*

". . . but Fletcher seemed to be the brains behind them, really. Landrum may have had the money, but Fletcher?

His talent dwarfed us all. So when he designed the sigil, modified it, we were all amazed. So simple, so elegant! Not just to hold the soul, to protect it in the body and prolong the life, but to enable it to be controlled while being held. A way to prevent hauntings should a psychopomp be delayed. A way to ensure no accidents occurred. A regular Church sigil made extraordinary by the addition of a new sigil, one made from rarely used runes, designed in such a way that they had a double meaning. None of us had ever thought of such a thing, but it sprang from Fletcher's mind fully formed."

A way to hold the soul in the body. To keep the body alive and the soul there until the psychopomp came for it.

She knew this. Had known it, especially after Hat Trick showed her the althea. But she saw it in her head now, the herbs burning in whatever was handy. The sigil branded onto delicate pale skin. The cloth over the mouth and nose, the peaceful death, the soul transferred to the owl—the greatest psychopomp—and taken wherever it needed to go.

And then released, fully formed. Released and controlled, released and bound with electrically charged wire, to service whoever paid the fee.

Oliver Fletcher was behind that?

But why the faked haunting, then? Someone with that much power and skill would surely be able to raise a few real ghosts. Could even control them, keep the Pyles from being seriously injured.

What the fuck was he up to?

Elder Griffin seemed to take her furrowed brow, her silence, for anger and disapproval.

"It was the accident," he said. "That is why they refused to reveal it. When Kemp . . . But I should explain. Cesaria, I hardly know how to begin. Suffice it to say that Fletcher and his friends—the three of them were inseparable—Horatio Kemp and Thaddeus Landrum were some of the most skilled students we've ever seen. And they ruled over us, walking as if always under a bright light.

"Until the accident. Until the day they ascended the tower on a dare and Kemp fell off. His body was broken, destroyed. His soul would have left . . . but Fletcher got there first. He carved the rune into Kemp's skin. It saved his life, Cesaria. Saved his life but made it not worth living. I cannot imagine how it would feel, being open to spiritual control, spiritual possession . . ."

He trailed off, his blue eyes staring at the wall above her head, while her skin crawled and her brain whirred like a blender.

Having your soul easily susceptible to magical control . . . She couldn't even imagine it. Worse, she imagined, than her addictions, than the feeling of throwing herself constantly on the rocky shore of her body's needs. At least her addictions brought her comfort and peace. Gave her a reason to get up in the morning, gave her something she could wrap around her like a blanket and hold close when she needed it. The Church may have given her purpose, but her pills made that purpose bearable, kept her head from breaking open under the weight of her life.

But as much as her needs controlled her, she had some free will. She had some choice. A puppet with fewer strings.

"It made him controllable," she whispered.

Elder Griffin nodded. "We were never certain if 'twas because of his gift or simply because of the sigil, but he became . . . addled. Spirits could enter his body, make him do things—not just powerful spirits, but any of them. He was that vulnerable. He took to wandering the streets at night, doing we knew not what, but a few times he returned with blood on his clothing, around his mouth, and could not recall from where it had come.

"Fletcher was beside himself with grief. In seeking to save his friend he had condemned him. He studied the sigil, devoted himself to it, bringing himself near unto death to find a way to undo what he'd done. But there was no way. And that was how we discovered that it was not just his modification that made the bearer vulnerable. The sigil, the basic one we all learned, did that in itself. Not to the same extent, oh, no. Nowhere near as much. But it expanded the possibility of possession, of spectral control. We removed it from our books, wiped it from our minds, lasered it from our bodies. Kemp was put in an institution. Fletcher and Landrum left the school. And we did not speak of it, not ever again."

"That's why Fletcher's Church education wasn't mentioned?"

He nodded. "We thought, to dredge it up . . . Tell me, Cesaria, do you believe Oliver is behind the haunting at the Pyle house? Is it indeed a visitation?"

She supposed it was possible. The actual ghosts could have been summoned, then filmed, their images forever replaying in the rooms of the Pyle home. Safer that way. Something a man as clever as Oliver Fletcher—a man who'd practically hung a sign over his head reading I DID IT when speaking to her—would have come up with easily, pulling it from his crafty brain like a dangerous sigil.

But that didn't feel right, either. And it definitely didn't match up with the eyeballs in her car or with Vanita.

She studied Elder Griffin for a minute. She'd trusted him, hadn't she? Not entirely, but as much as she was able. And he'd lied to her. He could have told her that day in the library. Could have passed her a note. He knew this was her livelihood, knew she needed the money this case would bring.

Knew what she'd be dealing with when he assigned the case to her.

She was so fucking sick of them all. Elder Griffin putting her in danger on a case through his reticence. Terrible taking her to Bump's to be blackmailed into putting herself in danger. Lex unfastening his jeans with one hand while he gave her pills with the other.

No, that wasn't entirely fair. Terrible had apologized. Lex had never made any bones about who he was and what he wanted from her. In his mind, she had no doubt, the connection between giving her drugs and giving her orgasms was tenuous at best. Frankly, she doubted that his jaunty ego would allow him to see it differently.

But he had used her. Kept her as a spy, her body made more valuable to him by the triumphant sense of putting one over on his enemies.

"Do *you* think Oliver would do such a thing?" she replied, stalling. To give him a straight answer at that moment would be committing herself to a course of action, and she wasn't ready for that. Not until she'd had a chance to talk to Fletcher, to investigate him further.

He sighed. "The Oliver Fletcher I knew wouldn't have." His blue eyes grew overcast with memory. "I didn't know him well, only one night . . . We were both at the café, a rainy night. I was—I am—a few years older than he. I believe he was . . . impressed by me, by the attention I paid him. We . . ." He shook his head, shutting away the memory while Chess's eyebrows rose.

Elders didn't have sex. Or at least, she never imagined they did, never mind that some of them were married. But Elder Griffin hadn't been an Elder then, only a student, and Oliver Fletcher was a handsome man.

A handsome man whose head she'd seen buried between Kym Pyle's legs. But who was she to judge? Absolutely nobody.

The discussion felt over. Chess stood up. "Thank you, Elder Griffin. For telling me. It'll help."

His smile refused to develop, was only an attempt. "You're welcome, dear. Fare well, Cesaria. Facts are Truth."

"Facts are Truth," she agreed, and let herself out.

But the facts and truth had never seemed more muddled.

Chapter Twenty-five

For it is Truth that things are not always as they appear. It is also Truth that things are as the Church tells you they are.

—*The Book of Truth*, Veraxis, Article 5

She turned down the radio when the Pyle house came into view, not wanting to blare the Replacements into the security guard's face. She'd thought the music would make her feel better, drown out her thoughts, but it hadn't. All it had done was insulate them, force them to grow louder so she could hear them over "Raised in the City."

Fletcher knew she'd been investigating the hooker deaths. Of course he knew; he'd been sending his pals around to harass her, to leave little presents for her, right?

But they hadn't killed her. Now she knew why. When Fletcher discovered she was vulnerable to blackmail, he'd told them to step back; if she died, the Church would assign someone else to the Pyle case, and a Debunker who could be controlled was far preferable to one who couldn't.

What was she supposed to do? She couldn't let Fletcher go on killing people. But neither did she look forward to seeing the expression on Elder Griffin's face when he realized she'd failed him. She'd do almost anything to prevent that, even after the way he'd let her down.

Just like Bump and Terrible, Slobag and Lex would do

anything to stop the murders. When she told them who was behind them . . .

Fuck, was she really considering this? Murder? Having Fletcher killed to—No, she couldn't. Could not.

But he was a murderer. The penalty for murder was death. If she didn't tell her drug-dealing pimp friends, if they didn't take care of Fletcher, the Church would, no matter if he sold her out or not.

That wouldn't be murder, though. It would be execution, legal and sanctioned.

She couldn't tell the Church what he'd been doing, because he'd expose her. She couldn't tell Bump what he'd been doing, because Bump would have Fletcher killed.

For the tenth time she picked up her phone, started to call Terrible. He would know what to do. Maybe he'd come along and get Fletcher to give her back the pictures and the negatives, help her . . .

Yeah, right. Terrible would be eager to help her, wouldn't he, after what he'd seen, what he'd heard? Now he knew she'd been betraying him for months, knew she'd listened to his speech—words she still couldn't believe he'd been brave enough to say, shit, she couldn't imagine what that must have cost him—and run over to Lex's place for sex? And then told him the next day that she wanted to be with him, but not just yet?

She couldn't blame him for feeling used, for thinking she'd been stringing him along in hopes of getting more information to give Lex. She hadn't exactly given him the benefit of the doubt when it came to Bump wanting her to do magic for him, had she?

What a mess.

The guard waved her in and she steered her car along that peculiar driveway, conscious of being watched. Faces hid behind curtains in the house, behind the one-way glass of the security booth. The entire building seemed coiled, ready to spring at her. She shivered, patted herself where she'd tucked one of Edsel's little bags into her bra with six pills inside, backups in addition to the three she'd taken ten minutes down the road. The search she'd been given last time had been thorough, but no actual fondling had occurred, so she figured that was safe enough.

If it wasn't . . . Hell, she was already being blackmailed. And Merritt had mentioned having to work today. Of course, there was every chance *he* would try to fondle her, but she'd deal with that if and when it occurred.

Merritt was on; he sat in front of the monitors in the security room, eating noodles from a little plastic bowl, with his legs up on the table. He smiled when she walked in, set his feet and bowl down so he could get up and greet her.

"Hey, Chessie. Wasn't sure you were coming today, after how much you drank last night."

He leaned in to kiss her, and Chess, unsure of what to do, let him. His lips on hers made her queasy, made her want to escape. What had she done? He was part of her case, a possible witness. Hell, for all she knew he could be involved.

She'd done so well for so long. Keeping her life compartmentalized, not letting anything get too out of control, not forgetting to take notes, to put things exactly where they belonged so she could find them no matter how fucked up she was. It was exhausting, but she'd done it.

And in the blink of an eye, in five minutes' time in a cemetery, everything had spun so far away from her she didn't know if she'd ever get it all back in place.

"Hi. Where is everyone?"

"Who? The other security staff? Or the Pyles?"

"Any of them."

He rested his forearm on the door by her head, while his other hand found her waist. "The Pyles have gone out for a little while. The staff . . . they're around, but I could lock the door."

Ugh. She slid away from him, almost spearing herself on the muzzle of one of the rifles on the rack. "I'm working today."

"You don't have to work all the time, right?"

"Today I do." One more reason to get this damn case over with. She could ignore Merritt's phone calls; she couldn't ignore him when he was reaching out to stroke her cheek. And she did not want to baldly break it off with him—not that there was anything to break off, but he seemed to think the night before had meant something—when she still might need his help.

"You're no fun." For fuck's sake, was he actually pouting? Yeah, *that* was sexy.

"Look, Merritt, I'm sorry." She forced the apology out; the words were razor blades scraping her tongue. She did not have time to coddle some infantile guy, not when even now Oliver Fletcher could be plotting another murder, very possibly her own.

"Maybe you can stick around another hour or so? I get off at six. We can go out to dinner, there's a nice place not far from—"

"Why don't we wait and see? I've got a pretty full day and, yeah, I'm still a little off after last night, so I might just go to bed early tonight."

"Why don't I come to your place? I'll bring food."

She crossed her arms over her chest, leaned away. Not too far away, not far enough to make him angry, but far enough that she didn't have to feel him breathe on her. "We'll see, okay? Maybe tomorrow or something. Hey, is Oliver Fletcher here?"

"Fletcher? Yeah, he's in the house somewhere. I think he might be in Mr. Pyle's office, you want me to check?"

"Check?"

"I can call over to the house and find out."

"Oh. Oh, sure." Her heart started beating again. For a second she'd thought there were monitors inside the house as well as outside, and that she and Terrible might have been recorded the other night.

Not that it mattered, but old habits died hard. So to speak.

Through the windows the landscape looked dull, tinged an odd pale sepia from the one-way glass. Unreal, like a painting, but too mundane a subject for art. Just a yard, with a few spindly trees here and there. Just a house, gleaming with fresh paint against the gunmetal sky.

Just her career and life hanging on the whim of the man inside.

"Yeah, he's in Mr. Pyle's office," Merritt said. "Said to tell you he's been waiting for you. Why's that?"

"Oh, he's waiting? I'd better not keep him then."

"Yeah, but how did he—"

She mushed her lips against his to shut him up, let him turn it into a deeper kiss than she wanted. Of course any kiss with him was deeper than she wanted, but whatever. Damn that Fletcher. He must have known Merritt would ask why he was waiting, knew it would make things more difficult for her. The arrogance of him, thinking he had her under control. Thinking she wouldn't know what he was doing, what he was up to. Thinking she would overlook murder to save her job.

She pulled away from Merritt, plastered on a smile. Mustn't keep the murderer waiting.

Fletcher sat behind Roger Pyle's desk, leaning back in the leather chair as though he expected a spotlight to go on over his head at any moment. Which maybe he did.

"Miss Putnam. How nice to see you."

She plopped into one of the delicate chintz chairs opposite the desk and eyed his ever-present whiskey glass, wishing she'd downed another pill before she came in. "Cut the shit, Fletcher. I figured it out."

His tidy eyebrows drew in. "Figured it out? I'm not sure what you mean."

"I think you do. I found out about your Church training. About the sigil. I know what it means, what it does."

Watching his face at that moment was like watching a street vendor preparing to sell old goods as new; the careful attempt to hide emotion, the fear that the truth might be found out before the money changed hands. Only Fletcher wasn't trying to put one over on her. He was genuinely dumbfounded. "How did you know about that?"

"You know how far back Church records go. And even if they didn't, Elder Griffin would have told me. Remember him?"

"Elder—Thad Griffin? An Elder?"

"I see you remember him, then. He certainly remembers you."

"What did he tell you?"

"He told me about you. Your friends Kemp and Landrum. Your sigil. Nice use of that, by the way. If he hadn't remembered you, I probably wouldn't have figured it out."

"What? I don't—"

"I'd like to know why, though." It was her turn to lean back in her chair, to let a self-satisfied smirk alter her features. The only thing she couldn't control was her anger, both at him and at herself.

It came back to her, sitting there, looking at his pale face. Those girls, killed, their bodies discarded on the street. He hadn't even taken them to the Crematorium where they could join the stack of shrouded corpses like toy logs against the walls. His buddy with the inked-up face had been able to break into the place once, so why not all the time? Once a body was in the room, covered in anonymous white, no one would know if it was legitimate or not, not in a place as big as Triumph City.

So why leave them, then? Why broadcast what he was doing?

"Haven't we already covered that? Why discuss it again?"

"I don't mean the haunting. I mean the girls. The hookers."

She'd run away. She'd find another job, another place to live. Nobody said she had to work for the Church, right? She could . . . she could find something, somewhere. And it wouldn't matter. Because no matter how low she sank, no matter what she became, she wouldn't be someone who let a man get away with murdering innocent women. At least she could feel proud of that.

"Hookers? Do I look like the kind of man—"

"Yeah, you do. You look like the kind of man who scares his friend to death in order to make him do what you want him to do. You look like the kind of man who assaults your friend's wife to bolster your fake haunting. You look like the kind of man who terrifies a teenaged girl. And yes, you look like the kind of man who murders hookers and leaves them lying on the street."

"What?"

"You heard me. I thought we were being honest here, right? I know what you've been doing. And I know why. And I have to admit, it confuses the fuck out of me."

"I don't understand." He did look befuddled. Chess didn't buy that for a second. She'd already jumped off the cliff; the only thing now was to see how far she fell.

"Why fake a haunting here when you could have just summoned some real ghosts? Why set up your little spirit bordello when you're trying to get Roger Pyle to leave? Why—"

"Miss Putnam, I have no idea what you're talking about. Spirit bordello? Dead hookers? I understand drug addicts get some crazy ideas in their heads, but this is—"

"Are you honestly telling me you didn't kill those girls?" She reached for her bag, found her camera in its pocket. He wanted to play photographic evidence? Fine. She could play that game, too.

"I haven't killed anyone. Really, I think perhaps we ought to rethink this whole thing. You're obviously far more unstable than I thought."

"I'm stable enough to bust your ass," she snapped, and showed him the camera screen.

It was a medium-range shot, wide enough to capture Daisy's blank, eyeless face and the sigil burned onto her delicate skin, narrow enough so the sigil's lines were still clear.

A gruesome image, yes. Chess was pretty sure she'd seen it in her dreams the night before, would keep seeing it in her dreams for years, along with other oldies but goodies: Randy Duncan, murdered by the Dreamthief; Brain, who'd trusted her and gotten killed for it. And now Terrible's disbelieving expression in the cemetery when he realized she'd been lying to him for months.

But the horror on Oliver Fletcher's face made a shiver run up her spine. He looked like he'd never seen the girl before. Worse, he looked like he was seeing something he'd never expected to see, like a man who'd just watched his family slaughtered in front of him.

"Dear God," he said, and the words were so hollow Chess hardly noticed the blasphemy. Fletcher didn't apologize for it. It wasn't unusual for people who'd grown up BT to slip up now and then and use an old expression; it carried a minor fine. "When . . . What is this?"

"It's a dead girl. A murdered girl." She didn't really know what to say. Nobody was that good an actor. His utter misery, his terror, filled the air and heated her tattoos, set the hair on the back of her neck on end like it was trying to escape. "That is your sigil, right? The one you designed? The one you used on your friend Kemp?"

He nodded. His gaze didn't leave the camera. "Horatio . . . oh, poor Horatio."

Unwanted sympathy trickled into her heart. She squeezed it ruthlessly away. He hadn't had any sympathy for her a few days ago, when he was making her metaphorically blow him to keep her job. "Poor because of what you did to him. He's in an institution, right?"

Now he looked up. His pupils were so dilated she could barely see the slate color of his irises. "No. He's not in an institution anymore. Based on this . . . based on this, Miss Putnam, I'd say he's in Triumph City murdering women."

Chapter Twenty-six

"How is that possible?"

He shrugged. His color was returning; he looked
almost normal. Whereas she felt like someone had
dipped her in wax and left her to cool.

"Horatio . . . I assume Thad told you about what
happened? About the sigil, and the tower?"

She nodded.

"He . . . developed an obsession with ghosts. Well,
with a lot of things. It's not important now. But we
discovered, eventually . . . he was killing people. Women.
He was . . . doing things to their bodies. Cannibalism.
Necro—need I elaborate?"

"Please don't."

"It wasn't him, Miss Putnam. You have to understand
that. It wasn't him, wasn't my friend Horatio. It was
whatever took him over at any given moment. He was
like a beacon, with his power and that fucking sigil . . .
I didn't know that would happen. Maybe I should have.
In my darkest moments I believe I should have. I was so
arrogant. So sure my power was strong enough to
protect me, to protect all of us."

An idea tingled in the back of her mind, but she
ignored it. At least for now. Best to see how things went.

"So what happened with Kemp? He got caught and institutionalized?"

Fletcher nodded. "Landrum and I set up a corporation together to pay his bills. Well, his additional bills—the Church paid for his actual keep. You didn't know that, I see."

She blinked. No point trying to hide it, he'd already seen her surprise. "No, I didn't."

"They did. The deaths were kept secret—they hadn't really made the news anyway—and the Church committed him. Landrum and I gave money to his family, we paid for his clothes and whatever else he needed. There were times when it seemed they'd be able to let him out, that they'd managed to fix the problem. His body—Last time I saw him you could barely recognize him for all the protective markings."

Protective markings . . . The man's face swam into her vision again, as if he were right in front of her. That was what covered his skin. She hadn't seen them well enough. "Why didn't they work?"

"Because," he said, and his sigh dragged the air down between them, "because he didn't want them to. By that point he'd formed a partnership with a spirit. Probably he's still working with her—at least I assume."

"Her?" She knew. She already knew. But she wanted to hear him say it, just to be sure.

"Yes. He worked with a female spirit. He told me about her once, when I visited him. I should have reported it, I know, but we never thought they'd actually let him out."

Chess reached for his half-empty glass and tossed the contents down her throat, grimacing at the bitter heat of it. Probably not the best idea when only speed and Cepts were holding her hangover at bay, but she had a feeling she would need it. Need the whole fucking bottle, for that matter.

"What was her name?"

"The spirit's? I don't recall exactly. Virginia? Va-something, anyway, he—"

"Vanita."

He nodded. "Yes, that was it. How did you know?"

"She was a madam."

"In—Oh, you're kidding. Really? And now they've—Well, fuck me. Makes sense, doesn't it?"

"Yeah. It makes sense. And you know what else makes sense? That you help me find them."

"Me? Why in the world would I do that?"

"Because this is your fault, that's why. Look, I get that you feel bad for what happened to your friend. Really. And I get that it was an accident. But this is your fault. You shouldn't have done what you did, you shouldn't have carved that sigil—"

"I should have just let him *die*?" He stood up and leaned over the desk, his eyes blazing. "I should have just let my friend die, is that what you're saying? Rather than do everything I could to save him? What the hell kind of person are you, to even suggest such a thing?"

"Do you think he's better off now?"

"I think he's *alive* now!"

"Yeah, alive and possessed, alive and staining his soul darker every minute. It's not even life, Fletcher, it's—suspended animation, it's slavery. You did that."

He came out from behind the desk, his body somehow larger in his casual button-down and unstructured jacket. California Cool becomes Murderous Rage Chic, if the look in his eyes was any indication. She took a step back, reached for the knife Merritt hadn't managed to find when he groped her in the security office. If he tried to touch her, she'd—

He did touch her, but she didn't finish reaching for her weapon, because he wasn't attacking her. Wasn't threatening her.

He was crying.

He leaned over her, rested his head on her shoulder, and clung to her, his tears soaking into her shirt.

What the fuck was she supposed to do with this? Hug him and say something comforting? He was blackmailing her and now she was supposed to take care of him like some kind of fucking nanny or something? She didn't know how to do that. What did people do to comfort each other?

She settled for patting him vaguely on the back and wishing she was anywhere but there. Although he did smell good.

Thankfully it didn't last long. "I'm sorry," he said into her neck. "I—This is quite a shock for me, you understand. I never meant to . . . If Horatio is killing people, killing women, it *is* my fault, isn't it? Because of the sigil, because of what I did to him?"

If he'd been her friend, she might have given him the lie. But he wasn't her friend. "Yeah."

"I never wanted this." He sighed. His grip on her loosened, but he didn't move away. "I may be an asshole—I would say don't bother disagreeing with me, but you won't, will you?—but I'm not a murderer. I don't want to be responsible for people dying."

"Then help me stop it." She wished he would get off her. His forehead was digging into her collarbone.

"I don't see how I can help."

His biceps felt bigger than they looked, hard and lean under that expensive jacket. She grabbed them and pushed, forcing him off her. "You know where he is, don't you? Where to find him? If we find him, we can find all of them. The girls, I mean. We can set them free."

"I can't."

"Yes, you can. Elder Griffin said you were talented."

"I don't do that sort of thing. Not anymore."

"Is that why you didn't summon real ghosts here? You could have, it would have been much simpler, you know."

"I—Yes. That's why."

"Get over it. I need your help. You know him, you're his friend. Maybe we can do this without anybody getting hurt."

"Get away from him."

Arden Pyle stood in the doorway of the office, her pale hair drawn back into a sloppy ponytail and her black shirt baggier than ever.

All these things Chess barely noticed. She was too busy focusing on the gun.

Fletcher turned from Chess, taking his hands from her waist and raising them slowly like flags at dawn. "Arden . . . Arden, honey, put the gun down."

"You promised. You said you'd take care of us."

"And I will, but I can't if you shoot me, can I?"

"I'm not going to shoot *you*," the girl said.

It was the sort of statement that deserved a big reaction, but all Chess could summon was a kind of weary anger. At this point, what the fuck did she care? Let the girl shoot her.

Although she couldn't help being pissed the end was going to finally come because of Oliver Fletcher. Because he apparently—Oh, yuck.

"Shit, Fletcher," she murmured. "She's fourteen years old, you asshole."

"Yes, and—Oh, no. She's—I'm not that twisted, Miss Putnam. Please."

"Stop talking!" The gun shivered in Arden's fist. Chess dragged her gaze away from it, down to see the way the girl's baggy shirt draped over her stomach. Her slightly protruding stomach . . .

The girl was pregnant. Fourteen and pregnant. Chess could certainly relate. No wonder Arden had a gun in her hand, no wonder . . .

No wonder she'd attacked her mother that night in the bedroom. Fletcher hadn't been in town that night, but someone had been in the Pyle bedroom. Someone who felt dead inside. Someone desperate.

"Arden." She took a careful step forward. "You don't have to do this."

The girl's blue eyes barely shifted. "What the fuck do you know?"

"I know shooting me isn't a good idea. Do you want to have that baby in prison? And get executed a month later?"

"Who cares."

Oh, for fuck's sake. She was not good at this. In fact, there were very few things in the world she was less good at than this.

What the hell was the matter with these people? How did they not see that of all the people on the planet, she was probably the least qualified to help them with their emotional problems? It was like asking a dog to do algebra.

Oliver stepped in and saved her from trying to explain to a child why she should be concerned with something Chess didn't care much about herself. "I care. That's why we're doing this, right? To get you away, so you can come stay with me? So I can help you? Don't mess this up now, not when we're so close."

Chess saw her cue. "Nobody's getting in trouble. I'm going to take care of everything at the Church. I can even recommend to your parents and to the Church you be allowed to live with Mr. Fletcher, okay? So don't—"

"Arden?"

Chess practically threw her hands in the air. Kym Pyle was joining the party, her light blue wool coat still thrown over her shoulders in the doorway of the office.

Chess wasn't sure what happened first. All she knew was Arden started to turn, her mouth opening. The gun moved sideways with her, its staring black eye finally focusing away from Chess.

Oliver leapt forward at the same time Kym did. Arden saw him, tried to yank the gun back.

It went off. Wood chips flew in slow motion from the doorframe.

Kym screamed. So did Arden. Another gunshot roared through the room, and another. Oliver stumbled. Arden fell.

Chess stood alone by the desk with her ears ringing. She couldn't hear them screaming but saw their faces, mouths open, faces pale save the blood that seemed to have speckled everything in the room.

It took her a minute to see where it had come from. Arden's foot—the damned kid had shot herself in her own foot. Fletcher's shoulder. Kym Pyle's hand—the bullet had gone through it to hit the wood, or ricocheted off and hit it, she didn't know. All she knew was that it was time to leave.

With Oliver Fletcher. Gunshot wound or no gunshot wound, she needed him to find Kemp for her, and if she waited until after he'd left the hospital, it would be too late. Her job gave her some influence there, but not enough to make sure Fletcher wasn't discharged and out of the District before she knew it. And what was she supposed to do then, go to his house all the way across the continent?

No, he would take off at the first opportunity and wash his hands of the whole thing, no matter how many tears he shed into her sweater or how responsible he might feel. They had to act now.

Merritt and three other guards came running, weapons drawn. Chess barely heard their voices over Kym and Arden's shrieks and the ringing in her ears from the shots. The room felt too small, crowded with bodies and stinking of gunpowder and blood and anguish, while

Chess stood and stared. It was almost interesting to see so much pain and for once not be part of it herself.

Something else she could do while attention was turned away, though. With her left hand she yanked the clasp of her bag, held it open, while she gathered Oliver's photos with her right and shoved them in. The camera's memory chip . . . He'd said something about the chip. Was it there, too?

No. She shuffled through the rest of the stuff on the desk as long as she dared but didn't see it. Oliver must keep it somewhere else. She'd have to see if she could get it from him later; she could always break into the Pyle house again with her Hand and look through his stuff.

Right now, though . . . It was dark outside, and they had to do what they could now. Had Oliver not been shot it could have waited, but no way was she chancing him getting away from her before they ended this thing.

She pushed her way past one of the guards and grabbed Fletcher's unwounded arm. "Come on."

"What?"

"Come with me. We need to find Kemp."

"You must be joking. I'm not going anywhere but the hospital."

"Yes, you are. More women could die, deaths you'd be responsible for."

"No way. I'm going—"

Chess leaned down, stared him right in the eye so he could see her determination. So he could see she really just didn't give a fuck at this point. "You're coming with me, or I'm calling the press. You want to turn me in? You go ahead. But you're just as interested in keeping this whole affair under wraps as I am, and you know it. So let's go."

She knew she had him when he blinked.

Chapter Twenty-seven

It's always good to keep some basic first-aid treatments in the home. You never know when you might need them, and helping others is the best and surest way to feel good about ourselves.

—*Mrs. Increase's Advice for Ladies*, by Mrs. Increase

Having Oliver Fletcher in her apartment wasn't her idea of fun, but they had to go somewhere, and she had a decent enough first-aid kit in her little bathroom.

No point trying to call Terrible. He wouldn't answer when he saw it was her. So she texted instead, a terse message to say she knew where the ghost house was and he should call her or come to her place.

Five minutes later she got a one-word response: "Fine."

Okay, so was he coming over or what? Shit, and she probably looked like she'd just crawled out of bed.

Fletcher was sitting on her toilet, cleaning the ragged flesh wound on his shoulder. Chess ignored him while she splashed cold water on her face and slapped on a little makeup. She felt like an idiot and it wouldn't matter one bit, but she did it anyway.

"Don't bother helping me, I can handle it," Fletcher snapped.

She glanced at him on her way out the door. "Good."

Should she call Lex? Probably. Well, definitely. But the thought of having him come over when Terrible was there . . . She'd call him when they knew where they were going.

A couple of Nips and a couple of Cepts, to calm her down and wake her up, and she was ready. Sort of.

"Miss Putnam? Seriously, will you help me here?"

Fletcher was still sitting on the toilet, bloody tissues scattered over the tile floor like flower petals. He was going to clean those up.

"I can't reach very well. And I'm in a lot of pain."

She sighed. "Turn around."

Dried blood surrounded the deep graze; the bullet had caught him at an odd angle. Chess grabbed a can of antibiotic spray and used it, ignoring his hiss of pain.

"I know you have painkillers, Miss Putnam. I think the least you can do is offer me some. I *have* just been shot, you know, and I'm still here to help you."

"Don't you have access to your own?" She dabbed his skin dry and grabbed a gauze pad.

"I don't know what you mean."

"Haven't you been drugging Roger Pyle?"

It was just a guess, but she didn't expect the answer she got.

"That wasn't me. That was Kym."

"Kym?"

He nodded. "You don't think I'm the only one who didn't want the Pyles living here, do you? She was hoping he'd—Hell, I don't really know what she thought. That he'd feel jumpy and sick and it would make him vulnerable, I suppose. As I said, she's not really the most intelligent woman in the world."

"Yes, you did say, didn't you."

"Excuse me?"

That was it. That was what bothered her before. "In fact, you went out of your way to point the finger at yourself, Fletcher. Right from the beginning. Why is that?"

"I don't know what you—"

"It was Arden, wasn't it. She started the fake haunting.

She's the one who scratched Kym in the bedroom that night, she set up, what, some kind of projector or something—like the one you screened your movie on, right? The night I was there?"

She didn't wait for him to reply. "And when she told you what she'd done, when you found out Roger and Kym were going to get the Church involved, you rushed to help her, because you knew that whatever she'd done might fool her parents, but it wouldn't fool the Church. You knew what a real ghost feels like. You knew the kind of investigating that's done for a haunting, and you knew there was no way she'd get away with it once the Church stepped in. Awfully altruistic of you, helping your friend's daughter like that. Just out of the kindness of your heart?"

He sighed. "Not really. She's mine, you see."

"She's—What?"

"Arden is my daughter, not Roger's. He's sterile. Kym found out, she came to me . . . I helped her. Arden doesn't know—Well, neither does Roger, for that matter. But when she needed help, she came to me, too. She'd already started this stupid haunting thing, rigged up one of Roger's old projectors. He's got a few of them lying around. I had no choice, really, but to try and help her."

"Yes, you did. They would have been lenient with her, and you know it. You were with the Church long enough to know that. She would have done a year in a Church program for underage offenders, at the most. And you wouldn't have been—oh. Right."

She caught his eye, knew he followed her thoughts. He nodded. "The DNA match. When they arrested her they would have put the family's DNA on file, and they would have found out she isn't Roger's. It would have killed him to know that. Would have destroyed Arden."

"And you, when the press got wind of it."

"That too, yes."

Shit. Arden all along. Some investigator she was, shit. "Who's the father of her baby?"

"I don't know. Some guy back in L.A. That's why she wanted to leave so bad. Not just to get away from her parents, but to get back to *him*. What can I say, she's fourteen years old. Can I have one of those pills now, please?"

She rolled her eyes, but let him follow her back into the living room and gave him a couple of Cepts and some water.

And sat, while the Nips sped her heart rate and set her toes tapping on the threadbare carpet.

She didn't have to wait long, at least. She'd only managed to play one Queers song in her head before the heavy knock made her leap to her feet.

The distance between the couch and the door had never seemed so far. What should she say? Should she even bother to say anything? Would he talk to her?

The sinking feeling in her stomach told her the answer even before she opened the door and found him there, hands in pockets, his harsh face set in stony, dead lines and his gaze focused so far past her she felt like a speck of dirt on a window screen.

"Hi." She stepped back, inviting him in. "We, um, that's Oliver Fletcher, he knows where we're going, so if you want to come in . . ."

Terrible shrugged and entered, subtly twisting his torso so as not to touch her when he walked past.

He hadn't looked at her at all.

Well, what the fuck did she expect, that he'd give her a big hug and tell her she was forgiven? They never even hugged normally. This probably wasn't the time he'd pick to start.

Fletcher stood up, wavering a little on his feet. Great. Just what she needed—a tipsy amateur witch. How much scotch had the man had back at the house? Had he eaten anything at all? His wound couldn't have caused that much blood loss.

"I'm Oliver," he said. "Have you ever done any security work? I'm always looking for—"

"Just gimme the knowledge so we get this done." Fletcher looked blankly at Chess for a minute, then said, "You want to know where Kemp is?"

"Kemp the one?"

"Yeah." She glanced at Terrible, waited for him to look at her. He didn't. "He's working with a murdered hooker named Vanita. Her spirit, I mean. Remember how Tyson had a host? I don't think it's the same exact arrangement, but . . . yeah, he's working with her."

Terrible's chin lifted and lowered, his only indication of surprise.

"Oliver knows Kemp, he studied at the Church too so he can help . . ."

"You coming then?" Terrible eyed Oliver up and down. "You come handle all, dig, you got the juice."

She bit her lip. "No, we're both going, he's going to help me." *Look at me, talk to me, something.*

He didn't. Just stood for a minute, absorbing what she'd told him, then shrugged. "Where?"

Chess looked at Fletcher, still standing with his feet planted a little too widely apart like he was having trouble balancing. What a lightweight. "Fletcher? Where?"

"What? Oh. You're assuming he's set up in one of our buildings? There's four in this part of town. One on . . . Second, I think, by the cemetery—What?"

Chess stiffened but just managed not to cringe. "Where are the others?"

"Let's see. Eightieth, that's a warehouse. I think the houses are on Mercer and Wharf. I understand the one on Mercer burned down or something recently, though."

"Wharf? By the docks?"

Fletcher nodded. "I assume so. Landrum handles the

purchasing. I only remember the addresses because I looked them up the other day, I was filling out some tithing tax forms."

Terrible looked at her for the first time, but his eyes still focused above her head. Like she wasn't really there, like she was invisible. "You got what all you need?"

"I'll get it. Can you, um, will you come help me? Some stuff is up on the shelf in my closet."

It wasn't fair, she knew. But if he wouldn't talk to her any other way—

"Fletcher here ain't little, aye? Figure he willin to give you the help."

Fletcher looked uncertainly from Chess to Terrible, and back again. "Yeah, sure. I'll help you."

Her bedroom was a total mess; she couldn't remember the last time she'd cleaned it. Just what she wanted, Fletcher seeing her dirty clothes strewn all over the floor, her unmade bed.

He ignored all of it, though, to give him credit, and handed her various boxes and bags from the top shelf as obediently as a child. "So what's the deal with the big guy, anyway?"

"What do you mean?" She'd need ricantha and althea, since they were already being used. Some hellebore would be good, too, and melidia and ajenjible. In fact . . . She grabbed the box where she stored her herbs and ingredients and upended it over her bag. Her psycho-pomp, the skull kept in its silk wrapping. Candles. Extra black chalk for sigils of protection. She had the dirt from Vanita's grave. She had her knife, but it might be a good idea to take a spare just in case, and she'd need to grab her portable first-aid kit, too.

What she did not need was to discuss the ins and outs of her relationship with Terrible—such as it was—with her blackmailer.

"Looked like you guys were friends, looks like now

you're not. Does it have something to do with the Asian guy?"

"How do—" Oh, right. The pictures. "None of your business."

"Just trying to make conversation." Shit, was he high? Yes, of course he was. High and chatty. This just kept getting better.

"Well, don't." She finished packing and zipped the bag. "Let's go."

It was so cold outside she expected ice to form on her eyelashes, but she left her coat in Terrible's car just the same. Not that it mattered. Nothing could warm her up after the frigid silence of that ride, with Assuck—a band he knew she disliked—playing so loud she couldn't hear herself think. Not that she really wanted to hear her thoughts at the moment.

Terrible watched her while she shouldered her bag, grabbed her stang from the floor where she'd set it. Fletcher stayed in the car, apparently waiting until the last minute before he left the warm interior.

She didn't blame him. This close to the docks the constant breeze stank of sewage and gasoline and the sour brine tinge of stagnant seawater. Nothing like the actual ocean, which she'd seen once . . . with Terrible.

She closed the door on that memory before it had a chance to open and looked around at the quiet street. Odd, that. She'd never been in this area before— Downsiders tended to stay in their own neighborhoods—but it certainly looked like the type of place that would be busy. Dive bars studded the rows of buildings, neon beer signs flickering in their darkened windows, but no crowds stood outside them. No kids wandered up and down the alleys looking for scraps of food, a place to fight or a place to fuck. Even the music drifting along the street seemed subdued.

And more than that . . . they were in the right place. She felt it, her tattoos tingling, ghost energy creeping along her skin like tiny secret fingers. Powerful. Powerful enough to send a shiver through her body that had nothing to do with the crystal-cold air.

"Is anyone else coming?"

Terrible shrugged. "Ain't you gave your boyfriend a ring up?"

Shit. She'd left herself wide open for that one, hadn't she? "He's not my boyfriend."

"Trick, then."

Ouch. "I haven't called him."

"Aye? Figured you'd give him the knowledge soon as you got any. Ain't that how it work?"

"No, it's—it doesn't 'work' any way. Terrible, if you'd just let me explain, if you'd just listen to me—"

"Maybe I *need time.*"

"Yeah?" Damn him. She needed to focus, needed to concentrate, and he wasn't helping. "Well, take it somewhere else. We have work to do, don't we?"

That was good. She thought it even sounded like she actually meant it, like her throat didn't ache and her eyes didn't sting and her belly didn't feel shriveled and dead.

And of course, he was right. She had been giving Lex information, of a sort. Nothing important. Nothing she didn't think it would help everyone for him to have. But how they'd met . . . how she'd agreed to sabotage Chester Airport . . . In the end she hadn't had a choice. But she doubted Terrible would see it that way.

She'd tell him, though. She'd tell him the whole thing if he would let her, and hope it made a difference.

"Aye. An let's get it done. Ain't exactly wanting to chatter with you, dig?"

"That makes two of us."

He stared at her for a minute, his face inscrutable, then

knocked on the window of the car, telling Fletcher to
come out.

That he did, weaving slightly. Chess frowned.

"Are you going to be okay, Fletcher? Maybe you
should stay in the car."

"Nonsense. Horatio is my friend. I should be there."

"Yeah, but—" Movement to her right caught her eye.

A man, skinny and dirty as a stray dog, made his way
out of an alley toward them. Normal enough, really; the
odds of standing on a Downside street and not being
approached by a panhandler or mugger or worse were
pretty slim, and they shrank the longer one remained a
stationary target.

She wasn't worried about muggers or worse, not with
Terrible there. The way things were between them, he
wouldn't save her because he wanted to, but they were
here to do a job and she knew he took that seriously. Hell,
her very presence here was proof of that, wasn't it, since
he looked at her as though he'd be happy to see her dead?

But something about their visitor bothered her,
whether it was the odd fixed stare or the way he seemed
unaware of what his body was doing. He ignored them,
ignored the Chevelle tilted up on the curb. Like they
weren't even there.

"Hey!" Terrible said, but the man didn't even blink.
His half-closed eyes stayed focused straight ahead, on a
point somewhere beyond their vision, something that
softened his face and made his mouth hang open despite
the cold.

He looked like a man about to fall into bed with a
woman.

Terrible and Oliver both must have thought the same
thing. The three of them looked at one another, realization dawning on their faces.

"The prostitutes," Chess said. "The tri—the men.
They're killing them."

"What a way to go." Oliver's smile faded when Chess and Terrible glared at him. He shrugged. "Well, it is, right? When you're my age you tend to think of such—"

Chess grabbed her phone. "We need more people. If there's going to be men there, even if it's only a few, and they're that fixated and probably armed, they could be dangerous."

"Aw, right. Ain't wanna make a move without Lex here, aye? Let him get his eyes in?"

None of the responses she thought of were sufficient, so she just glared at him and dialed. "I suggest you call Bump and let him know."

"Ain't give a fuck what you suggest."

Lex answered, his usually smooth, rapid speech muffled and slow. "What's up, Tulip?"

She explained the situation as fast as she could, glancing over her shoulder. Terrible was on his own phone, his black steel gaze following her as she paced. Stripping her.

"Aye, okay," Lex said. "Guessing I'll get over there, me. Hang on, aye?"

"Yeah."

She stuck the phone back in her bag, pulled out her black chalk. "Come here, both of you. We're going to need some protection."

Chapter Twenty-eight

Oliver, his face almost hidden by magic symbols, smoked a cigarette against the side of the Chevelle. He really was good; he'd done his own arms and showed Chess a few tricks she hadn't thought of. What a shame things at the Church had turned out so badly for him, she thought, and had to stop herself from smiling. Earlier she'd been convinced Fletcher was a murderous pedophilic blackmailer; turned out he was just a blackmailer. Everybody had their flaws.

At least he was there. She could almost forgive him for forcing her to add yet another lie to the stack she'd already told the Church, just because he was there and willing to help.

Too bad not everyone was so quick to forgive.

Terrible sat on a stack of crates along the curb, his long legs stretched before him, his arms folded over his chest. She needed to mark him, to scrawl protective runes and sigils across his skin to keep him safe, but the thought of actually doing it . . .

Well, that was a lie. She didn't have to. She could have asked Oliver to do it. His memory was good enough, even if he was high. He certainly had the power to put behind them.

She *wanted* to. That was it, the fact and truth of it. She wanted to mark him, because she wanted to touch him again. Because somewhere in the back of her mind she thought if she could touch him, if she could get close to him and look him in the eyes, she could explain. She could have him back. Even if he didn't want her anymore, maybe he would be her friend again. She missed him. It had only been a day and she missed him.

"Pitiful," she muttered, but the chalk still shook a little in her fingers as she planted herself between his legs. "Look up."

He glanced up, then away.

"Terrible. Tilt your head back. Come on."

He didn't move for a minute, such a long minute she started wondering if she might have to call Oliver after all. Then he gave a half-nod, as though he'd decided something, and angled his head back, eyes to the sky.

Not looking at her.

Chess bit her lip and leaned forward.

He flinched when the fingertips of her left hand came to rest on his neck, just below the jawline. Like it hurt to have her touch him.

Which maybe it did; she wasn't feeling too good herself.

And here she was again, with the scents of his pomade and smoke and soap filling her nose, feeling the vein throb beneath his skin, hearing his breath catch and seeing his eyes darken when he realized she'd heard it.

She scrawled a basic protective sigil on his forehead, her focus shifting at that moment from him to what she was doing, putting as much power as she could behind it. Next came a few runes, one to lend him strength, one to dispel fear—not that he needed either of them, but it made her feel better to do it.

Her left hand slid around to the back of his neck, her fingers tangling in his hair to shift his head. His sideburn brushed against her wrist; could he feel her pulse pounding?

She stepped closer to him, closer than she'd intended, until her knees wedged between his thighs and his chin hovered right around her breasts. If he looked down, or even straight ahead . . .

She swallowed. Down the side of his brow to his cheeks she moved the chalk, adding anything she could think of to protect him, to dispel as much of the power they were about to face as she could.

She cradled his face in her hand, wished stupidly she could keep doing this. With his breath heating the tender skin of her inner arm, his mouth silent, his angry eyes focused elsewhere, she could almost pretend nothing had changed. With his body so close to hers, so close his broad back sheltered her from the wind, she could almost imagine they weren't here on the street, they were somewhere else, somewhere warm and dark where sheets whispered against their bare skin.

Her entire body tingled. Power, some of it; she was summoning as much as she could, letting it flow from her to him through her hands and the chalk. But the rest . . . The rest was simply her, wanting him, arousal sizzling up her spine and along every nerve ending, flooding her lungs and stomach and all points lower.

"Other side." Was that her voice? It sounded dry and hoarse, both too quiet and too loud on the dead street.

He obeyed, his face lifting, and their eyes met. The chalk fell unnoticed from her hand.

He still wanted her. She saw it in the burning depths of his gaze. Felt it in his body almost touching hers, in his slightly too heavy breath and rapid pulse. He was angry, oh yeah, that was there, too. But he still wanted her, and he knew she wanted him. Knew she wasn't just trying to protect him, she was trying to seduce him.

For that one long moment they just stared at each

other. Her fingers were numb and shaking; all the same they moved, holding his jaw, her head tilting down of its own volition, trying to get closer to his. Her hair fell forward to hide them in their own private world. Just a few more inches and they would be kissing, just another couple of tiny inches . . .

Something brushed the inside of her leg; his hand. Oh shit, his hand, and it slid up past her knee, farther, until her mouth opened and she gasped, a soft cry she couldn't stop, and his hand wedged against her, hard, sending shocks through her entire body. She knew he could feel how hot she was through her jeans and she was falling into his eyes, falling so her lips tingled with the heat from his because only a hairsbreadth separated them.

He tensed, swallowed. "Chess. Got an ask for you."

"Yeah?" It took her two tries to get the word out.

"I got some pills on me, dig. Figure I hand em over, I come back your place on the later and fuck you? Ain't sure how much you charge, but—"

She slapped him. Hard enough to make her hand scream, hard enough to make her entire right arm go heavy and sore. He had a jaw like a chunk of concrete, the asshole, the total fucking—

Oh shit. He jerked up from his perch on the crates, eyes flashing, face flushed around the pale mark of her hand. His arm rose, drew back.

Chess started to duck, knowing she would be too late. She'd hit Terrible. Nobody hit Terrible and lived to—

The blow didn't fall. Instead the crates lifted, shot through the air toward the seedy bar to her right. Wood flew when they splintered against the pockmarked bricks, the crash just slightly louder than Terrible's growl.

"Fuck!" Oliver—shit, she'd forgotten he was even there—ducked, staring at them both like they'd just turned on him with guns. "What the hell is the matter with you two?"

"Ask her," Terrible said. His thick finger pointed at her like an accusation. Which it was. "Goan, ask her."

"Fuck you, Terrible. Fuck you."

"Fuck *you*, you lying little bitch."

"Asshole."

"Feels shitty, somebody play you the lead on, aye?" His eyes narrowed. "Make you feel stupid?"

He opened his mouth to say more, but Oliver spoke again, straightening his torn, bloody shirt as if he was about to give a speech at a black-tie dinner.

"Can I remind you both what we're facing here? And that I have friends and family in the hospital? This isn't exactly the way I'd choose to spend my evening, even without you at each other's throats."

"Fuck you, too," she said, but without vehemence. She couldn't manage it; as her anger faded, misery poured in to replace it, and the tingle in her eyes and ache in her throat told her she was about to start crying. She'd thought . . . She'd been so stupid, but she'd thought for a minute there . . .

She turned away from them both, not wanting them to see her. Wishing she could disappear, wishing they didn't have to be there so she could visit the pipes and obscure the pain in a cloud of thick honey-sweet smoke. Wishing she could swallow every pill in her box and make this all go away.

Seeing Lex's car pull up didn't make her feel any better. Seeing his face made it worse.

"What the hell—" she started, then remembered. Terrible had knocked him out, hadn't he?

Looked like he'd done more than that. The entire left side of Lex's face was bruised and swollen, his eye nothing more than a suggestion beneath his brow.

"Hey, Tulip," he said, and Chess cringed. The last

thing she wanted was to hear his pet name for her. Or to have Terrible hear it.

Lex saw her look, glanced at Terrible, who stood with his arms folded and his face turned away. "Broke my jaw, he did. All full of wires."

At least that's what she thought he said, since the words were slurred and dim and his jaw didn't move. No wonder he'd sounded so subdued on the phone.

"Shit." She reached for him, but pulled back. "Sorry."

He shrugged. "Ain't like I never thought he might, aye? Just bad luck."

"Not really."

"What?"

"It wasn't really bad luck. We were—well, I was—set up. I'm pretty sure, anyway. By the guy doing this, running this house. He left a message for Terrible, I don't know how."

"Ain't gonna ask neither, aye?"

"No."

Several men had gotten out of the car with Lex; they lined up behind him, their handsome bronze faces immobile, their eyes pegged on Terrible.

A few more men arrived, men Terrible had called, apparently. They eyed Lex's men like tomcats protecting their territory.

Figuring they ought to get moving, Chess quickly marked them all up the way she had Oliver and Terrible. Lex worried her a bit; being unable to touch the left side of his face made it harder to squeeze everything in, but she went down his neck to his chest instead while Terrible's gaze burned holes in the back of her head.

He hated her. Sure, he still wanted her; he was a man, and men didn't just stop wanting to fuck somebody they wanted to fuck. At least not in her experience. But their friendship, the feeling she'd had of being on the verge of something more than that, something she'd never thought was possible for her . . . gone. Gone for good. She'd be lucky if he bothered to help keep her safe tonight, and if he did, it would only be because of what he owed Bump and the dead hookers and missing men.

And Lex? She had no idea what to do about him. She knew what she *should* do, which would be to end it. But what difference would that make now? Wasn't like Terrible would forgive her as soon as she did.

And she *liked* Lex. Maybe they weren't compatible in every way, and maybe they both *knew* there was no real future for them—Hell, no maybe about it; they both knew. But he made her laugh and he turned her on, and he was decent company who didn't ask questions or try to have deep, meaningful conversations with her. In a lot of ways he was the perfect pseudo-boyfriend.

But if she didn't give him up, there would be no chance of righting things with Terrible, not ever.

So did she stick with the acceptable sure thing, or give it up for the possibility—just the outside chance—of something . . . else?

She sighed. No point in thinking about possibilities, really. She'd ruined everything. She'd known what the consequences might be and had done it anyway. Self-destruction was one thing, but she was turning into a one-woman wrecking ball.

She grabbed a couple more pills, washed them down, and surveyed her ragtag troops. "Okay," she said. "Let's go."

The house would have been easy to find even without the line of men patiently curling from the front door around to the side. Easy to find, because Chess felt its call, faint like a soft erotic whisper against her skin, growing stronger and blacker with every step.

A house like any other, one of many lining the broken streets. Blistered, peeled paint that might once have been white or gray still clung in splotches like a festering rash to the walls; a few rickety bars remained of what had once been a porch railing. It should have looked dead, another empty corpse to be disposed of.

Chess knew better, though, and for that reason she saw the house through its greenish-black magic haze like a predator, watching and waiting, its hooded eyes half-closed in feigned somnolence.

No lights came from any windows; several doors down the charred remnants of a similar house still smoked. Burned down, she guessed, when its inhabitants left their heater running or their candles lit in their haste to sample Vanita and Kemp's treacherous wares. Good thing they'd set up this far on the edges. Had they used a building in the middle of Downside, half the population would have been sucked into their trap.

She turned and checked their men. She and Oliver had worked together to invent an anti-arousal sigil that seemed to be working—certainly none of them were joining the line, although a few of them looked a little dazed—but she had no idea how long the effect would last. Once they got inside . . .

She shook her head. Time for that later. First they had to get those men out of there. They were too much of a distraction, too much of a threat, to leave on the scene.

"Okay." She set her bag down and folded her arms. At least for the moment she could forget everything else and focus on this, on her work. "I want to cast a circle around the entire building, so I don't have to do it individually when I'm inside. Oliver, do you think the sigil will break the spell they're under?"

"I'm not sure. I suppose we could try."

"Okay. Do that, and let's see. I'd rather not draw too much attention. They probably already know we're here, but still."

Oliver took the piece of black chalk she offered him, wandered over to the line of men. Chess held her breath.

The man Oliver picked ignored him until the sigil on his arm was complete. Oliver glanced back at her as if to ask what she thought, but before she opened her mouth the man shook his head, glanced around him as though he had no idea what he was doing, and stepped out of the line.

Excellent. "Okay. Oliver, get them all marked. I'm going to start the cast, okay?"

"How bout I go along, me?" Lex had his knife out and ready; beneath his shirt she saw the bulge of a gun.

Terrible snorted, turned away. Chess ignored him. "Yeah, okay. But no talking. I need to focus."

She set up her stang facing east on the pavement, fixing the iron base and placing the candles on either side.

Something was wrong here. She didn't know what, but something was definitely not right, and it was more than the fear creeping up her spine or the misery over what had happened with Terrible—shit, did she really think he was going to just forgive her, after what she'd done to him?—or simple sadness over the deaths of so many people.

No. Something was wrong, and she didn't know what it was. But she had a distinct feeling she was about to find out.

The bag of salt she'd brought, big and heavy as it was, still wouldn't be big enough to cast as thick a line as she would like all the way around the building, and the intermittent breeze wouldn't help. She'd have to drop it thin and hope she could power it enough to hold.

Another psychopomp would have been nice, too. Oh well. Nothing could ever be easy—

The shouts behind her hit her ears at the same time her other senses rang angry alarms through her entire body. Too easy. It *was* too easy, wasn't it, to assume that one sigil was enough? To assume that whatever enchantment hung in the air around this place would be dispelled with one stupid sigil?

Yeah, it totally was. Her upper body twisted, and she saw the fight begin.

Chapter Twenty-nine

To use a wild psychopomp is a serious crime; to cause the death of a psychopomp is a grave one, and puts both the life and soul of the murderer in jeopardy.
— *Psychopomps: The Key to Church Ritual and Mystery*, by Elder Brisson

Men. The men standing in line, going from docile lust zombies to angry mob in the space of a second. Men in robes like the one worn by Kemp at the Crematorium poured from the doorway of the building. Not so many, maybe five or six in all, but their power hit her like a fist in the stomach. They were all hosting, all of them, given superior strength by the spirits sharing their bodies. And fuck, when they died, those spirits would rise—

She couldn't help. Couldn't do anything but cast the circle as fast as she could in order to get to work. Without the circle, the psychopomp could escape, could run loose in the city and take whatever souls it wanted. Could do murder—murder for which she'd be liable when they caught the psychopomp and discovered it was hers.

"*Septikosh, septikosh,*" she murmured, wanting to stay quiet and keep herself out of their focus as long as possible. Beside her Lex pulled out his gun, caught her eye; she nodded and kept moving, letting the salt trickle from her fingers.

They rounded the corner, Chess keeping her mind focused as much as she could on her circle, on the words of power spilling from her tight throat. Energy stood her hair on end. The power in this place, oh shit . . .

Every step she took felt like a step toward her own death. Her vision darkened around the edges; it wasn't just the strength of the magic here, it was the sheer filthy malevolence of it. Protections were all over the damn place, no surprise there—that was what set the men out front off, wasn't it, they probably had an alarm set for unfamiliar magic—and she wasn't sure how easily they'd break, if they would break at all.

She'd have to deal with the protections or wards when they came up. If she made it that far. She still didn't know who was inside watching, where Kemp and Vanita were.

Around the next corner, to the back of the building. No lights here, and the moon hid somewhere in the broken concrete skyline. Shadows threatened and beckoned along the patchy bricks on the ground, turning the mundane shapes into looming hulks waiting to leap out at her.

Her hair brushed against her face, and she paused just long enough to yank a ponytail holder out of her pocket and use it. The movement shifted her gaze to the right . . . to the high-wheeled Dumpster against the wall . . . to the arm hanging out of it.

She'd seen a Dumpster like this by the Crematorium, hadn't she? Of course. Those missing bodies had to go somewhere, right? And she'd wondered herself why the killers hadn't taken the prostitutes there. They were too busy dumping the men, it appeared. Their Dumpster was full.

With that macabre realization came the faint stench of decay, one with which she'd become way too familiar a few months before. She tried to ignore it and kept going, her steps slow and steady, her voice still calm. Behind her the line coalesced. Her luck and her salt were both holding out for the moment.

Lex moved constantly at her side, scanning the area,

staying alert. It reassured her. She let herself focus on the magic and forget the rest.

It was coming, growing inside her and in the air around them. Sweat broke out on her skin. Her heart pounded, her body itched like she'd gone too long between doses. If there'd been any food in her stomach, she probably would have brought it back up; every step was like walking through deep slime sucking at her legs, trying to pull her down.

Faintly over the beat of her heart and her own voice came shouts, the men fighting in front of the building. Another problem to ignore, at least until she finally left the alley and walked back into the meager light.

Bodies in front of her, surging and tumbling, anger and violence heavy in the air. It forced its choking way into her, sent adrenaline pounding through her veins. Not good. Magic required calm, required focus, and showing any sort of emotion around ghosts was a bad idea. Especially fear.

And ghosts there were. Either some of the house guards were dead, or they'd summoned more ghosts to fight with them, or both. Translucent forms flitted in and out of the crowd, appearing and disappearing.

Not for the first time she was thankful Oliver was there. Without him . . . Without him everyone might have died. Would have died, because of her and her lack of foresight. She'd given him some graveyard dirt and asafetida, but it hadn't occurred to her to hand it out to the others. That was what too much emotion could do. Kill people.

Lex tensed. The gun cocked. Chess held out her hand, caught his eye, and shook her head. Not until they were seen.

Which would be in about ten seconds. No getting out of it; to finish the cast she needed to walk awfully close to the fight.

Blue light sparked from her fingers as she etched a quick sigil into the air, an attempt at rendering Lex and herself unobtrusive. Whether it worked she couldn't tell, not with so much energy pounding through her already.

They made it within a few feet before they were spotted. One of the guards spun around, his mouth opening, hands already rising. In one of them a dagger caught the edge of the moon.

Her left hand was still full of salt. With her right she grabbed some graveyard dirt.

The gun went off. The sound barely hit her ears when a hole appeared in the guard's forehead, his features below it fixed in surprise.

The entity he hosted slipped from his falling body, rage blasting from it like cold from a high-octane freezer. Chess forced herself to stand still, to wait, until it got close enough for her to hit it with the dirt.

The respite only lasted a second. If their mere presence hadn't been enough to attract attention, the gunshot certainly was. The fighters turned en masse and came at them, and only the knowledge that if she gave up now, she'd only have to come back later kept her from running away.

Run she did, though, ducking in and out among the bodies, her mouth forming words of power that meant little more than nonsense syllables in her weary, semi-panicked state of mind. Her salt line thickened and thinned; she moved too erratically to keep it even.

Through the haze she saw Terrible, had time to register the blood pouring down the side of his face before he disappeared from her sight again. Bodies jostled her, elbows catching her ribs and arms, feet almost knocking her over. She could only hope she wasn't leaving huge gaps in the salt line, that it would seal into the ground properly.

Somehow she thought it wouldn't, but there was nothing she could do about it.

She drew her own knife from her pocket, ducked under the last few fists. Almost time to close the circle.

Oliver caught her eye, saw the weapon in her hand. She made a slicing motion with it and pointed to herself, hoping he'd know what she meant.

He did. He nodded, cut around the fighters to the edge. The crowd had definitely thinned. Slow-moving ghosts hung around the edges, a few of them outside her salt line, all of them held by the dirt and Oliver's words of power. Should she send her psychopomp after them before she went inside? Or would that be a waste of time?

Unless . . . Her gaze traveled up, to the familiar sight of birds circling the building, riding the air currents above the fighting men. Psychopomps. Wild ones, whose use was not recommended in ritual; she'd never heard of anyone actually doing it, save with an owl like the one Kemp and Vanita used, and even then she knew they'd trained it, worked with it extensively. They must have.

These were common birds: sparrows, pigeons, crows. She thought she glimpsed a hawk, but it disappeared before she could be certain.

Oliver shouted something she couldn't make out. He was struggling, weariness apparent in his hunched shoulders and slowed movements. If he ran out of energy, if he were injured or killed, the ghosts would be unstoppable.

Okay, then.

The last of the salt fell through her fingers, completing the circle. Magic swirled around her, the wind died. Time to seal it.

Her knife's handle was warm, a little slick from sweat. She raised her left hand palm up over the salt line. With her right she placed the point of the blade on her left pinkie, beside the healing wound from the graveyard.

"With salt I make the circle whole. With blood I make the circle whole. With my power I seal the circle that it may hold strong and be not broken."

On "blood" she sliced herself, a quick, hard movement that opened the pad of her fingertip. Blood welled in the cut, dripped over the edge, and hit the salt.

Her entire body shook. The black magic guarding the house was reacting to her magic; she felt pulled in two directions, battered from both sides like a piece of meat caught in a garbage disposal. A scream forced its way out of her mouth, past her tight lips. Her head was about to explode.

From a million miles away she heard Oliver's echoing shout. Shit. It was hitting him too, of course. If it immobilized him—He was powerful, yes, but he was not a witch despite his education and natural ability. She could fight this—at least she thought she could—but whether he could, she did not know.

She flung her left hand up, watching her blood leap from it into the air. "I call on the escorts of the dead! *Ornithramii mordreus*, I command you!"

Power slammed into her like a wall, hard; unseeing, unfeeling and cold as death itself. Her body screamed, every muscle and nerve vibrating with agony as it struggled to absorb the blow. Too much, way too much, she was going to fall apart, dissolve into nothing. Her mind overloaded, the small remaining conscious part of it screaming at her, pounding its fists, trying to get control before she went insane.

Without her knowing why or how, the words burst from her again. "*Ornithramii mordreus*, I command you! By my blood and by my power I command you!"

Abruptly the power left, swooping out of her with the same rage with which it had entered, leaving her struggling to stand, still battered by the dark welcome Kemp and his ghost had left for her.

Overhead the birds screamed.

She had them. She thought she had them. Deep in the back of her mind she felt them, angry and curious in equal measure, fighting against her control.

It made her sick. They were chaos, they were a hive-mind, and she didn't know how long she would be able to hold them. Couldn't stop being amazed that she'd been able to catch them in the first place, couldn't stop hearing the warnings of Elder Bewick about how unpredictable wild birds were in ritual and the dangers of attempting to use them.

Danger was relative. She could use the birds and possibly die, or she could not use them and certainly die. Along with everyone else.

She set her firetray down and heaped herbs into it, wolfsbane and ajenjible, sandalwood, black cohosh and hyssop and bat nut. Her lighter flared to life, and she touched the flame to the herbs.

Fire leapt from the tray, blasted a few seconds of heat onto her skin. In her hasty bag-packing she'd thrown in some dehydrated earthworms, hard and twisted like scraps of tree bark, and she threw those onto the fire, a small offering to echo the larger one she was about to make.

This time she sliced across her palm, barely noticing the pain through the throbbing of magic in her veins. Her body beat in time to it, her head pounding. Wings fluttered in her eyes, feathers touching her body. Not the birds, but the power of the birds, their essence, fighting her control.

"I offer appeasement to the escorts for their aid," she said, watching her blood fall onto the fire. Waiting to see if her sacrifice would be accepted.

The birds fell silent.

Chess looked up. They still soared overhead, their wings flashing moonlight, but they made no other sound. In her head their frantic energy calmed. Still wild, still unpredictable, but—for the moment—accepting.

"Escorts of the dead, I command you, take those souls which do not belong. By my blood, by my power, by my sacrifice, remove them from this world and take them back to their place of silence!"

The birds turned. For the first time since she'd passed them, Chess allowed herself to look at the fighting men.

They were barely visible. Black smoke filled the air around her, the physical manifestation of the dark wards. She'd been so caught up with the birds she'd barely paid attention, but when she stopped she still felt it, whispering around her, trying to sap her strength.

Terrible's head moved above the crowd; he still stood, still fought. She caught a glimpse of Lex's spikes, of Oliver's pale, exhausted face, of a few others she recognized.

But everywhere were bodies, and everywhere were ghosts.

The birds swooped as one. Oliver's head turned in time to see them, in time to see the hole opening behind him. His lips formed words she could not hear, his arms rising and lowering, pushing the living away from the open gateway.

Ghosts flailed and fought to no avail. The birds did their job, their wingspans seeming to grow as they dove, as they clutched the lost souls in sharp talons and dragged them from the world of the living.

Chess felt each flexing of claws, each lifting of wings, as if her body had suddenly sprouted those parts. Her body was moving, imitating, carried away by the strength of the magic coursing through her.

It seemed to happen so slowly, to take so much time,

but as the hole closed on itself she realized it had taken just seconds.

And not all of the birds had gone. Half of them still circled the building, waiting for her next command.

Too bad she didn't know what that could be—but she figured there was only one way to find out.

Oliver appeared from the swirling black fog, followed by Lex and, a moment later, Terrible.

"Should we go in with you?"

Chess nodded. She didn't want to speak. Wasn't actually sure if speaking would break her connection with the birds, and didn't want to find out.

They left a few of their men still fighting the last stragglers, walked across the narrow, cracked stoop, and opened the weatherbeaten front door.

Chapter Thirty

Dust filled her nose at the same time the sex energy, so much stronger inside than out, hit her body. The result was a sort of shuddery, gasping sneeze, and she struggled to regain control. The men looked around uneasily, or at least Oliver and Terrible did. True to form, Lex appeared unconcerned.

They stood in what had once been a lovely entry hall. A lone candle burned in an iron sconce at the far end, casting flickering light across the grimy floor. Wallpaper hung in tatters from the water-stained walls; piles of shreds and chunks of plaster lined the baseboards.

Music filtered into the room, too faint for her to pick up the tune. Violins, she thought. Something orchestral. She couldn't tell where it came from. She didn't hear anything else. Every nerve in her body twanged and shuddered, waiting for Kemp, for Vanita, for the ghosts. For whatever existed in this house.

To their left, an empty room with broken floorboards revealing gaping blackness below. A shrouded chair, a broken mirror so old and filthy it looked more like a blank gray eye staring at them.

Without speaking they headed toward the end of the

hall, toward that single flame. The door flapped on its hinges behind them.

And all the while Chess felt the birds overhead waiting for their passengers. Felt their indifference. They didn't care who lived or died, they only waited to clean up after it was over.

A staircase curved up on their right, its banisters catching the candlelight and shining it back. The wood felt solid enough, but the stairs creaked.

Not that it mattered. The ghosts knew they were here. She was certain Vanita and Kemp knew, too. It was a trap, but it was a trap they couldn't refuse to walk into, not unless they wanted more people to die. She couldn't let that happen. None of them could.

Of course, it was easy to be so definite when she hadn't yet seen what awaited her at the top of the stairs. When she did, it was all she could do to keep her feet under her.

The men gasped, but whether from the blast of sexual power or the sight before them Chess didn't know, and she couldn't bring herself to care.

For some reason she'd thought the ghosts would be upright. Instead, iron frames were fixed around the edges of the single beds, flush with the mattresses. From the top and bottom of each frame, cuffs extended, threaded with wires, circling the wrists and ankles of the ghost on each bed. Electric current running through the wires gave them solid form; their skin was silvery white, eerily pale as they writhed on the beds. They appeared sculpted from moonlight.

Ten of them, or a dozen; she wasn't capable of counting at that moment.

Chess didn't recognize them. Was glad she didn't recognize them, didn't connect them with the living women they had once been or the empty bodies she'd seen on the cold streets. It wasn't the triumphant greed on their faces. It wasn't the way their skin glowed as they sucked the life force from the magic-trapped men above them.

It was the eyes. Naked, bloody eyes, slightly shriveled and blackened now but still recognizable. They'd been placed in the women's sockets, a sick joke in the unreal perfection of their faces.

Chess's mouth went dry; she could do nothing but stare for one long, sickening moment at the unearthly horror before her.

The ghost on the nearest bed was terrible, and beautiful, and desire built in Chess to go to her, touch her, experience for herself what that perfection felt like. Someone moved behind her, then stopped; perhaps impervious Lex had caught whoever it was.

Perhaps whoever it was had simply seen the man above the ghost, his flesh seeming to melt away, his eyes hollow and dead in his agonized face. Or maybe they'd seen the viscous stain on the mattress as overused body parts exploded again and again, as they chafed and went raw and finally bled. Every bed, every ghost, was smeared with blood and semen, with tears and saliva. The mattresses stank, the floors were thick with a glistening, congealing stew of human fluids.

Still the men's hips kept moving, still their hands roamed over the bodies beneath them. Transfixed. Trapped. Caught in an ever-tightening finger trap they could not escape from no matter how hard they tried. Bile rose in Chess's throat, sharp and sour; she forced it back down, forced herself to focus on ending the horror instead of absorbing it further into a soul that had already seen far too much of it.

Should the psychopomps come in first, or should they try and get the men away and then bring them in? Of course, she didn't know if she *could* get the men away, nor was she certain the birds wouldn't simply shuck the men free of their bodies like ears of corn and carry them into the City as well.

Or even if there would be enough left of them to live if she did free them. The man before her was barely more than skin and bone, his lips shriveled back from his teeth, his skin shining through the thin downy hair on top of his head.

They should probably try to free him just the same. If they freed all the men, she could simply call the birds in. The iron cuffs and electric current wouldn't pose a problem for—

The crash slammed her knees to the filthy carpet. Before she knew what had happened she was leaping back to her feet and flinging herself forward purely on instinct. Her skin burned and itched, her tattoos were hot to the point of pain. She wanted to scream but was too scared.

She didn't know how, and she didn't know what happened next, but she did know without a doubt that whatever black magic guarded this place had been tripped.

Thick, grimy glass filled the window in front of her. Through it she barely made out the shadows of the birds outside in their endless circles. Still under her control. Waiting.

For now, anyway. Shit, she had no idea what to do. No idea, and it was getting hard to breathe. Hard to think. Her legs shook beneath her, her vision blurred. The spell, the protection, was feeding on her.

Feeding on all of them. Through the doorway of the bedroom she saw Lex and Terrible's men, still standing in the hall, bracing themselves on the rickety banister, on one another. If she didn't get her shit together, they would all die.

"Oliver!" Where was he? Was that dust in the air, making it thick and dark?

No. The screaming pain of her tattoos, the creeping

terror up her spine, told her that. Ghosts. More of them, who knew how many, called into being by the curse or Kemp or simply because they sensed death and fear in this place and wanted to join the party.

Before she could think about it, before she could second-guess herself, she smashed the window.

Glass drove itself into her arm, into her hand and shoulder. A scream tore from her, as if her flesh itself was screaming.

Birds poured in through the window. Over the pain she felt them feeding on her blood, connecting her to them more strongly. Felt their greed, their coldness. Felt, with a sinking horror, the malevolent spell fight them.

Kemp and Vanita had turned the house into a spirit home, a guardian. The psychopomps could not do their job; magic blocked them, forced them into impotence. They buzzed angrily around the room, wings beating the air, their rage apparent. Their rebellion apparent; she would lose them in a few minutes. Already she felt them slipping away, straining to break her control despite their pleasure in her sacrifice.

And they were feeding. Even if the house wasn't already sucking her energy away, the birds were. It was getting harder to hold them, harder to see, harder to move. She needed help. Needed someone who could share some power. Oliver. He had power and he would know how to help, right?

She had no idea what was happening in the hall, if the men were still there, if they had succumbed to the house's thrall. Feathery wings battered her face, her bloody arm, her legs, as she fought her way through the flock and back to the hall, her nostrils dry and caked with dust.

Hands grabbed her, spun her around. She screamed. Her fist connected with solid bone. Oliver, holding his nose, glared at her. Only the whites of his eyes were clearly visible.

No time to apologize. "The house is protecting them!" she shouted. "It's a spirit house, we have to break it."

He nodded. Blackmailer or no, she really owed him something after this.

His hot, sticky hand grabbed hers, forming a skin connection. Through it she felt his power slip into her body and meld with hers. The darkness before her eyes cleared. Her muscles responded.

Together they moved forward. The heart of the house, the seat of the spell. That's what she needed to find. Vaguely she knew Terrible's and Lex's men were following them, felt Lex at her side with his knife ready.

A shape appeared before them, forming itself from the air. Vanita. Her pale skin glowed in the darkness, too perfect for life. Her figure in its black dress disappeared in the black fog. She was all around them, filling them. Impossible to escape, no chance, just give up . . .

Pain exploded in her torn arm. Her head snapped up to see Oliver's face inches from hers. Had he punched her? Fucker.

He was right, though. This was not the time to give up. Blood dripped down the fingers of her free right hand as she reached into her bag, found the herbs and dirt she still carried. This wouldn't be enough, and she knew it; somehow Vanita was connected to the house as well, and she would not be sent to the City until the house's spell was broken.

But if Chess could freeze her, slow her down, steal some of her power, they had a chance.

"*Arcranda beliam dishager!*" Chess flung the grave-yard dirt at that smug, glowing face, followed it with ajenjible and powdered crow's bone, and grabbed her Ectoplasmarker from her pocket. Ready.

Vanita did not disappear, but she faltered. It was enough. Behind her Chess saw what she needed. A doorway, one from which darkness radiated, one that made her legs weak. That was where they needed to be, she knew it.

She dared to look away long enough to find Terrible, little more than a hulking shape in the shadows. "The door," she told him. "Break the door."

He nodded.

She flung herself forward, into Vanita. Icy cold ripped her breath from her lungs; evil stole her sight. She faltered, blind, rummaging around inside a ghost, certain at any moment she would fall. She would be lost, lost forever, lost in the endless darkness . . .

I am already lost. The words shouldn't have given her strength, but they did. There was nothing this bitch could do to her that hadn't already been done, nowhere lower she could go. She turned the thought into a mantra, let those negative words and images she tried so hard to forget flow free through her mind, and found her skin warming again and the darkness falling away and she saw Terrible battering at the door, throwing his huge body against it again and again. The frame buckled; the walls groaned. Her skin, her tattoos, vibrated as the spell weakened.

Vanita watched, too, and in that moment when she was distracted Chess took her chance. Vanita's body was translucent, but her hands were solid; Chess used her Ectoplasmarker to scribble the passport she'd designed earlier to direct her psychopomp onto that spectral hand, completing it just as Vanita noticed and yanked herself away with a wail.

Too late.

Terrible crashed through the door. Foulness poured through the open frame, thick greenish-black, choking.

Her knife seemed to jump into her palm. She pulled energy from Oliver, from the air, from the well of blazing anger in her soul, and entered the room.

The house roared; she felt it shake through her entire

body. She ignored it. Ignored, too, the fight taking place behind her, around her, as Vanita struggled to stop her. Ignored her terror that Kemp would show up any second and kill her. Oliver moved, his hand still in hers, but his voice just a rumble in the general din. She didn't have much time.

Runes decorated the floor, wall to wall. Terrible had already come in contact with some of them; she felt them burn through the soles of her shoes.

"*Baredia lachranta. Baredia lachranta emplorascum.* By my power I command it." The wound in her left palm still bled; she gritted her teeth and deepened it, increasing the flow. Her blood sizzled and spat when it touched the boards at her feet.

"*Baredia lachranta resticatum.*"

The floor shook. It was working. Working, but not fast enough. Her knees hit the rune-covered wood, now wet with her blood. She dug the point of her knife in, started carving over the runes and symbols as she spoke their names aloud: "*Ashtaroth, septikosh, higam, spadirost.*"

Vanita screamed. Chess's blood kept spreading over the floor, sinking into the gouges she made. It wasn't enough, she didn't have enough. Oliver's face was pale beside her, his hand shaking in hers. He was almost empty, it was hard for her to breathe, she needed more power—

She still had the birds. They'd be furious, but she had them, and she was going to use them. Wild feathers filled her mind, her body. She shook with them, unsure for a minute if she was still human, but their energy coursed through her, and she saw something—something squirming in the corner of the room.

A cat. A dead cat, swarming with maggots. The spell's sacrifice, its rotted flesh feeding the magic, hidden by a visual glamour until she'd weakened the spell enough to fade it out. Rational Chess was disgusted; the rest of her simply saw it, knew what needed to be done.

She lunged forward, lifted her knife, and drove it into the corpse, shrieking with fury and power and fear. With a tremendous echoing groan—Chess felt it all the way to her toes—the spell broke.

The birds screamed, swooping through the air with new purpose. From the rooms came the shouts of the zombie men, angry their prizes had been stolen from them, or relieved to be free, or both—she couldn't tell and didn't care. All she knew was she had a job to do.

She yanked her own psychopomp from her bag, set the skull on the ground, and took up a handful of the dirt from Vanita's grave. "I call on the guardians of the City of the Dead. I call on the escorts. Aid me; collect this soul from where it does not belong."

There was too much magic in the air already; the psychopomp formed from the skull in an instant, roaring and leaping from the floor. Chess jumped back, turned around to see Vanita trying to run away. She threw the dirt.

"Vanita Tailor, I command you to return to your place of silence. By my blood I command it, by my power I command it. I call on the escorts of the City of the Dead to take you there, and it shall be done!"

Vanita tried to run but couldn't. The dirt trapped her, held her, until the great black dog leapt up and caught her dress in its teeth.

Through the fog and the smoke Chess watched Vanita shrink, watched her being dragged through the hole. It closed around her, around them, the skull rattling back to the floor, the magic releasing in a breath-sucking rush.

For a minute they all stood staring at one another in the waiting silence.

Then they ran.

They flung themselves down the stairs, the wood

splintering beneath them as the building's magic died. Oliver's hand still rested in hers; she felt how weak he was, how much he'd given her, and had time to feel thankful and a little sorry before the ceiling collapsed behind them.

They spun around the corner and ran faster, the door in sight. Freedom beckoned, freedom and air and even the dim moonlight again, the normal world. Her lungs ached, her entire body hurt, but she ran for that door as hard and fast as she could, dragging Oliver with her, dragging them all with her.

Out the door and onto the pavement, turning in time to see the house fall. It collapsed all at once, like an object dropped from a great height. One minute it was there and the next it was nothing but a pile of rubble, housing the fading, pitiful shouts of the ghosts' victims. Beside it, birds carried their souls into the still-open hole, dim, flickering light catching their bodies.

Chess took a breath. The stench of sour water and garbage had never smelled so good, so fresh. She couldn't get enough. One more breath and she would free the birds, then they could leave.

She had just enough time to register the figure emerging from around the side of the wreckage. One second to realize it was a man, his naked body scrawled head to foot with magical symbols and runes.

Then something hard and heavy slammed into her, knocked her down. Her wounded arm, still spiked with glass, hit the concrete; she tried to scream, but there was no air in her lungs.

Gunshots echoed, shouts. More gunshots. Something hit her in the leg, too hard and deep for pain. All she felt was shock—shock and dizziness and the certainty that something bad was happening, something unforeseen—

Terrible. His body above her. More shouts. Wetness oozing through her sweater to her skin, and she knew what it was and what had happened and now she could scream, she pushed his heavy weight from her and could not stop screaming.

His eyes were closed. His body was still. She picked up his hand, tried to get him to look at her, to talk to her, but he would not, and her mind refused to accept it and her eyes refused to see it and she heard wings, heavy wings, and she looked up and knew the birds had left her control.

The hawk was coming.

Chapter Thirty-one

Physical death is but a pathway to the City of Eternity; the psychopomp is an escort to a life of freedom and peace.

—*The Book of Truth*, Veraxis, Article 66

Its powerful wings stretched wide as it soared down, not in a hurry, ready to claim its soul. Terrible's soul. He was dying, he was dead. The knowledge hit her so rough and deep it made the gunshot wound in her leg seem like nothing at all. She could not let this happen. Would not let this happen.

Her hands didn't shake as she reached for his gun, tucked into the waistband of his jeans against his still-warm skin.

"Chess, what are you—"

"Tulip, c'mon now—"

Hands on her shoulders, gentle hands. They were trying to help, she knew, but they were wrong. They didn't know how to help her. She shook them off, lifted the gun, pulled back the slide. He'd only let her shoot this one a couple of times, but she could do it. Oh, yes, she could do it.

Oliver shouted again, but she barely heard it. Heard nothing but the beat of her own heart, pounding triple-time like she'd snorted a bagful of speed, as she raised the gun, sighted down the top just like he'd shown her, and fired.

Missed. The hawk swerved off to the left, still coming.

Any second now it would claim its prize, any second. Fuck, she couldn't—

She fired again. The hawk fell without grace, its head gone, its wings useless to stop its descent. It hit the pavement and lay still.

"Chess! You can't do this, you can*not*—"

Chess spun around, still holding the gun, and put Oliver Fletcher right in her sights. Gave him her eyes, let him see she meant it. The sound of the slide pulling back again echoed off the street. "Don't tell me what I can't do."

"You don't know what—"

"Fuck off, Fletcher." It came out as a moan. How much time did she have? He was wasting her time. "Just fuck off."

"Chess, I know how you feel, fuck, you know I do, but you can't—"

She switched the gun into her left hand, grabbed her knife with the other. "I can't lose him. *That's* what I can't do. I can't—I can't—"

Her fingers scrambled at Terrible's shirt, ripped it open. Blood on her fingers, blood on his chest. So much blood, she was too late, another psychopomp would be on its way, she had to hurry.

Someone grabbed her arm, tried to pull her away. She yanked herself free—it seemed so easy—and dove forward, the point of the knife over his heart.

"Chess, please," Oliver said. "*Please.*"

She ignored him.

She'd studied that sigil, traced it with her eyes. Knew it by heart. The knife moved as if by its own accord, making the triangle, adding the runes, swerving over the top. She left out Oliver's modification, used only the Church sigil, the one they used before. It was safe— surely it was safe—and if it wasn't, she didn't care, because if she lost him, she would die.

"*Kesser arankia*," she whispered, in a voice that barely sounded like hers. "By my power I bind."

Nothing happened. She heard wings. Too late. She was too late, she'd done it too late, she'd committed a capital offense in killing a psychopomp, and she'd done it for no reason at all because she was too late, and her entire body convulsed on itself and the knife fell from her stiff fingers and she couldn't breathe.

Terrible's chest rose beneath her hand.

The last person she expected to see by the side of her bed was Oliver Fletcher. At least, he was the last person she expected to see until she realized Roger Pyle sat next to him.

"Hey," she croaked. Roger grabbed the glass of water by her bed and handed it to her.

"No, thank *you*," he said, cutting off her next words. "For keeping my family and friends out of prison."

What?

"He knows," Oliver cut in. "About our deal."

"I could hardly help but find out something was going on, what with my wife and daughter being shot in my home, right? And the doctor told me about . . . well, that I'm going to be a grandfather." Roger shook his head. So he still didn't know Arden wasn't his, then. "I still can't quite believe that."

Chess had no idea what to say. He was glad his family and friends had worked together to trick and terrify him? On what planet was that good news?

He must have known what she was thinking, because he said, "I know it's hard for a girl like you to understand. But . . . they're my family. They never meant to hurt me, they just couldn't get me to listen to them any other way. I made a mistake, forcing them to move out here. They made mistakes, too. Just because you make mistakes doesn't mean you don't love someone."

Yeah. She knew that. She focused on the cup in her hands, wished they weren't in the room so she could grab a couple of Cepts from her bag. The one good thing about the hospital was the free drugs. The bad thing was they were so damned careful in handing them out. No matter how much pain she pretended to be in, they wouldn't give her the pills until exactly six hours had passed. Pedants.

But she had a secret supply, courtesy of Lex. That meeting had been awkward, to say the least, but he'd come, he'd given her her pills, given her a kiss. What happened next they'd just have to see.

And her leg and arm didn't hurt that badly anyway. The only reason she was still there was her job. No way the hospital was going to take a chance on letting a Church employee go until she was completely healed.

"I'm glad," she said finally, because it seemed Roger expected a reply. "I hope everything works out for you."

"Me too."

Okay, this was kind of weird. Did he know *why* she'd agreed to let his family off the hook? Shit, they'd never even come up with a decent cover story—Oh, wait. She looked at Oliver.

"We're blaming it all on Kemp, right? And you're here to tell me what you told them?"

He nodded. "Basically. We're saying Kemp summoned the ghosts for revenge, because of my involvement. I've already spoken to Thad Griffin. And you were at that house because of me. I begged you to go with me."

"And Elder Griffin was . . . He's okay with that? I mean, am I going to—"

"I don't think you'll have any problems with him, no." His eyes held hers for a moment. No, he couldn't mean *that*. Elder Griffin wasn't the type who'd overlook a crime because of sex. She knew that. But a favor for an old friend? That she could see.

"Thanks."

"Least I could do, I guess. Oh, and . . ."—he glanced at Roger—"Your friend . . . his bills are paid, okay? We're taking care of it."

She bit her lip. Her friend . . . He'd pulled through. Been awake. Refused to see her. She'd tried twice the day before, but the first time the door had been closed and the nurse had told her he was sleeping, and the second time some buddy of his had shooed her away.

He wouldn't see her. He'd saved her life, and she'd saved his, but he wouldn't talk to her.

It had to mean something, though, right? That he'd saved her? That in that last minute he'd seen Horatio Kemp with a gun, and his thought had been to protect her, to shelter her? Didn't that mean something?

Oliver's eyes showed he knew what she was thinking. Mercifully, he did not speak.

"Anyway," Roger said. "I wanted to come and say thanks. And you're always welcome to visit, if you like."

"Thanks, but I don't travel much. One day, maybe—"

"Oh, no. We're moving back to L.A., but we're keeping the house. We'll spend summers here, I think. If you ever find yourself out that way, please feel free to say hello. I'd like that. I think we all would."

This kept getting weirder and weirder. "Okay, thanks."

He shook his head. "You gave me back my family. We're talking again. You could have turned us all in, ruined our lives and our careers. Hell, you could have sold the story to a tabloid. You didn't. I appreciate that."

She opened her mouth to tell him it hadn't exactly been her choice, but closed it again. It was nice to think something good had come out of all this mess. That at least someone's life had been improved. Her job didn't lend itself to happy endings. Her life . . . well, that went without saying.

They chatted for a few more minutes, then the men stood up to leave.

"One more thing." Oliver held something out to her. "I thought you might like to have these."

It was a flat, square package, thick as a magazine. The pictures—another set, she guessed—or maybe she hadn't managed to grab them all at the Pyle house that night. She nodded.

"If you ever need anything, give me a call. Please. My card is in there."

"Yeah, okay. And thanks, really."

They shook hands. Oliver leaned over and kissed her forehead, and the men left.

She opened the package. Yep, the pictures. All of them. And the memory chip. Nice of him. Of course, he had a lot more than that to hold over her head at that point.

At the bottom were two copies of one photo, a close-up enlargement. She and Terrible, the night they'd gone to Bump's place, just before he'd knocked on the door. Joking with each other.

Their bodies were so close they almost touched, so it was hard to tell where he ended and she began. The breeze had lifted her hair from her shoulders and brushed back her bangs so her eyes looked larger, totally focused on him.

And he was smiling down at her, that grin that changed his entire face.

Tears stung her eyes and she brushed them away. Two copies Oliver had made of this one. Maybe she felt like getting up and going for a little walk anyway.

She slid off the bed and sneaked a couple of pills. Maybe this was a stupid thing to do. It probably *was* a stupid thing to do, but she didn't care at that point. What difference would it make? She'd already made a total ass of herself, sobbing and screaming and telling a crowd of men—one of whom she was fucking—that her life would end if Terrible died.

Terrible's room wasn't far from hers, just a few doors down the hall. His big, tube-ridden body dwarfed the bed.

He looked okay, she thought critically. Not too pale. Whether that meant anything, she wasn't sure.

In her stocking feet she padded over to the bedside, listening to him breathe. Listening to the steady beeping of the IV machine in the corner. What she'd done . . . it had been worth it. Totally worth it, despite the possible consequences. She'd killed a bird. If that was discovered, she'd be in prison for a long time, possibly even executed. But she didn't care. Didn't care at all, because he was alive.

She reached out and brushed the hair back from his eyes, half wanting him to wake, half hoping he wouldn't.

He stirred, mumbled something she didn't understand, but didn't wake up. That was fine, too.

He wouldn't see her, wouldn't talk to her. That hurt far worse than the hole in her leg. So did knowing that this might be the last time she'd ever touch him, maybe even the last time she'd ever be this close to him.

But she'd be dead now if it weren't for him. When it came down to it, no matter how angry he was, no matter how badly she'd hurt him, he'd used his own body as a shield. Sacrificed himself for her.

And she'd done the same in return. That had to mean something, right? That no matter how it might feel, their story wasn't over?

And right now, that was enough. What she would do about Lex she didn't know. What the consequences of that sigil on Terrible's chest might be, she didn't know. Hell, there were lots of things she didn't know; she never had.

But right now she knew Terrible had died to save her. Some part of him, no matter how small, still cared about her at least as much as the rest of him still wanted her. And she still wanted him, more than she'd ever thought she could want anyone, and she wasn't scared.

So that was a pretty good start.

She set the picture on his bedside table, where he would see it when he woke up, and padded back down the hall to her own room. It was his move now.

She just hoped he would make it.

Her bed waited for her; she climbed up, ignoring the twinge from her healing leg. The nurses would be by in another hour or two to give her more pills; she had a stash from Lex, a TV bolted to the wall, and a stack of books Elder Griffin had sent. She was alive. Nobody was going to take her job away. Nobody was spying on her anymore.

Maybe it wasn't a happy ending. But it was a hell of a lot better than she'd expected.

Yearning for your next Unholy fix?

Read on for a sneak peak inside the next
novel in Stacia Kane's dark and sexy series:

Coming soon from Voyager

Chapter One

The guillotine waited for them, its blackened wood dark and threatening against the naked cement walls of the Execution Room.

Chess limped past it, trying not to look. Trying not to remember that she deserved to kneel before it, to place her neck on the age-smoothed rest and wait for the blade to fall. She'd killed a psychopomp. Hell, she'd killed *people*.

Only the death of the hawk meant automatic execution.

But nobody knew about that. At least, nobody with the authority to order her death knew about that. She was safe for the moment.

Too bad she didn't feel safe. Didn't feel the way she should have felt. The dull ache in her thigh with every step she took in her low-heeled Church pumps reminded her of the almost-healed gunshot wound; her limp reminded everyone else, drew attention to her at a time when she wanted it even less than usual.

Elder Griffin's hand was warm at her elbow. "You may sit while the sentence is read and carried out, Cesaria."

"Oh, no, really, I'm—"

He shook his head, his eyes serious. What was that about? Granted, an execution wasn't exactly a party-it-up event; very few Church events were. But Elder Griffin looked even more solemn than usual, more troubled.

He didn't know, did he? Had Oliver Fletcher told him about the psychopomp, about what she'd done? If that bast—No. No, she was being stupid and paranoid. Oliver wouldn't have told him. When would he have? As far as she knew, the two men had only shared one conversation since that night, the night she'd killed the psychopomp, the night Terrible had been—

Her breath rasped in her chest. Right. This wasn't the time, or the place. This was an execution, and she had testimony to give, and she needed to calm the fuck down and give it.

So she sat on the hard, straight-backed wooden chair, breathing the disinfectant stink heavy in the room, and watched the others file in after her. Elder Murray, the rings painted around his eyes as black as his hair, almost disappearing against the rich darkness of his skin. Dana Wright, the other Debunker who'd been at the bust at Madame Lupita's, her light hair curling around her face.

For Lupita herself, no one came. Any who might have cared about her, who might have wanted to be there for her in the last moments of her physical life, had either already been executed themselves or were locked in their cells in the prison building.

Last—last before the condemned woman herself—came the executioner, his face obscured by a heavy black hood. On his open right palm rested a dog's skull—his psychopomp, ready to take Madame Lupita down to the spirit prisons. Clenched in his left fist was a chain, and at the end of that chain was Madame Lupita, her legs and wrists shackled together with iron bands.

The door thunked shut behind them, the lock popped; it would not open for half an hour. Time enough for the execution to take place and the spirit to be taken to the City of Eternity. The timelocks had been instituted in the early days of the Church, when a series of mishaps had led to a ghost opening the door and escaping. Like everything the Church did, the timelocks made sense, but Chess couldn't help the tiny thrill of panic that ran up her spine. Trapped. Something she never wanted to be.

The executioner fastened the chain-end he held to the guillotine and began setting up the skull at the base of the permanent altar in the corner. Smoke poured from his censer and overpowered the scent of bleach and ammonia; the thick, acrid odor of melidia to send Lupita's soul to the spirit prisons, ajenjible and asafetida, burning yew chips to sting Chess's nose. The energy in the room changed, power slithering up her legs and lifting the hair on the back of her neck, that little rush that always made her want to smile.

She didn't, though. Not today. Instead she pressed her teeth together and looked at the condemned woman.

Lupita had changed since Chess saw her last, in that miserable, hot little basement that stank of terror and burned herbs and poison. Her big body seemed to have shrunk. Instead of the ridiculous silver turban Chess remembered, Lupita wore only her own close-shorn hair; instead of the silly sideshow caftan, her bulk was hidden beneath the plain black robe of those sentenced to die.

But her eyes had not changed. They searched the little crowd, found Chess, and glared, hatred burning from their depths so hot Chess almost felt it sear her skin.

She forced herself not to look away. That woman had almost killed her, slipping poison into her drink; had almost killed a roomful of innocent people, summoning a rampaging, violent ghost. Fuck her. She was going to die, and Chess was going to watch.

Something slithered behind Lupita's eyes.

Chess's breath froze in her chest. Had she seen that? That flash of silver? That flash, which meant Lupita was Hosting a spirit in her body?

Her eyes widened; she stared at Lupita now, focusing. Waiting. It shouldn't be possible. Lupita hadn't been Hosting when she was arrested—they would have caught that immediately when she was brought in—and there was no way in hell she would have been able to pick up and bond with a spirit in the Church prisons. It simply wasn't possible.

The flash didn't reappear. No. She was imagining things. All the stress, the tension of her personal life— what there was of it—and the overbearing sympathy of the Elders and the other Debunkers, crushing her beneath their concern for her leg and their good intentions. Add to that a few extra Cepts and a Panda, and half a Nip to keep her awake . . . No wonder she was seeing things. What was next, pink elephants?

Elder Griffin stood before the guillotine, cleared his throat.

"Irene Lowe, also known as Madame Lupita, thou hast been found guilty by the Church of the crime of summoning spirits to earth. Further, thou hast been found guilty of the attempted murder of Church Debunker Cesaria Putnam. Cesaria, is this woman responsible for those crimes?"

Chess stood up, despite the protests of her right thigh and Elder Griffin's slight frown. "Yes, Elder."

"Thou testifiest this based on what?"

"I saw this woman commit those crimes, Elder."

"And thou swearest thy word to be Fact, and Truth?"

"Yes, Elder. I do."

Elder Griffin gave her a curt nod, turned next to Dana Wright while Chess sank back onto her chair. A woman was about to die based on her word. When her word—

the word of a junkie and a liar, the word of someone who'd betrayed her only real friend in the world—wasn't worth shit.

He was never going to speak to her again. She'd given up calling the week before. She'd given up hoping she might see him out at Trickster's or Chuck's, given up hanging around the Market in the cold waiting to see if he turned up. He was still out there, of course. People had seen him.

People who weren't her. She'd never known anyone could avoid another person so thoroughly. It was like he could sense her coming.

Shifting movement in the standing crowd drew her attention back to the proceedings. The execution itself was about to take place.

The room thrummed with power now, beating like a heart around them, steady and slow and thick. No need for a circle; the room itself was a circle, a fortress with iron sandwiched into the cement walls.

Elder Griffin started pounding the drum, letting his hand stay in the air for so long between beats that Chess felt herself waiting, breathless, unable to move or allow her lungs to fill until the next heavy thump. The room's magic slid into her, finding those empty spaces and filling them, making her something more than she was. It felt good. So good she wanted to close her eyes and give herself to it completely, to forget everything and everyone and do nothing but exist in the energy.

She couldn't, of course. She knew she couldn't. So instead she watched as the executioner's psychopomp formed, the dog growing out of the skull, flowing like a river from a mountain peak to become legs, a tail, hair sprouting glossy and black over the bare skin and bones.

The drum beat faster. Drums . . . there had been drums at Lupita's séance that night, played by a duo of speedfreaks with eyes like ball bearings. Now the drums again, keeping monotonous, dragging time under Elder Murray's voice.

"Irene Lowe, thou art found guilty and sentenced to die by a tribunal of Church Elders, and this sentence shall now be carried out. If thou hast any last words to speak, speak them now."

Lupita shook her head, staring at the floor. Chess reached out with her own power, trying to get some sense of something from the woman. Some fear, some anger. Anything. Lupita was too quiet. Too calm. This didn't feel right.

The executioner helped Lupita to her knees, placed her neck on the divot. The drum beat harder, louder even than Chess's blood in her veins or the thick sweet magic air rasping in her lungs. Louder than her own thoughts.

She reached out further, letting her power caress Lupita's skin, trying to find something—

Oh, fuck!

Her leg gave when she leapt to her feet, almost falling over. "No! No, don't—"

Too late. The blade fell, its metallic *shnik* slicing the air as cleanly as it did Irene's neck, thudding into place like the slamming of a prison door.

Irene's head tumbled into the basket. Blood erupted from the stump of her neck, poured over her head, over the dull cement floor.

Her spirit rose; her spirit, the spirit that had been Madame Lupita. The dog lunged for it, ready to drag it below the earth, into the prisons outside the City of Eternity.

The other spirit rose as well. The spirit Lupita'd been Hosting. The one there was no psychopomp to take care of, no graveyard dust to subdue. The one an entire roomful of Church employees were helpless against in that room with its iron walls and locked door.

Chess's scream finally escaped, bursting into the air. It was drowned out by the others, the shouts of surprise and fear.

Elder Griffin dropped the drum. The dog grabbed Lupita's spirit—she had a passport on her arm, she was the one he'd been summoned to retrieve—and dove into the patch of wavering air behind the wall. The last thing Chess saw of Lupita was her mouth stretched into a horrible grin as she left them all to die.

The ghost hovered in the air before the guillotine. A man, his hair slicked back from his forehead, his eyes blank, his face twisted with savage joy. Elder Murray shouted something, she couldn't be sure what; her skin tingled and itched and threatened to crawl away from her body entirely. A powerful ghost, too powerful. What the fuck was he, how the fuck had she—

"I command you to be still!" Elder Griffin's voice rang out, echoed off the walls, speared through Chess's body. "By my power I command it!"

It wouldn't work. She knew without even looking that it wouldn't. But the executioner . . . did he have another skull? Some graveyard dirt?

Dana screamed. Chess glanced over and saw the ghost fighting with Elder Murray, its mouth open in a ghastly smile, its eyes narrow with effort. The ghost held the ritual blade in its hand, the one the executioner had used to summon his psychopomp.

No time to watch. No time to look at them, and it wouldn't do any good anyway. The room was filled with noise and energy and heat, a confusing mish-mash of images her brain couldn't process. She focused on the smoking censer, the stang in the corner, the black bag beside it. The executioner dug through it frantically, pulling things out—

Someone fell into her, she tumbled to the hard floor with a thud.

More screams, more shouts. Something clattered to the floor. The energy was unbearable. It wasn't a rush anymore, wasn't a high. It was an invasion, shoving her around, distorting her thoughts and her vision and infecting her with everyone else's panic.

She had to calm down. Her hands refused to obey her. Her tattoos prickled and burned, as they were designed to do. The ghost's presence set them off, an early warning system she was usually grateful for but would gladly have done without at that moment. Chaos reigned in the execution room, it carried her along on a wild riptide of blood.

Okay. Deep breath. Pause. She closed her eyes, dug down deep to the emptiness in her soul. The place where things like love and happiness and warmth should be, the place that was an almost empty room for her, the place where only two people lived, and one of them hated her.

But it was enough. It was enough to have that moment of silence, to tune out the terror and noise around her and find her own strength.

She opened her eyes. Her limbs obeyed her. She sprang to her feet, ignoring the pain—and almost lost her hard-fought calm.

Elder Murray was dead. His body lay stretched across the floor like a corpse ready for cremation. A gaping bloody wound leered at her from his throat.

Behind him the executioner slumped against the wall, his robe soaked with blood. She barely saw him through the ghost, blazing white, bloated with the energy he'd stolen. Chess groaned. A ghost with that much power was like an ex-con on Cloud-laced speed—unstoppable, without feelings, without logic. A killing machine who wouldn't stop until he was forced to.

And they were locked in with it.

Oh, shit—they were locked in with *them*. The iron walls kept the spirits of Elder Murray and the executioner locked in just as surely as the rest of them; Chess saw them out of the corner of her eye, faint shapes struggling to come into being.

There was a chance they wouldn't be hungry, that they wouldn't become murderous, but the odds were about as good as the odds that she'd be able to fall asleep that night without a handful of her pills. In other words, not fucking good at all. In a minute or so the ghosts would find their shapes, find their powers, and things would go from worse to totally fucking awful.

Blood spattered the walls, dripped off the shiny blade of the guillotine and ran in thick streams along the cement. It dripped from the ceiling where it had sprayed from Elder Murray's neck; it formed a glistening pool around the body, outlined footprints in a dizzying pattern, and smeared around the broken remains of the dog's skull. Fuck. No psychopomp. Did he have another?

Elder Griffin was covered with blood. Dana too, her eyes wide. But Chess wasn't the only one who'd rallied. Dana's eyes were dark and fierce with determination; Elder Griffin fairly glowed with power and strength.

Chess caught Dana's eye, jerked her head toward the bag. Dana nodded and took a step forward.

"By my power I command you to be still," she said, each word loud and clear. "I command you to go back to your place of silence."

The ghost turned to look at her, and Dana edged back, drawing it away. Chess inched to the left, trying not to catch the ghost's attention. She had to get to that bag. Had to get to the bag or they would all die. Maybe they'd die anyway, but she was damned if she wasn't at least going to try to save them. Life might be a pool of shit, but the City was worse—for her anyway—and she had no intention of going there. Not that day.

Her feet in their stiff shoes slipped in thick blood; the scent of it filled the air, a coppery tang beneath the herbs. How long would those burn, and was there more?

The ghost moved toward Dana, who kept talking, words of power flowing from her mouth. He clutched the knife in one semi-solid hand, blood dripping down the blade and covering his spectral skin. Viewed through him it looked black, like ink.

She glanced at the ghosts of Murray and the executioner again. They were almost fully formed now, slowly squirming into being like maggots erupting from a slab of rotting steak. She—they—didn't have much time.

Dana screamed. The ghost jumped at her. Elder Griffin leapt to the side, joining the struggle, as the ghost attempted to slice Dana's throat.

Chess dove for the bag. More herbs first—she grabbed the little baggies, dumped them on the dying fire in the censer. The smoke thickened. Another psychopomp, please let him have a spare. She threw things from his bag, not watching where they landed, the hair on the back of her neck practically pulling itself out of her skin. She couldn't hear much, what was happening? Were Dana and Elder Griffin dead? Oh, shit—

Her hand found something solid and her body flooded with relief. Another skull. Thank the gods who didn't exist, he had a spare. She yanked it out, tore at the inert silk wrapping it, barely glanced at it as she set it down.

A roar behind her. The ghost had spotted her. Dana and Elder Griffin tried to hold it, but it made itself transparent and sprang at her through the guillotine. She ducked out of the way. "I call on the escorts of the City of the Dead," she managed, stumbling, trying to keep within reach of the skull but away from the ghost's grabbing hand. "By my power I call you!"

The skull rattled. Chess pushed more power out, as much as she could—not an easy task when trying to keep from being turned into an energy snack for a rampaging dead man.

Another problem faced her as well. No passport. The spirit hadn't been accounted for, didn't have a marking on his body; there was a chance the dog wouldn't know which spirit to grab when it came. It had happened to Chess once before, a few months previously, and the dog had gone after her. She would never forget that feeling, the horrible sensation of her soul being pulled from her body like the peel off a banana . . .

Not to mention the additional spirits forming not five feet away, the executioner and Elder Murray.

"No passport!" she managed to say, and Dana's eyes widened. She glanced at the knife in her hand, raised her eyebrows, and Chess nodded because she had no choice.

Dana tossed the knife. The ghost spun around when it clattered to the floor, leapt for it. Chess grabbed the executioner's Ectoplasmarker and popped the cap, held it ready in her fist, and shouted.

Just as she'd thought, the ghost wheeled back around and came after her with the knife. Dana and Elder Griffin moved, Chess didn't see where. She was too busy watching the ghost, seeing his solid hand raise over her head, grabbing his wrist with her left hand and bringing the marker up with her right.

He didn't have a passport—they hadn't expected him, hadn't designed one. Oh fucking well. The blade hovered above her eye, its point tacky with coagulating blood, while she scrawled a series of Xs on the spectral skin. The ghost's face twisted with rage.

Now for the worst part. With every bit of strength she had left she pushed herself to the side, to the skull, and, dropping the marker, brought her right hand to the blade's point.

She hadn't expected it to hurt instantly but it did. Ow, it really fucking did, and her blood poured from the wound onto the skull, and she shoved all of that pain and all of her power into her next words.

"I offer the escorts an appeasement for their aid! Escorts come now! Take this man to the place of silence, by my power and by my blood I command it!"

The dog roared into being, huge and shaggy, its fangs bared. This wasn't just a dog, it was a wolf, what the fuck was the executioner doing with an unauthorized psychopomp—

The ghost's eyes widened. His mouth opened in a silent scream as he tried to jump away, all thoughts of killing forgotten. The dog—the wolf—went after him, its body moving low and fast like the predator it was.

The ghosts of the executioner and Elder Murray were fully formed now, huddled in the corner. Chess could see the last vestiges of sanity, of who they were in life, draining away, could see them trying to hold on.

It didn't matter. The wolf howled. A hole ripped open in the thin veil between her world and the spirit one, the wolf snatched the original ghost in its massive jaw. Ectoplasm burst from the ghost's body under the wolf's teeth. The ghost screamed, an act somehow more horrible because of its silence.

The wolf turned toward Elder Murray and the executioner. They huddled together, trying so hard. Tears sprang to Chess's eyes. She'd never known Elder Murray well, never dealt much with him, but his last act was to struggle to retain some humanity, and she couldn't help the surge of affectionate sadness, of pride, that threatened to overwhelm her.

Dana and Elder Griffin were beside her, Dana squeezing her hand. The wolf leapt, still clutching their unwelcome visitor in its teeth, and caught Elder Murray and the executioner in a bizarre sort of bear hug; he carried them through the wavering hole and it snapped shut behind them, leaving the three still alive to stare open-mouthed at where it had been.

Printed by RR Donnelley at Glasgow, UK